Absolution

By
Ramsey Keller

Published By Arkhos Atlantic

ISBN-13: 978-0692668078 (Arkhos Atlantic)
ISBN:0692668071

DEDICATION

This book is dedicated to my Uncle,
Reinhardt Peter Keller, who inspired me, and
encouraged me to always keep writing.

Contents

Chapter 1 – Hope and Despair

September, 1806 – Ohio Territory

"HEAVE!!" Nathan shouted as he strained against the back of the wagon. His older brother John tugged furiously on the oxen's reins, at the front. The animals were slipping and sliding, trying to gain some footing. The wagon remained hopelessly stuck. It was up to its axels in the quagmire.

The oxen were tired, and the mud was deep. A thick fog was developing; damp, cold mists were boiling up the hillside from the valley where the storm-swollen Muskingum River ripped through the fertile bottom land below. The sun had already set, and darkness was enveloping the daylight, while the brothers struggled with the stranded wagon on the narrow, rutted trail.

The storm was intensifying. In his frustration, Nathan gave one last gut-wrenching shove against the tail-gate of the Conestoga. Catching the young man off guard, the wagon unexpectedly lurched forward; bouncing out of the muddy rut, which had held it fast for more than an hour.

"God bless your strength, brother!!" John Stillman yelled back to Nathan, who was now sprawled out, face down in the mud. John peered around the side of the wagon to see why Nathan hadn't answered him.

"Um ... the wagon's up here, Nathan. Are you comin'?" John stifled a laugh as Nathan struggled to his feet, wiping the mud from his eyes.

"Very funny ... yes, very humorous indeed." The younger brother continued to mutter and complain, "I save the day, and you make jokes. Let's just catch up to the others and find a place to hunker down tonight. I've had it."

"They're up on that ridge by now. I just hope they've found a clear place where we can make camp." John climbed up into the wagon and gathered the reins. Nathan walked alongside the overloaded Conestoga.

John Stillman, at twenty-nine, was responsible for the welfare of his brother Nathan, who was four years younger. It was their mother's mandate upon leaving Pennsylvania. This sometimes caused passionate contention between the brothers.

"Listen, John! Did you hear that?"

"Hear what?"

"Sounded like gun fire."

"It's probably just thunder."

"Stop ..." Nathan raised his hand. "There it is again."

"You're right! It's trouble. Come on ... cut across this hill, we'll get to them faster!" John shouted; immediately jumping down from the wagon, and running toward the bluff.

Nathan quickly tied off the oxen. He grabbed the rifles and powder from the wagon and followed John up the hillside toward the ridge. The gun fire could be heard clearly now; and they could see the faint glimmer of flames through the trees at the top of the hill. Nearing the summit, the sound of bloodcurdling screams prevailed over the noise of the thunderous storm. Crawling on their bellies, John and Nathan slipped onto the ridge.

"Oh, God! Oh, my God ..." John choked the words in a whisper, "we're too late!"

Nathan crushed John's arm in a death-grip; silent; helpless.

Crouching there in the tall grass, they were impotent observers; witnessing the gruesome slaughter playing out in front of them. There was nothing they could do to stop the bloodbath. The gunfire had ceased. Friends and neighbors were being scalped, mutilated, and burned.

Nathan and John remained paralyzed with fear. Silent tears mixed with the rain, and ran down their faces. Neither uttered another word in the midst of the terror. Through the torrent and the smoke, the brothers watched several Shawnee renegades escape into the forest. The rain had quickly extinguished the fires, and the five wagons stood like smoldering black ghosts in the haze which blanketed the ridge. As the intermittent lightning flashed above them, John and Nathan caught fleeting glimpses of the bodies; the bodies of friends, strewn about the summit road alongside their burned-out wagons.

Once the Indians had left the area, John and Nathan waited a few moments; wanting to be sure all of the Shawnees were gone. When it was apparently safe, they jumped to their feet and ran to the road, frantically looking for any signs of life. The young men stumbled around in the blackness, searching for movement – listening for sounds. They checked each person, hoping beyond hope to find someone alive.

There had originally been six wagons – thirteen adults and six children, including a four-month old child.

"John, where's Maggie Waters? Here's Elizabeth and Hannah; and their ma and pa are over there, but I can't find Maggie!"

"She's not here?" John ran to the Waters' wagon, searching the area for one more body.

"The Sturges' baby isn't here, either." Nathan spoke softly, covering Will and Nancy Sturges with a scorched quilt he pulled from their wagon.

"Nathan!! Listen!!" John was skirting the edge of the forest just beyond the wagons. "Did you hear that? I thought I heard someone cry out!!" He stood frozen; listening intently. "There it is again – did you hear it?"

Both men bounded into the thick woods without thinking of their own safety. As the sound became clearer, the soulful weeping was obvious. And then they spotted her.

"Maggie!" Nathan ran toward the girl, who was huddled against the trunk of a huge Oak tree. She sat motionless, sobbing, and clutching a bundle wrapped in a woolen blanket. She was seemingly oblivious to the approach of the brothers. A dead Shawnee lay at her feet. A pitchfork was embedded in the warrior's chest.

"Maggie! It's all over, girl... You're safe." Nathan sat down beside the girl and cradled her in his arms, holding her securely – safely.

Maggie didn't speak, nor did she respond in any way.

"What's she holdin'?" John leaned closer, straining to see through the blackness.

Nathan reached over and lifted the corner of the blanket, which shrouded the object Maggie was clinging to.

"It's the baby! It's the Sturges child!" Nathan said, quickly pulling the blanket back over the child's face. He jumped to his feet gagging, and he began to retch.

John wrestled the baby from Maggie's grasp; she wouldn't give it up easily. The blood-soaked blanket was sticky and cold in John's hands. In the darkness, he could barely make out the gash in the child's throat. It had been slashed.

"Come on Nathan, let's get out of here. I don't want to end up like the others! We can come back in the mornin' when it's light."

Nathan scooped Maggie up in his arms, and they made their way back to the road. John put the dead baby into the Sturges' wagon, and tarried just long enough to whisper a short prayer, commending the souls of his slain friends into God's care.

They walked the road in silence. The rain had finally stopped, but the air was still cold and heavy with drizzle. They heard the mournful cry of a wolf, echoing across the hills.

"Let's move the wagon off the road a bit – out of sight," John said. He shivered in the cold dampness, briskly rubbing his biceps with crossed arms. "I sure hope that firewood in the wagon is still dry – we need to dry out our cold bones."

"Yea, but is it safe to build a fire? What if those injuns see it?"

"Well, little brother, they'll probably just figure the wagons are still smoldering." John ran his hands through his long wet hair, smoothing it back off his face. "How's Maggie doin'?"

Nathan shifted Maggie's body in his arms, so he could see her face. Her eyes were wide open, but staring blankly. "I don't know, John. It's like she's not really here. She's lookin' at me, but I don't think she's seein' me."

John untied the oxen and led them into the forest, moving the wagon a short distance from the road. They situated it in a grove of old pine trees, where the limbs draped down over it, conveniently hiding it from view. The light rain had finally stopped.

John climbed into the wagon, and Nathan hoisted Maggie up to him. He grabbed a quilt and wrapped it tightly around the girl; then he laid her on the feather bed in the front corner of the wagon.

"The wood's dry," John said, tossing a couple of logs from the wagon. "Here's the tinderbox, Nathan. Go ahead and try to get a fire started while I get Maggie settled." John rustled through the supplies and pulled out a lantern. "Nathan," he said, leaning outside the back of the wagon, "come and light this lantern."

Nathan appeared at the wagon's end with a sprig of pine branch, which was fully enflamed. John gratefully lit the lantern and handed the branch back to Nathan. Finally, there was some light in the oppressing darkness.

Nathan busied himself getting the logs started. The warmth from a fire would be a necessary blessing.

Maggie moaned softly, and John hurried to the front of the wagon with the lantern. He held the light above the girl and looked down into her sad, swollen eyes.

"Maggie, you're safe, girl. Nathan and I brought you to *our* wagon. Are you all right?"

"Mama... Papa... Where are my sisters?" Maggie choked on the words.

"I'm so sorry, Maggie." John stroked her forehead softly, moving the curly wet strands away from her eyes. "Are you hurt anywhere?"

"Oh God ..." Maggie tried to raise herself up, but sank back onto the featherbed. "I saw it! I saw it all! I didn't help... I ran! Oh God!"

"It's OK, Maggie. There wasn't anything you could have done. It's a miracle you saved yourself. Your family would have wanted you to."

"I'm so cold, John."

"Nathan's gettin' a fire started so we can warm you up, Maggie. You still haven't answered me... Are you hurt anywhere?"

"I don't know... I'm kind of numb. I'm so cold."
The girl was shivering violently.

"Nathan ..." John stuck his head out of the
wagon. "Help me get Maggie to the fire."

The brothers managed to move the girl close to
the warmth from the fire. John brought a bottle of
whiskey from the wagon.

"We've all got to get into some dry clothes, or
we'll get pneumonia," John said, pouring more
whiskey into the cup. He took a long drink of the
whiskey then handed the cup to Maggie. John
pulled Maggie's shoes off and then wriggled out of his
own boots. He turned to Nathan and pointed a
demanding finger at the young man. "Nathan, you
go to the wagon and get changed. I'll stay here with
Maggie." John reached over and gave Maggie's hand
a reassuring squeeze. "While you're in there, see
what we've got that might work for Maggie." He
propped the boots and Maggie's shoes up on a rock,
close to the fire.

"Barkin' orders like a damned general!" Nathan
said, shaking his head in disgust as he headed for
the wagon.

Nathan emerged shortly, dressed in warm dry
clothes. He was carrying more logs to add to the
fire. "OK big brother. It's your turn. I laid some
things on top of the trunk for Maggie – so don't
bother with those. I cut the legs and sleeves to try
and make them fit her better...not good... but at least
doable." Nathan put a log on the fire and stirred the
coals a bit. He glanced over at Maggie. The girl was
trying desperately to stifle the grief which was

overwhelming her soul. Her body was shaking violently from cold and shock.

"Maggie... Come here... Come closer to the fire and sit with me." Nathan placed a log beside him, and motioned for Maggie to sit down on it. "Come on, girl... Come warm yourself."

Maggie stood up slowly, pulling the quilt tight around her chilled body. "Oh, Nathan... What am I going to do?" She stepped over to the fire and peered pensively into the flames. "What's going to become of me?" She turned slowly and looked Nathan squarely in the eye. "I think I should have died too. I should have .....I wish I would have..."

"Good Lord, girl!" Nathan jumped to his feet and grabbed Maggie's hands. "You don't know what you're saying! You've been through hell tonight, and you're just not thinking clearly." He looked down into Maggie's sad green eyes. She appeared so lost. "Maggie... You know John and I love you like our very own sister." He fidgeted with the girl's fingers. "You don't need to worry about anything, Honey. John and I will always take care of you." He let go of Maggie's frail hands and pulled her close to him, giving her a warm, firm hug. "We'll make sure you're well taken care of – I promise!"

"What's going on out here?" John asked, climbing down from the wagon.

"She was askin' how much longer you were gonna be. She's cold," Nathan interrupted, stepping between Maggie and John assertively. He turned to Maggie. "Now you can get out of those wet clothes. The dry ones are on top of the trunk." Nathan swept

Maggie into his arms, and hoisted her into the back of the Conestoga before she could say another word.

"Did I miss something?" John asked, scratching his head. "You said something to make her start cryin' again, didn't you? You never know when to keep your mouth shut!" He poked a stubby finger into Nathan's shoulder.

"You didn't miss a thing, big brother." Nathan answered John; his tone sounded distant. He was distracted by the silhouette on the canvas of the wagon; relieved that John's back was turned to it. Nathan smoothed his mustache thoughtfully. "You know... I don't think we should have let her drink whiskey, John." Nathan couldn't take his eyes off the canvas. "And it's not like she doesn't have plenty of reasons to be upset right now! For God's sake ... she just lost her entire family – What the hell do you expect? Poor little girl's feeling lost and alone – She didn't need *ME* to make her cry – Life does *THAT*!"

"Ok... I'm sorry, Nathan. Now then, here's the plan ..." John assumed his dictatorial role again. "You get some sleep, and I'll take the first watch. When I can't stay awake anymore, I'll wake you up, and you can take over. How does that sound?"

"Does it make any difference what I think?" Nathan said, grabbing hold of the tailgate of the wagon, and stepping up onto the wheel.

"Wait, Nathan... Maggie may not be dressed yet. You'd better check before you go in there."

"She's dressed," Nathan answered dryly; and he climbed up into the wagon.

As the sun rose over the ridge, Nathan and John were preparing to return to the sight of the slaughter, to bury the dead and salvage what they could. It was a grisly chore, but a responsibility which couldn't be avoided.

"I don't want Maggie to see that mess," John said, sipping hot coffee. "Do you have any idea how we're going to do this without her going into hysterics again?"

"Now you want my suggestion?!" Nathan asked in astonishment. "You make all the easy decisions, and expect *ME* to take care of the tough ones!"

"Well, we can't leave her here alone... And we really can't let her come along... And it will take *BOTH* of us to get the job done... Nathan, I'm at a loss." John stood up and stretched.

"Tell ya what, John," Nathan said, running his fingers through his hair, which was a matted mass of blonde curls. "I thought about that very problem ... thought long and hard. And I *do* have a suggestion." He stood up and faced his brother. "This might sound crazy, but we're going to have to knock her out – put her to sleep. Some of that tonic Mama sent along might just do the trick. That stuff could put a horse to sleep. It's the only thing we can do. If all goes well, she'll sleep right through it." He shoved his hands into his pockets and cocked his head to one side, waiting for John to make his usual critical comment.

"That's a very good idea, Nathan!" John said, in a matter-of-fact tone. "But what if she wakes up before we're done?"

"Just a chance we'll have to take, I guess."

John scratched his head, looking thoughtful and worried. "I guess so."

"That's what we'll do then," Nathan replied; trying not to show his surprise.

"OK. You feed the oxen, and I'll pack the gear; we'll get Maggie secured, and head on up to the ridge." John barked his orders like a sergeant, as usual.

Nathan shook his head in disbelief. "Some things just never change," he muttered, under his breath.

"What'd you say, Nathan?"

"I said we need to get Maggie to drink some of that tonic."

"Ah... You're so right. Go get it. I'll make some tea right quick, before she wakes up."

Nathan sighed. "Good Lord, it never stops." He walked over to the wagon, and began rummaging through one of the cargo boxes, looking for the tonic.

By the time Nathan returned to the fire with the medicine, John had a cup of tea ready. "I made it good and strong, so Maggie won't taste that gawd-awful stuff," he said, setting the cup down on a nearby tree stump and reaching for the bottle Nathan was holding.

"Better let me do it, John. I don't want her to have too much. It won't take more than about ten drops."

"Give me the damned bottle, Nathan, and go get the honey."

"You get the damned honey, and I'll take care of the damned bottle!" Nathan said, glaring at his older brother.

John's expression changed instantaneously from determined to complete astonishment. He looked as if Nathan had thrown ice-water in his face. "Um ... well... I guess that'll work," he said.

"Are you two arguing?" It was Maggie. She was leaning out the back of the wagon, looking disheveled and unstable.

John hurried to get the honey, and Nathan quickly added the tonic to the cup of tea; blocking Maggie's view by turning his muscular broad back to her.

"Morning Maggie," Nathan said, pivoting around to face her. He offered the cup to the sleepy girl. "Made you some tea ... um ... John's gettin' the honey."

"Yes, ma'am... Here it is, to sweeten your tea." John quickly stirred a heaping spoon full of honey into the steaming cup.

"So you weren't arguing?" Maggie asked, taking the tea in both hands and sniffing its fragrance.

John stuttered nervously. "Oh no ... no ... we don't argue."

"That's right, Maggie, we were just having a discussion... We get pretty passionate about our discussions sometimes... Remember? It wasn't even important. Isn't that right, John?"

"Nathan's right, Maggie. Now drink your tea. It'll warm your belly."

Maggie disappeared back into the wagon with her cup, and the brothers breathed a sigh of relief.

John packed up all the gear, while Nathan fed and watered the oxen, checked the harnessing, and loaded everything back into the cargo boxes. It took about thirty minutes, which was long enough for the drug to take effect.

John nodded to Nathan, and Nathan called out, "Maggie ... are you ready to roll?"

There was no answer. Nathan moved the canvas covering aside, and looked into the wagon. Maggie was lying across the old feather-bed, and didn't respond to his voice. He climbed inside and checked to make sure the girl was indeed breathing.

"OK, John. Let's do it," Nathan said, jumping down from the Conestoga.

The brothers walked in silence, leading the oxen-drawn wagon up the grade toward the ridge. It was a sunny day, and there was a warm wind blowing in from the south, but the dark, cold reality of what they were about to encounter, weighed heavily on Nathan's heart. He was dreading the task which waited at the hilltop. As they neared the summit, his attention was drawn to the sky; vultures were circling, indicating the location of the carnage.

"John ... I was thinkin' ... it might be a better idea to just dig one grave ... bury 'em all together ..."
Nathan's voice trailed off into his sorrow. He drew his sleeve across his eyes to wipe away any evidence of tears.

"Yes," John said.

There, just ahead, in the middle of the narrow, muddy road, was the nightmare they had escaped, only the night before. Now they were duty-bound to provide a proper burial for their friends and neighbors who hadn't been as fortunate. Sorrow and guilt was the high price they paid for their own survival.

There was a small clearing just beside the road. The men worked in silence. The rain-soaked ground was soft, so the toil of digging the grave was easier than they had anticipated. Although the exterior of the wagons were burned and charred, there remained salvageable quilts and comforters inside them. That bedding was used to wrap the bodies. The heart-wrenching work continued for an hour or more before the last person was gently laid into the mass-grave. John and Nathan covered the bodies with the earth and then tamped it down securely.

"We need a marker," John said quietly. "Let's try and move that stone." He pointed to a large sandstone beside the road. "Maybe we can roll it."

Moving the heavy stone was harder than digging the grave, but the men finally accomplished their task. They set the stone up on end at the head of the grave, facing the road. Nathan retrieved a chisel and a hammer from one of the wagons. He thoughtfully carved these words into the face of the sandstone: *'Pennsylvania families killed by injuns – September 28, 1806 – Waters, Sturges, Riggle, Porter, and Smith. Rest In Peace'*.

Finishing the stone, Nathan brushed away the dust and the fragments. Without saying a word, he walked to the side of his wagon and pulled a Bible out from one of the cargo boxes. He opened it to his favorite passage and handed it respectfully to his older brother. John accepted the book, and the two men bowed their heads in a silent prayer.

Then John began to read:

> "Who shall give account to him that is ready to judge the quick and the dead? Beloved, think it not strange concerning the fiery trial which is to try you, as though some strange thing happened unto you:
>
> But rejoice, inasmuch as ye are partakers of Christ's sufferings; that, when his glory shall be revealed, ye may be glad also with exceeding joy.
>
> Amen."

Nathan's mind wondered back to the Pennsylvania farmland. He remembered growing up next door to the Waters family. Benjamin Waters owned a large farm besides being a busy country doctor. Since he had no sons, John and Nathan spent all of their free time helping out on the Waters' farm. Nathan managed a smile; remembering how old Ben Waters used to tease his wife about giving him *good-for-nothing daughter*s instead of sons. Ben always said, Maggie was the closest thing to a boy he got out of the deal. Maggie certainly had been a tom-boy. Nathan wiped at the tears in his eyes as John finished a prayer.

The sadness was palpable as the brothers began cleaning up the site. They moved the burned-out wagons off the road. There were three horses, a milk cow, and two oxen which appeared unscathed, so the men tethered them together. Feed and water salvaged from the other wagons was given to all the surviving animals. The injured ones were set free, and the dead ones were rolled over the hillside. Then there was the gruesome task of looking through the wagons to see what could still be usable. Cookware, stoneware, farm implements, tools, money, grain, whiskey, medicine, and food were all items which could not logically be left behind. In this wild country, staples and necessities were always in short supply.

"Good Lord, John, I feel like a thief!" Nathan said, as they fastened a perfectly good plow to the side of their wagon. "It doesn't seem right."

"I know, little brother, but it would just be a waste to leave it all to rot ... or for someone else that will surely come along."

"I don't know... These things will just serve as a bad reminder whenever we look at them. ...Don't know if it's really worth it."

"Nathan, when we get into Zanesville, you'll see how valuable these items are. You just can't get things you need out here. I've heard stories of several families having to share one plow, or one good bucket. Put your conscience aside, and just let's get this done and be on our way."

Nathan wriggled out of his shirt, and wiped the sweat from his face with it. The sun was nearing the eleven o'clock position, and the day was quite warm compared to the previous days.

"How long do you reckon we'll stay in Zanesville before going on to Newton?" Nathan asked, dipping some water from the barrel and pouring it over the top of his head to cool himself. "Our land should be close in around Newton, shouldn't it?"

"We'll just stay long enough to get the information we need and re-supply. The land office is there. It'll probably take us a day or two to get from Zanesville to Newton. I just hope the weather holds out, so we can find our stake, get needed clearing done, and put up a cabin before it gets really cold." John threw a couple of bags of grain into the back of the wagon.

"Shhhhhhhh!" Nathan punched John hard in the shoulder. "No sense wakin' Maggie before we get good and far away from this cursed place!"

"Well, I'm finished. Do you see anything else we need to take with us?" John took a final look around.

Nathan surveyed what was left and shook his head slowly. "Nope, I think we've collected enough. Let's get out of here."

John tied the rescued animals to the back of the Conestoga, and Nathan proceeded to get the forward oxen moving. The wagon lurched ahead, and the wheels began to turn, moving westward along the narrow road called *Zane's Trace.*

"There's a pretty steep decline comin' up, shortly... Once we get 'er down to the bottom, we'll stop," John said, looking over at Nathan. "Should be a creek down there, where we can wash up. I sure could use a cool dip!"

"That sounds good to me." Nathan looked down at the blood stains covering his hands and the crimson spatters on his trousers. "But I would rather have a hot bath, lots of soap, and some clean clothes. I'd just like to wash this whole memory out of my mind."

"Pa used to tell us stories like this. Remember? I never thought we would have to experience it, though." John shook his head sadly. "You just don't think about that stuff when you're a kid. I remember when he told us about him and Uncle Peter coming up on a whole settlement that'd been attacked in Bucks County. Took 'em three days to bury the dead. Funny ... I remember thinkin' what a hero Pa was... I don't feel much like a hero." John's voice sounded shaky as he spoke.

"Yep, I remember that story. Seemed like Pa enjoyed tellin' it, too. Maybe he was made of tougher stuff than us. I dunno... I don't think heroes puke their guts up like I did. Or cry like a baby. And I'd just as soon not talk about it, or think about it ever again."

"I understand what you're saying, little brother. But maybe it's all part of bein' a man. ... Seems like life has a way of toughening ya up. I don't enjoy it, but just consider the whole episode like a growin' pain ... Ya know?" John wiped his eyes with the back of his hand. "Yep, this kinda stuff'll make ya hard as nails ... like Pa."

At that point the wagon was going down a steep hill.

"Nathan, you climb up in the seat and work the brake. I'll handle the oxen. We just need to take it slow and steady. Mud can be tricky on the downhill."

Nathan jumped up into the wagon seat and took hold of the brake with both hands. Even though the wheels could be locked, the mud was slippery and the heavy wagon was inclined to slide. It was all the men could do to control which way it would skid; and try to stop it by attempting to turn it from side to side. Nathan prayed the oxen would retain their footing in the muck. It was touch and go, and it was a slow descent. He tried not to look beyond the edge of the road and into the deep ravine below. For over an hour, the men fought the grade. More than a few times, the wagon slid precariously close to the brink.

John pulled the wagon to a stop in a clearing at the bottom of the hill; next to a lazy, wide creek, that meandered through the fertile, green valley.

"Damn!! I'm glad that's over!" Nathan said, jumping down from the wagon seat.

"You go and get Maggie, and I'll unhitch the oxen, and get the other animals over here for a drink and a rest," John said, untying the livestock at the back of the wagon. "After you get Maggie situated, see what you can rustle up from the food bin."

"... Sure thing, Masta!" Nathan replied sarcastically.

Nathan climbed into the wagon and sat down on the featherbed next to the sleeping girl. Maggie didn't stir.

"Maggie ..." Nathan said, leaning over her. "Maggie, wake up."

He couldn't help but admit that this was one beautiful young woman. *Not* a little girl any more. Her shiny black curls framed the delicate features of her face. Her skin was smooth and white, her cheeks glowed faintly pink, and her full lips were so inviting that Nathan felt an overwhelming temptation to kiss them. This was not the same little girl he remembered growing up with – wrestling with – fighting with.

Nathan gently brushed his lips across her cheek, and he whispered into her ear, "Maggie ... Wake up."

"What the hell are you doin', Nathan?!" It was John. He was standing at the end of the wagon, looking inside.

"She won't wake up," Nathan said, trying to conceal his embarrassment.

"Well, bring her out here. Maybe the fresh air and sunshine'll rouse her."

Nathan scooped the sleeping girl up and carried her to the opening. He carefully climbed down out of the covered wagon, and walked over to the creek bank with Maggie in his arms. She felt warm and soft against his bare skin. He just stood there savoring that feeling. He buried his face in her hair and breathed in the lavender scent mixed with the smell of smoke. He remembered the conversation from last night. At that moment, Nathan swore to himself, and on his own life, that he would love and care for Maggie as long as he lived. It was an epiphany moment. A life-changing decision had been made.

Maggie's eyes fluttered open. She put her arms around Nathan's neck, and nuzzled her face against his chest. She moaned softly.

"OK, is anyone hungry?" John broke the spell. "How's Maggie feeling?"

"I'm feeling a little sick," Maggie groaned. Her voice was almost inaudible.

"Well, that's to be expected. You'll feel better after you eat something. It's what whiskey will do to you." John winked at Nathan when he said it.

Nathan put Maggie down, steadying her while she gained her balance. The girl looked confused as she surveyed the landscape.

"Where are we?" she asked.

"We're about five miles from Zanesville," Nathan replied.

Maggie started backing away, looking around like a frightened animal. "My family – – Where is my family? I want to say good-bye! Nathan, I've got to say good-bye to them. I can't just leave them!"

"Maggie, calm down, Honey. John and I gave them all a proper burial. You were sleeping, and we just didn't want to wake you up ... not after all you've been through." Nathan reached for Maggie's hand, but she yanked it away.

"How could you?! How dare you assume I would just leave my family behind, on some God-forsaken road, in the middle of nowhere?" Maggie was crying hysterically now. "What if it was *your* family? Would you have preferred to sleep, rather than say one last good-bye – – Or say one last prayer in their honor? What were you thinking?!! What were you both thinking?!!" She began pacing. "You take me back! Take me back there right now!! I've got to say good-bye!!"

"Maggie, we can't do that... We've come too far to go back now." Nathan reached for Maggie again; and again she pulled away. "It was treacherous just getting to this point," he spoke as calmly as he could. "Be sensible, Maggie... Just simmer down, girl... Someday I'll take you back there, but not today. And don't forget, Honey, your family *was* my family. They practically raised me and John!"

John walked quietly up behind Maggie and caught hold of her around her waist, picking her up and holding her fast against his hip.

"Put me down!" She began screaming – kicking and flailing her arms.

John and Nathan both stood over six feet tall and were broadly built, muscular Swedes. It was no contest for Maggie, who weighed all of one hundred nine pounds and stood five feet four inches tall.

"I'll put you down when you calm yourself, young lady," John said firmly. "You're making enough commotion that those savages will be back here in a heartbeat. You settle yourself right now." John looked at Nathan and shook his head. "Let's just take her back there and leave her," he said, winking at his brother.

Upon hearing that, Maggie suddenly stopped squirming in John's grip. "Oh no you won't!" she said, in a determined but calmer voice. "I'll not go anywhere with either one of you. You're inconsiderate, unfeeling, stupid, unchristian, and um ... you're both cruel!!"

"Well then ... let's see," John said thoughtfully, "shall we just leave her here, Nathan? I don't think we want to be charged with kidnapping. What say you?"

"As always, big brother, you are definitely right. We don't need to get ourselves into that kind of trouble. I say, if she doesn't want to go with us, we shall just continue on without her."

"It's settled then," John said, dropping Maggie abruptly. She hit the ground with a thud.

"I hate you both!" she said, glaring up at Nathan. She scrambled to her feet and ran toward the Conestoga, with tears streaming down her cheeks.

"Hey!" John shouted, "You stay out of my wagon, girl!" John turned to his brother looking seriously concerned. "Nathan," he said in a low voice, "she's going to cause us more misery than we already have. You've got to get that girl under control."

"... Me!? What makes you think I can control her!?" Nathan yelled.

"Keep your voice down, man," John said, looking over to the wagon. "Where'd she go?"

Nathan walked quickly to the back of the covered wagon and looked inside. Maggie wasn't there. He glanced around frantically, hoping to see her somewhere along the road. There was no sign of her. "She's not here!" he shouted in alarm.

"She has to be!" John ran to the wagon. "My god, maybe I was too hard on her. I was just trying to get her to cooperate – – Now what?"

"You're an idiot! I should have never played along with it!" Nathan slammed his fist against the side of the wagon, and cursed John in silent rage.

"Well you didn't seem to have any better ideas!" John said, grabbing his rifle and powder from the wagon and heading back up the hill. "I just hope we find her before some injun does."

Nathan took his gun and jogged toward the creek. John was carefully examining the muddy trail for footprints going up the hill, which they had

24

recently descended. Nathan was looking for signs of broken branches, or indentations in the soft sod along the creek bank. There was no evidence that Maggie had been in either place.

Suddenly shots rang out, abruptly breaking the silence. Nathan turned on his heel and raced toward the road, ascending the hill. Just as he spotted John kneeling by the side of the road near some brush, in the process of reloading his gun, he heard another shot. Nathan was aware of a searing pain in his right side. He felt the cold mud on his skin as he dropped, sinking into the muck. As if a million miles away, he was barely aware of more gun fire. He couldn't move. He knew he was losing consciousness. Blackness was closing around him. He felt his rifle being pulled from his grip, and he tried to open his eyes.

"Lay still, Nathan. Play dead." It was Maggie's voice, but then she was gone. *'Was he imagining things?'* He couldn't tell. At that point, he surrendered to the dark void which was swallowing him.

Maggie disappeared into the forest and quietly circled around toward the brush pile where she had last seen John. She remembered, as children, how John and Nathan would use bird calls to communicate with one another when hunting. She especially remembered a call John made up. He named it the *chicken hawk mating scream* and he had devised an answering call for Nathan to use in response. As she neared the brush pile, she pursed her lips and made that very same bird-call, hoping

John would recognize it and not shoot in her direction. She crouched down low, and remained very still, listening for John's answer. Everything was silent. She tried again.

Finally, to her relief, she heard the correct answering reply. She repeated the first call. John responded. Maggie made her way toward the sound, keeping a sharp eye out for the Shawnees. As she advanced every few feet, she would repeat the call, and John would answer. She was kneeling under the broad leaves of a large bush, loading the gun, when she spotted two Shawnee warriors in her direct line of vision. One was creeping toward the brush pile where she was sure John was hiding. The other one was just beyond it. The Shawnee nearest her seemed to be taking aim with his musket. The renegade behind the brush was raising a tomahawk into the air. Maggie had to make an instant decision. Just as she raised Nathan's rifle, a shot rang out from the brush and the Indian aiming the musket fell to the ground. Maggie let go on the Shawnee with the tomahawk and he also fell. John jumped from the brush pile, and ran in Maggie's direction. She stood up, and as he passed by, he caught her arm, dragging her along. She could barely keep up. They ran to the road where Nathan lay bleeding.

Without saying a word, they lifted Nathan to his feet; one on each side of him; dragging the unconscious man down the road to the wagon. John hoisted Nathan into the Conestoga, and Maggie climbed in behind. Within seconds, the oxen were harnessed and the wagon was being pulled at breakneck speed across the creek and down the bumpy road. John didn't let up on the oxen as he employed the whip to their rumps. The wagon lurched and jostled from side to side on the uneven road, nearly tipping over at times.

Inside the wagon, in spite of being literally thrown around by the bumps and weaving, Maggie managed to drag Nathan to the bed and was diligently attending to his wounds. She thanked God the ball seemed to have missed any major organs and had exited through the fatty tissue on the far right side of his back. As she probed the exit wound with her fingers, she found some small bone fragments, and she concluded that a lower rib had been shattered. She removed the bone splinters and poured whiskey into the wounds. The bleeding was easily stopped with pressure. Maggie tore a piece of sheet from the bed and bound Nathan's wounds tightly. She wrapped his ribs as firmly as she could with a muslin curtain she found in the trunk. Finally, she raised the bottle of whiskey to her lips and took a long, slow drink of the brew. It burned her throat, and she could feel the heat all the way to her stomach. Breathing a long sigh, she lay down on the bed beside Nathan and tried to steady him; while the wagon rumbled and rattled along the rough road.

They finally arrived in Zanesville. The little town was sparsely settled. The wagon passed several crude cabins and a few temporary lean-tos along the main trail through the village. A couple of taverns, a back-smith shop, and a land office had been established only within the last two years.

John drove the oxen down to the end of the road at the river's edge. There he spotted the inn. He jumped from the wagon and disappeared inside the residence of Jacob McKray, the owner. Within minutes, four men emerged from the double log structure. Dragging Nathan out of the wagon, they carried him inside. Maggie was left alone with her thoughts. After some time, she climbed down from the back of the wagon and looked around. The oxen were covered in a thick layer of foaming sweat. Their feet and legs were bruised, swollen, and bleeding. She hurried to the front and unhitched the animals; she was glad the others had been left behind.

Maggie led the pair of oxen to the river's edge and allowed them to walk into the cool water, just long enough to rinse the mud and blood from their legs. It took all of her strength to keep the animals from drinking. She led them back up the bank, and tied them off at a post beside the cabin.

A boy came out just then. He was a tall, lanky, black child, and he looked to be about thirteen years old. His bright smile put Maggie at ease immediately.

"Can you get me a bucket, please?"

"Yes, ma'am," he replied.

"I think we should wet these poor animals down. Can you do that?"

"Sure can."

"OK. I'd really appreciate your help. But please don't let them drink but a sip. If you let them drink too much, it'll kill them."

"I know that, ma'am." The boy laughed, and he gave Maggie a sideways kind of look and paused before candidly asking, "Ma'am, why are you dressed like that?"

Maggie abruptly remembered she was wearing Nathan's cutoff clothes. She straightened the shirt nervously. It was stained with blood and mud. She smoothed her curls back from her face with her blood-stained hands. Maggie was embarrassed, knowing full well how wretched she looked at this moment. "Well ... it's a very long story... Rainstorm, injuns, ummm ... Nathan got shot... Do you have any idea where I might find some proper clothes?" Her throat tightened into a knot and she was trying not to cry.

"My name is Marky." The boy smiled at Maggie. "My mom's name is Caroline. If you go right in that door there," he said pointing to the door at the side of the cabin, "I'm sure she'll have something that will do."

"Marky, my name is Maggie, and I certainly do thank you for helping me."

Maggie forced a smiled, and left the boy in charge of cooling down John Stillman's exceptional pair of oxen.

She walked to the door and knocked softly. Caroline Green opened the door, and her eyes widened when she saw the girl standing there, dressed in men's clothes, and caked with blood and mud.

"Are you Caroline?"

"Yes. Yes I am – Honey, do you need some help?"

Maggie immediately broke into sobbing. "Yes ... I do ..." Her voice trailed off as she stood there crying.

Caroline, threw her arms around Maggie and hugged her tightly. "Now, now... Whatever it is, we'll fix it." She led Maggie inside and sat her down at a table. Caroline hurried to gather up some leftover stew, a loaf of bread, and a mug of fresh milk. She set the food in front of Maggie and sat down across from the girl. "Now, first you eat and then we'll talk," she said in a soft yet determined voice.

Caroline Green was a tall elegant Negro woman. She had smooth chocolate colored skin, and high cheekbones; giving her the semblance of an Indian princess. Her silky black curls were tied into a pile on top of her head with a red ribbon. She was dressed in a blue flowered frock that had a crisply starched white pinafore over it. Her quiet strength, grace, and sweet disposition endeared her to everyone who was fortunate enough to know her. She and her deceased husband had come from Maryland to the Ohio territory with Jacob McKray and his family. Although the Greens had originally been slaves, the McKray's had granted them their freedom. Mr. And Mrs. Green, however, stayed on with the McKray family as hired help.

On the other side of the inn, the only doctor in the area had been asked to examine Nathan. Dr. Mathison lived across the river in Springfield, and just happened to be attending a meeting at the inn. The doctor was a jovial man; he was short and stocky, and the prominence of his belly preceded him wherever he went. His bushy eyebrows accentuated large, twinkling, steel-grey eyes. His shaggy sideburns made his face look much broader than it actually was. He wore a pair of wire spectacles, which were continually slipping down off his nose. Although he was in his late forties, everyone assumed he was much older.

Nathan had regained consciousness and was trying to make sense of what happened.

"Stillman, you are a lucky man," Dr. Mathison said, sponging Nathan's side with a solution made with apple cider vinegar. "Looks like the girl patched you up right good." He dressed the wounds and bound Nathan's ribs again. "That ball didn't hit any organs – went clean through. I'm wondering how she figured out your rib was busted. She wouldn't have tied your ribcage so tight, otherwise." The doc scratched his head and shoved his glasses up a little further on his nose. "Did she have any medical training in Pennsylvania?"

"Her Pa was a doc," Nathan said, grimacing from the pain.

"Well, now I understand." The doctor took a small packet out of his bag and emptied the powder into a cup of water. He stirred it until it dissolved and handed it to Nathan. "Drink this. It'll make that pain easier to live with. I'll leave some here. The girl can make sure you get a measure when you need it. I'll be back tomorrow to see how you're doing." He packed his black bag and stood up to leave. "Oh ... by the way ... tell the girl I'm looking for an assistant. If she's interested, she's got herself a job. And I just want you to know ... she very well could have saved your life with her quick thinking. Being

31

tossed around in that wagon, having a busted rib...
You could've ended up with a punctured lung if you
hadn't been bound as securely... like you were."
With that, he placed a few packets of "Bitter Powder"
on the table beside the bed, turned, and left the
room.

John and Nathan stared at each other in silent
amazement.

"She saved my life, too," John said sheepishly.
"I didn't know there was an injun behind me, ready
to open my skull with a tomahawk. I only saw the
one in front of me. I shot the one I was lookin' at.
She got the one behind me. She shot that heathen
right between the eyes! The tomahawk fell in my
lap."

"Thank the good Lord." Nathan moaned. "And
to think ... we taught her to shoot." Nathan
struggled to speak, and could barely keep his eyes
open. "Um ... But where had she been?"

"Good question," John said, pulling the blanket
up over Nathan's chest. "You get some rest. We'll
talk about this later."

"Maggie, girl, am I to understand that your entire
family was killed out there on the ridge? I mean,
we've only had one serious problem with Shawnees
in the last few years. Must be something up with
those savages. The men folk in town will probably be
plenty upset to hear about this. Last time we had a
problem, the whole town went out, brought four
injuns in, and hung 'em in that tree right out there.
Are you sure they were Shawnee?"

"Yes ma'am … no doubt about it." Maggie began to cry again, thinking about her parents and her sisters, buried in a mass grave at the side of the road. Her heart was breaking.

Caroline stood up and walked over to where Maggie was sitting. She knelt down and took hold of the girl's hand. "Things like this happen, Maggie. We're all aware of the dangers when we leave our homes back east to come out here. Your folks knew the risks and so did you. You just have to make yourself go on. Try to put this tragedy behind you and make a good life for yourself here. It's what your family would want you to do." Caroline squeezed Maggie's hand firmly. "Once this Indian problem is taken care of, I'll take you up to the ridge myself. Then you can say a prayer at your family's grave, and say good-bye. You have my word."

"But I don't know how to go on without my family," Maggie said. She choked the words out between sobs.

"Well, Honey, you've got the men who rescued you. Didn't you tell me they'd always been like brothers to you?"

"I don't ever want to see them again! Neither one of them!! Not ever!!"

Caroline decided to change the subject. "Let's just get you cleaned up. That is, if you've had enough to eat. Do you want some more stew?"

"No thank you."

"Alright then, come with me, and we'll get you fixed up." Caroline grabbed a bucket of water from the corner, and she led Maggie into a back room. It was small but cozy. The bed had a colorful quilt on it. There was a dresser at one side of the room, and a comfortable looking rocking chair sat in the corner. The bedroom smelled clean and fresh; it was a calming scent; like sunshine and freshly cut wood.

Caroline opened a chest and took out a bath blanket and a bar of lye soap. She poured the water from the bucket into the large wash basin sitting on the dresser. There was a bottle of rose water beside the bowl, and Caroline added a few drops of the perfume to the water.

"Now, Maggie, you get washed up while I go find you some clothes. I'll be right back. You can bolt the door behind me. Will that do?"

"Yes... Thank you so much Caroline."

The tall, graceful, black woman left the room, and Maggie diligently bolted the door behind her.

Maggie first looked around the little bedroom to make sure there wasn't an uncovered window; then she wriggled out of the dirty clothes, leaving them in a pile on the floor. Stepping over the heap, to the dresser, she studied her face in the mirror. Her eyes were red and puffy, and she had a bloody scratch across her right cheek. She splashed some water on her face. It smelled like fresh flowers. She plunged her head into the deep bowl, scrubbing her hair with the soap and then rinsing it until it was squeaky clean. She continued until her entire body was finally scrubbed spotless. She wrapped the bath blanket around her and sat down in the big old rocker to wait for Caroline's return.

Everything seemed to be playing out in slow motion. Shock and despair takes a strange toll on one's sensitivities. Maggie sat quietly; trying to understand her own feelings. She was experiencing a numbness she had never known before. It was an unfamiliar detachment. She thought it absurd that her tears had turned to ice water, and her blood was running cold in her veins.

There was a soft knock at the door. "Maggie, it's me."

Maggie trudged over and unlocked it. Caroline came in with an armload of clothes. "I think these should fit you just fine," she said, dropping the load onto the bed. "There's a brush there, so you can fix your hair. I'll be in the kitchen if you need me." With that, Caroline left the room again.

Maggie bolted the door and turned to the bed to look through the clothes. She chose a pink calico dress with a delicate white lace collar. Caroline had even included a pair of shoes and an apron. There was also a flannel night gown, robe, and night cap. Maggie tucked those under the fluffy pillow on the bed. The two other dresses she draped over the rocker.

Maggie dressed quickly and brushed out her long dark hair. The curls fell in ringlets around her face, accentuating her huge emerald-green eyes. The clothes fit surprisingly well, and Maggie was sincerely grateful for Caroline's generosity.

"Well, how do I look?" Maggie did a slow twirl, for Caroline's approval.

"My, my!" Caroline exclaimed. "Is this the same muddy little girl that was here just a while ago? You sure don't look like the same child! You clean up real nice." Caroline laughed. "Oh! I almost forgot... Marky was asking about you. I told him I'd send you out when you were ready."

"Ok... I'll go see what he wants," Maggie said. "He was taking care of the oxen for me." She hurried outside to find Marky.

Maggie looked around for the boy, but didn't see him anywhere. She did, however, find the oxen. They were standing quietly in a sturdy pen and looking perfectly healthy. She was relieved. Maggie noticed the familiar and pungent smell of camphor and eucalyptus. She entered the pen, and discovered that Marky had lovingly wrapped the legs of each animal with liniment soaked cloth. She remembered how her Pa had done the very same thing, and how she helped him on numerous occasions when their beautiful Belgium draft horses were overworked. She relished the memory. She allowed herself to be absorbed in the daydream.

Suddenly a gun shot rang out.

Abruptly startled from her musing, Maggie screamed and whirled around, sucking in her breath. She grabbed hold of the gate to steady herself. The color drained from her cheeks.

Hearing the scream, Marky quickly forgot about the fat old goose he just bagged. He dropped his muzzleloader and ran over to the enclosure, grabbing Maggie's arm. He could see she was on the verge of fainting. "Oh no!!! I didn't mean to scare ya, girl!! He struggled to keep her on her feet. "Help! Somebody... Help!!" he yelled, as loudly as he could.

John emerged from around the front of the inn. He, too, had been surprised by the sound of gunfire. When he saw Marky trying to hold Maggie from falling, he wasted no time coming to assist the boy. He scooped Maggie up, and with the girl in his arms, he ran for the inn. Caroline, who had also heard the shot and the scream, was instantly at the door.

"What on earth happened?" she exclaimed, holding the door open for John. "Is she shot?"

"No, Mama ... I shot a goose over by the bank. I guess it scared her real bad. I'm sorry! I didn't even know she was out here."

"Young man, you get your behind out of here! I'll deal with you later," Caroline scolded.

Maggie was regaining her senses, and realized it was John holding her. "Put me down, you heathen!" She wriggled to free herself as John lowered her onto a chair at the kitchen table. "I don't need your help! Just get out of my sight."

"I was worried, Maggie. I didn't know if you'd been hit," John said.

"Well, I wasn't. Now just go." She spat out the words with all the hatred she could muster.

John looked at Caroline, shaking his head in bewilderment. "She's a headstrong woman," he said quietly. "I'll just be about my business ... I guess... If you need me, I'll be in the front."

Caroline walked over to John and laid her hand on his arm in a gesture of understanding. "Miss Maggie just needs someone to blame for losin' her kin.... Lashin' out at those closest to us is just our nature... you know?" she whispered.

"Thank you for looking after Maggie. I just don't know how to remedy this. I guess I'll never understand women." He turned and walked out of the kitchen, scratching his head.

"I'll be just fine with you and your brother out of my life!" Maggie screamed after him.

Caroline turned and gave Maggie a disgruntled look, raising one eyebrow, and shaking her head. "Miss Maggie, I think you need to rest a bit. You've been through way too much today. Why don't you consider lying down for a while? Dinner will be ready in about an hour." Caroline felt Maggie's forehead with the back of her hand. "You look feverish to me."

"I'm OK ... just angry," Maggie said. She brushed the curls away from her face and stood up slowly. "Do you have any tea? I could really use a cup."

"I sure do, Maggie," Caroline said. She hurried to the fireplace and ladled some hot water, from the big black kettle, into a mug. "A nice cup of hot tea will probably do us both some good," she said, filling another cup. Caroline took the cups to the table and put some tea leaves and honey into each one.

"That smells wonderful," Maggie said, sniffing the comforting aroma. "Do you mind if I take mine outside?"

"You go right ahead, girl. Just be careful – and don't you stray too far, ya hear?"

"Yes ma'am."

Maggie took her cup and stepped outside. The flowers in Caroline's herb garden, just beyond the cabin door, were closing their petals as the late afternoon shadows descended on the flower beds. Her attention was drawn to the river. It resembled a fiery, orange-red ribbon, emanating golden sparks, which bounced and danced on the rippled surface. The sun setting in the west was a huge crimson orb. Its reflection on the Muskingum River was spectacular. She couldn't remember ever seeing a sunset so dramatic. Maggie walked to the river bank and sat down on a rock. She sipped her tea, holding the cup in both hands, enjoying the sensation of the heat on her fingers. Everything seemed so peaceful here. The river sang as it splashed down over the rapids, endlessly pursuing its union with the Ohio River some sixty miles distant.

The evening was warmer than she expected, and there was a slight breeze blowing in from the south. She was aware of the faint fragrance of pine in the air. Maggie raised her head and breathed in the aroma. She was acutely reminded of her beloved Pennsylvania mountains. She wept quietly.

Chapter 2 - Moving On

When Nathan opened his eyes, the rising sun was bathing his room with yellow-grey muted light. The greased paper on the window filtered the sunshine, casting strange spotted shadows across the floor. It was a familiar sight. Nathan felt a subtle melancholy. He realized he was homesick.

He tried to sit up, but found it was too painful. He managed to roll onto his left side. Using his left arm, he slowly raised his torso, and with some work, he swung his legs over the side of the bed. Nathan sat there holding his ribs tightly, breathing shallow, and praying the pain would subside. He glanced over at the table beside the bed. The packets of "Bitter Powder" were still there. He stared at the pitcher of water and the cup, knowing full well they were beyond his reach. He would need to maneuver closer to the table in order to obtain the medicine he wanted so desperately.

John was sleeping on the floor, stretched out on a pile of quilts at the other end of the room. Nathan debated whether to wake John, or try to get to the powder on his own. He attempted to stand up.

"Gawd!!" he yelled. The pain ripped through his torso like a white-hot knife. He collapsed back onto the bed screaming in agony.

John jumped up from his bedding, not quite sure what had jarred him awake. Staggering around like a drunken sailor, trying to get his bearings, and still half asleep, he glanced over at his brother. Nathan was writhing in pain, and moaning like a woman giving birth. John rushed to the table and quickly mixed some of the medicinal powder into a cup of water. He raised Nathan up; just enough for him to drink it.

"Nathan, what the hell did you do?" John asked, lowering Nathan back down onto the pillow. "You know you're not supposed to get up." He set the cup down on the table with a bump. "I just hope to God I mixed that right. Doc said to have Maggie do it, but I don't think she'd help us if we were hangin' over a cliff by our fingernails. I saw her last night, and if words could kill, I'd be a dead man."

"What?" Nathan moaned.

"Your little Miss Maggie is still mad as hell at us... And holdin' onto a grudge like it's a lifeline. She made it real clear she doesn't want to see either of us ever again. I mean ... she said it in no uncertain terms."

"*MY* little Miss Maggie?!! What the hell is that supposed to mean?" Nathan tried to sit up. "Oh gawd!!!!! I don't think you mixed enough of that stuff in the water," he groaned, and resigned himself to just lie still on the bed.

"Wait a while for it to take hold. I'm not givin' you any more for a while." John picked up the packets and shoved them safely into his pants' pocket. "You think I didn't see what was going on between you and Maggie? Think I'm blind, huh?" John said, turning back to Nathan.

"Don't know what you're talkin' about. Maybe you were seein' things... You know ... hallucinating?" Nathan squirmed under the blanket, trying to get comfortable. "John ... umm ... I need a bucket. I gotta go."

John got the slop-jar from the corner and handed it to Nathan who drew it under the covers. John continued the conversation. "Well, makes no difference anymore... I can tell ya one thing for sure, now... You won't be havin' any more romantic interludes with that little girl! She'd sooner stick a knife in you than look at ya!"

"Oh gawd!" Nathan winced. John's words plunged into his heart like a dagger. "Take this jar, and give me some more of that damned medicine!"

John retrieved the pot, but ignored Nathan's pleading for more pain killer. He busied himself with folding up the quilts strewn about the floor.

There was a knock at the door, and Doc Mathison walked right in. Maggie followed in behind him. "Good mornin' to ya boys," Doctor Mathison said, plopping his black bag down on a chair. "How's the patient?"

"He's a pain in the ass," John replied, not seeing Maggie standing behind the doctor. "He's the biggest baby this side of the Ohio River! Whinin' and complainin' like a little girl."

"Like a little girl?" Maggie echoed, stepping up beside the doctor.

"Ummm... Sorry 'bout my language, Maggie... I didn't see ya there," John stammered.

"Not to worry... I wouldn't expect anything better, from a heathen like you," she snapped.

"Let's take a look," the doctor said, loosening the binding around Nathan's ribs. "You boys recognize my new assistant, huh?" He chuckled mischievously.

Nathan bit his lip, trying not to show his discomfort, as the doctor removed the dressings. "Doc ... the pain killer isn't working," he moaned.

"Maggie, mix up some of that Bitter-Powder for the boy. It's there in the left side of my bag. And please ... I know you'd like to see him dead ... but don't over-do it. OK?" Stifling a chuckle, Doc Mathison tried hard to sound serious.

Nathan's eyes widened. "Um ... Doc ... maybe YOU should mix it, huh?" he whispered. He could feel his mouth going dry from fear.

"... but Doc, I just gave him some. He said it wasn't helpin' but it's only been a few minutes. Aren't you afraid he'll get too much?" John shouted.

"Now, now, boys... Maggie's perfectly capable. Don't worry." Doctor Mathison poured a vial of antiseptic over the wounds and placed a clean dressing on them. "She saved your life once, Nathan... I don't think she'd waste all that effort by killing you now," he said, smiling.

"Don't bet on it!" Maggie said soberly, handing the cup to the doctor.

Doc looked at Maggie and grinned. He took the container from her. "... And to answer your question, John – – a double dose won't hurt him," he said. The doc held the cup to Nathan's lips. "Here ya go ... drink this, Nathan. In no time, you'll feel nothing."

"Yea ... that's what I'm afraid of," Nathan said. He hesitated for a moment, but the pain was too much for him. He gulped down the solution, praying Maggie hadn't poisoned him. The drink was extremely bitter; more so than what he had been given before. Nathan swallowed the last drop, closed his eyes, and raised his hand. "Bye," he whispered. A luscious dizzy feeling was rising from his toes, up his body. It was like a warm bath getting deeper and deeper; creeping higher and higher; finally bathing his entire body in the most delightful sensation he had ever felt. His hand fell heavily onto the bed.

John gasped. "Nathan... Oh my God! Is he dead?" He grabbed his brother's shoulders and shook him violently. "Nathan!"

"I didn't kill your brother," Maggie said. "Not that either one of you deserve to breathe ... but if you don't stop shaking him like that ... *you* might just kill him."

Doctor Mathison eased John's hands from Nathan's shoulders. "He's going to sleep for the rest of the day ... maybe even most of tomorrow, John. But I promise you, he'll feel much better when he wakes up. Sleep is the best thing for the healing process." Doctor Mathison slapped John on the back. "Don't worry, John. He'll be just fine. I'll come back tomorrow evening and check on him." He turned to Maggie and smiled. "Maggie, girl... I want you to bind up those ribs, again... And please ... be gentle ... alright?"

"I'll behave, Dr. Mathison. I promise," Maggie grinned.

Dr. Mathison grabbed his bag and left.

"John, get me a basin of hot water and a sponge from the kitchen, please," Maggie said, pulling a chair up to the side of Nathan's bed.

"Umm... Sure," John conceded, and headed for the kitchen. It wasn't in his nature to take orders from anyone, especially a woman; but in this case he decided to guard his tongue and his manners just to keep the peace.

Left alone in the room, Maggie sat down beside the sleeping Nathan, studying his face. His features were strong and masculine. His jaw was well defined, as if chiseled by the hand of God. He had the most exquisite cleft in his chin. His skin was a tawny bronze color, from working long hours in the sun. His bushy blonde mustache accentuated his large mouth and full lips. Nathan kept it neatly trimmed, and the sides grew straight down to his chin, framing his entire mouth. There were matching dimples on each side of his face, just below his cheek bones. She looked at his hands. They were possibly the largest hands she had ever seen. He was muscular from head to toe. Nathan Stillman was a very handsome man. Maggie breathed a sigh, and a single tear slid down her cheek.

Nathan stirred; regaining consciousness. Suddenly, he grabbed Maggie, dragging her off the chair and pulling her body across his chest. His massive arms held her fast against him.

"Nathan!" Maggie shrieked. "Let me go! What are you doing?!" Maggie struggled to free herself.

Nathan's eyes were glassy and he was trying hard to focus on Maggie's face. He put one hand behind her head, and pulled her face down closer to his. He stared deeply into her eyes, as if trying to find the Maggie he had once known.

"Nathan, please let me go ... you don't want to hurt me, do you?" Maggie knew the drug was affecting the man's thinking. She strained to pull away.

"I wouldn't hurt you, Maggie... I'm gonna love ya Honey ..." His words were garbled.

Without warning, he pulled her face down further, and covered her lips with his. He kissed her. Maggie frantically wriggled to escape, but his kiss became a magnet, pulling her into him instead. Before she realized what was happening, she was responding to it; craving more; she stopped fighting him – – but only for a moment. Knowing she was in a potentially dangerous situation, she gathered all her strength and managed to pull free. She stood up and backed slowly away from the bed; half afraid that he would come after her. Maggie stood silently, watching Nathan suspiciously. Her heart was racing. To her amazement, he seemed to be unconscious again. She was relieved to see John enter the room.

John brought the bowl over and set it on the table beside the bed. Caroline had also given him a bath-sheet, which he laid on the foot of the bed. "Do you need any help?" he asked in a quiet voice.

"No, thank you. This is just fine," Maggie answered breathlessly. She quickly straightened her dress, and hoped John didn't notice her rapid breathing. She could feel the heat from her flushed cheeks.

"Maggie ..."

"I don't want to talk to you."

"Well, I think you *NEED* to talk to me."

"John, I told you... You're NOT my friend anymore. Now just leave it at that."

"Maggie... You're like my own sister, and I don't intend to let this go on."

"No ... not like your sister! Or you would have never deprived me of saying a proper good-bye to *OUR* parents!"

"Look, damn it to hell!!" John yelled at Maggie. "Nathan and I were tryin' to protect you. Maybe we made a huge mistake. Maybe we weren't thinkin'. You're not the only one who was traumatized! Do you think it was easy for us to have to clean up that bloody mess? Do you think it was easy for us to do what we *had* to do? - - Not what we *wanted* to do? Why don't you just stop bein' so damned self-centered and selfish ... and think about what *ME and NATHAN* went through... And what we were tryin' to do by NOT lettin' you see your Ma and Pa, and your sisters all bloody, and mutilated, and DEAD!!!!" John swung his arm across the table, sending everything on it crashing to the floor. "NOW I wish to hell, we'd taken you right into the middle of that carnage and rubbed your gawd-damned nose in it!!!"

John turned to the girl and sternly poked his finger into her chest, causing her to lose her balance and sit down heavily on the chair. He looked Maggie right in the eye and said, in a slow, cold tone, "Have you even considered that it is *YOUR* fault that my brother is layin' there, right now, with holes blown clean through him because we were out lookin' for *YOU*, while *YOU* were throwin' your immature temper-tantrum? Which, by the way ... was the reason those savages found us out there." John whirled around on his heel. "You can just keep on actin' like the spoiled, self-indulgent, BRAT you are!! I've had it with your shallowness!" John threw his hands into the air in exasperation and left.

Maggie sat there for a long time, in a state of shock and disbelief. Wave after wave of shame and embarrassment washed over her consciousness. Finally, she laid her head down on the bed, beside Nathan's unconscious body, and she cried. All the grief, all the hurt, all the anger melted away in her tears. It was the first time she actually realized what *SHE* had done. In her self-absorbed vengeance, she had totally ignored the fact that it really was all *HER* fault. She was the one who caused the commotion, *SHE* had attracted the Shawnees to their location. And it was *HER* childish antics that nearly got both brothers killed. Most importantly, she understood *WHY* Nathan and John didn't want her to see her family, and relive the massacre.

"Oh Nathan!" she said. "I'm so sorry. I'm so very sorry ..." Her voice trailed off into soulful sobbing.

Maggie succumbed to an entirely different kind of grief. It was an agony she had never experienced before; a sorrow that gripped her very soul; an anguish which drowned her hopes, and her dreams, and her perception of self-worth. She was painfully aware of a self-loathing which surpassed any hatred or disgust she had ever felt for another other human being. Her actions were deplorable; unforgivable, and she knew it.

"John is absolutely right – – and completely justified," she cried out, into the empty room.

After a while, Maggie composed herself enough to clean up the shattered pottery and glass on the floor, and then, tend to Nathan. She bound his ribs tightly, but gently. Maggie was thankful that Nathan remained asleep. She gathered her things, and she left the room.

It was late afternoon the next day, when Dr. Mathison arrived at the inn. Maggie had been watching for him, with the good news that Nathan was recovering faster than she had expected. Although she only peeked into his room from time to time, and hadn't actually talked to him, she was relieved to see him up, sitting in a chair, and eating the hot meals Caroline prepared for him.

Dr. Mathison pulled his buggy to a stop, climbed down, and tied his horse to the post.

"Good afternoon, Miss Maggie."

"Good afternoon to you, Dr. Mathison," Maggie replied.

The doctor walked to the back of the buggy and untied a beautiful, little bay mare. "Do you ride, Miss Maggie?" he asked, leading the filly around to the front.

"Yes sir... Why?"

"Because this horse is for you," he said. He extended the reigns to the girl.

"Excuse me?"

"Well, if you're going to assist me ... you'll be making some house visits, and running errands for me. Seems to me you'll be needing a way to get here and there. Right?"

"Yes sir… But I …"

"Yep… Here's a list of some of the families I make visits to on a fairly regular basis." He pulled a wrinkled piece of paper from his coat pocket, and handed it to Maggie. "I just make sure the kids are growin' right, and I take them tonic every other week. The ones at the bottom are old folks I check in on to make sure they're doin' OK. There'll be times when you'll need to come with me … to help with the serious stuff … like birthing babies, accidents, surgery… You know. Your Pa did it all, didn't he?"

"Well… He …"

"This'll work out great. Give me more time in my office with those who can come in to see me. It's those folk outside of town, who can't make it in to the office so easy. Those are the ones you'll be seeing. What say you, Maggie?"

"I think …"

"Good. We'll sit down later, and I'll write out directions … make sure you can find those farms." Dr. Mathison reached in the buggy and pulled out his black bag. "Let's go see the patient, shall we?"

Maggie didn't even bother trying to answer the doctor. She tied the mare to a post and followed Dr. Mathison inside.

When they walked into Nathan's room, he was sitting in a rocking chair, by the window. Nathan looked up in surprise. "Dr. Mathison… Good to see ya," he said. He nodded to Maggie, acknowledging her presence.

"Good to see you out of bed, Nathan." Dr. Mathison walked over and felt Nathan's cheek with the back of his hand. "Still a little fever... How's the pain?" he asked.

"Much better, thanks."

"Where's that big brother of yours?"

"He went over to Springfield to take care of some business. He'll be back shortly."

"Did Maggie take good care of you while I've been gone?" The doctor chuckled.

"Don't know, sir. I was out of it all yesterday and most of today." Nathan glanced up in Maggie's direction, and then quickly back at the doc. "She must have. I mean, I'm not dead." He managed a smile. Maggie glanced over and caught him studying her. He had a roguish expression on his handsome face.

"Well, let's get a look at your side, and get those dressings changed. Can you make it over to the bed?" Without waiting for an answer, Dr. Mathison was already helping Nathan to get up. "Maggie, bring my bag over here, and get the batting out. Oh ... and the antiseptic, too."

Without saying a word, Maggie did as she was asked.

She couldn't help remembering Nathan's kiss, and in the most secret part of her being ... she longed for more. It was her first real kiss! She wondered if he remembered kissing her. She pretended it never happened.

"How soon before I can travel, doc?" Nathan asked. "John's gettin' antsy."

"What's your hurry?" The doctor lifted the dressing and took a close look at Nathan's wounds. He poured the antiseptic over them and wiped away the drainage. "Hmm... Well, Stillman ... if things go well ... I'd say within a few more days." Dr. Mathison pushed his spectacles up further on his nose. "So ...?"

"So what?" Nathan had a confused look on his face.

"So what's the hurry?"

"Oh... Well, we've got some land out by Newton and we may need to do some clearing; and we have to put up a cabin before winter sets in. That is ... if we can find the stake. I guess the plat's off the trail, and we need to locate it. That's what John's tryin' to get some help with, right now."

"Maggie, can you finish dressing this, and bind him good and tight?" The doctor stood up, and walked over to look out the window. "You know ..." he said thoughtfully, "I've got to make a trip to Newton next week. I have a patient near Uniontown who needs tonic and herbs. I take 'em out there every couple of months." Dr. Mathison turned back around to face Nathan. "I could go sooner... I know some other people in that area. We'd probably get you and John settled faster, if we all worked together."

"Owwee!!" Nathan yelled.

Maggie jumped back in surprise. "I'm really sorry... I didn't mean to hurt you... Doc said to bind you tight... I ... I ..."

"Now Maggie ... I told you to be nice," the doctor said, in a stern voice.

Maggie looked up at Dr. Mathison and saw his sly wink. "Oh, all right. If I have to ..." she sighed, playing along with the doc.

"Here, girl... I'll finish this up. You'd better go get that mare fed and bedded down before dark." The doctor took the binding strips from Maggie's hand. "And don't disappear... I want to talk to you when I'm done here."

"Alright," Maggie said, reluctantly heading for the door.

"So, Nathan ... what do you think about getting my friends to help you and John get settled?" He finished pulling the wrapping tight around Nathan's midsection, and tied off the ends. "If you want my help, just let me know. I've got a couple of midwives who cover my office for me when I'm out of town... I'll have to make some pretty quick arrangements, if you and John want me to accompany you."

"Are you sure it wouldn't be a bother for you?"

Dr. Mathison extended his hand and Nathan shook it firmly. "Stillman ... after what you fellas have been through ... I'd be honored to help you. And besides that, I want to keep an eye on that wound for a couple of weeks." The doc started packing up his bag. "Oh ..." He stopped and turned back to Nathan. "Did you hear what happened with that Indian problem up on the ridge?"

"Not sure what you mean."

"About twenty of our best citizens, from here and from Springfield, went up there looking for the savages that attacked you and your group. Tracked 'em for about ten miles... Clear over past Taylorsville. Seems they were a renegade bunch from down south, around Chillicothe. Nine of 'em. They won't be causing any more problems. Killed 'em all."

"Thank God." Nathan breathed a sigh of relief. "I'm glad to hear it."

"Yep ... I thought that'd make you feel better." Dr. Mathison picked up his bag. "I'll be back tomorrow. Maggie's got the pain killer, if you need it. Talk to John and see what he says about my offer." With that, he walked out of the room.

Dr. Mathison found Maggie in the kitchen talking to Caroline. When he walked through the door, Caroline's face lit up with a huge Smile.

"Doc, you're just in time for dinner! I'm so glad you're here," Caroline said, grabbing the doctor's arm and ushering him over to the table. "Sit yourself down, right here."

"Who am I to turn down one of your wonderful meals, Missy Caroline Green?" Dr. Mathison said, with a chuckle.

"I thought you'd see it my way," Caroline answered. She set a large plate of stew in front of the doctor, and a big mug of fresh buttermilk.

"Oh my, my, my... You do know how to spoil me," he said.

"Doc... I'll never stop thanking you for saving my Marky... You know that." She placed a loaf of fresh baked bread on the table. "I will be eternally grateful. You *ARE* my hero."

"Mine, too!" Marky shouted, bursting into the kitchen. He ran over and gave Dr. Mathison a big bear hug.

"Marky, my boy... How's your foot feeling? And how's that old dog Sam?" The doctor grabbed Marky's leg and swung it up onto his lap. He quickly slipped the boy's shoe off, and removed the sock. "Hmm... Looks pretty good, if I do say so myself," he said, pushing his glasses up on his nose.

Maggie sucked in her breath at the sight of Marky's foot.

"Oh, Miss Maggie," the doctor said, frowning at the girl, "you should have seen it before we got it all fixed up. Isn't that right, son?"

"Sure is, doc," Marky agreed. "It looks much better without those mangled old toes. It was a little hard walking for a few weeks, but it's just right fine, now!"

"Marky had a pretty serious run-in with an old mother bear, a few months back," Caroline said, squeezing Maggie's hand reassuringly. "Sam didn't fair very well either ... but his intervention gave Marky a chance to get away. If it hadn't been for Doc Mathison, Marky and Sam probably wouldn't have made it. Didn't you notice Sam is missing one of his ears and an eye?" Caroline reached over and tousled Marky's hair. "Yes sir... Those two are a fine pair. Marky and Sam... Just like old war buddies."

"You're right, Marky... It looks right fine to me, too," the doc agreed. He gently lowered Marky's foot to the floor. "Now get that shoe back on before you get a splinter in your foot."

"Yes, Maggie... You'll soon find out that everyone loves Doc. Not many lives in these parts that haven't been touched by this angel of a man." Caroline patted Dr. Mathison affectionately on the shoulder.

"Oh for God's sake, Caroline... I'm no saint and you know it. Makes it right hard to live up to all that praise you people keep spreading around about me."

Maggie covered her mouth to stifle a giggle.

While Dr. Mathison and Maggie were eating, Caroline and Marky served the rest of the guests staying at the inn.

"Maggie, my girl, do you think you can handle that schedule I gave you?" the doctor asked, reaching for another piece of bread.

"I'm sure I can."

"Well ... There's something else I've been thinking about." He slapped a big knife full of butter on the bread and spread it around. "How would you like to move into my office? I've got a stone cottage over in Springfield and there's a little apartment ... um ... a cabin, off to one side. I lived there while I built my house. Actually, it's attached to my house, now. I think it would be right convenient for both of us." He shoved the bread into his mouth and grinned at Maggie. "Caroline sure is a fine cook."

"I ..."

"Of course you'd want to see it before you make up your mind. Would you like to come over to Springfield tomorrow and take a look?"

"Well ..."

"Good. Come over about one o'clock. Bring Marky with you. He knows the way."

"OK... I'll ..."

"Yep – I'll see ya tomorrow, Maggie. Now you take good care of Nathan tonight. He's a pretty special fellow." He stood up, buttoned his waistcoat, and grabbed his bag. He gave Maggie a pat on the back, and was out the door, leaving the girl to wonder if she'd ever get a word in edge-wise with that man.

Maggie cleared the table for Caroline, and then went into the main part of the inn, to gather the dishes from the tables there. She saw John come in the front door and sit down with Mr. McKray, the owner. She watched as John counted out some coins and then neatly stacked them in little piles. He moved the money toward Mr. McKray. McKray picked up the coins, put them in his pocket, and then shook John's hand. John looked over at Maggie, but didn't acknowledge her in any way. His expression was cold, and he looked away quickly. Maggie returned to the kitchen with a heavy load of plates, cups, and cutlery, stacked on a tray. She set it down on the dry sink. Although she didn't want to face John, she knew Dr. Mathison expected her to check on Nathan before bedtime. Maggie stood for a long while, trying to muster the courage to go and see about Nathan. Finally, she dried her hands with a towel, straightened her apron, and headed for the room on the other side of the inn.

She knocked at the door softly.

"Who is it?" It was John's voice.

"It's me... Maggie. I came to check on Nathan."

"Nathan's fine. He's sleepin'... And we don't need your help any longer. Go away."

Maggie turned around slowly. She could feel her throat tightening into a painful knot. She hurried to her room and fell across the bed. She cried herself to sleep.

"It's perfect!" Maggie cried, looking around the cheerful little cabin. "I love it!"

"I like it, too," Marky chimed in.

"I thought you would, Maggie," Doc Mathison said. "It's not much, but it *is* comfortable, and it couldn't be any closer to work." He grinned, and winked at Maggie. "My office is right through this door, right here," he said, opening the door. "I'll put a bell on a string, so I can ring for you when I need you." He stopped, and looked over at Maggie. "I mean, if that's OK with you."

"It's perfect!" Maggie repeated herself.

"Good. I'll give you a dollar a week, free room and board, and I'll take care of your mare. How does that sound?"

"It's perfect!"

"Maggie... Is there an echo in here, girl? I mean, can you tell me what you really think?"

"I'm sorry, Dr. Mathison... I love the cabin, the bell is fine, and the entire arrangement suits me perfectly."

"All right, then. Let's shake on it."

Maggie shook the doctor's hand. She couldn't stop smiling.

"Can I come visit you, Maggie?" Marky asked. "You know ... I'll help you get settled. Why... Me and Mama have lots of stuff you can use here."

"You and your mom will be welcome here anytime," Maggie assured Marky.

"OK kids ... you can start bringing your stuff over whenever you want." The doc sat down at the little table in the middle of the room. He pulled a piece of paper from his pocket and smoothed the wrinkles out with his hands. "Look here, Maggie. Here's some notes... Where to find things you'll need. How to get to those families outside of town. Read it over and see if you understand everything." He shoved his spectacles up. They seemed to be always slipping down on his nose. "Elizabeth Williams and Susanne Jackson will be here for the next few weeks. I'll be out of town. They'll help you if you need it. They're both midwives and very good midwives ... I trained them of course." He chuckled. "I've got some patients to see right now, so here's a little money, in case you need anything." He dropped several gold coins onto the table. "That should hold you." The doctor left without any further instructions.

Maggie looked at the money, and then at the door. Confused, she ran to the doorway just in time to see the doctor's buggy rolling down the street. "Why would I need that much money?" she asked, looking at Marky.

Marky just shrugged his shoulders. He didn't say a word.

Maggie returned to the center of the room, and took another look around, in disbelief.

"I think it's wonderful, Marky... What do you think?" Maggie twirled around the room in a little dance.

"It's perfect!" Marky shouted.

"I think there *IS* an echo in here," Maggie teased.

The next morning, Maggie packed the little bag Dr. Mathison had given her. She mounted the pretty bay mare, and started her rounds for the day. Maggie only had three families to visit, so she expected to be back before noon. Then, she could start taking things over to her new home, in Springfield. Caroline had given her quilts, dishes, pots, and cooking utensils. Marky had a list of items Maggie had instructed him to see if he could purchase from the people in town.

The morning went smoothly. Everyone Maggie visited was very hospitable. She was relieved to find them all in good health. She dispensed the herbs and tonics, and arrived back at the inn by noon, just as she had hoped. She fed and watered the mare, then turned the horse out, into the paddock.

"Boy am I hungry!" Maggie cried, bursting into the kitchen. "Caroline, I had such a marvelous time." Maggie ran over and hugged Caroline tightly. "You should have seen the baby I got to bathe... And the old blind man who can see with his fingers!"

"Aw... That would be Charlie Kessler," Caroline said, patting Maggie affectionately on the back.

"Why yes! That was his name." Maggie poured herself a cool cup of water, from the pitcher on the cupboard. "I've got to check on Nathan, and then

Marky and I are going to take my stuff over to Springfield. I'm so excited!" She noticed Caroline suddenly looked distressed. Maggie stepped back and stared intently into Caroline's eyes, sensing something was wrong. "Nathan's all right, isn't he?"

Caroline hesitated for a couple of seconds, and then said, "Oh yes ... Maggie Girl. He's just fine. As a matter of fact, he and John left this morning for Newton." She waited pensively for Maggie's response.

"Newton? So soon?"

"Um huh. Doc Mathison went, too."

"Doc went to Newton?" Maggie put her hand down on the table, to steady herself.

"Maggie ... are you OK, child?" Caroline put her arm around Maggie and walked her over to a chair. Maggie didn't protest, as Caroline helped her to sit down. "Do you want a cup of tea?"

"No ... um, no thank you, Caroline. I don't care for any tea." Maggie looked at her hands, and then rubbed her palms together as if she were trying to warm them. "Did Nathan say anything? I mean did he mention me?" Maggie's voice sounded small, and was beginning to crack.

"Yes, Maggie, he did." She reached into her apron pocket and pulled out a long golden chain with a large, heart-shaped locket hanging on it. "He asked me to give you this," she said, handing it to Maggie, "and he said to tell you ... if you ever need him, he'll be there for you."

Maggie slowly took the locket from Caroline's hand. She opened it, and looked at the miniature portraits inside. It was her mother and father. She closed it up, and held it against her cheek, squeezing her eyes shut tight.

"It was my Mama's locket ..." Maggie choked out the words, fighting back the tears.

"I know," Caroline whispered.

"She never took it off."

"Well, it's a beautiful necklace."

"She would have had it on when they killed her."

"Let's not think about that, Maggie," Caroline tried to change the subject. "Let's think about how lucky you are to have the locket ... as a token of your mother's love. I'm sure she would be happy to know you have it. And it was really sweet of Nathan to keep it for you."

"Nathan ..." Maggie groaned. And then the real story poured out from Maggie's heart. She admitted it was her fault that Nathan had been shot. She told Caroline about her childish outburst, and how she screamed and yelled at Nathan and John. She confessed that the Indians would have never found them if she had just been quiet. Then, she told Caroline about John chastising her; pointing out the ugly truth; making her realize how one-sided her perception had been.

"I want to die. I didn't get a chance to apologize," Maggie said. "I wouldn't blame them if they never forgive me... I don't think I'll ever forgive myself," she cried. "I'll probably never see Nathan again... And he'll never know ... um ... he'll never know ..." she stammered.

"Never know what, Maggie?"

"How much I love him," Maggie whispered. Maggie completely broke down; gut-wrenching sobs shaking her body. She struggled to catch her breath.

Caroline hurried over to the cupboard and pulled out the jug of "medicinal" whiskey. She poured some in a cup and brought it over to Maggie.

"Maggie … I know Nathan leaving so abruptly is hard on you. I want you to drink this, and then lie down for a while. It'll calm you, Little Girl."

Maggie obediently drank the whiskey. It burned all the way down, but then the warmth seemed to be strangely comforting. Caroline guided the girl to her room, and helped her into bed. Maggie closed her eyes and prayed she would go to sleep and never wake up.

"My life is over," she murmured, as she drifted off to sleep.

"No … Maggie … your life is just beginning." Caroline spread a quilt over Maggie, and tucked it in around her shoulders. She noticed the locket was entwined in the girl's fingers; gripped tightly. It was an anchor to the past.

Chapter 3 – Finding The Stake

"OK, men. We go north on the trace to that off-trail by Crooks' tavern, at Jonathan's Creek. We'll follow Kent's Run, up toward Adamson's place. You know where that fork is? That's where we'll follow the north fork. Should only be about a mile upstream from there." Thomas McCollough tapped his finger on the map which was spread out across a barrel.

"I certainly appreciate your help, Tom," Dr. Mathison said. "I still don't know how you managed to get so many men together on such short notice."

"Well, Doc ... I know how crucial it is to get these boys settled before the first snows come. Good Lord, I remember my first winter in this god-forsaken place. Good thing I didn't bring my family with me." Thomas looked over at Nathan and John. "Yep ... had the good sense to leave them back in Virginia, 'til I got the cabin up and a good crop in. Brought 'em here in the summer... Been five years now. Built a real house last year. It just takes good planning." Thomas rolled up the map and tucked it under his arm. "Any questions, boys?"

"Tom, we've already got the wagons loaded up. We just need to do a quick re-check ... Make sure we've got all the tools. Remember last time we did this... Jack forgot the chains?" William Redman said, stepping forward. He was a huge man, standing over six foot five and built like a lumber jack. He picked up a large knapsack loaded with food supplies, and threw it over his shoulder. "Nathan ... John ... I just want to warn you, now ... I'm always the one elected as chief cook. It's not too late to change your minds." He grinned and winked at Nathan.

"Don't let him fool ya! He's ten times the cook my Becky is!" Samuel Wilson laughed. "He makes the best damned biscuits this side of the Ohio River."

There were twelve men in all, gathered in Thomas McCollough's barn, not counting Nathan and John. Five wagons were lined up outside and ready to roll. The men filed out of the building, each one stopping to shake hands with Nathan and John.

It was six o'clock in the morning, and a dense fog had settled over the countryside during the night. The air was brisk, and the sun was just beginning to rise, over the hills. The sound of the horses and the creaking wagons echoed across the valley, as the group made their way down the narrow, crude road. A flock of noisy geese, flying south, in formation, broke the monotonous clatter of the wagon wheels. As they neared Crooks' tavern, the familiar smell of corn liquor from the still, permeated the air.

"Smell that? Sure wish we had a jug of it to take with us," John said, batting at a spider web which was stretched out across the road, and sticking to his face.

"Well, just be thankful we still have *our* whiskey." Nathan gave the reins a quick snap, and the oxen picked up the pace. "We *do* still have it, don't we?"

"Yep, little brother. It's in the wagon."

"Looks as if we're about to turn off the trace, up ahead," Nathan said, pointing at the wagons toward the front. "Gawd I hope that trail isn't rougher than this one. My side is starting to ache."

"I think you just want some more of that pain killer." John laughed. "I was afraid of that."

"Well ... a little whiskey ... a little pain killer ... erases the ghosts in a man's mind. Ya know?"

"No, Nathan ... I don't think that's the way to wipe out bad memories. I think readin' the good book and a whole lot of prayin' would be a better way to get rid of those images."

"Yea, well ... you deal with your goblins your way ... and I'll deal with mine, *MY* way."

The line of wagons turned off the main road and onto a dirt trail running parallel to the creek called "Kent's Run". As Nathan had suspected, the trail was rough and barely wide enough for the wagons to get through in places. The area was densely wooded; an impenetrable tangle of huge oaks, bushes, and underbrush. Low-hanging branches from old-growth trees often needed to be cut, in order for the wagons to pass. Here and there, large trees had fallen across the path. The men used axes and saws to reduce the obstacles, many times having to unhitch a team of horses, and use them to drag the tree-trunks out of the way. It was slow going, and the sun was nearly at the noon position when the men reached the fork in the creek.

Tom McCollough was on horseback, and trotted up to John and Nathan's wagon. "This is it, boys. We'll go along the right-hand fork, from here. I was back there hunting, last spring... My sister owns twelve hundred acres out here. It get's rougher up ahead. We'll go about a mile ... according to the map, your property starts where a smaller creek empties into this one. We should be able to find a marker about there."

"Thanks Tom," John said. "I don't have any idea how we could do this without your help ... and the help of your neighbors."

"Think nothin' of it... That's just how we do things around here. Every one of us has been in your situation. We've all helped each other out. Believe me .... If folks keep settling this area ..., you'll get *your* turn to help *them* out." Tom laughed heartily, and reined his horse around to join the others up ahead.

It took nearly an hour more, before they finally reached the boundary of the Stillman property. There, sticking out of the ground ... was a large stake, nearly three feet tall. It had been pounded into the creek bank where a smaller stream emptied into the larger one. The stake had a faded red handkerchief tied to it, like a flag. They had arrived at their destination.

The wagons pulled to a stop, and the men wasted no time unhitching the horses and leading them into the creek for a cool drink. John jumped down from his wagon and released the oxen's yokes. As John led the animals away, Nathan remained on the wagon seat, surveying the landscape, and thanking God for all he saw. The creeks were perfectly located at a natural clearing. The smaller stream ran through a meadow, gently sloping downward to the edge of the larger waterway. The water in the main creek was about three feet deep, and the current was fairly swift. Nathan could see the bottom through the crystal clear water. It was covered in large flat stones, without mud and silt. The brook which emptied into it was just as clear, although less than half the width and depth.

"Well, Stillman... What do you think? It's all yours ... pretty much as far as you can see from here." Dr. Mathison interrupted Nathan's daydreaming. The doctor had ridden in a wagon with Samuel Wilson, who was tending his team. "Sam said to tell you he'd give you twice what you paid for it," the doctor said, chuckling.

"Well sir... I never imagined it could be this grand," Nathan said. "Don't think I'll ever sell it. Nope... this is a keeper."

"What do you think, Will?" Dr. Mathison called out to William Redman, who was coming toward them.

"It sure is a beautiful piece of property, Nathan. Good place to raise a family... Good place to plant a few generations, I reckon," William Redman said, brushing the burrs off of his pants. "I can't wait to get you guys settled in, here. I'd betcha within a week ... two at the most, we'll have a cabin and a barn put up 'cause we don't have to do a lot of clearing. The Good Lord sure did prepare the way for you boys!" William shaded his eyes, and looked across the meadow. "Yep... that right there is a perfect place for your cabin-site. I'll bet that brook's spring-fed. We'll put the cabin right close to it, and build a spring house there." He pointed to a flat place close to the tree-line and next to the stream.

John Stillman and Samuel Wilson finished tying off their animals, and joined the others, congregated at the wagon with Nathan, Doc Mathison, and William Redman.

"You men probably worked up an appetite gettin' here .... So I guess I'll start a fire and see what I can rustle up for us to eat," William said.

Everyone cheered loudly, and Will headed off to his work.

Preparation and planning was the agenda for the rest of the afternoon. Wagons were unloaded, and the men began taking measurements. Stakes were pounded into the ground and cord was strung from stake to stake. Teams of men split off, to scour the field for sandstone, suitable for foundations, fireplace, hearth, and stepping stones. Others went into the forest to mark trees for felling; for the logs which would be used for the cabin, barn, smokehouse, and springhouse.

Work started early the next morning. Each man knew exactly what he had to do, and everything was progressing like a "well-oiled machine".

The cabin, barn, smokehouse, and springhouse were finished during the next ten days. Each man had his task down to a science. A hunting party filled the smokehouse with plenty of game that would last for months; it was situated above the coals – beginning to cure already.

The final evening was a night of feasting and celebration.

The next morning, everyone was up at the crack of dawn. The property was alive with activity. Some of the men were putting the last touches on their handiwork, while others began loading up their wagons and preparing their teams for the trip back to their own farms. Dr. Mathison was helping John and Nathan organize the household implements that they unloaded from the Stillman wagon.

"Doc," Nathan said, "I need to talk to you before you go."

"Now that sounds serious... What is it Nathan?"

Nathan took a small map out of his trunk, along with a metal box. He walked over to the table and pulled out one of the chairs. "Sit down, doc," he said.

Dr. Mathison sat down, and Nathan spread the map out on the table.

"First of all, I want you to know I'm sure you're a man I can trust. After all – I trusted you with my life," Nathan said. "This is about Maggie Waters."

"Aw .... It's about the lovely Maggie!" Dr. Mathison said, peering at Nathan over the top of his glasses, and looking very wise.

Nathan opened the box and took out a paper. "This is her father's land patent ... six hundred acres. I guess the land belongs to Maggie now, since she's the only one from her family who survived the massacre." Nathan pointed to a spot on the map. "This is her property... Butts right up against ours. I don't know what she'll want to do with it ... keep it ...

sell it ... whatever ... but the thing is – it's hers."
Nathan sat down next to the doc. "Now ... I never got
the chance to give these things to her ... things that
belonged to her family ... but I want you to see that
she gets all of it." He opened the box and pushed
over to Dr. Mathison.

"Good Lord!" The doctor gasped, peering inside
the container in disbelief. "How much gold is in
there?!"

"I didn't count it, but Mr. Waters was a wealthy
man. A doc, like yourself, only he practiced in
Philadelphia for a good many years after the
rebellion. Then he set up a practice in Bucks
County; spent years taking care of the country folk.
He thought he could make a difference out here in
the wilderness. He just never got the chance."
Nathan dug into the box of gold coins and pulled out
some jewelry. "These are her parents' wedding
rings. I thought it best to let some time pass before I
gave those to her. I had to take them off the bodies
myself. Lord it was a gruesome chore." He blinked
hard, to see through the tears welling up in his eyes.
He laid a gold pocket watch, two more rings, jeweled
hair combs, and some earrings on the table.

"Nathan, Maggie is a lucky girl to have you for a
friend." Dr. Mathison pushed his spectacles up on
his nose. "Any other man would have kept it all for
himself."

"No sir... I couldn't do that and sleep at night.
John and I gathered up all the land patents and
warrants we could find in the other wagons, and
turned them into the land office in Zanesville. The
man there said they'd make sure the heirs of those

families got them. We didn't take rings or jewelry from any of the others. It's just ..." Nathan hesitated. "... It's just that Maggie is special to me. I had to save these things for her." The young man's emotions were hard to conceal.

"Well, my boy... I can assure you, I'll get these to Maggie." The doctor reached over and patted Nathan on the shoulder. "I certainly do respect your honesty, Stillman... And you have my word... I'll see to it that Maggie gets her inheritance."

"Thank you, Doc." Nathan shook Dr. Mathison's hand firmly. "I was sure I could count on you."

"Nathan, can I ask you a personal question?"

"Depends on what it is."

"Is there something between you and Maggie Waters? I mean something more than a friendship?"

"Funny ...." Nathan said, shoving his hands into his pockets, "... that's what I keep asking myself."

When everything was finished, and all the work was completed, the group of men came up to the cabin. Each one was carrying a gift.

Tom McCollough stepped forward and offered a huge burlap sack to John. "John ... Nathan ... this is a bag of cornmeal... I ground it myself. You'll be needing it, until you get your own crop of corn in. I believe there's enough here to get you through the winter. Please take it with my blessing."

John accepted the bag. He set it down on the porch and shook Tom's hand. "I don't know what to say, except thank you .... For everything."

"What's this?" Nathan asked. "It's *us* that should be giving *you* all gifts."

Samuel Williams walked up on the porch and handed Nathan a heavy wooden box. "Boys .... These are the best seeds in the county. Every year I've had bumper crops of vegetables and corn. Every harvest, I save extra seeds and share them with my friends. You are my new friends, and I hope your crops will come up strong and plentiful. Everything is labeled, so you'll know what you've got. Just put this box down in your cellar, and the seeds will be fine for spring planting."

Nathan set the box down and both brothers took turns hugging Sam.

William Redman gave John and Nathan a large pail of salt, and Rev. Manley set a barrel of flour on the porch. Doc Mathison made sure the boys had plenty of his medicinal herbs. The other men left various items which included potatoes and turnips, onions, honey, tea, and moonshine. It was a poignant experience for Nathan and John. They had never known such sincere generosity.

After thanking each man individually, one last time, the brothers walked with the group, down to the narrow path where the wagons were loaded and ready to go. Nathan and John watched their newly found friends mount their horses, climb up into their wagons, and head off down the trail; leaving, to go back to their own homes. It was a bittersweet moment. The men of Newton had concluded an incomparable act of kindness and goodwill; freely given, and with no thought of recompense.

Watching the wagons disappear into the distance, Nathan felt a vague melancholy. He regretted leaving Maggie Waters back in Zanesville, and wished desperately that he hadn't.

Chapter 4 – The Fever

BANG... BANG... BANG ...

"Maggie... Maggie!" Marky was yelling and pounding on Maggie's door.

Maggie sat straight up in bed, awakened abruptly from her nap. "I'm coming," she called.

Maggie ran to the door, lifted the bar, and opened it to find Markey standing there. He was crying and very distraught.

"Maggie ... you've got to come to the inn! It's Mama... She's real sick!"

"All right, Markey," Maggie said, pulling on her hooded cloak. "What made her sick?"

"Two guys came to the inn a week or so ago... Hurry Maggie!" The boy grabbed Maggie's arm and literally yanked her out the door. "These two guys came – one was sick. Mama thought he just had a bad cold ... she tended him. But he had a really bad fever, Maggie. He got a real bad belly ache, too. Then he got these red spots on his belly."

"Wait, Marky ... get my bag."

Marky ran back into Maggie's room, grabbed the bag and was back in an instant. Maggie was already up in the horse-drawn cart, by the time Marky returned.

"Maggie... The man seems to be a little better, but Mama's burning up!" The boy snapped the reins and the horse trotted off toward the ford in the Muskingum River.

"Marky, how long has Caroline had a fever?"

"Started three or four days ago," he said, steering the horse into the river at the ford. "I think Mr. McKray is getting' it, too. He didn't look so good today... He was walking around holding his gut."

The sure-footed horse pulled the cart across the rocks, in the shallows of the river. "Mama says she aches all over, Maggie. I don't think she can get out of bed."

"Are you sure the man was sick before he got to the inn?"

"Yep... His friend had to carry him in, when they got there."

"Do you know where they came from?"

"The one guy said they'd come from Marietta. He said his friend started getting sick a week before they got here."

"And the friend doesn't show any signs of the illness?"

"Nope... He seems just fine."

They made it across the river. The cart bumped along, up the bank on the Zanesville side of the Muskingum. Marky shook the reins and the horse picked up the pace, trotting down the path toward the main road which ran through the town.

Marky pulled the horse to a stop in front of the inn. He jumped down from the little wagon and hurriedly tied the reins to a post. Maggie hurried into the inn, and went straight to Caroline's room.

"Caroline... Caroline... Tell me how you feel, where do you hurt?" Maggie set her bag down, and felt her friend's forehead. "Oh Lord... You *do* have a bad fever!"

"Maggie... I'm so glad you're here. I ache everywhere ... I'm so cold, too"

"What about your stomach, Caroline? Does your stomach hurt?"

"Yes," Caroline moaned.

"Marky, listen closely. Here's what you need to do for me..." Maggie turned to the boy. "Stir up the fire in the kitchen and swing the big pot over the coals. Put eight cups full of vinegar, eight cups of molasses, eight cups of whiskey, and plenty of tansy bitters in the pot... I want it to boil." Maggie reached out and took Marky's hand in her's; she squeezed it reassuringly. "Then I need you to find all the silver coins you can get your hands on... Beg if you have to.... Knock at every door you come to ... ask for the silver. Explain that we've got fever in the town... Tell everyone you see to stay inside, until we tell them it's OK to come out. Tell them it's a quarantine situation. Once you get some silver, I want you to throw the coins into the pot with the other ingredients and let it all boil together. Do you understand?"

"Yes, Maggie."

"Good. Get going."

Maggie filled a basin with fresh water and sponged Caroline down, to cool the fever. She discovered the woman's glands on her neck were swollen. Raising Caroline's blouse, Maggie wasn't surprised to see the purple-red tell-tale blotches on Caroline's light brown skin.

"Oh my... Caroline... It's what I suspected, when Marky told me about the man."

"What is it, Maggie Girl?" Caroline reached out for Maggie's hand.

"I think it's typhoid. I've seen it before. We had an outbreak in Bucks County a couple of years ago." Maggie took her friend's hand in hers.

"Oh, NO!!" Caroline cried.

"Well, just try to stay calm. I'll do what Pa did. He was real good at treating it. I just hope we caught *yours* in time. Why didn't you send for me sooner?!"

"Marky wanted to, but I wouldn't let him .... We know how busy you are with Doc Mathison out of town and all ...."

Maggie found another quilt and spread it across the shivering woman. "I need to check on the others. I'll be back. You just try to sleep."

Maggie discovered there were three others coming down with the fever. She questioned the sick man's friend, and found out he was indeed fine. His companion seemed to be past the critical stage of the infection and Maggie was sure he would recover. She found another man with a very high fever who was complaining of severe cramping, and retching over a bucket. Mr. McKray was warming himself by the fire. He was wrapped in quilts, and drinking whiskey from a jug.

"Mr. McKray, tell me how you're feeling," Maggie said, laying the back of her hand on his flushed cheek.

"I feel like I've been trampled by a herd of buffalo," he grunted. He raised the jug and took a long swig of the liquor.

"How's your stomach?"

"... Doesn't hurt as bad as it did before I got some whiskey into it. It's these damned chills that are getting the best of me."

"Well, you've got a pretty high fever, sir." Maggie gently eased the jug out of Jacob McKray's grip. "I'm making a tonic that should help. My pa taught me how to handle typhoid."

"Typhoid?! Are you talkin' about typhoid fever, girl?!!!" McKray exclaimed. He was visibly alarmed.

"Yes sir. I believe that's what we have here. I think the traveler brought it with him."

"Are we gonna die, Miss Maggie?" Jacob asked, slurring his words slightly.

"Not if I can help it, sir."

"What about Caroline?"

"She's very sick. We'll know in a day or two."

"Oh God!" McKray moaned. "She's one hell of a good woman. Been with me from the beginning – She and her husband... Good people." He rubbed his forehead. "And her boy, Marky... Is he OK?"

"Well, sir... Marky's been exposed. He may or may not come down with it. That's just how it is. I'll do everything I can to keep him healthy, though."

A few miles up the road, a rider was approaching Zanesville. He was riding a tall, highly spirited black horse, which ran like the wind. The man's long coat floated behind him in the wake, as the magnificent ghostly steed galloped down the road. The rider and the horse were phantoms; riding through the surreal shadows cast by the simultaneously setting sun and the rising moon. The horse, at times, slowed to rear up, in an intricate ballet, reaching high into the air and dancing on its hind legs along the trail. It was apparent that the rider and the horse were intimately bonded. It was clear that both were free spirits -- an enigma to all they encountered, and each possessing the soul of a maverick. Like an apparition, the duo glided down the main street to the inn. The rider jumped off the tall black stallion and looped the reins over a post.

The stranger knocked at the door to the inn. Maggie hurried over and opened it.

"Evenin' ma'am," the man said tipping his black, broad-rimmed hat. "I know it's late, but I was wondering if you might have a room available."

"I'm sorry sir," Maggie said, "but we have a problem here. Seems everyone is coming down with the fever. I doubt that you'd want to stay here."

"I don't intend to sound presumptuous, but what kind of fever?" The man peered over Maggie's shoulder, into the cabin.

"Sir... I think it might be typhoid. I'm sure you don't want to expose yourself to it."

"Ma'am, I'm a doctor. May I come in?"

Maggie caught her breath in relief. "Oh! Thank God! Please *do* come in. We have four people in here who I'm sure have it... One might be a carrier." Maggie backed up, opening the door wide.

The man walked into the inn and glanced around. He looked to be in his late twenties. He was a tall, well-built man, and he carried himself with an air of confidence and authority; if not pure arrogance. He wore a long black duster, and knee-high boots. He was very well dressed for a traveler.

"Maggie! Look!" It was Marky. He burst through the door and ran up to Maggie, showing her the twenty silver coins he held in his cupped hands.

"Oh, Marky... That's wonderful. You know what to do with them. And check on your Mama while you're at it."

"Yes, Maggie," Marky said. He ran off toward the kitchen.

The stranger laughed, watching the long, lanky boy scurrying away; and then he looked back at Maggie. "So... Your name must be Maggie. Hello, Maggie," he said, smiling and extending his hand. "My name is Miles Deihl. I'm on my way to Lancaster, from Boston."

Maggie placed her hand in Dr. Deihl's hand and curtsied politely. "I'm Margaret Waters, from Bucks County. My friends call me Maggie."

"Well, Maggie from Bucks County... It's a pleasure meeting you. I'll just get my bag, and then you and I will see to our patients. What do you say?" The handsome doctor smiled and winked at Maggie.

"All I can say is thank you. I'm so glad you're here."

The doctor went outside and Maggie went to check on Caroline.

Maggie sponged Caroline down, with the cool water, one more time. The woman was still shivering, and her cheeks remained flushed from the fever. Caroline's breathing was labored and she gasped from time to time, trying to get more air.

"Caroline, hang on..... for Marky," Maggie whispered.

Maggie went to the kitchen and found Marky there, stirring the tonic which was boiling in an iron pot, over the fire. She gathered eight cups from the shelf and set them on the table.

"Marky, I want you to put one ladle full of the tonic into each cup... Then you can help me pass them out to everyone here."

"OK, Maggie," Marky said, grabbing the pot's handle with a rag. He lifted the pot from the crane and carried it over to the table.

"What do we have here?" It was Dr. Deihl. He was standing in the kitchen doorway with an inquisitive look on his face.

"Um... It's a tonic my pa used for the fever," Maggie said. "It will keep those who don't have it from getting it... And it can help those who have already caught it."

"What's in it?" the doctor asked.

"Whiskey, molasses, vinegar, tansy bitters, and silver," Marky answered, sounding very knowledgeable. "Maggie's pa was a doc. He taught her how to do what he did. Now she works for Dr. Mathison... She's his assistant."

"That's very impressive," Dr. Deihl said. He looked at Maggie and smiled. The young doctor's penetrating eyes were blatantly scrutinizing the girl from head to toe.

Maggie blushed. "Well, it sounds impressive, but I assure you ... I'm only a novice. Dr. Mathison is out of town, or he would be in charge." Maggie put a ladle full of the tonic into a cup and handed it to Dr.

Deihl. "You'll need to drink this much, three times a day, until this outbreak runs its course." She handed a cup to Marky. "... You, too, Marky." She raised her own cup, held her nose and gulped down the contents. "You see?" She grimaced. "That's how it's done."

"If it tastes as bad as it smells, I don't think I want any," Marky said defiantly.

"Drink it," Maggie ordered. "I'll take some into your mama. After you drink yours, I want you to make sure everyone here gets a cup of it."

"All right, Maggie," Marky conceded.

Maggie filled a cup and disappeared into Caroline's room.

"After you ..." the doctor said raising his cup to Marky.

The boy took a deep breath, held his nose, and poured the thick liquid down his throat. "That wasn't so bad, after all," he announced, once he swallowed the medicine.

"Well, I guess if you can do it ... I will try," the doctor said. He took a deep breath and tossed down the tonic. "Hmmm ... you're right. Not bad at all." He looked surprised. "Come on boy, I'll help you dispense the medicine to the sick."

The next ten days were exhausting for Maggie, Marky, and Miles Deihl, as they cared for the sick. No one else came down with the fever, and those who had it seemed to be recovering, except for one traveler and Caroline. Marky checked with the families living in and around Zanesville, and no one else was ill. The general consensus was that the two travelers from Marietta had brought the fever to Zanesville.

"Mr. Cover isn't getting any better, Dr. Deihl," Maggie said. "In fact I think he's worse. And I'm terribly worried about Caroline."

"Well ... I didn't want to resort to it, but I think we need to bleed them," Dr. Deihl said.

"My pa didn't believe in bleeding people."

"Why not? It's been done for centuries."

"He said it only weakened his patients. He said it did more harm than good."

"Well, then, Miss Maggie ... what would you suggest we do?" He sounded irritated.

"I don't know. I'm too tired to think." Maggie looked down at the floor, and tried to hide the tears welling up in her eyes.

"I think you need some sleep." Dr. Deihl walked over to Maggie and encircled the girl in his arms, holding her securely. "If you don't get some rest, you won't be any good to any of us." He tipped her chin back and looked into her tired, sad eyes. "You go lie down for a while, and I'll tend to the sick." Miles gave Maggie a reassuring hug, and then reluctantly released her. "Now go," he ordered.

"You're right. I do need a nap, but what about you?"

"Don't worry about me. I'll get some sleep after you wake up."

Sometime later, Maggie awoke to the sound of soulful crying. It sounded like Marky. The girl rose from the bed and ran out of the room, following the sound. She was led to Caroline's bedroom. Marky was on his knees at Caroline's bedside. Heartbreaking sobs shook the boy's body. Miles Deihl was standing silently at the foot of the bed. Caroline wasn't shivering anymore.

Two days passed, and Mr. Cover died. Mr. McKray was feeling better, and so was the traveler who had been the first to succumb to the fever.

Caroline Green and Mr. Cover were buried in the cemetery at the top of the hill above the main street. In later years, the hill was called Pioneer Hill and the grave yard was named Pioneer Cemetery.

The people of Zanesville banded together to give Caroline a beautiful funeral service. She was laid to rest beside her husband, Jonathan, who had drowned in the Muskingum River just two years earlier. Everyone loved Caroline Green, and losing her was a tragedy, especially for her now orphaned son, Marky.

No one knew Mr. Cover, or if he had family to be notified of his passing; but here in the pioneer wilderness, a group of loving strangers stood in as a surrogate family, to say a heartfelt good-bye.

There was a damp chill in the air, as gray clouds descended, embracing the town in a dreary autumn mist. The village mourners made their way down the hill from the graveyard. Some walked while others rode in carriages and carts. The silence was deafening; only to be broken now and then by the soulful whinnying of a horse, or the creaking and jangling of a wagon. It was a single file procession of black, crepe-draped testaments; a silent tribute to those left behind; on the hill; in the earth.

Dr. Deihl slipped his arm around Maggie and pulled her closer to him; trying to console the weeping girl. The carriage moved slowly down Main Street with the rest of the wagons. Maggie rested her head on Miles' shoulder. She appreciated his strength and composure. They rode in silence, as an unspoken bond was being established.

Miles Deihl turned the carriage onto the lane that led to the river's ford; heading for Springfield – to Maggie's cabin.

Chapter 5 – Two Doctors in One Town

"Maggie, you're a strong woman," Miles Deihl said, helping Maggie down; out of the cart. "I feel privileged to have gotten to know you, these past couple of weeks."

"I don't think it's strength, Dr. Deihl. I believe it's more a matter of acceptance."

"Well, that may be true. You've certainly had your share of trials to overcome... I mean ... to accept."

"What else can I do?"

"Good question." He rubbed his chin thoughtfully. "You know, it seems as if everything has worked out for you, though. Opportunities ... such as securing employment with Dr. Mathison, a cozy place to live and all. Things could be worse." Miles opened the door for her.

"Won't you come in, and have a cup of tea with me, Dr. Deihl? I really don't want to be alone right now."

"Maggie, I would prefer you call me Miles." He laughed, stepping into the cozy room.

"Well then... Miles... won't you sit down?" Maggie smiled. "Give me your coat."

She took Dr. Deihl's coat and scarf, and she wriggled out of her cloak. Miles Deihl watched her intently, as she laid them on the bed at the other side of the room.

She stirred the coals in her fireplace and swung the crane over the fire. Soon the pot of water was boiling. Maggie brewed the tea, and set the cups on the table.

"I feel so sorry for Marky," Maggie said, sitting down across from Miles.

"It was very kind of Mr. Spangler to offer him an apprenticeship. He'll be just fine. He's got a place to live and a nice family to look after him. Once he learns the trade, he'll be a fine blacksmith. Mrs. Spangler seems to really like the kid."

"He's a good boy. Caroline raised him properly." Maggie said, as she poured the tea. "How could you not like him?"

Dr. Deihl took a long drink of the brew. "So, Maggie ... is there anything you can't do well?" He paused. "By the way, this is very good tea." He took another drink, studying her intently, over the rim of his cup.

Maggie blushed. Miles Deihl was an extremely attractive man. He was the epitome of the term "*tall, dark, and handsome*". His piercing brown eyes made Maggie uneasy, though. She always felt like he was looking into her soul. He had a distracting way of making her acutely aware of her femininity. It was the way he looked at her, the way he spoke to her, and the way he always seemed to find an excuse to touch her. Although he never touched her inappropriately, there seemed to be a subtle sexual inference in his approach, along with a disposition of possessiveness.

"There are, in fact, so many things I can't do well, but wish I could," the girl sighed.

"Probably... only the things you haven't yet tried." He smiled and winked at Maggie. "I'll bet you'd make a great mother."

"Excuse me?" Maggie was surprised by the statement.

"I'm sorry," Miles apologized. "I guess I was just thinking out loud."

There was a knock at the door. Maggie welcomed the intrusion.

"Maggie, are you in there?" It was Dr. Mathison.

Maggie jumped up and ran to the office door and excitedly flung it open. "Oh Doc! I'm so glad to see you!" Maggie cried.

"I'll bet," he said. "I heard what happened while I was gone. I'm sorry I wasn't here to help you through it."

"Doc, I want you to meet Dr. Miles Deihl. He's from Boston. He's going to start a practice in Lancaster."

Miles stood up, extending his hand to Dr. Mathison.

"Good to meet you Mr. Deihl," Doc Mathison said, shaking Miles' hand. "I understand you and my Maggie, here, staved off a full blown outbreak of the fever. I'm happy I have the chance to thank you in person."

"I was glad I could help. But in truth, I don't think Maggie needed my assistance... maybe just the moral support. She actually handled it all." Miles casually slipped his arm around Maggie's waist, and squeezed her against his side.

Maggie's face turned red, and she wriggled free. "I made some tea, Dr. Mathison. Would you like a cup?"

"That sounds wonderful, Maggie. I could use a good hot cup of tea," Dr. Mathison said, glancing at Miles Deihl with a disapproving look on his face. He pulled out a chair and sat down across from the other doctor. "So, Dr. Deihl... Where did you study medicine?" He eyed the younger man critically.

"I studied in Boston, sir. ... Under the direction of Dr. Daniel Horn."

"Aw yes," Doc Mathison said, pushing at his glasses. "I've heard of him. So when are you leaving for Lancaster?" he asked bluntly.

"I'm not quite sure, now," Miles said, smiling at Maggie. "My plans may change."

"Well, you ought to try to get to Lancaster before the weather turns bad," Dr. Mathison insisted.

"Actually, I'm considering spending the winter over in Zanesville. I find that little town quite hospitable." Miles met Dr. Mathison's gaze defiantly.

"Zanesville is definitely an up and coming town, Dr. Deihl... But how would you sustain yourself?"

"Well I *AM* a doctor," Miles said.

"Yes, but this is an extremely small community. Do you think there's a need for two physicians?"

"Why not?" Dr. Deihl asked, leaning in toward Dr. Mathison; anticipating his reply.

"Shall I make more tea?" Maggie deliberately interrupted. She could feel the tension building between the two men.

"No thank you, Maggie," Dr. Deihl replied, rising to his feet. "I'd better be getting back across the river before dark." He picked up his hat and turned to Dr. Mathison. "It was a pleasure meeting you, sir," he said curtly.

Maggie hurriedly grabbed Miles Deihl's coat and scarf from the bed and handed them to him at the door.

The young doctor planted a lingering kiss on Maggie's cheek and left.

Maggie turned and grinned at Dr. Mathison. "Hmm ... that went well."

Doc raised an eyebrow and frowned. After a moment of silence, Dr. Mathison composed himself.

"Maggie, I've got something to show you." He left the room, returning with the metal box Nathan had given him. "Sit down Maggie... Ummm ... please."

Maggie sat down at the table and watched as the doc opened the box. He took out the land patent and the map.

"OK, miss Maggie," he said, spreading the map out on the table, and pointing to a square on the paper. "This land is yours, young lady. This is the land that was bought and paid for by your Pa. Now it's all yours... Six hundred acres."

"I don't understand," Maggie said; confused. "Where did you get this?"

"Nathan gave it to me with direct orders to see that you get it." The doctor pushed the open box over in front of Maggie. "He said to give you this, too."

Maggie peered into the box, bewildered by what she saw.

"He said he wanted to give it to you himself, but he just didn't get the chance."

There was a long silence, as Maggie sorted through the contents of the box.

"I don't know what to say, Dr. Mathison," Maggie said, choking back her tears, and clutching at the locket hanging around her neck.

"Do you realize you are a wealthy woman, Maggie?" Dr. Mathison pointed to the box. "There's a fortune in gold in there ... plus you own six hundred acres of prime bottom land."

"Mine?" Maggie asked in a frail voice.

"Yes, my dear... It's all yours," the doc confirmed. "I couldn't believe it when Nathan gave all of this to me ... made me swear on my life that I'd get it to YOU. Any other man would have kept quiet and stolen this fortune. Do you know what an honorable fellow Nathan Stillman is?"

"Yes, I've always known." Maggie wiped her eyes with her apron. "I wish I could thank him."

"Well I certainly think you should!" Dr. Mathison smiled knowingly at Maggie. "Now the question is ..., what shall we do with all this treasure?"

"Dr. Mathison, would you consider keeping it safe for me? I don't know what to do with it. Maybe you can advise me."

"Well, first of all, Maggie ... you need to decide whether you're going to keep the acreage or sell it. I've seen it, and I can tell you, it is definitely choice property. It's got plenty of water, and the lay of the land is perfect for cultivation and pasture. If you decide to keep it, then I'd use some of your money to invest in livestock ... sheep would be perfect. If you decide to sell it, I have friends down around Newton who would be willing to pay top dollar for it. Maybe even Nathan ... it butts right up against the Stillman spread." Dr. Mathison cocked his head to one side, rubbing his chin thoughtfully. "I think you should take a look at it before deciding. What do you say?"

"I'd love to see it," Maggie said. "It's all Papa talked about... For months it's all he had on his mind. And you're right about sheep – – that was *his* dream. He wanted a flock of Merino sheep. They come from Spain, but are the very best. He said that's why we needed so much land ... for the sheep."

"Well, then ... it's settled. When the weather breaks, next spring, we'll make the trip to Newton," the doc said, slapping the table. "Too bad it's too late to go, now."

"Why can't we go now?" Maggie asked. She looked pleadingly at the doctor.

"Maggie, winter is upon the doorstep."

"Why would that stop us?"

"We could get caught in a snow storm, or a freezing spell. It's a long trip. We could freeze to death on the trail." Dr. Mathison patted Maggie's hand. "Take my word for it, Maggie ... you don't want to be traveling in bad weather ... and around these parts, you never know when it will turn ugly ... and you never know how ugly it will turn."

Maggie sat there for a moment, frowning. "All right, doc. I'm sure you know best."

"Good. Now, we've got lots of catching up to do," Dr. Mathison said, leaning back in the chair. "Tell me everything that happened while I was gone."

"No... First tell me about Nathan," Maggie grinned.

"Aw... Just as I had suspected," the doctor said, raising an eyebrow. "And to think I was beginning to worry about the good Dr. Deihl!"

"Worry? Why would you be worried about Dr. Deihl?"

"To be honest ... I have a problem with his intrusive behavior where you're concerned."

"You don't like him?"

"No."

"Well ... Dr. Mathison, you certainly don't mince words, do you?"

"I consider myself a very good judge of character. It's that simple."

"And you approve of Nathan?"

"Yep." Doc crossed his arms over his chest, and nodded his head *'yes'* very slowly and deliberately. He thought for a moment; then pulled his glasses off, and laid them on the table. "Did you know that his Swedish name, *Stillman*.... actually means *man of few words*?" Dr. Mathison chuckled. "His name certainly fits him!"

Maggie smiled at the doctor, and he winked back at her.

Dr. Mathison and Maggie Waters spent the next two hours catching up on events, and making plans for the coming weeks.

Maggie went to bed that night thinking of Nathan's kiss; her first kiss.

Chapter 6 - The Kiss

Miles Deihl stopped by from time to time, to visit with Maggie and have a cup of her special tea. He always made her laugh, even though she felt a vague apprehension when he was near. It was an uneasy feeling that she wasn't always able to hide. It seemed to Maggie, that Dr. Miles Deihl enjoyed watching her struggle with it – what ever it was. Sometimes they would take long walks along the river bank, discussing the medical arts. Miles Deihl was a fine doctor. Medicine was one of his passions, and so was Maggie.

Early one November morning, Maggie saddled her mare and headed off, to start her weekly rounds. The little bay filly was feeling feisty in the cool autumn air. The filly trotted briskly down the main street of Springfield, arching her neck and holding her tail high. Maggie was about a mile out of town, when she heard the sound of another horse galloping up behind her. She pulled her mare to a stop; knowing it was prone to jump and dance around when other horses were at a lope. The horse loved to run.

"Good morning, Maggie." It was Miles Deihl. He trotted his beautiful black stallion up beside her. "Where are you off to, this early in the day?"

Maggie was surprised to see the doctor so far from town. "Oh... Good morning to you, Miles," she said, trying to control the mare, which was unwilling to stand still; going in circles and trotting in place.

Miles Deihl reached over and took hold of the mare's bridle. "Whoa!" he commanded, giving a stern jerk on the leather. The filly immediately quieted down.

"Thank you," Maggie said, "she's pretty high-spirited ... especially on cold days like today."

"So, where are you off to?" he repeated his question. The mare started to act up again. "Give me the reins, Maggie. I don't want to see you get dumped. This mare needs a little discipline." He pulled the reins from Maggie's hands, before she could argue with him.

"I've got some errands to run for Dr. Mathison. I have to go out to the Hennesy farm. It'll take me an hour or so to get there. I really need to be going... Now if you'll hand me my reins ...."

"I think I should ride with you. That is if you don't mind. Your horse seems to be unmanageable ... and that worries me. Besides, I think that's too far for you to be riding alone, even on a well-behaved horse."

"I can handle my horse," Maggie insisted. "She'll calm down shortly. Any way ... I'm sure you have better things to do."

"Actually, I can't think of anything better than spending time with you." The young doctor grinned and winked at Maggie.

"I'm flattered, Miles... But I really don't need a chaperone. I'm perfectly capable of executing my responsibilities on my own." Maggie was adamant, and she was becoming impatient with the man's insistence.

"You're really quite lovely when you're angry, Maggie Waters," Miles said, jumping down from his horse. He tied the mare to his saddle, and walked up to Maggie, literally dragging her down from her side-saddle, and into his arms. "Now, Miss Maggie ... you're going to ride with me. We won't debate the issue any longer," he said, hoisting her up onto his stallion. He climbed on behind Maggie, and gathered his reins around her.

"Just wait a minute, Dr. Deihl!" Maggie struggled to compose her bruised dignity. "Let me down!"

"Not on your life!" Miles Deihl laughed. He transferred the reins into his right hand and encircled Maggie's trim waist with his left arm. He pulled her tightly against his hips, tapping his heels into the stallion's sides. The big stallion trotted off down the road. "You need to understand how dangerous it is out here for a girl alone ... like you. I'm just trying to protect you, Maggie," Miles apologized. "I don't enjoy making you angry with me, but sometimes a man just has to do the right thing."

Maggie was silent. The girl was bewildered by the doctor's tenacity and strength of will. She relaxed against the warmth of Miles' muscular body, as he continued to hold her firmly in his grasp. The horse was at a walk, now, and the gentle swaying was strangely comforting. The doctor continued to speak to her, but she wasn't listening. She was reeling in the sensation of his breath against her ear and the warm closeness of him. Maggie closed her eyes and felt an unfamiliar, delightful stirring in her body.

Miles heard Maggie's involuntary and almost inaudible moan. He nuzzled his face against her skin and drew his lips around to the nape of her neck. He felt her tremble. Instinctively recognizing Maggie's reaction, he slid his left hand down onto her thigh, while planting warm kisses along the back of her neck. He felt the girl's body tense. He waited to see if she would contest his advance, but she quickly relaxed.

Suddenly, a blood-curdling scream came from the forest beside them. It sounded almost human and immediately broke the spell of the moment. The horses began snorting and stomping; reacting in alarm.

"What was that?!" Maggie cried, looking around in panic.

"Sounded like a cougar!" Miles said, kicking the stallion in the sides. The horse reared slightly, and then broke into a run. The little mare followed; having no trouble keeping up.

When Miles was sure they had put enough distance between them and the growling animal, he pulled his horse to a stop and jumped off. "Are you all right, Maggie?" he asked, lifting her down from the saddle.

"Yes ... but ... that really startled me," she admitted.

"You see? That's what I was talking about. If you had been out here all alone, I guarantee your mare would have tossed you, and then run off, leaving you to that creature's mercy!" Miles pulled her hard against him, and held her tightly. "You're a head-strong woman, Maggie Waters. Maybe this will teach you a lesson! You're not as tough as you think you are." He buried his face in her hair and breathed a sigh of relief mixed with frustration.

"Well, I have to admit it... I was frightened ... but I would have been OK. The mare has more sense than you give her credit."

"You just don't seem to comprehend the danger," he said. "You need someone to look after you, Maggie."

"I'm a big girl, Dr. Deihl, and I can take care of myself."

Miles dropped his hold on Maggie, and walked several paces down the road, cursing loudly, waving his arms around, and ranting. His exasperation was obvious. His behavior was anything but the controlled aloofness Maggie was used to seeing. After blowing off some steam he walked back to face a bewildered Maggie.

"Look," he tried to sound calm, "it's not just the forest animals you need to be wary of, Maggie. You are *NOT* capable of protecting yourself!! You're naïve and inexperienced. I proved that, back there. Any man, who knows anything about women, would have had his way with you. You would have given in without the least opposition! Now tell me that's not true, Maggie!!" Miles pointed a convicting finger at Maggie. "You knew full well what I was doing, and you didn't even *TRY* to stop me!"

Maggie was suddenly ashamed and humiliated. Her cheeks burned with embarrassment. She was speechless.

"What's the matter, Maggie? Cat got your tongue?" Miles mocked. "Do you see what I mean? I know the truth hurts sometimes, but for god's sake, girl ... you need to be careful. The animals around here are not always the kind that walk on all fours! I don't want to see *ANYONE* take advantage of you. You need to understand that I really care about you! I think I would kill any other man who tried to lay a hand on you."

Maggie stood quietly, looking down at the dusty road, unable to meet Miles' gaze.

Dr. Deihl untied Maggie's mare and handed her the reins. "Mount up, Maggie. We're wasting time."

When Maggie and Dr. Deihl reached the Hennesy farm, Sarah Hennesy ran out to meet them. "Hello Maggie," she called. "I was afraid you weren't coming."

"Sarah, how are you?" Maggie asked.

Miles led the horses over to the cabin and tied them to the post.

"I'm fine, but Ben is feeling poorly. He cut his leg splitting wood, and it looks bad."

"When did he do that?" Maggie asked, walking up the steps and into the cabin. Miles Deihl followed the women inside.

"Three days ago," Sarah replied.

"Hello Maggie girl," Ben called out. He was sitting in his rocking chair, by the fire, with his leg propped up on a log.

"Sarah ... Ben ... this is Dr. Deihl. He's a friend of mine from Boston," Maggie said.

Miles stepped forward and shook Ben's hand. "Pleasure meeting you, sir," Dr. Deihl said. He nodded politely to Sarah. "Mind if I have a look at your leg, sir?" he asked Mr. Hennesy.

Ben Hennesy lifted the poultice his wife had applied to his leg. The gaping cut was about five inches long and oozing blood. The tissue around it was an angry red-purple color, and there was slimy, yellow pus inside the gash. Dr. Deihl laid his hand above the injury. The skin was hot to the touch.

"Maggie," Miles said in a low voice, "do you have a needle and thread in your bag?"

"No," Maggie replied, "but I have some vinegar and a little whiskey."

"Well, we can use the whiskey," the doctor said. Miles turned to Sarah. "Mrs. Hennesy, your husband's leg is infected and we need to clean out the dead tissue and close up the wound. I want you to boil some water, get me a sharp knife. I also need tongs, a needle, and some thread."

Mrs. Hennesy looked to Maggie for approval. Maggie nodded, and Sarah went to gather what Dr. Deihl had requested.

"Mr. Hennesy, this is going to hurt. Do you want some whiskey to drink before I get started?" Miles patted Ben reassuringly on the hand. "If we don't get this cleaned out, you could lose your leg ... or the infection can get into your bloodstream and kill you."

"Do what you need to do, Doc," Ben said. "Maggie, hand me my jug from the cupboard, will you please?"

Maggie uncorked the jug, and handed it to Ben Hennesy. Without saying another word, Ben took several long drinks of the liquor.

"Maggie, do you have bandages in your bag?" Miles asked.

Maggie took some batting and several strips of binding from her bag. She laid them on a table beside Ben. Sarah returned with a knife, the tongs, a needle, and some thread. The water was already boiling, over the fire. Dr. Deihl tossed it all into the scalding water. He dipped the pair of tongs into the hot water; holding them in place for a minute, and then laid them on the batting.

Maggie watched intently as the doctor walked over to the basin and began washing his hands with the lye soap laying there. When he returned to the fireplace, he used the tongs to fish the items out of the hot water, and laid them on the clean batting.

"Mr. Hennesy, you may want to take a few more drinks of that stuff," Miles said. "Maggie, go ahead and pour some of your whiskey into the wound. Sarah, it's OK if you'd like to wait outside. As a matter of fact, I think you should."

Just as Ben was taking another long drink from his jug, Maggie proceeded to drown the wound in whiskey.

"Owwww!!!!!" Ben screamed, blowing the liquor out of his mouth, and all over Maggie.

"I'm so sorry, Mr. Hennesy, I didn't mean to hurt you!" Maggie apologized.

At that point, Sarah Hennesy hurried outside and scurried down the path; away from the cabin and out of earshot of her husband's screaming.

Miles stood in front of Ben Hennesy, and quietly took the jug from his hand, giving it to Maggie. The girl stood up to put the jug away. She turned around just in time to see Dr. Deihl pull back his fist and let go with a sucker-punch to Ben Hennesy' jaw, knocking him out cold.

Maggie was shocked, but didn't say a word.

"A man's got to do what a man's got to do," Miles said calmly, smiling at Maggie. He sat down on a log beside Ben's leg and went to work.

Dr. Deihl took the sterilized knife and carefully cut away the necrotic tissue from the injury, stopping now and then to pour more whiskey into it, to wash it out. When he was finished he laid the knife in the hot coals, on the hearth. With the skill of a seamstress, he neatly stitched the gash tightly closed. It was then, to Maggie's astonishment, that Dr. Deihl took the knife from the fire, and laid the side of the blade onto the wound. The sizzling sound and the smell of the burning flesh was more than Maggie could handle.

Miles watched the color drain from the girl's face, and she began to sink. He jumped up and caught Maggie, before she hit the floor. She had fainted. The doctor carried her over and laid her on the bed, then returned to his work. He chuckled quietly as he bandaged Ben's leg and cleaned up the mess. He washed his hands again, and then attended to Maggie. He bathed her face with cold water to revive her.

"What happened?" Maggie asked weakly.

"Looks as if you couldn't stomach the cauterization procedure... It's an old Indian trick," Miles said, laughing out loud, while helping her to stand up. "Now try to pull yourself together, and go get Mrs. Hennesy."

By the time Maggie returned with Sarah, Ben was awake. He looked dazed and confused, but it was obvious he was glad it was over.

"I'm sure your leg will heal just fine, Mr. Hennesy," Dr. Deihl said. "Maggie or I will be back in a couple of days to check it, and change the dressing. In the meantime, keep it elevated and stay off of it."

"OK, Doc. Sure do appreciate it," Ben said, slurring his words. "What do we owe you?"

Miles looked at Maggie. "You're Maggie's patient," he said.

"Dr. Mathison will handle your bill, Mr. Hennesy. Here's your tonic he wanted me to bring you," Maggie said, handing two brown bottles to Sarah. "We've got to be going, but you take care now."

"Thanks again," Sarah called out, as Dr. Deihl and Maggie left for home.

They rode side by side in silence. The sunshine had taken the chill out of the morning air, and it felt more like a spring day than November. As Miles and Maggie approached Springfield, the heavy smell of wood, burning in the fireplaces, filled the air;

reminding them, it was, indeed, the beginning of winter.

When they arrived at Dr. Mathison's office, Maggie dismounted and tied her mare to the rail outside her door. Miles Deihl just sat quietly atop his elegant black steed, watching Maggie.

Maggie stepped up to her door and opened it. She turned and looked back at the handsome doctor. "Don't you want to come in for a cup of tea?"

"I thought you were still angry with me. You haven't said a word to me, since we left the Hennesy farm."

"I'm sorry, Miles... I've been thinking ... that's all."

"It's been my experience that women become dangerous when they're allowed to think!" The doctor laughed.

"You can be so insulting, Miles Deihl!" Maggie hissed.

Miles bowed low, over the side of his horse and tipped his broad-rimmed hat to her. "Good day, my lady," he said, grinning broadly. He gave the horse's sides a gentle nudge with his heels, and trotted away.

Maggie spun around and went inside, slamming the door behind her. She threw her bag across the room and stamped her foot in vain defiance; but just then, there was a soft knock at the door. Maggie quickly composed herself and opened the door to find Dr. Deihl back again, and standing on her doorstep.

"What .....?" Maggie began.

Without saying a word, Miles Deihl stepped inside, pulled Maggie into his arms, and kissed her.

The chemistry between the two exploded. The intensity escalated. It became a blistering kiss. He pressed her hard against him. She felt the strength of his body; hot against hers. She felt his passion; a passion demanding her response. He kissed her until she was dizzy with desire, and when she could barely stand, he released her.

Maggie took a step back, unsteady on her feet, and breathless from the encounter. Her mind was flooded with questions.

"I just wanted to say a proper good-bye," he whispered hoarsely; grinning a mischievous grin. Then, he turned on his heel, and he left, as unexpectedly as he had returned. Maggie stood motionless at the door, confused and disorientated.

Chapter 7 - Zanesville Is Burning

Big fluffy snowflakes were drifting downward from the low gray clouds, only to be caught back up by the wind, and swirled around in a silent ballet of white. The first snow of the season was accumulating quickly.

Miles Deihl tugged at his collar, pulling it up higher, to protect his neck from the icy cold. He quickened his step. When he left McKray's inn, the sun was only beginning to set, but now the remaining daylight was being obscured by the whiteout. The wind was picking up and the temperature was dropping. The snow stung Miles' skin, driven by the strengthening gale. He pulled his scarf across his face. When he finally reached the tavern, he flung the door open and was literally blown into the room. Everyone stopped what they were doing to look toward the door, which Dr. Deihl was struggling with, against the wind, to close.

"We were about to start the card game without you, Doc," Martin Slagor shouted from the bar.

Miles stomped the snow from his boots, and handed his hat and coat to the plump, scantily dressed bar maid who traded him a tall mug of ale. "Thank you, my dear," he smiled, gladly accepting the pewter cup. "That's some storm out there! You're going to have to warm me up, Darlin." He grabbed the girl around the waist and yanked her against him, laughing.

"Ok, Doc ... you'll have time for that later. Let's get this game started," Mathew said, pulling a chair out from a table, and slamming a deck of playing cards down on the tabletop.

Several other men joined in; each taking a seat, and placing piles of coins in front of them. Miles released the barmaid, sending her off with a swat on the bottom. He sat down with the others and placed his money on the table, too.

"Daisy, bring us a round to get us started," Daniel O'Riley yelled. He shuffled the cards and dealt one card, face up to each man. An ace landed in front of Dr. Deihl. "Looks like you win the deal, Doc," he said, shoving the deck over to Miles.

The game continued for hours, while the wind howled outside the tavern. The more the men drank, the more reckless they played, which gave Miles Deihl the upper hand. He was drinking less and winning more. The company was good and the conversation was entertaining. The fire roared in the big fireplace at the end of the room, warming the drafty tavern and bathing it in cozy light.

Just as the men were about to call it a night, the door flew open, and Silas McGregor entered the establishment, covered with snow. His beard was a solid mat of ice, and little icicles clung to his bushy eyebrows. The gust of wind from the opened door blew the cards off the table, and onto the tavern floor.

"Silas! What the hell?!!" Martin Slagor shouted. "Close the damned door, man!"

Silas closed the door and scuttled over to the bar. "Whiskey!" he demanded, throwing a coin at the barmaid. "Who won?" he asked, turning to the table where the group was sitting.

"Doc won again!" Daniel O'Riley answered. "Where have you been? We thought you'd be here to play."

"Been down at McKray's... Had me a big steak and a pile of mashed potatoes." Silas tossed down the cup of whiskey, and then shook the snow from his beard. "Listen to this! I was sittin' there enjoyin' my meal, and Dr. Mathison was talkin' to Jacob McKray. I couldn't help but overhear 'em... They was sittin' right across from me. Seems that little girl, who works for the doc fell into a fortune." He slammed his cup down on the bar and shoved another coin over to Daisy. "Yep... He says she's got six hundred acres of prime land down by Newton, and over twenty thousand in gold coin."

Miles Deihl was jarred upright in his chair. His attention was peaked. "Where'd she get that kind of money?" he asked, trying to sound nonchalant.

"I guess her daddy was pretty well-to-do. You know he was killed up there on the ridge, with the rest of her family ... and others. Well, the young men that she and her kin was travelin' with, salvaged it all, and gave it to the doc to give to her. He said she's going to invest in a herd of Merino sheep, and go to farmin' down in Newton."

Daisy filled Silas' cup again, and he tossed it straight down. "She's a beauty for sure ... wouldn't mind gettin' my hands on that little filly. Uh huh! Now, to find out how wealthy she is ... well that just makes her all the more appealing! Ya know what I mean?" Silas bought another whiskey. "Yep, she's just ripe for the takin'." He winked at the men, running his thick tongue over his cold lips. "Maybe she'd pay me for my servicin' her?"

Miles Deihl instantly rose to his feet. His first impulse was to put his fist into Silas McGregor's filthy mouth, but he quickly decided against it; not wanting to betray his feelings for Maggie Waters. "Daisy, come here you sweet thing," he called out. "Let's you and I go upstairs and have us some fun."

In an instant, Daisy was at Miles' side, and arm in arm, they walked toward the stairs.

Just then, the tavern door was flung open, and Jack Douglas shoved his head inside. "FIRE!" he shouted. "The tannery's on fire. Hurry!! We need help!" He was gone as quickly as he had appeared. All the Zanesville men jumped up, grabbed their coats, and ran outside.

"Aren't you going with them, Doc?" Daisy asked, rubbing her bosom provocatively against Miles' arm.

"I don't see how my presence will make much difference there ... when I'm definitely needed here," he grinned, running a finger across the exposed swollen cleavage of Daisy's breasts.

Further up the main street, at the foot of the big hill, giant flames roared and leaped to the sky. Scores of men were running toward the fire, carrying buckets and blankets. Soot was raining down on the snow-covered ground, and the air was full of caustic black smoke, mixing with the snowflakes which continued to fall. The fire had already spread to adjacent structures, and was racing ever closer to the Spangler's blacksmith shop on the next block.

There was a spring at the foot of the hill, and the men formed a bucket brigade running from the water source to the tannery. The cold air made the work agonizing, as the water sloshed and then froze on the hands and bodies of the brave firefighters. Some of the men, soaked blankets in the spring, and worked feverishly, beating out the red hot embers which kept blowing in every direction, and igniting new fires. The citizens worked relentlessly, but in vain. The flames were insatiable as they claimed building after building. The entire upper part of Zanesville was soon a blazing inferno.

Reverend Wilkins fell down on his knees, praying earnestly for God's intervention, as the fire advanced rapidly toward his little log church. The Spangler family, along with Marky, were desperately moving their belongings from the blacksmith shop into the street, and trying to get the horses to safety.

Maggie Waters and Dr. Mathison arrived at the scene in a flat-bed wagon. Elizabeth Williams and Susanne Jackson, the midwives, were with them. They immediately began helping to load several of the injured and frost bitten men into the wagon. Many of the firefighters were having difficulty breathing, due to inhaling the toxic smoke.

"Maggie ... you and Elizabeth take these men to Jacob McKray's inn. I'll borrow another wagon, and Susanne and I will bring more," Dr. Mathison shouted over the noise of the wind, the roaring of the fire, the crashing of collapsing structures, and the screaming.

Maggie obediently climbed up into the wagon. She glanced around at the incomprehensible chaos, and concluded that *this must be what hell is like.*

Elizabeth climbed up onto the wagon seat beside her, and Maggie gave the reins a hard snap. The horses quickly made their way back down the main street.

Halfway to the inn, Maggie spotted a familiar figure walking quickly toward the fire. She pulled the horses to a stop, and stood up in the wagon. "Dr. Deihl... Dr. Deihl," she called out waving her hands in the air.

"Maggie! Where are you going?" Miles yelled, running over to the wagon filled with injured men.

"I'm taking these men to the inn. They're in bad shape. Can you help us?"

Miles Deihl jumped up into the wagon without answering. He scooted Maggie to the side and snatched the reins from her hands. "Heyaw!" he shouted, cracking the whip on the horses' rumps. The team reared slightly, and then broke into a run. They arrived at the inn within minutes.

The injured were taken inside and examined by Dr. Deihl.

"Here's what we need, Maggie," Miles said, rolling up his shirt sleeves. "Lots of salt water ... buckets of salt water. Mix about two cups of salt into each bucket of water. Then I need lots of batting. I need lots of snow, too. Elizabeth, I want you to build the fire up ... move the three men with frost bite closer to the fireplace. Get their wet clothes off and wrap them in blankets." The doctor washed his hands in a basin which was sitting on the hearth. "Then get some rope... Bind the wrists of these four guys who are having trouble breathing. We're going to raise their arms above their heads... It should help. Once you get the ropes around their wrists, I'll throw it up over the rafters. OK girls ... let's go."

Maggie and Elizabeth began gathering up the necessary supplies, while Dr. Deihl began work on the four men who had been burned.

"Give them each a big cup of saltwater to drink, and then give me the buckets and the batting," Miles said, ripping the shirtsleeve of one of the burned victims.

He poured salt water over the man's hand and arm, and then wrapped cotton batting around them. He took a dipper and saturated the cotton with saltwater.

"Maggie," he said, handing the dipper to her. "Keep the cotton wet with the saltwater." The doctor then moved on to the next man. Upon cutting the man's pants-leg, he was dismayed to see that the burn was extremely serious. "Elizabeth, go out and get me a bucket of snow, please," he called.

Once Miles had the snow, he washed and bandaged the man's blistered leg. He wetted it down with the brine and then packed it in snow. "Keep the snow coming, and keep the saltwater on it."

Next, the doctor moved on to the men who had inhaled too much smoke. He tossed the ropes up over the rafters in the cabin room, and pulled the men's arms above their heads, tying off the ropes to keep their arms comfortably elevated. "Sorry guys," he said, "this shouldn't be too uncomfortable... Is it making it easier to get your breath, yet?"

The men admitted that although it seemed absurd, it really did help their breathing.

Miles had just finished up, doing what he could for the men, when Dr. Mathison came in with more injured firefighters. Seven men had to be helped into the cabin. One of them had a badly mangled hand, and another man had a deep gash on his head. Both were bleeding profusely.

"Is the fire out, Dr. Mathison?" Maggie asked, hurrying over to help the older doctor.

"I'm afraid not, Maggie," he said. "I think it will just have to burn itself out. The wind is absolutely wreaking havoc up there." Dr. Mathison put his bag on a table. "The good thing... is ... I think this group is all that remains of the injured from up there ... for now, anyway." He looked over at Miles Deihl. "Thank God you're here, Dr. Deihl. We need all the help we can get. I see you have things under control." Then, Dr. Mathison eyed the ropes critically, and added, "Are you afraid these men will escape?"

"No sir," Miles said, "it's a trick I learned from working with coalmine fires. Helps expand the lungs ... makes it easier for them to breath."

"Excellent, Dr. Deihl. I see you can teach me a thing or two. Thank you!" Dr. Mathison chuckled, pushing his glasses up on his nose.

Miles looked over at the door, and was surprised to see Susanne Jackson helping Silas McGregor into the cabin. The man's foot was wrapped in an old shirt, and the blood was seeping through the material. Just seeing Silas' sneering face, rekindled the anger Miles had felt back at the tavern. Susanne helped McGregor to sit down on one of the chairs. Maggie knelt in front of Silas, and diligently unwrapped his foot. Blood spurted into the air, and continued to gush out in rhythmic, rapid intervals. The man was moaning with pain, but his mood seemed to lighten, immediately upon seeing Maggie Waters.

Miles Deihl could feel the rage burning into his awareness, as he watched the uncouth McGregor speaking flirtatiously with Maggie.

"Maggie, I'll see to this one. You go and soak that batting with the saltwater," he said sternly. Maggie stood up and returned to her other patients.

"Aw doc... Why'd ya have to go and spoil my fun?" Silas whispered.

"Let's have a look," the doctor said, ignoring Silas' question. "Looks pretty bad. How did it happen?"

"A damned beam fell on it."

"Dr. Mathison," Miles shouted, "We've got a bleeder here. You want to take a look?"

Dr. Mathison was busy suturing up another man's hand. "You go ahead, Dr. Deihl. Do what you need to do."

"Maggie, put the wide knife into the fire," Dr. Deihl shouted across the room. "And get me a small needle; and I'll need a very fine silk thread, if you can find some." Dr. Deihl took hold of Silas McGregor and helped him down onto the floor. "Just lie still, now," he said in a low voice, "this is going to hurt, but you'll be all right."

Maggie knelt down beside Miles, and watched him apply a tourniquet to Silas McGregor's upper leg. Then he spread the gash wide open and poured whiskey into the wound, exposing the blood vessel he was looking for.

McGregor let out a blood-curdling scream and passed out.

Miles grabbed the two severed ends of the bleeder with both hands, and pulled them up, holding them tightly together and pinching off the bleeding end. Maggie was amazed. She had never actually looked at an artery before.

"OK, Maggie... First of all, I want you to go and wash your hands. You *NEVER* touch an open wound without first washing your hands!"

Maggie ran over to the basin and scrubbed her hands, returning to Miles' side quickly.

"Now then... I want you to hold these ends together, just like I'm doing. Can you do that?"

Maggie nodded, and took a deep breath. She carefully retrieved the severed ends of the artery from Miles' hands, and held them together.

"Pinch the one that's bleeding, Maggie. That will stop it."

Miles poured more whiskey over the wound, and began to skillfully sew the tiny ends together in a "whip-stitch" style, working around the edges until the artery was finally intact. He performed the intricate work with skill and confidence. Maggie couldn't help but think that Dr. Miles Deihl was born to be a surgeon. His hands were steady and his concentration was intense. He removed the tourniquet and finished closing the jagged edges of the gash in the man's leg.

"Now, Maggie ... go and get the knife," he said quietly.

Maggie did as she was told, and returned with the red-hot instrument.

"All right, now... I want you to lay the flat part of the knife onto this wound while I push the sides together ... and hold it there with some pressure until I tell you. And please don't pass out, this time." He looked at Maggie and grinned. "Aw yes... And try not to burn me ... or yourself."

Maggie took a deep breath and placed the red-hot knife onto the wound, between Miles' hands. She was careful to keep the knife away from Dr. Deihl's fingers. There was that awful searing, sizzling sound again – – and the smell of burning flesh. Maggie prayed she could hold out. It seemed like an eternity.

"That's it," Miles said. "You can let go now."

Maggie dropped the knife and collapsed into a heap on the floor, in a dead faint.

"Oh Maggie ... what am I to do with you?" the young doctor whispered, smiling down affectionately at the girl.

With the bleeding under control, and the wound closed and bandaged, Miles scowled at Silas McGregor. Dr. Deihl leaned close to the man's ear. "I'll just patch you up for now, McGregor ... and kill you later," he whispered.

When he was finished, he scooped Maggie up into his arms and carried her over to where Dr. Mathison was working.

"What shall I do with this?" Miles asked. He looked at Dr. Mathison and chuckled.

"Good Lord ... what happened to her?" Dr. Mathison asked, looking alarmed.

"She helped me cauterize McGregor's laceration. She actually did a very good job. At least she waited until it was finished before she fainted." Miles said, grinning broadly.

Both doctors burst out laughing, and they laughed until their sides hurt.

Maggie stirred in Miles' arms. "Ooooh ... what happened?" Maggie moaned, regaining her senses. The girl looked embarrassed.

"Maggie, Sweetheart, seems you fainted," Dr. Mathison said.

"Oh no... Not again," Maggie sighed.

"It's OK, Maggie," Miles said, "we got the job done. Actually, I couldn't have managed it without your help." Dr. Deihl lowered Maggie slowly, allowing her body to slide down against his. Once her feet were firmly on the floor, he continued to hold her close to him, pretending to steady her. "Are you all right now?" he asked, and then he winked at her playfully.

Maggie's flushed cheeks betrayed her as she stood there, held fast by the doctor. She could feel the warmth of his very masculine body against hers, and she was remembering his kiss. Miles Deihl was studying her intently. He looked amused.

"Maggie, are you sure you're feeling all right? You're trembling. You'd better sit down," Dr. Deihl said. He helped Maggie to a nearby chair. With his back turned to Dr. Mathison, Miles grinned that handsome broad grin, and winked at Maggie again.

Maggie blushed. "I'm just cold," she said nervously, knowing full well that Miles Deihl knew otherwise.

Jacob McKray walked into the cabin, just then, accompanied by several other men. They were covered with soot and snow, and they all looked exhausted.

"Well, the fire's finally out," Jacob announced, in a tired voice. "Not much left up there, though." He wiggled out of his coat and shook the snow from it. "It's still snowing hard as hell. Looks like we've got about nine inches... We'll have more than a foot before it's over."

The group that came in with Jacob McKray settled down at a table in the corner; they ordered a large jug of whiskey.

Dr. Mathison walked over and threw an arm around Jacob's shoulders. "So I guess we're snowed in for the night."

"Looks that way. How are your patients?"

"We finally have things under control here, and I could sure use a drink ... how about you, old friend?"

"Yes, Doc... A drink sounds good," Jacob said. He tossed his coat over a chair and sat down at the nearest table.

"Make that three," Dr. Deihl added, sitting down heavily, at the same table. "Is it always so chaotic in this town?"

"Are you reconsidering staying?" Dr. Mathison asked hopefully. He poured three cups of whiskey from a jug he'd taken down from the cupboard, and handed one to each of the men.

"Well ... you asked me if this town really needed two physicians. Do you remember?" Miles grinned. "After tonight, I've decided this town could use a dozen doctors!" He gestured at the bodies strewn around the floor of the inn. Even the midwives had given way to exhaustion, and were stretched out, asleep by the fire.

"Here's to Zanesville and good doctors," Jacob McKray said, raising his cup high and laughing.

"... To Zanesville!" Dr. Mathison chimed in, raising his cup, too.

"... To a fine little town!" Miles added, bumping his cup against the other two.

"Maggie, would you like a cup of whiskey to warm you up?" Dr. Mathison asked, looking over at the tired girl. "I heard you say you were cold."

"Yes, Maggie," Jacob McKray said, "have a cup of whiskey with us, and then you can sleep in your old room. It's vacant, and the bed is clean and cozy. You look like you're worn out, little girl."

"I think I *will* take some, Mr. McKray. But just pour me a little," Maggie said tiredly.

Dr. Deihl slapped a stern hand down on the jug Jacob McKray was about to pick up. "No. Maggie... I don't think you should drink whiskey. What you need to do, is just go to bed and get a good night's sleep," Miles interrupted.

"Come on Doc, you sound like you're her father. She'll be fine. I'll just give her enough to take the chill off," Jacob said, frowning at Dr. Deihl.

"I'm sorry, Jacob... I just can't condone giving the lady whiskey," Miles said. "As a matter of fact, I think she would be better off sleeping in her own home tonight." He looked over at Maggie and shook his head. "Get your wrap, Maggie. I'm going to take you home."

"You can't be serious," Dr. Mathison said, slamming his cup down on the table. "We're having a blizzard, man! You don't even know if you'll be able to cross the river!"

"It's a snowstorm... *NOT* a blizzard... And we'll take my horse. He's as sure-footed as they come." He stood up and grabbed his hat and coat. "Let's go Maggie," he demanded.

"Just wait a minute, here," Maggie said, jumping to her feet, her green eyes blazing. "I think I can make my own decisions. You don't order me about like that!"

"Maggie... I'm just concerned with your welfare. Now please, humor me, just this once." He walked over and bent near to Maggie's ear. "I don't want you here with these men when they get all liquored up, Maggie!" he whispered. "Now please ... I've seen what can happen. Just get your cloak and come with me."

Maggie looked over to the corner where the group of men were drinking from the large jug. They were already getting loud and belligerent. She looked back at Miles Deihl. "All right, Miles. You can take me home," she conceded.

Maggie put her cloak on and pulled the hood up. She walked over to Dr. Mathison and laid her hand on his shoulder. "Miles' is right, Doc... I really need to go home. I'll see you tomorrow."

"OK, Maggie," Dr. Mathison said. "But if he's not back here in an hour ... I'm coming after him." He gave Maggie a deadly serious look.

"I'll be fine. Good night everyone."

"Guard my cup," Miles said. He laughed and pointed a finger at Doc Mathison. "I *WILL* be back to finish my drink."

The snow was still coming down, when Maggie and Miles mounted the big black stallion, and started off toward the river, to Springfield. The wind had calmed down, and everything seemed eerily silent. Miles held Maggie firmly against him, as he reined the horse toward the river's ford.

"It's lovely," Maggie said, wistfully.

"Not exactly the dangerous blizzard Doc Mathison warned us about, is it?" Miles laughed.

They crossed the river and trotted down the street to Dr. Mathison's office. Miles jumped off the horse, and then lifted Maggie down. He tied the stallion to the post and walked Maggie up to her door.

"I'm going to get the fire going, Maggie... Then I've got to get back to the inn," he said opening the door for her. Miles went straight to the big fireplace and stirred the coals. He laid two large logs on top of them and then turned to look at Maggie.

"It's so cold," she said shivering.

"I can fix that," Miles smiled, helping Maggie out of her cloak. He wrapped his arms around her and held her tightly against his body. "Hmm," he mused, "you don't feel cold to me. As a matter of fact you feel deliciously warm." He looked down into her big emerald-colored eyes, and marveled at how expressive they were. He kissed her lightly on the forehead, and squeezed her tighter. "You are definitely warming *me* up, Maggie Waters!"

Maggie giggled. "You're incorrigible, Miles Deihl!"

"No... I'm just honest. I want you ... plain and simple. I want to be the one to make love to you the first time. I want to be the one to father your children. I want to be the *ONLY* man you'll ever *know*. I want to marry you, Maggie Waters"

Maggie was shocked by his words. She started to pull away, but he covered her mouth with his, and she was suddenly being devoured by another one of his ever passionate kisses. She was drawn into that bitter sweet persuasion of yearning and desire. The world was spinning out of control as she surrendered to her own passion. Miles found the strength to stop, while he still could.

"Maggie! You're going to be my undoing, if you keep this up!" He gasped, moving away from her.

"*ME?*!!"

"Yes, *YOU!*" He rubbed his chin and looked at her angrily. "You bring out the worst in me. You make me want you in an agonizing, urgent way. I don't want to hurt you by giving in to that! I want you to be my *WIFE* ... and I don't want to take you before that time comes... I try my damnedest not to dishonor you! This has got to stop." He opened the door, and then stopped and looked deeply into Maggie's eyes. "I *will* have you someday, Maggie. I can't promise you I can always be a gentleman where you're concerned, though. I'm trying to give you time to grow up – – to mature a little." Miles shook his head in exasperation. "This is an honest warning from a desperate man. Don't play with fire, Maggie."

He left; slamming the door behind him.

Once again, Maggie found herself standing at the door, dazed and confused.

Chapter 8 – Educating Maggie

Thanksgiving came and went without much ado. Maggie was keeping busy helping Dr. Mathison with his patients, and getting the pharmacy started. The demand for Doc's tonics and herbs had grown to the extent that delivering them all was just too much work for the pair. In the little spare time she found, Maggie tutored Marky, who was doing a good job at the blacksmith shop, but had been neglecting his education.

"Maggie, open the door!"

Maggie ran over and flung the door open. It was Miles Deihl. He was standing on her doorstep holding a freshly cut evergreen.

"I brought you a Christmas tree, Maggie. Let's put it up and decorate it." He grinned, dragging the tree into the room.

"I don't care about Christmas," Maggie frowned. "Thank you for thinking of me, though." She looked sad.

"Maggie! There's more to life than work! Come on, be a sport," he said, propping the tree up against the wall.

"I haven't seen you in weeks, Miles. Where have you been?" Maggie asked, helping him off with his coat. She shook the snow from it and hung it over a chair.

"I had to go back home to Boston and take care of some business," he answered, catching Maggie's wrist as she walked past him. "I missed you," he said, bending over to kiss her on the cheek.

Maggie dodged his lips playfully, and grinned up at him, "You warned me ... remember?"

"What?!"

"You told me not to play with fire, Miles Deihl. You said that, the very last time I saw you! Well, I certainly don't intend to get burned ... so ....."

Miles grabbed Maggie roughly, picked her up in his arms and carried her over to her bed. He held her there, watching her expression change from mischievousness to apprehension. Maggie's eyes grew wide with fear, as Miles slowly lowered her to the bed. The girl squirmed in his arms, trying to escape. Just as she was about to scream, Miles abruptly dropped her onto the bed and burst into uncontrollable laughter.

"Oh Maggie! That was priceless! You should have seen the look on your face!!" Miles continued laughing until he could barely breathe.

Maggie scrambled off the bed and marched up to Dr. Deihl. She stamped her foot and slammed her hands onto her hips in anger. "How dare you make fun of me?!!" she shouted. "That was an awful thing to do to me!"

"Why? Did you want me to finish the job?" He laughed even harder. "Maggie... Don't you know by now, you are too inexperienced for me to waste my time and energy on?"

"What's that supposed to mean?!" she demanded.

"It means if I want sex... I'll find someone who knows how to satisfy me! Not someone I have to teach!" Miles slapped his leg in glee, as he continued to laugh. "I just don't have time to waste, Honey. You're safe... I was only playing!"

"You're horrible, Miles Deihl!" Maggie shrieked.

"And you're absolutely radiant when you're angry!" Miles grinned. "I love how sparks literally shoot out of those big green eyes of yours! Don't be too hard on me... I was just having some fun."

"At *my* expense!" she said, sitting down at the table, and resting her chin on her clenched fists.

"Oh Maggie... Where's your sense of humor, Sweetheart?" Miles said, squeezing Maggie's shoulders. "Relax. Let's have some fun. Would you like to go for a ride in the sleigh? I brought it."

Maggie turned and looked up at the handsome doctor. She couldn't help thinking he was unquestionably more fun to be with, than anyone she'd ever known. She also realized he was just as dangerous. He was her *'spider in a jar'*.

"All right. Let's go for a ride," Maggie agreed. She didn't want to admit she'd missed his company.

Dr. Deihl grabbed Maggie's cloak and threw it around her shoulders. He put his own coat on, and grabbed the broad-rimmed hat he always wore.

Outside, Miles lifted her up into the sleigh, and then climbed in beside her. It was barely snowing, but the air was biting cold. Dr. Deihl spread a heavy quilt across their legs to keep them warm. He slipped his arm around Maggie and pulled her closer against him.

"Damn, Maggie... We might freeze to death out here!" he said, grinning at the girl. He gave the reins a snap, and his horse trotted off down the snow covered street.

"Maybe you can teach me how to keep you warm," Maggie said, teasing the doctor.

"Don't start with me, Maggie!" Miles snapped.

"I'm serious, Miles."

"What is it you want from me?" Miles asked, looking perplexed.

"I want you to tell me how to please a man," she said bluntly.

"You can't be serious!"

"Well, how else will I learn? I mean, other than actually doing it?" She looked up at the doctor and grinned. "I mean ... if it's such a terrible chore to have to physically *TEACH* a virgin how to satisfy a man ... why not just *TELL* her beforehand?"

"You *ARE* serious, aren't you?"

"Yes."

"Hmm ..." Miles looked thoughtful. Moments passed. "Well .... The first thing you have to understand... is that although men want to *marry* virgins ... they want to *make love* to whores."

"Oh NO!" Maggie exclaimed. "Then, how on earth are they ever happy at home with their wives?"

"Well, you see ... not very many married men *ARE* happy at home. That's why there will always be prostitutes."

Maggie was silent for a long while. She sat there, quietly thinking. Miles held his breath, waiting for the next question. He was positive it would be shortly forthcoming.

"OK, Miles," Maggie began, "what's the difference between a wife and a whore?"

"That's easy, Maggie ..." He laughed. "A wife thinks making love is a *duty*, and a whore thinks making love is a *privilege*."

"Why?"

"Why, what?" Miles looked confused.

"Why don't wives consider making love a privilege?"

"I suppose because they've been taught that sex is not to be enjoyed... Or maybe their first experience went badly. Usually if a woman's first experience is a bad one, they're psychologically damaged for life ... they'll suffer a life-long aversion toward lovemaking. That's a man's fault!"

"Well, if God created it, and the Bible says that the marriage bed is undefiled ... doesn't that mean it should be enjoyed?" Maggie said, shrugging her shoulders.

"You'd think so. But then there's that thing about it being only for procreation – not enjoyment. I never did understand why it had to be so complicated for some folks!"

"How would you turn your wife into a whore?" Maggie asked innocently.

"Oh for god's sake, Maggie! Do you really expect me to answer that question?"

"Yes."

Miles stopped the sleigh and turned to the girl. "First of all, are we talking about *ME*, personally? Or just any man?"

"*YOU* ..." Maggie giggled.

Miles shook his head incredulously. He gave the reins a shake, and the horse began to move again.

"Are you warm enough, Maggie? Looks like it's starting to snow harder." Miles was hoping to change the subject.

"You didn't answer me, Miles."

"Maggie, to answer that question would be to betray all good men everywhere!" He laughed. "I'm obliged to remain true to my gender!"

"Tell me, please!"

"I'd rather show you," he said, with a chuckle.

Maggie slapped Miles on the arm, playfully. "Please, Miles... Tell me how ANY man could turn his virtuous wife into a wanton whore."

"Maggie! Such language!!!!" Miles sounded sincerely shocked.

"Sorry." Maggie felt a flush of embarrassment. "I just want to understand, Miles."

"I don't think it's something you need to understand, Maggie. Not right now, anyway!"

"I think you don't have the answer. That's what I think!"

Miles pulled the sleigh to a stop, under a huge oak tree on the river bank. The entire landscape looked like a work of art. The snow continued to fall, and the glistening ripples in the Muskingum River glittered and danced in the muted light. The air was cold, stinging and biting at the skin. The fragrance of pine mixed with freshly burning wood from the nearby cabins, permeated the air. Miles pulled Maggie close to him, and kissed her gently.

"Listen to me very carefully because I won't repeat myself," Miles said, sternly.

"All right," Maggie agreed.

"Any man, who knows how to *really* please a woman, can turn *any* woman into a whore. And I use that word *whore* loosely. What I mean is ... a woman who loves to make love and is always willing – not a *prostitute.*"

"How does a man learn to please a woman? Does it come naturally?" Maggie asked, her eyes growing wider.

"You see! That's the problem, Maggie. It doesn't come naturally. If it were that easy, there wouldn't be all these frigid wives making their husbands' lives miserable!" Miles looked at Maggie and laughed loudly, shaking his head in exasperation. "Men are taught by women! Experienced women – – older women – – women who aren't afraid to enjoy their men. Those women have no reservations when it comes to asking for, and getting exactly what they need to satisfy themselves sexually. They teach men what men need to know. Those men, in turn, satisfy their wives to the extent that their wives crave and desire their husbands' advances." Miles looked at Maggie. "Now do you understand?"

Maggie sat quietly, leaning against Miles' warm chest. Her curiosity was satisfied for the moment. She turned to Miles Deihl and slipped her arms around his neck, looking into his piercing brown eyes. She kissed him affectionately on the mouth. Then she thought of one more question. She leaned back, studying his attractive features. He braced himself for the next round of inquisition.

"Who taught *YOU* to please a woman?" Maggie asked.

"I didn't say I knew how, did I?" He smiled.

Maggie thought for a minute. "Oh. I guess you didn't say you did."

"Now that we've got that settled ... is this conversation over, Maggie?"

"Thank you for humoring me, Miles. I've just been so curious about those things. My Mama didn't like to talk to us girls about sex. You could just about see her squirm in her skin, if you dared ask her a question about it. I think it was sweet of you to help me. It's just that now I've got a thousand more questions in my mind ... and ...."

Miles dragged Maggie into his arms and covered her mouth with his, just to stop her from talking. He was amazed at the almost instantaneous passion that was aroused in them both, whenever they kissed. He was drowning, in that intoxicating fervor Maggie alone could elicit from the depths of his soul. Without warning, he abruptly stopped.

"Maggie Waters, you are a very bad girl!" he whispered hoarsely, against her ear. "I've got to take you home, or we're both going to be in serious trouble." He gave the reins a quick snap and the horse began trotting along the river bank.

Maggie collapsed against the doctor and remained completely silent all the way home. When the sleigh reached Maggie's house, Miles carried her from the sled, right up to her doorstep. He set her down and kissed her softly. It was pure affection, and Maggie felt it.

"We'll decorate that tree tomorrow, Maggie. I've got to go," he said, and he left in a hurry. Maggie watched the sleigh disappear down the street.

Miles drove the sleigh to the ford, where he unhitched his horse, saddled it, and crossed the river, leaving the sleigh for tomorrow. He rode straight to Slagor's Tavern and ran inside.

"Daisy, Darlin! Let's go Honey, I need some attention!" Miles said, grabbing the buxom barmaid by the hand and dragging her up the stairs.

The next morning, when Maggie opened her door to leave, she discovered a large package, wrapped in red silk cloth, on her doorstep. She picked it up and took it inside. It was a beautiful, leather bound medical book from Miles. There was a note tucked inside. It read:

Dearest Maggie,

> *I'm sorry I'll miss Christmas with you. I've been unexpectedly called away. I'll be gone for a few weeks, but I'll be back to quiz you on what you learn from this book. Please enjoy it, and think of me often.*

Merry Christmas,
Miles

Maggie held the book against her chest, remembering the sleigh ride last night.

Chapter 9 - Storm Clouds Are Gathering

Spring came quickly. The winter had been an extremely harsh mix of snow and ice. As the snow melted, the creek rose, claiming ever more land as it approached the cabin.

"I can't even see the road, Nathan. I sure hope it stops rising, or we'll float right out of here. Maybe we should have built us a boat, instead of a cabin!" John laughed, standing on the porch, looking out across the meadow.

"Well, at least it's not raining," Nathan said.

"Have you checked the cellar to make sure the water hasn't come in there?" John turned, looking at his brother.

"No... I never thought of that."

"We need to start plowing next week, and plant the week after that. If the seeds get ruined – I don't even want to think about that!" John said, jumping off the porch and disappearing into the cellar.

"Well?" Nathan yelled.

"It's still dry down here, thank God," John shouted back.

The brothers were a week behind schedule when they finally started plowing the fields. The water, however, left the soil wet and easily tillable. What appeared to be a disaster, with the water receding so slowly, had turned into a blessing.

"Gidup there!" Nathan yelled, as the oxen pulled the plow effortlessly through the virgin soil.

The smell of the black, wet loam, stirred the man's senses, awakening his determination to succeed at this farm. It was a beautiful day. The sky was clear blue, without one cloud in sight. The trees along the road were coming alive with budding leaves, and the birds flitted restlessly from tree to tree, searching for a place to nest. The entire valley was in the process of rebirth. A warm breeze lifted Nathan's spirits, and the sun warmed his very soul. The winter had been cruel, and the spring brought with it, the welcomed relief from the bone-chilling cold. Nathan could hardly wait to get the crops in, and then watch them grow.

John was working the plot which would eventually become the vegetable garden. It was up near the cabin. The brothers had missed working in the sunshine. Neither one of them ever minded hard work.

Winter time always took its toll on a man's disposition, and John prayed that sunnier days would be the catalyst to stop Nathan's nightly drinking.

Before the month was over, John and Nathan had managed to get all the crops in and the fencing up. They put in corn, wheat, tobacco, and hemp. John planted the vegetables, which were already starting to sprout. The fruit trees looked strong, but there would be no fruit for two or three years. It would, however, eventually be a wonderful orchard.

The lengthening days and balmy nights were filled with a new-found joy and anticipation.

It was the second week of June. It had been a hot day, and the humidity hung heavy over the land. Black clouds were gathering in the western sky, as the Stillman brothers finished up the day's work.

"Looks like a storm brewing," John said, looking up at the darkening sky. "Hope it's not as vicious as that last one!"

"Storms here are quite different than the ones we had in Pennsylvania, aren't they? Why do you suppose that is?" Nathan asked.

"Probably because this is pretty flat land – not like back home, where we were sheltered by the mountains. The hills would have cut down the force of the wind, don't ya think?" John surmised.

Lightning flashed in the distance and the temperature began to drop. The deep rumbling sound of thunder echoed across the valley.

"I think this is gonna be a bad one, John," Nathan said, pointing at the tree tops whipping around violently, as the wind picked up.

"Let's get the oxen into the barn, before this gets any worse," John called, already sprinting toward the paddock.

By the time the men reached the barn, huge pieces of ice were falling like stones from heaven, and the wind was howling through the rafters. The oxen were distressed by the pounding hail, lightning and thunder; and they resisted the brothers' efforts to get them sheltered. Once inside, John and Nathan stood in the doorway, watching the intensity of the storm as it continued to build. The noise was deafening, with the oxen bawling nervously, the wind screaming through the building, the hail stones beating against the wood, and the thunder crashing in huge explosions.

"Nathan... We've got to get to the cellar!" John shouted.

"We can't go out in this!" Nathan yelled.

"Come on! We've got to make a run for it!" John screamed.

The air was thick with flying debris as the men ran for the cabin. When they reached the cellar, they crouched in a corner and prayed the storm would pass quickly, and the buildings could withstand the assault. The brothers hunkered down there for what seemed an eternity; but in reality it was only a few minutes.

Suddenly everything was quiet. As quickly as it had descended on the valley, it was gone. John went to the cellar door and peered out. The air was dead still. No sound could be heard. John stepped outside and looked around at the destruction.

"Nathan!" he cried. "You won't believe this!"

Nathan ran outside to where his brother was standing. The fields were littered with all kinds of rubble; pieces of the barn, tree limbs, fence rails, dead birds, and things which couldn't even be identified. The barn roof was gone, although the rest was still standing. The oxen had somehow managed to get into the cornfield, but seemed to be all right. The boys walked through their fields; inspecting the damage to the crops, which were just beginning to come up. Had it been two weeks later, they would have lost everything to the destructive hail storm.

The trees across the road had been stripped bare of their leaves; looking like stark gray skeletons, on an alien landscape; several had been completely uprooted and tossed like mere twigs about the road.

"Good Lord!" Nathan gasped. "What would you call that?"

"I'd call it one hell of a wind storm," John said quietly. He rubbed his forehead, wondering how the cabin was able to withstand such a storm. There didn't seem to be any damage to it, except for a couple of the clapboards that were missing from the roof, and the paper had been torn off the windows.

"Well, big brother, we've got a mess to clean up. And I'm just thankin' God we're alive!" Nathan said, kicking at a piece of the rocker that had been snatched from the porch, and ripped to pieces by the wind.

"How many of these are we goin' to have to endure?" John said, looking up into the sky. "Nobody bothered to warn us of a storm like this. Makes me wonder what else we don't know about."

"I know exactly what you mean, John." Nathan leaned on his brother's shoulder, taking stalk of the devastation around them. "Let's go catch the oxen."

Summer was beautiful on the Muskingum River. The town was alive with playful children and busy shop keepers. Zanesville was growing and so was the population. Dr. Mathison and Dr. Deihl were both necessary components of the community. Although not on friendly terms, the two physicians worked together when it was required.

With the coming of summer, came the seasonal ailments; especially the agues. Ague was a debilitating and chronic illness which came in the summer and lasted until nearly winter. Zanesville seemed to be a hotbed for the complaint.

Jacob McKray had invited the doctors and a few of the town's people to attend a meeting at his inn, for the purpose of addressing the ague problem. They were all sitting around a huge table, discussing ways to stop the spread.

"Maggie, I'm thinking we should brew up a batch of your Pa's tonic and try it on some of these sick folk," Dr. Mathison said thoughtfully.

"Well it certainly worked on the typhoid," Miles Deihl admitted, rubbing his chin. "I still think the problem originates in the swamps around here. If we could just get enough men together and dig trenches to the river, we might be able to drain them."

"Or why not just fill them in?" Maggie asked.

"Because they're probably spring-fed, and not just a catchall for runoff," Miles said.

"He's got a point, Maggie," Doc Mathison agreed. "If the swamps are the problem, then they would most certainly need to be drained into the river." Dr. Mathison pushed at his spectacles. "Dr. Deihl, what is it about the swamps that you think could possibly cause ague?"

"I'm not sure if it's the gasses or the insects," Miles replied. "Either one could do it."

"Well, that's true enough," Doc Mathison admitted.

"So where do we start ... if we're going to try and get this thing under control?" Jacob McKray asked.

Doc Mathison scratched his head. "I'd say, brew up a big batch of Maggie's tonic and get it dispersed to everyone showing any symptoms, and then ... ..."

"And then try to get volunteers willing to help get the swamps drained," Miles interrupted.

"Yes. Exactly," Dr. Mathison said. "We'll attack the problem from both views, and see if we can make a difference this year."

"Too bad we didn't approach the problem in the spring," Miles said. "We may have been able to stave off some of this illness that's already affected our neighbors."

"You're right, Miles," Maggie agreed. "But then ... I don't believe anyone actually thought the problem could be solved so easily. I mean ... if, indeed, the problem can be solved."

"We'll just have to try, Maggie. And then we'll wait and see." Miles grinned at the girl.

The next few weeks passed quickly for Maggie. She couldn't even count the batches of tonic she had brewed, and dispensed to people suffering from ague. She felt a sense of pride, as one by one, patients began to improve.

Maggie hadn't seen much of Miles Deihl since he returned from Boston this time. He had taken on the responsibility of supervising the trenching project which took up much of his time. There were three large swamps in the process of being drained. Maggie missed his humor, and the fact that they always enjoyed such stimulating conversations. She had learned so much from him. His medical knowledge far surpassed Dr. Mathison's.

It was Saturday afternoon, and Maggie had just finished working with Marky, going over his math lessons for the week. Once the boy had gone home, Maggie decided to take a walk along the riverbank. She loved walking under the willow trees, and watching the geese and the ducks gliding through the water. The day was warm, but there were some clouds gathering. The air was filled with the fragrance of honeysuckle growing in abundance along the river. The Muskingum River sang as it passed over the lower rapids, swirling and gurgling, falling down onto the rocks at the level below.

Maggie stood quietly on the river bank, watching the endless flow. She felt at peace there; the sound and the smell of the river soothed her mind. Maggie found a large flat rock and sat down on it. She took off her shoes and let her toes dangle in the water, which felt surprisingly cold.

She noticed a man walking toward her, but she didn't get up. When he approached her, she realized she had never seen him before. He looked unkempt and appeared to be intoxicated. Maggie immediately sensed she should leave, but it was too late. The man reached down and caught her arm, yanking her to her feet.

"Hey, little girl ... what'cha doin' out here all alone? Where's your daddy?" he grunted.

"Excuse me," Maggie said, politely. "Please let go of my arm. That hurts!"

"Oh ... my... Excuse me ...," he mocked, grabbing at her with his other hand.

Maggie struggled to free herself from the stranger. He was a largely built, middle aged man, and he was much stronger than she was. She began to cry, and she was about to scream for help, when Miles Deihl suddenly emerged from the trees. His eyes were blazing and his face was blood red with rage. Without hesitation, Miles rammed his fist into the man's face, knocking him easily to the ground. The stranger was so drunk, he thrashed about in the dirt, spitting blood and cursing, while trying to get up. Miles grabbed Maggie's shoes, caught her hand, and ran, almost dragging her, down the path and out of the drunken man's range of vision.

It started to rain, as they neared the ford, where Miles' beautiful black horse was tied. Without saying a word, he lifted Maggie up into the saddle, and climbed on behind her. They rode across to the Zanesville side of the river, and then headed down the path toward Harvey's Ravine. When they reached the bottom of the canyon, Miles jumped off the horse and pulled Maggie down, and into his arms. He still didn't say a word. He just stood there, holding her close to his heart.

It was raining harder now, but it was an exhilarating rain. It felt wonderful, and fresh, and cooling. Maggie looked up at Miles, blinking her eyes hard to see through the rain. He was glaring at her angrily.

"Put your shoes on, Maggie," he said bluntly, handing them to her.

Maggie obediently slipped them on her feet. Miles caught hold of her hand and they walked along the path in the pouring rain. Miles led his horse behind them. They walked in silence. Maggie sensed that Miles needed time to calm his temper. She had only seen him this angry on one other occasion. They turned onto another path which ran steeply up the hillside.

From the top of the hill, Maggie could see the entire Muskingum valley, and both towns with the river meandering between them. Miles stood there quietly gazing at the picturesque scene. He breathed deeply, and seemed to relax, but he still didn't speak.

The two of them were drenched. Maggie's hair hung in dark wet ringlets, and her now transparent cotton clothing clung tightly to her body. Maggie could easily make out the rippled muscles across Miles' abdomen, and the swell of his biceps through his dripping shirt. He looked gorgeous in the rainstorm. His straight black hair was tied at the back of his neck, but the front fell across one eye, and his skin glistened gold.

Miles and Maggie stood silently on the hilltop until the rain stopped and the sun began to peek through the clouds. A haze was filling the valley, as steam rose from the scorched earth.

"I wanted you to see this," Miles finally spoke. "And there's something else. I want to show you what I discovered."

Maggie didn't say a word as Miles led her back down another pathway. Maggie could hear the sound of rushing water, and looked around to see where it was coming from. What she saw, took her breath away. It was a gorgeous steep waterfall, which had cut a deep gorge into the hillside next to where they were walking. The hill was covered with honeysuckle and the fragrance permeated the air.

Miles tied the horse to a bush and led Maggie back to where the water was gushing over a cliff. He pulled her along with him, as he walked around the falling water, and went in behind the cascade. There, veiled by the falls, was a cave. It was huge, like a secret room hidden in the hillside.

"Oh! I wish we had a torch!"

"Someday we'll bring one, and explore the cave," Miles responded.

Miles took both of Maggie's hands in his and looked into her eyes. "You know I warned you about men who are predators. If I hadn't seen you from the other side of the river ... who knows what might have happened to you. I just crossed over to say hello. I had no idea you would be in trouble. You were just lucky this time. But what about the next time, Maggie?"

"I'm sorry, Miles. I walk that path so often, I never thought ..."

"That's the problem, Maggie!" he interrupted. "You don't *THINK*!"

"Well, I understand now. I won't walk alone anymore," Maggie promised.

"Where I come from, *ladies* never leave their homes without an escort. This is really hard for me to handle... It's like an entirely alien culture."

Miles looked down at Maggie's dress, and didn't say anything for a long time. He just stood quietly staring at the girl. Finally he couldn't resist. "Uh Oh, Maggie... Look at YOU!!" He laughed. "Do you realize you might as well be standing there naked?"

Maggie looked down, and was horrified to discover that her soaking wet, pale pink dress looked paper-thin; her entire body was on display; showing through it. She ran around behind the doctor, trying to hide.

"It's a little late, Maggie." He laughed harder. "You certainly left *NOTHING* to my imagination, including the perfect nipples on those pert little breasts of yours!"

Maggie was beside herself with embarrassment. Miles was tugging on her arm trying to pull her back around, in front of him. Maggie began to cry.

"Oh Maggie... You shouldn't be ashamed of such a beautiful little body. You're perfect, and I loved seeing it. Please don't cry! I didn't mean to embarrass you." He pulled his shirt off over his head, and handed it back to Maggie. "There, now. Will that make you feel better? Just put it on over your dress."

Maggie gratefully wriggled into Miles' shirt which covered her clear to her knees. She was still crying when she allowed him to look at her again.

"Have you forgotten I'm a doctor, Maggie?" Miles chuckled. "Do you have any idea how many naked bodies I get *paid* to have to look at ... some of them I should charge double ... for having to endure the task. I liked looking at yours! That was a refreshing experience for me! And I'm not even going to charge you... That's how nice it was!"

"I hate you!" she snarled. "You enjoy embarrassing me! That's cruel and sadistic!"

"You don't hate me, Maggie." Miles grinned. "You just don't know how to handle my honesty."

"I want to go home," Maggie cried, choking out the words.

"Are you going to stay mad at me, Maggie?" Miles asked.

"Yes!"

"Why? Because my eyes happened to be open, when you stood right there in front of me?"

"No! Because you ... because you ..."

"Because I told you I could see through your dress?"

"Yes!!"

"But if I hadn't told you, then anyone we encountered on our way home would see it, too! Would you have preferred that?"

"NO!!"

"Well, then... What would you have had me do?" Miles laughed at the ironic logic. "I'm damned because I *did*... But I would have been damned if I *didn't*. Seems I got caught in a *lose – lose* situation."

"I don't know!" Maggie cried. "No man has ever seen me naked before ... that's all."

"Not even your doctor?"

"That's different!"

"Well, if it's any consolation... I didn't ask for it."

"Shut up!"

"It's not as if I don't know what's under your clothes, Maggie! My hands have memorized every inch of your body."

Maggie collapsed to the ground crying in humiliation. Miles pulled her back up onto her feet. He held her by her shoulders and shook her gently.

"Damn it, Maggie! It's time for you to grow up and act like a woman!" He cupped her face in his hands and forced her to look at him. "You don't have some secret weapon under your clothes. You don't have anything new and special that other women don't have. So what the hell is going on in your head? Why make such a big deal out of this? You have a normal body. It's a very nice body, but it *IS* normal. And it's certainly not anything I haven't seen countless times before! Maybe not *YOURS* ... but you have to understand that yours is really no different than most others!"

"I don't know what's wrong with me... I don't want to talk about this anymore. I just want to go home."

"You're just a product of how you were raised, Maggie!"

Miles grabbed Maggie's hand and led her back to his horse. He literally threw her up into the saddle and climbed on behind. The trip to Maggie's house was uncomfortably silent. Miles seemed to be lost in deep thought, the entire way.

Once inside Maggie's house, Miles' frustration got the best of him. He grabbed Maggie roughly and pulled his shirt off of her. She tried to get away from him, but he refused to let her go.

"Maggie, I'm going to teach you something you really need to learn!" Miles said angrily.

In the struggled that ensued, Miles actually ripped the dress from Maggie's body, leaving her naked and vulnerable.

"Scream, Maggie!" Miles demanded. "Go ahead Maggie... Why don't you scream for help?"

While holding the girl with one strong hand, he unbuttoned his trousers and shoved them off, along with his boots. Now, they were both totally undressed. Maggie squeezed her eyes tightly closed, refusing to look at Miles' nakedness.

"Look, Maggie! I'm as naked as a jaybird! Open your eyes and look at me. Scream for Dr. Mathison! This is what you're so afraid of? Naked bodies?"

"Let me go!" she hissed at him.

"No. I don't intend to let you go until you understand there's nothing scary or dangerous about being naked. It might surprise you to know the human body isn't some sinister sexual tool, either!!"

"I'm going to scream!"

"No you won't."

"Let me go!"

"I'd feel much better if you *would* scream. Then I'd know you've learned the lesson I'm trying to teach you!"

"Please, Miles, let me go! I *WILL* scream!"

"You want to know WHY you won't scream... You won't scream because you're afraid Dr. Mathison will come in here and see your sacred naked body! Isn't that the truth, Maggie? Even if I decided to rape you,

you wouldn't scream. You'd do anything to protect your damned modesty!!"

"Please let me get dressed!" Maggie pleaded; still keeping her eyes tightly closed.

"Open your eyes, Maggie. You need to look at us. We're built like normal human beings. We're no different than anyone else on the planet. We all have the same body parts!"

"I don't want to look."

Miles led her over to the table and sat her down on a chair. He pulled another chair up beside her and he sat down, too.

"Now, Maggie... You and I are going to have a casual conversation about medical terminology. We're going to sit here totally nude, and we might even discuss anatomy."

"You're cruel!'

"This is the *kindest* thing anyone will ever be willing to do for you! I swear it! Someday you'll thank me for this! Open your eyes."

"NO!"

"Ok, you're making this harder than it has to be," Miles said. His impatience was obvious. "If you don't open those beautiful green eyes of yours, I'm going to carry you outside and show the entire neighborhood how special your body is ... and as an added benefit, they'll get to enjoy mine, too!" He laughed at the thought of it.

Maggie's eyes flew open. "You wouldn't dare!" she snarled.

"Aw... That's better," he smiled. "Now keep your eyes open and look at me." Miles stood up and Maggie squeezed her eyes closed immediately. "Not good," he said, scooping her up in his arms and heading for the door. Her eyes flew open again. "How long do we have to play this silly game, Maggie?" he asked in frustration.

"All right," Maggie said weakly. "I'll look."

Miles sat her back down in the chair and stood in front of her with no compunction. He even turned in a slow circle, making sure the whole time that she kept her eyes on his perfect, naked physique.

"I have a nice body, don't I, Maggie?" Miles said, grinning.

"Yes," she whispered. Her cheeks were turning a bright scarlet color.

"Now, you do that. Stand up and turn around for me!"

"I can't do that."

"Well, maybe you'll do it for your neighbors, then?" Miles laughed.

Maggie jumped to her feet and made a quick turn, sitting back down in a hurry.

"Nope. That was much too fast. You have to do it slowly, like I did."

Maggie rose from her chair, wishing she was invisible. She stood in front of Miles and turned around as slowly as she could.

"Now, Maggie... Ask me if I think you have a nice body."

"Miles, do you think I have a nice body?" she forced the words.

"Yes, Maggie, as a matter of fact, I love your body... Thank you for sharing it with me!" He grinned.

Maggie slapped him hard across the face.

Miles grabbed the girl and pulled her over his knees and actually spanked her hard on the bare bottom. Maggie yelled and struggled free, slapping him again. Again he spanked her; this time leaving large red welts on her flesh. After that spanking, she just laid there, across his lap, crying like a child. Miles could barely keep from laughing. Then, Maggie was quiet for a long time, and Miles knew she was thinking. At this point he was preparing for anything.

Strangely, Maggie's thoughts went back to the massacre on the ridge and her outburst with Nathan and John Stillman. She remembered how she had overreacted and nearly got all of them killed. Looking back, now, she knew Nathan and John had been traumatized, too; and they were only trying to protect her from further pain. But she lashed out with blame, in a childish tirade. There were other times, she recalled, when she'd blown things completely out of proportion. Admittedly she did have a tendency to see events more dramatically than they actually were. It was a matter of *her* perception. Miles was correct in his assessment. She *had* exaggerated the consequence of the incident in the rain.

Suddenly Maggie wriggled off of Miles' lap, stood up and looked him right in the eye. "Would you like a cup of tea, Dr Deihl?" she asked quietly.

"Oh Maggie! I would absolutely love to have a cup of tea!" he said, trying not to show his surprise. This is exactly what he was hoping for.

Maggie went to the fireplace, stirred the coals, and swung the iron pot of water over the fire. She took two cups from the cupboard and brought them to the table. She prepared the tea the same way she had, so many times before. Miles watched her in amazement. He knew that after a while, she would forget her painful reticence. She just needed the distraction of a beneficial spanking to help her along.

"This is good tea, Maggie," Miles said grinning at the girl sitting across from him.

"Thank you," she replied. "Would you like some more?"

"No, thank you. I'm going to have to head home, Maggie. I'm really tired," Miles said, reaching for his pants.

Without warning, Maggie jumped up, snatched Miles Deihl's trousers from the floor, along with the boots and shirt. She scampered to the door, opened it, and tossed them outside.

"I'm sorry you have to leave so soon, Miles." She grinned impishly, while standing there totally naked.

"Oh NO! I've created a monster," Miles sighed. He stood up slowly, trying to decide how to handle this situation. "I free you from your false sense of modesty, and this is the thanks I get, huh?"

"That's for spanking me!" Maggie said, rubbing her bruised bottom.

"Well you slapped me."

"I'm sorry. You were making fun of me again."

"Maggie, I was just teasing you. I would never make fun of you. I honestly *DO* love your body. I just wanted to see your reaction when I said it," Miles admitted. "Anyway, I've got to go... NOW ..."

"What ... no good-bye kiss?" Maggie giggled.

"Um... Maggie, I can't kiss you good night, until I get my clothes on." He grinned and winked at the girl, playfully.

"Why?"

"Don't start with the questions, Honey! I've got to get out of here!"

Maggie was about to continue her interrogation, and Miles knew it.

She didn't get the chance. He scooped her up into his arms laughing, and carried her over to the bed. Maggie's skin felt hot against his; burning him; but it was *HIS* inferno. *'Now who was playing with fire?'*

Miles finally collected his determination and dropped Maggie onto the bed. He turned around and walked out into the night, picking up his clothes outside Maggie's door. He pulled on his trousers and jumped onto his horse. He prayed to God the neighbors didn't see him.

Maggie lounged on the bed laughing out loud, thinking about Dr. Deihl leaving her house with no clothes on. She deeply respected his tenacity in preserving her virginity, especially when it meant wondering out into the night naked. She laughed so hard she had to hold her aching sides.

Maggie resolved to admit that Miles Deihl actually did manage to teach her a valuable lesson in regard to false modesty – and the freedom from it. She couldn't believe she had ever held such a childish concept about the human body. Miles Deihl was a remarkable man, besides being an extraordinary doctor.

Chapter 10 – The Initiation

The drainage project was a success. The swampland was dry and there were no new cases of ague in Zanesville. With the project completed, Miles Deihl again made plans to leave town on one of his regular business trips.

"Are you going to make some time for me?" Miles asked. He stood on Maggie's doorstep grinning. He was holding a large covered basket.

"Only if you're going to take some time off to spend with me!" Maggie laughed, and pulled the young doctor inside. "I'm glad to see you. You've been so busy lately, I've been feeling neglected."

"I know, Maggie, and you're probably not going to like what I'm about to tell you." He bent down and kissed the girl gently on the lips. "I'm leaving tomorrow for Boston, but I thought we could have dinner together tonight." Miles put the basket on the table and pulled the cover off, in a grand gesture. "... A glass of wine madam?" He took a bottle from the basket and handed it to Maggie. "Would you care for a slice of Devil's Food Cake, my dear?" The doctor carefully lifted a beautiful chocolate cake from the basket. "Oh no ... that's dessert! ... Here we go ... let's try this juicy roast beef ... and some potatoes ... and green beans ... and fresh baked apples." Miles set the items on the table, one by one, with great flare and drama. He then stepped back, and bowed low to Maggie. "Does it please my lady?"

"I don't know what to say, Miles! This is a lovely dinner!"

"You don't need to say anything. Just give me a big kiss."

Maggie threw herself into the doctor's arms and kissed him enthusiastically.

"What a fellow has to do, just to get a kiss!" He smiled down at Maggie, and kissed her back, pulling her closer.

Maggie squirmed against him. "What on earth is poking me?"

"Oh ... I forgot something." Miles reached into his side pockets and pulled out candlesticks and candles. He set them on the table, placed the candles in the candlesticks and lit them. "It wouldn't be a romantic dinner without candlelight, now would it?"

"Oh, Miles... You've thought of everything. This is just perfect!" Maggie cried, clapping her hands together gleefully.

"I want tonight to be perfect because I may be gone longer than usual. I don't want you to forget me while I'm gone." He kissed Maggie on the forehead, and grinned. "I thought ... maybe I could make this a memorable evening."

"Don't be silly, Miles. Every evening with you is memorable!"

The food was excellent and the conversation was lively as usual.

"Dinner was wonderful, Miles. Thank you so much."

"I'm glad you enjoyed it, Maggie."

She got up and opened the cabin door to look outside. It was a balmy night and the stars were just beginning to appear. Maggie turned to Miles, smiling. "Let's go for a walk down along the river," she said.

"If that's what you want, then that's what we'll do," Miles said, grabbing Maggie's hand and pulling her out onto the street.

They walked slowly, hand in hand, in the twilight. The town was quiet, as if asleep for the night, already. Only the occasional barking of a dog, in the distance, broke the silence. Miles held Maggie's arm securely, helping her down the riverbank to the path that ran along the water's edge. This location was Maggie's special place; a place of fantasies and daydreams; a secluded trail leading to her secret sanctuary. They headed toward the destination – – the private retreat; hidden by low hanging willow branches; carpeted with cool thick grass; and surrounded with high banks covered with honeysuckle.

Maggie reached out and moved the willow branch aside, anxious to enter her fanciful kingdom. She froze.

"Someone's in here," she whispered.

Miles stepped through the opening in front of Maggie, and peered into the enclosure. He immediately grabbed the girl's hand and yanked her back out and onto the path. "Come on Maggie," he said, quietly, "you don't need to see that."

"What were they doing?" Maggie asked innocently. She pulled back, trying to see.

"He's kissing her. Come on, Maggie... Let's go home."

"Miles! I want to see!" she whispered defiantly.

"Why do you care what two lovers are doing in a private place like this? If they wanted people to see them, they wouldn't have come here!"

"Because I can't believe what I saw! I just want to look one more time... Maybe my eyes were playing tricks on me ... in the shadows."

"Maggie! Your eyes weren't playing tricks on you. You saw exactly what you think you saw." Miles couldn't help laughing – – He hoped the couple hadn't heard him; and he didn't want them to know he and Maggie were discussing their private tryst; and he certainly didn't want to disturb them.

"Miles, please... Just let me peek!" Maggie pleaded. She pulled harder.

Miles knew, full well, he would be in for another intense round of inquisitions if he allowed Maggie to spy on the couple. But he also knew she would continue to badger him if he didn't. He reluctantly released his hold on her, and she immediately disappeared into the lair.

Miles waited patiently outside; on the path. Moments passed. Suddenly, to his dismay, Miles heard a female softly squealing in delight, and the squeals soon escalated into screams of pleasure. He knew the sound too well – – and he was absolutely sure that it wasn't Maggie screaming. At this point, Miles realized the trouble he was about to encounter, when Maggie started her questioning. She would invariably confront him about what she had witnessed. His mind was racing; trying to devise answers to unasked questions. He held his breath, knowing that any minute he was going to have to face Maggie's interrogation once more.

Maggie flew out of the enclosure, running into the doctor; nearly knocking him down. Her eyes were the size of saucers, and her mouth was wide open. She was trying to speak, but her voice refused to cooperate. Miles took her by the hand, and literally dragged her back down the path to the riverbank, where they climbed up to the street, and stopped.

"Well, Maggie? Are you satisfied, now?" Miles shook his head in exasperation. "I told you... That wasn't something you needed to see!"

"I... I can't... I just can't... Oh... I didn't... Miles!!"

"Is that right?" Miles laughed at Maggie, as she continued to stutter and stammer. "I'm glad to see you're expressing yourself so well!"

"You... You... I... I just... You knew!"

"Yes I did." Miles began laughing so hard he could barely stand.

"Oh... Oh my! They were ... he ... he was... She ..."

"Yes, Maggie... They certainly were." Big tears were running down Miles' face, from laughing so hard. "The bottom line is ... did they enjoy themselves, Maggie?"

Maggie shook her head enthusiastically; "*yes*". She had given up trying to speak.

Miles finally regained his composure. He wiped his eyes with his handkerchief, and grinned at

Maggie. "Let's go home and have a glass of that wine. I'm worn out, Maggie." He put his arm around the girl's shoulders, and steered her toward her home.

Miles poured the wine into the cups and handed one to Maggie. They both sat down, staring at each other in silence. Miles was waiting for it to start. Maggie didn't say a word. The questions were there, in her eyes, but hadn't reached her lips.

"Well, Maggie... Aren't you going to taste your wine?" he asked. Miles took a long drink from his cup, peering at the girl over the rim.

Maggie took a sip. Then she gulped the entire cup down, and filled it again, herself.

"No ... No... Maggie! Don't overdo it, Honey... You'll get sick."

"It's good."

"Too much of a good thing is never actually *good*." Miles took another drink of his wine. "I'm glad to see you can speak, now." He shook his head, remembering her quandary, and he chuckled. "Sometimes I wonder... Will you ever listen to me? Just trust me when I tell you something isn't good for you?"

"Are we talking about the wine?"

"Not only the wine," Miles said.

The silence that followed was intriguing. A myriad of expressions subtly crossed Maggie's face, as she sat there so quietly; obviously deep in thought.

Miles leaned back in his chair, anticipating the next round of Maggie's incessant curiosity and questioning. He took a deep breath and tried to relax. Still, the questions didn't come. He began to perspire. Whether from the wine or the anticipation of being in the 'HOT SEAT' again; he wasn't sure.

"Maggie, I think it's awfully warm in here ... Or maybe it's the wine." Miles stood up and pulled off his shirt; up over his head in a single effortless action.

Maggie's surprise was palpable, and her cheeks immediately flushed bright pink.

Miles just stood there, studying Maggie's reaction.

He untied the ribbon that bound his long dark hair at the back of his neck. He shook his hair free.

Maggie's eyes widened. She had never, in all the time she had known the doctor, seen him without his hair tied neatly back. He looked untamed; wild and exciting. His dark eyes were accentuated by the black mane, falling across his forehead, around his face, and over his broad shoulders. His lips looked fuller – – His jaw more defined – – His facial features more prominent. Maggie poured herself another cup of wine, and filled Miles' cup, too. She continued to stare at him, as she drank it.

"Um... Miles... What were we talking about?" Maggie squirmed in her chair, and took another long drink of the wine. Miles' inquiring gaze made her uneasy. She could feel little beads of perspiration breaking out across her own forehead. Still, she couldn't take her eyes off him. Golden, rock-hard muscles protruded on his arms, and stood out across his bare chest, and abdomen; his body glistened in the muted candle light. He was a dark wild thing; exuding raw sensuality and emanating an inaudible primal groaning.

"We were talking about excesses." Miles finished the wine in his cup. He continued to watch Maggie.

"Miles, I just have to tell you... You are a very handsome man. I'm sorry. I just have to say it." Maggie fidgeted in her chair. "I've never seen you with your hair loose like that. It makes you look completely different... Like a stranger. It scares me a little."

"I scare you?"

"Yes."

"Would you feel better if I tie it back the way it was?"

"Maybe ...Well... No. I like it, but it's not *YOU*."

"That's silly Maggie! So you think looks define the person?"

"Now you're confusing me." Maggie wiped her brow with her apron.

"I'm sorry, Maggie. I promise you... I'm *ME*. Nothing about the *real me* changed, just because I let my hair down." Miles grinned and winked at Maggie.

Maggie stood up and walked over to where Miles was standing. She gathered his hair into her hands, running her fingers down through it. She was surprised at how heavy and glossy it was. "On second thought...I love it!" she said. "I wish you never had to tie it back!" She pulled a handful of it up to her nose, and breathed in the scent of him. "Oh God ... I really do love it!" She exhaled the words; her voice sounded low and hoarse. Something was happening to her senses, and Miles was keenly aware of what it was. He allowed her to continue her musing, knowing he had adroitly set the ambiance for the culmination of his attempt to dominate Maggie's will; and rule her heart and her body.

"Maggie, what are you thinking?"

"I'm thinking that you are handsome, and mysterious, and ... I'd love to kiss you!" She looked up at Miles and giggled.

Miles caught her into his arms and kissed her; it was a long loving kiss. Neither wanted it to end.

Miles pulled away from Maggie. "Would you like to know what I'm thinking, Maggie?"

"What are you thinking, Miles?" She smiled

"I'm thinking that I'd love to kiss you from head to toe... the very same way the man in the hideaway was kissing his lover."

Maggie's surprise was obvious, but her body betrayed her restraint. She slowly slipped her arms around the handsome doctor's neck again. She offered herself to his desire, with no reservations.

"You won't forget me while I'm gone, will you Maggie?"

"How could I?"

"Did I succeed in making this a memorable evening, Sweetheart?"

Maggie started to cry.

"Maggie... Why are you crying? You know I can't leave you here like this... I want tp remember your smile – – not your tears!"

"I don't want you to leave."

"You're crying because you don't want me to leave?"

"Yes."

"I'm confused, Maggie. You don't want me to go to Boston? Or you don't want me to leave here?"

"Both."

"Well, what can I do to make you feel better?"

"Just stay with me tonight."

"You know I can't do that! How would it look?"

"I don't care how it would look! I just want you to stay ... and hold me all night."

"Believe me Maggie... There's nothing I'd rather do, than hold you in my arms all night ... but we don't need people saying bad things about us. You know ... no matter how innocent it might be -- and I use that term loosely.....me spending the night here would be inappropriate."

"Please, Miles?"

"I'm sorry Maggie, but I can't do it. *Your* honor is as important to me as my own. If I didn't give a damn about your honor, you wouldn't still be the virgin you are!" He sounded agitated.

"All right, Miles. I just don't want to be alone... but I'll submit to your peculiar sense of honor, if I have to." She forced a smile.

The Doctor gave Maggie a big hug, and kissed her lovingly. He picked up his shirt and tossed it over his shoulder.

"Good night, Maggie. I'll see you when I get back. Please try to stay out of trouble while I'm gone! OK?" He grinned.

"I'll try."

Chapter 11 - The Confession

Summer was over and autumn was transforming the leaves on the trees into glorious and varied shades of orange, purple, red, and gold. The countryside was buzzing with harvesting. All of the neighboring farmers brought their produce to the town market and it was a festive time for merchants and citizens alike.

It was October, and Maggie hadn't seen Miles Deihl for weeks. She often wondered why he was always traveling to Boston. He would say he had business to take care of, but never volunteered more information.

Maggie walked down the street in Zanesville, looking over the tables of produce. Now and then she purchased a bundle of vegetables, or a package of fruit. Her basket was beginning to get heavy, and she decided it was time to head home. Just then she felt someone tugging at her overflowing basket.

"Here, let me carry this for you, Honey." It was Miles Deihl. He was grinning that familiar, handsome grin of his.

"Miles! When did you get back?" Maggie asked, trying not to show her delight in seeing the doctor.

"I got back yesterday. Did you miss me?" he asked; smiling.

"Why are you always going to Boston? You were gone such a long time, this time!"

"You didn't answer me, Maggie. I asked you if you missed me." He winked at her.

"Yes, I suppose I did," Maggie answered. "Now answer my question. Why are you always running off to Boston?"

"If you'll invite me to your place for a cup of tea, I'll answer your question."

"Would you like to come home with me, and have a cup of tea, Miles?"

"Where's your mare, Maggie?"

"She's right over there, Miles. Where's the black?"

"I'll go get him, and meet you at the ford,"

Maggie set the cups on the table, and poured the tea into them. Miles Deihl sat down and remained silent.

"Are you all right, Miles?"

"Yes, why?"

"You just seem so subdued. It's not like you." Maggie took a drink of the tea.

"I have a lot on my mind, Maggie."

"And you haven't touched your tea."

Miles picked up his tea and took a long drink. "It's good, as usual."

"Well, are you going to tell me why you go to Boston all the time?"

"Yes I am, Maggie," Miles answered. "But first, there are some other things you need to know about me."

"It's true, Miles... I really don't know anything about you. It just never seemed important. You're my friend and that's what counts."

"Well you may consider me just a friend, Maggie ... but I intend to be your husband someday," he said, smiling. "That's why I've decided to let you in on some secrets."

"Well, I don't think I'll be ready for marriage for about a hundred years!" Maggie said, playfully. "Oh – but, secrets ..." Maggie leaned across the table, toward Miles. "I've always had a feeling there were secrets." Maggie's eyes were wide with anticipation.

"First of all ... my stallion's name is Seminole. I always thought it curious that you never asked me if he had a name."

"That's an odd name. What does it mean?"

"It means *wild one* or *runaway*." Miles grinned. "Don't you think that's appropriate for him?" He hesitated thoughtfully. "And, for myself, as well?"

"Yes, as a matter of fact!" Maggie agreed. "I think the name suits you both perfectly. But why do I need to know the name of your horse?"

"Why did you never ask me his name?" Miles looked at Maggie, inquisitively.

"I'm not sure... I guess it didn't seem important, since I never heard you call him *anything*? Why don't you call him by name?"

"Because it's a secret," Miles said bluntly.

"Why would your horse's name have to be kept secret?"

"Oh, Maggie... I'm not sure how to explain this to you, Sweetie. I've wanted to tell you for a long time, but ..." Miles reached across the table and covered Maggie's hands with his. "I wasn't sure how you'd react ... or if I could trust you not to tell anyone."

"All right, Miles," Maggie said looking into the young doctor's serious eyes. "If you don't feel comfortable telling me ... then, I don't want to know. But on the other hand ... if you decide to tell me, I give you my word, I'll never repeat what you say."

"OK, Maggie," he said. "I'm going to tell you the entire story."

Miles stood up and walked over to the fireplace. He stared into the flames for a long time before speaking. Maggie sat silently, waiting for Miles to continue.

"My father was Scottish mixed with Upper Creek blood. He met my mother in St. Augustine, Florida. My mother was Seminole ... the daughter of a Lower Creek chief." Miles turned and looked at Maggie, waiting for her reaction.

"*Creek chief?*" Maggie repeated. "Are you saying that you're part *Indian?*"

"Yes." He turned back to the fire. "There's an indigenous group of people who are mostly from the deep south... They finally settled in Florida. They're called Seminoles. They're actually made up of Creeks, Yuchis, Yamasees and a few aboriginal remnants."

"So that's what makes you so ruggedly handsome!"

Miles spun around in surprise. "...Not the reaction I expected, Maggie."

"What did you expect?" she smiled.

"Well... With what happened to your family, and your friends ... I wasn't sure if ...."

"Miles! It was the Shawnees who killed my folks," she interrupted him, intuitively knowing why he was hesitant in divulging his parentage. Maggie jumped up and ran over to Miles. She hugged him tightly, and smiled at him admiringly. "Why would you have worried?"

"I was only worried that you wouldn't allow me to finish my story!" Miles laughed.

"I'm sorry! Go ahead, I'm listening." She remained standing with him, her arms around him affectionately.

"The white settlers kept moving further south, and even into Florida. There was ... still is ... a horrific conflict between the Upper Creeks and the settlers. The Lower Creeks are for the most part, neutral. The whites want the land. The Seminoles want to retain what's rightfully theirs. The white settlers killed both my father and my mother ... just for the land." Miles looked down at Maggie. "That's what we have in common, Maggie."

"Oh Miles! I'm so sorry!" Maggie whispered, remembering her own loss.

"I was only fourteen when it happened. My grandfather, who was a Lower Creek chief, and also a Christian ... had an English friend who was a surgeon... Dr. Daniel Horn. Dr. Horn took me to Boston, and he and his wife adopted me ... raised me. Mr. And Mrs. Horn were older when they took me in, but still managed to be perfect parents. They made sure I had the very best up-bringing and education. My step-father taught me everything I know about medicine. I worked with him. They were wonderful people, Maggie, but they're both gone now. I lost my step-mother three years ago. My step-father died last year." Miles looked sad, for the first time since Maggie had known him. "What I want to tell you about my trips ... is ... I *don't* go to Boston. I pick up medical supplies and take them to Florida. I do what I can for my people." The doctor took a deep breath, and sighed. "It's really dangerous right now. It looks as if civil war is brewing between the Upper and Lower Creek tribes. I hope it doesn't come to that, but the situation isn't good."

"Is that why the secrecy?" Maggie asked.

"Yes. If war does break out ... being part Creek could be dangerous to one's health." He forced a smile. "Another problem is that the Upper Creeks are joining England ... against the United States. There's another war coming, Maggie." Miles was silent for a moment; thinking. "And then ... there's the Shawnee chief, Tecumseh ... he's trying to unite all the eastern tribes to fight against the whites ... instead of against each other. I'm sure Tecumseh will align his forces with England, when the time comes. He hasn't been able to convince the Lower Creeks to join him yet. I hope they don't because if they do... I'll be in more danger. You see, if they're fighting the United States, and I get caught helping them, I could be hung for treason."

A shiver ran down Maggie's spine and Miles felt it.

"Don't worry about me, Maggie," he said, enfolding her in his muscular arms. "I didn't tell you this to make you worry. It's just that there's a possibility I could leave for Florida someday, and never return. I need for you to understand that ... if you were to never see me again ... it wouldn't be because I chose to stay away from you."

Maggie didn't know what to say. She yielded to the strength of Miles' embrace. She buried her face in his chest and held on to him tightly. Miles' tenacity, his decisiveness, the passionate way he approached his every objective, caused Maggie to question her own fortitude; her own significance. She had never been as committed to even *one* cause, never devoted herself wholeheartedly to *one* vision. Dr. Miles Deihl was unconditionally resolute about his every endeavor. Maggie knew it would be futile to try to discourage Miles from helping the Seminole people. She began to sob.

"Maggie? Don't cry."

"I just don't understand you, Miles Deihl!" she said, sobbing into his chest. "Even if I *allowed* myself to care for you ... it would be a never-ending competition – me against your damnable commitment to what you call duty, along with your damnable honor and destiny! ... And to your obsession with medicine. I want a man who will be devoted to me ... and ONLY me! It's such a travesty, Miles! You could never belong to anyone! Not to me, not to any woman."

Miles released Maggie, and backed away from her, appearing shocked and surprised.

"Well, now, Maggie Waters," Miles said, looking at her critically, "that's a very narrow view of love, don't you think? I believe you have *love* and *ownership* a bit confused. You're absolutely right... Nobody will ever *own* me. Nor will anyone ever possess my heart ... or my soul. I'll always, and only, belong to myself! I'm willing to share myself, but that's the extent of it. That's what real love is, Maggie. It's *sharing* one's self with another."

Maggie was silent, while she tried to grasp the significance of Miles' argument.

"I'll just leave you to ponder that, Maggie. Maybe when you grow up, you'll be able to understand what I'm talking about." He laughed. "But, I do still love you ... in spite of your flawed reasoning."

Miles left without giving Maggie his usual good-bye kiss. She suddenly felt empty and alone. The word *love* haunted her. The interpretation of the word itself was ambiguous, to say the least, as was the actual expression of that word.

Chapter 12 – Reclaiming Lost Dreams

The harvest was plentiful and was finally finished. The brothers congratulated each other on a job well done by throwing a harvest party, and inviting all the neighbors. The feast was a huge success, and everyone was glad to see that Nathan and John had had such a profitable season. The families attending the feast, reminded the boys of happier times in Pennsylvania. The Stillman brothers couldn't help but miss the sense of family; so acutely absent from their little farm.

The last corn and pumpkins were harvested just as the weather began to turn cold. John and Nathan were not looking forward to another harsh winter, but tried to remain optimistic, in hopes that this coming winter would be a milder one.

Samuel Wilson took their excess corn and grain to market for them, and had returned with enough money for the brothers to invest in more livestock next year. Will Redman, accompanied the boys to the mill in Lancaster, where they got their wheat and corn ground into flower and meal. They would have more than enough to last until the next harvest.

As the weeks passed and the days grew shorter, the brothers stocked up on supplies, stored the fruits of their labor, and prepared for the coming cold. Right on cue, winter roared in, just as it had the year before. And along with the short dreary days and cold weather, came Nathan's seasonal melancholy.

John noticed Nathan had stocked up on enough whiskey to get him through the winter. Nathan's drinking problem appeared to have started when he was wounded, and John was sure the drug intended to take away the pain, had facilitated his addiction to drinking.

Nathan Stillman sat comfortably by the roaring fire, reading his Bible. John was outside getting more firewood. It had been snowing for hours, and the wind was whistling through the un-chinked cracks around the windows. John came back in carrying an arm load of wood.

"Has it let up any?" Nathan asked.

"Not yet. If anything, it's getting worse. I checked on the oxen. They were making a hell of a ruckus. Their water was frozen, so I broke the ice, and gave them extra grain. They settled down some, after that." He dropped the logs onto the hearth, and took off his buckskin jacket. "I hope they'll be all right," John said, brushing the snow out of his hair.

"I suppose you want to bring them in here?" Nathan growled.

"Very funny!" John quipped, tossing a log onto the fire. "I've just never seen them act like that."

"Well, the way you baby those creatures! I'm surprised you're not sleeping out there with them."

"Naw... It's too drafty in that barn for me. We need to put some doors on it."

"Well, it's pretty damned drafty in here, as well," Nathan said, pulling the rocker closer to the fire.

"I know it's drafty when the wind blows this hard... We've got to finish those windows, Nathan."

"I'll add that to the list," Nathan replied dryly.

"What is your problem, little brother? You've been in an ugly mood for months, now!"

"I can't stop thinking about Maggie. We shouldn't have left her back there, in Zanesville, all alone."

"You've been thinking about her all this time? For over a year?!" John shoved his hands into his pockets. "I wouldn't waste my time worrying about that spoiled little wench!" John spat the words out, as if he had a bad taste in his mouth. "She nearly got us both killed. Or have you forgotten? And ...."

"... and she saved our lives!" Nathan interrupted.

"... and we saved hers. What do you think would have happened to her, if we hadn't found her in the woods after that massacre?!"

"Well, it just wasn't right... We shouldn't have abandoned her back in Zanesville last year."

"Have you forgotten, Nathan ... she didn't want anything to do with us, back there?"

"I think she was just upset... trying to deal with everything that had happened. She wasn't herself."

"I think she deserved everything she got," John said, pouring a cup of whiskey and tossing it down.

Nathan jumped to his feet, and faced John. "You self righteous ass! Are you really in a position to pass judgment?!" He grabbed John's collar and twisted it tightly. "You call yourself a God-fearing man?!! Then how could you make an ugly statement

176

like that?!!! She saw her entire family murdered. She was left alone and afraid." Nathan let go of John's shirt, and sat back down in the rocker. He looked at his brother with an expression of pure disgust. "But for the grace of God, it could have happened to YOU!!" he said in a quieter voice.

"Nathan... I ..."

"Shut up! Just shut up!" Nathan shouted. "I made a vow to take care of Maggie Waters – no matter what. And YOU!! You convinced me to do otherwise. I've regretted that decision ever since we settled here." He shook his head sadly. "Now I've got to do the right thing. I can't live with myself if I don't! To hell with you, John!! To hell with you!!" Nathan grabbed the jug of whiskey as he did so often. It seemed to be his only consolation these days.

John didn't say another word. He took off his boots and went to bed. Nathan fell asleep in the chair by the fireplace. The storm continued to howl outside the cabin.

The sun was just beginning to rise when Nathan was jarred awake by the scream of an animal which seemed to echo across the valley and penetrate the walls of the cabin. He jumped up and grabbed his gun from the rack on the wall. He quickly loaded it. John was right behind him. Nathan opened the cabin door slowly, and looked outside, just in time to see the big black cat limping away from the barn. It was dragging its back leg, leaving a bloody trail across the snow.

"Oh God!" Nathan yelled. "It's a panther!" He aimed the rifle and fired, hitting the cat in the side. It went down instantly. "Take that you black devil!" Nathan snarled. He grabbed his coat and bounded out the door.

One of the oxen was bellowing wildly, and trying to break through the fencing in the paddock. There was no sign of the other one. John ran to the barn, while Nathan crept up to the panther to make sure it was dead.

As Nathan poked at the big cat with his rifle, he could hear John screaming and cursing in the barn. Nathan immediately went to the pen and caught hold of the frightened ox, speaking softly, stroking it soothingly and calming it down. He examined it closely and found it to be uninjured. He grabbed a rope and led it back to the cabin, tying it to a post, there at the porch. When he returned to the barn, he found John kneeling beside the bloody carcass of the other ox. The animal's throat had been ripped open, and it was covered with deep claw marks. John was distraught. He continued to cry and curse.

"Get up John," Nathan said calmly. "We're going to have to get it butchered. No sense wasting the meat."

John stood up slowly, not taking his eyes off of the dead animal. "I knew something was wrong last night. I knew it. I should have done something ...."

"Like WHAT?!" Nathan grabbed his brother's shoulders and shook him. "What could you have done? Sleep out here in the middle of a blizzard, and guard them?! Put yourself at risk?!! Now get hold of yourself and let's get to work."

"I can't," John said bluntly.

"Yes you can... And you *WILL!!*" Nathan shouted. "Just be thankful the other one is all right. At least we didn't lose both of them!"

Once the butchering was completed and the mess cleaned up, Nathan led the lone ox back to the barn. It was reluctant to enter the enclosure, as if remembering the encounter with the panther. It took some prodding, but the animal finally went in, and Nathan immediately put the poles in place to secure the pen. On his way back to the cabin, he lingered outside the smokehouse, where John was still at work. The black-panther skin was hanging, spread out on the side of the building, like an ominous warning to any other big cats in the area to stay away.

"We should get a good price for that panther skin," Nathan said, sticking his head inside the smokehouse. "Maybe even enough to replace the ox."

"I doubt it." John said, not bothering to look up from salting the meat. There were massive slabs hanging over the hickory fire. "You're a dreamer, Nathan. Pa always said that about you."

"Well, we'll see," Nathan muttered, leaving John to his chore.

Nathan went to the back of the cabin and sorted through a pile of extra logs and puncheons. He chose several large pieces of wood, and dragged them inside the cabin, one by one. With axe and hatchet, he tore into his project like a man obsessed. After two hours of non-stop work, Nathan stepped back to admire his handiwork. Just then, the cabin door opened, and John walked in.

"What the hell?!!" John asked, laughing and slapping his leg.

"It's a sled!" Nathan answered indignantly. "I'll put it together outside. I had to build it this way, or I'd never get it through the door. I need you to help me carry it out."

"Drag it out yourself... I'm going to get washed up." John shook his head in disbelief. "I'm out there working my ass off, and you're in here playing carpenter! I don't know what you think you're going to do with a sled ... but I'm not even going to ask. You should have been out there helping me!"

"Fine!" Nathan shouted.

Nathan defiantly began hauling one huge half of the sled out of the cabin. John pretended to ignore his brother's effort. By the time John finished cleaning himself up, Nathan had managed to get the other half outside, and completed assembling the sled. He was greasing the runners with bear grease, when John appeared at the door.

"Nathan," John said, grinning, "that really is a fine piece of work. I'm sorry I was so short with you."

"I don't need your approval any more than I needed your help," Nathan said curtly. He turned the sled over and onto the runners. He fastened the poles to each side, and made sure they would fit the yoke. "Now, I'm going to bed," Nathan said, pushing John aside, as he walked into the cabin and collapsed onto the bed.

When John arose the next morning, Nathan was gone, along with his gun, the sled, the ox, and all of the pelts which had been hanging on the side of the smoke house. John made a pot of coffee and sat down in the old rocker in front of the fire. He thought about the argument they had had two nights before, and the remarks he made about Maggie Waters, knowing Nathan obviously cared deeply for the girl. He regretted calling his brother a dreamer. He was sorry he hadn't offered to help Nathan with the sled. Now he was wondering if Nathan would come back at all.

John tried to keep busy the entire day. He chinked and daubed around the windows and doors. He made himself a list of things to do, such as finishing the loft and several other chores which had been put off. Late in the afternoon, he heard a horse approaching, and he opened the door of the cabin and looked out. It was Tom McCollough. He rode up to the porch, leading a handsome chestnut gelding behind him.

"Afternoon John," he called, grinning broadly. "I understand you and your brother had a bit of a tiff." He laughed loudly, as he jumped off his horse. "He sent this *peace offering* to you." Tom led the gelding up to the porch and handed John the reins. "Yep ... bought this fine horse and all the tack from me, and asked me to deliver it to you. He said he'd be gone a few days, but he'd be back. Said he's gonna replace that ox you lost to the cat, even if he has to go clear to Marietta to get one."

"He's a fool!" John grumbled.

"I don't think so," Tom countered. "That boy is one hell of a carpenter. While he was in Newton, half the men at the tavern put in orders for sleds such as the one he was driving. The boy left with a fortune in deposit money. I'd say he's got eight sleds promised. Now, that's not the mark of a fool, John!" Tom pointed a stern finger at John. "Nathan is a natural born business man. Your Pa would be sorely proud of him." He looked intently at John. "You should be proud of him, too, John. He's a good man ... like you."

"Well, we have our differences," John admitted sheepishly. "And he drinks too much."

"Brothers always have their differences, John."

"I was pretty hard on him. Said some things I shouldn't have."

"I heard the whole story. He said some things he regrets, too."

"I just don't understand why he has to be so damned touchy ... especially about that Maggie Waters girl! He hasn't seen her for over a year."

"Did you ever stop to think the lad is in love?"

"In *LOVE*?!!"

"It's clear to me. I can't believe you haven't figured it out!" Tom laughed. "Or maybe it's because you've never been in love, huh?" Tom slapped his leg and laughed loudly. "How old are you and Nathan?"

"Um... Well, no ... I don't think I ever was in love ..." John scratched his head thoughtfully. "I turned thirty last month, and Nathan's twenty-six."

"Well, love makes a man crazy. Becomes the reason for everything he does, thinks, says... Yep, it's all-consuming. You wait... Your turn's comin' soon enough. You boys are at a ripe age for it to happen. It'll change your entire life, in the blink of an eye. I promise! Men aren't meant to be alone. They need their women!"

"I thought he felt more like a brother to Maggie. I mean, I thought he felt responsible for her, like kin. I knew he cared... But *LOVE?* That explains a lot. Thanks Tom. Now I finally think I understand."

"Well, John ... I've got to get back. Is there anything you need before I go?"

John walked down off the porch and gave Tom a bear hug. "Tom, you've given me everything I could ever need. Thank you so much, sir... I appreciate your wisdom."

"Don't mention it, John. Just go easy on the boy when he gets back. If he can't talk that little gal into coming home with him, he's *really* gonna be a bear to live with... That's for sure!" Tom mounted his horse and turned to leave, but then stopped and looked back at John. "You know where I live and I don't want ya to be a stranger! As a matter of fact, we're having a kind of party at my house Saturday. I'd sure like to see ya there. Will ya come, John?"

"I'll be there! Thanks again!" John called.

As John watched Tom McCollough ride off down the road, it began to snow again. The clouds were dark and another storm was brewing. John's prayers were with Nathan.

John led the big gelding to the barn and made sure it had plenty of grain and water.

"Well, old friend ... welcome to the Stillman plantation," he said, patting the horse's neck. "I think I'll call you Tiff, if that's OK with you. Yep ... you're new name will be Tiff, in memory of the *tiff* that brought you here, to me."

John chuckled to himself, walking back to the cabin. Once inside, he stirred the coals and put a couple of logs on the fire. He sat down in the old rocker and propped his feet up on a handsome three-legged stool Nathan had made. He opened his Bible and began to read. As the sun settled in the west, John soon nodded off to sleep. Although it was snowing and cold outside, it was warm and cozy in the cabin. No more drafts from un-chinked windows and doors.

Chapter 13 – Blood in the Snow

The weekly card game at Slagor's Tavern in Zanesville was wrapping up. The men counted their coins and determined, on this particular evening, that Silas McGregor was the winner. Silas bought everyone one more drink for the road, while he bragged about his winnings.

"I'd give it all back for one more peek down Maggie Waters' bodice," he snickered. "Yep, she and the doc, here, fixed my foot up right good ... but just looking at that little girl's endowments ... if you know what I mean ... made me feel like a new man."

Silas had been ranting about Maggie Waters all evening. Miles Deihl could barely control his temper, although he forced himself to laugh, along with the other men, when Silas McGregor made those slanderous remarks about Maggie. The doctor's blood was boiling with rage, as he threw on his coat and grabbed his hat to leave.

"Good night gentlemen," Miles said coolly. "Good night, Daisy, my sweet." He winked at the bar maid.

The rest of the group soon left the tavern. The snow was coming down heavily, and a stout breeze was blowing in from the west. The streets were empty in the little town, and all was quiet.

Silas McGregor hummed a tune, as he turned his mule down Harvey's Path and headed into the pitch-dark ravine. Suddenly, he was savagely yanked off the mule's back, and he barely felt the razor-sharp knife, swiftly and smoothly severing his throat. He was aware of someone rummaging through his pockets, but he was unable to speak, as the blood gurgled and gushed from his neck. He lay helpless in the snow, waiting for the end – so slow in coming. He marveled in amusement, that his very last thoughts were of the hogs he'd butchered during his lifetime. So, it seems, they didn't suffer much after all. He smiled at the thought, closed his eyes, and surrendered to death.

Nathan stopped the ox in front of Dr. Mathison's office, and climbed down out of the sled. He hesitated outside Maggie's door, wondering what kind of a reception he might receive. It was late, and he was sure Maggie would be in bed. He wanted to go to McKray's Inn, but there was no way to get the sled across the river's ford. He didn't have a choice. He was at Maggie's mercy. Nathan took a deep breath and knocked softly on the door. He waited. Again, he knocked, this time a little harder. Again, he waited.

"Who's there?" It was Maggie's voice, but she didn't open the door.

"It's Nathan Stillman."

The door was instantly flung open, and Maggie Waters threw herself into Nathan's arms, hugging him tightly.

"Oh Nathan! I was afraid I'd never see you again! I've got so much I need to say to you!" she cried, burying her face against his neck.

Nathan was overwhelmed with surprise and relief. He wrapped his arms around the girl and held her warmly against him. She continued to cry. He finally recovered his voice and said, "Maggie ... it's all right ... really. Can I come in?"

Realizing they were standing on her doorstep in the snow, and she was in her nightgown, Maggie released her hold on Nathan and led him inside, closing the door behind them. She grabbed a shawl and threw it around her shoulders, and then just stood there, smiling from ear to ear, staring at Nathan.

"Maggie ... I have to admit I wasn't expectin' a very warm welcome. Not after the last time I saw you."

Maggie reached out and took Nathan's hand in hers. "Nathan, I'm so sorry. I was so wrong. I desperately need your forgiveness."

"There's nothin' to forgive, Maggie. Do you think I'm so callous I don't understand what grief can do to a person? I never once took your anger personally. I knew it was only part of your grievin' process. I just kept you in my prayers and in my heart ... hopin' someday we would be friends again."

Maggie reached her arms up and around Nathan's neck, hugging him. "Nathan, I'm not going to let you go until you tell me everything you've been doing!" She laughed. "You'll just have to pry me loose, if you don't tell me."

"Well, Honey ... you're goin' to have to let me loose for a few minutes, anyway. I've got my pelts out in the sled, and I don't want anybody to steal 'em. Can I bring 'em in? And can I put my ox in Doc's barn for the night?" Nathan gently removed Maggie's arms from his neck. "I would have gone to McKray's Inn, but the sled wouldn't make it across the river. I'm really sorry to impose."

"Of course you can bring your pelts inside. And I'll help you get the ox into the barn. And I'm so very glad you came here, instead of going to the inn... I can't tell you how happy I am to see you, Nathan!" Maggie said, slipping her shoes on. She dropped the shawl and pulled her cloak over her nightgown. She lit the lantern and handed it to Nathan. Together they went outside to see to the ox, and bring in the pelts.

Back inside, Nathan stirred the coals in the fireplace, and laid another log on the fire. Instantly the room brightened. He had nearly forgotten how beautiful Maggie looked in the warm glow of a blazing fire. He couldn't take his eyes off her. He watched as she wiggled out of her cloak and again wrapped the shawl around her shoulders. Her long black, shiny curls reflected the light from the fire, and her huge green eyes dazzled in the glow. Maggie was acutely aware of Nathan's stare. She stopped what she was doing and looked back at him, remembering her first kiss. Slowly she walked up to where Nathan stood. Standing on her tip-toes to reach him, she cradled his handsome face in her hands and kissed him softly on the mouth. Her shawl fell to the floor.

Nathan instinctively caught Maggie up in his muscular arms, and spontaneously responded to her kiss. He kissed Maggie deeply, first affectionately, and then passionately. He could feel a conflagration building in his soul. He had dreamed of this moment for a long time. He had only imagined what it would feel like to hold Maggie in his arms this way. Nathan was certain Maggie didn't have any idea what she had ignited in his being. He knew if he didn't stop now, this inferno would become uncontrollable. Slowly he withdrew his kiss, and looked deeply into Maggie's innocent eyes. Tears were streaming down her flushed cheeks. She buried her head in his chest and wept. Nathan cradled her there in his embrace for a long time, confused by her tearful response.

"What's wrong, Maggie?" Nathan asked. "Whatever it is, I'm sorry I upset you."

"You didn't do anything wrong, Nathan," she said. She continued to weep. "I'm just so happy and surprised to see you again ... it's been so long."

"You're cryin' because you're *happy*?" Nathan cupped her chin in his hand and tilted her head so he could see her face. He looked at her inquisitively.

"Yes. I missed you so ... when you left without me!" she cried. "I was horribly miserable and lonely, so I tried to forget you. I just got on with my life. I was certain I'd never see you again."

"I've missed you, too. But when I'm happy, I don't cry!" Nathan laughed. "Maggie ..., let's sit down and talk."

"Nathan, I've got so much to tell you."

Nathan and Maggie talked for what seemed like hours. Maggie told Nathan about the fever outbreak, and Caroline's tragic death; she described the fire; they talked about her plans for her land, and the Merino sheep. Nathan described the land, and the neighbors, and the Stillman cabin. He told her about the harvest, the panther attack, and his quarrel with John.

"Maggie ... would you like to come home with me?" Nathan asked in a quiet voice. "I've been thinkin' a lot about my promise to always take care of you.... back when we were just gettin' here. Do you remember?"

"I remember," Maggie said, looking down; her cheeks turning pink.

"Well, I can't bear the thought of leavin' you behind again." Nathan reached across the table and took Maggie's hand in his. "Would you consider marrying me?" Nathan cocked his head to one side and grinned at the girl. "Do you remember when you were a little girl... you asked me to marry you? You said '... *You need a wife ... and lots of children to help out on our farm.* !'" He chuckled. "Do you think we can do that?"

"Yes, I do," Maggie said without looking up.

"Yes ... you want to come home with me? ... or Yes ... you still want to marry me and make lots of children?"

Maggie wrestled with her heart. She had known Nathan all of her life. He had always been there. It was the natural culmination and transition from their childhood. Her parents would approve, and Dr.

Mathison would approve. He was an honest, decent, God fearing man.

'Why was she hesitating?'

She thought of Miles Deihl, whom she had only known a short while, although it seemed she had known him for years. She argued with herself for what felt like an eternity – but was only moments.

'Could she give up her relationship with Miles Deihl? Could she be happy with Nathan, when Miles was so much more fun to be with? Could she find the same excitement and stimulation with Nathan that she had with Miles?'

But the biggest question was this: *'Would she have the quiet, stable life with Miles that she was guaranteed to have with Nathan?'*

As the minutes passed, Nathan was beginning to feel a nervous uneasiness. He wondered if Maggie would decline his proposal.

Maggie decided to do the logical, acceptable, and prudent thing.

She jumped up and ran to Nathan, climbing into his lap and throwing her arms around his neck. "Yes!!! I want to go home with you, and I DO want to marry you!" Maggie planted a big kiss on Nathan's cheek. "I've always wanted to marry you, Nathan! Since I was a little girl... I've wanted to be your wife!"

Nathan planted a kiss on Maggie's cheek, and laughed. "All right, then ... tomorrow I have to find another ox to replace the one the panther killed. I also need a milk cow and a good riding horse. I'm goin' to see what I can get for my pelts at Munro's tradin' post. I've got plenty of money with me, from the deposits on the sleds I promised to build ... so I won't have any problem buyin' what I have to have."

Nathan gave Maggie a hug. "You'll need to pack up what you want to take... Tell Doc Mathison – of course, I think he already suspected this would happen!" He laughed. "The sled's big enough to carry everything you want to take. We'll leave as soon as I get the rest of what I came for." He grinned at Maggie.

"Oh Nathan... I wish I could have gone with you from the beginning!" She was thinking of the handsome Miles Deihl; regretting some of the things she'd allowed to happen.

"We could talk about that all night, Maggie. But right now, we'd better get some sleep. We've got a lot to take care of tomorrow." Nathan looked around the room. "Do you have any extra bedding? I'll make me a bed on the floor."

"Nonsense!" Maggie said. "You'll sleep in my bed – not on the cold floor! I trust you Nathan. Don't you trust me?"

"Well of course I trust you, Maggie. I'm just not so sure I can trust myself!" He laughed nervously.

"Here's what we'll do. I'll sleep under the quilt, and you'll sleep on top of the quilt ... with another quilt over you, of course. That's how Mama used to put us to bed when we were little... Remember? It was you, John, me, and my sisters; all in the same bed?"

"That's funny, Maggie. Yes I do remember!!" They both had a good laughed, remembering their childhood experiences.

Maggie was awakened by an insistent rapping on the office door. The sun was well up, and it felt as if she had just gone to sleep. The girl dragged herself out of bed, pulled her shawl around her, and scurried over to the door connected to Dr. Mathison's office. She opened it.

"Maggie ... can I come in? I've got something important to speak to you about!" Dr. Mathison didn't wait for permission, he walked right into the room, but stopped short when he looked at the man in Maggie's bed. "Maggie!! What on earth ...?"

"It's Nathan, Dr. Mathison," Maggie quickly explained. "He arrived late last night, and couldn't get across the river with his sled. Nothing happened between us... I swear it!!"

A look of relief swept over Dr. Mathison's face. "Aw... That explains the sled outside. ... but, I'm not so sure this is the best time for Nathan to show up, here," the doctor said, sitting down at Maggie's table. "Maggie, Miles Deihl is telling everyone in town you're going to marry him. How can this be true?!"

"He what?!!" Maggie said, looking shocked.

"That's right. He's saying the two of you are getting married!" The doc shoved his spectacles up on his nose. "You know I don't like that man!"

"Oh my!!! I never agreed to marry him. He told me he *wanted* to marry me... He didn't *ASK* me!! You know I've always loved Nathan. NATHAN and I are getting married. As a matter of fact, I was going to tell you today. He's taking me back to Newton with him."

"I'm really happy for you Maggie. Nathan's a very good man. You know how I feel about him," Doc said.

"Well thank you, Doc!" It was Nathan. He swung his feet over the side of the bed, and ran his hands through his matted blonde curls. He rubbed his eyes, and grinned at Dr. Mathison.

"Do you always sleep with your boots on, Nathan?" Dr. Mathison chuckled.

"Only when I go to sleep in a strange woman's bed," Nathan quipped.

"Are you saying I'm *strange*?" Maggie asked, pretending to be hurt.

"Maggie ... you give the word *strange*, a whole new meanin'!" Nathan laughed. "Now ... who is Miles Deihl, and what's this story he's tellin'?"

Maggie's eyes widened. She tried to think of a way to explain her friendship with Dr. Deihl. Her silence was damning. Her face turned red.

"Maggie?" Nathan persisted. "It would probably be a very good idea if you were to explain it to me ... before I have to pay *HIM* a visit and have *HIM* explain it to me!" Nathan was deadly serious, and Maggie knew it.

"Umm... I thought he was my friend," Maggie began, "and then he started to act different ... a little possessive." Maggie stammered, trying to find the right words. "And then he ... he ..."

"He *WHAT*?!" Nathan shouted.

Dr. Mathison squirmed in his chair. He was feeling uncomfortable, like an intruder. "Nathan, maybe I can shed some light on this topic," the doc interrupted. "Dr. Deihl is a very street-wise man –

according to the bar maid at Slagor's Tavern – he could charm the skin off a rattlesnake. Anyway, like I told Maggie two or three weeks ago ... this man is bad news — maybe even dangerous. I didn't like him the moment I met him. And his attitude with Maggie was way overly possessive. It was almost as if she was being set up from the beginning. I told Maggie just what I thought." The doc stood up and patted Maggie on the shoulder. "Somehow, Miles Deihl found out about Maggie's inheritance. Jacob McKray told me this morning ... that Deihl came in late last night, all liquored up, talking about how he was going to marry Maggie and use her money to invest in an office, and start a hospital. I think he's been planning this for some time, now. I think he intended to try and sweep our Maggie off her feet." The doc scratched his head, and looked Nathan straight in the eye. "Nathan, we both know that Maggie, here, could never hold her own with a street-wise womanizer."

Maggie remained silent, analyzing all that Dr. Mathison had said. ' *Could he be right about Miles? Surely not! Was it really only the money he wanted? NO! Miles had plenty of money of his own. He could be a womanizer, though. What was that about the barmaid? Maggie's mind was spinning. How could Miles betray her like that? He was her best friend – – or was he?*'

Nathan shoved his hands defiantly into his pockets, and he stared intently at the floor. His face was nearly purple with rage, and the veins in his neck were engorged. His anger was conspicuous. "All right, Maggie... What did he do to you?"

"He kissed me," Maggie said, in a barely audible voice.

"How many times?" Nathan said, quietly.

"I don't know ... different times."

"Is that ALL he did?" Nathan continued the inquisition.

Maggie was silent, remembering the ride to the Hennesy farm and how Miles Deihl had put his hand on her thigh. She would never be able to tell him about being nude with the doctor, though!

"Maggie!! I asked you ... is that *ALL* he did?"

Maggie managed to look at Nathan, tears welling up in her green eyes. "He put his hand on my thigh, once."

"And what did you do, then?" he demanded.

There was another long silence. Maggie began to sob.

"Maggie!! What did you do when he put his hand on your thigh?!" Nathan shouted.

"*NOTHING!* I did nothing!! I was shocked and surprised... I didn't know what to do. We were on his horse ... and then there was a cougar ... and he took his hand off, and the horse ran. Nothing else happened *that* day! I swear it, Nathan!!" The story regarding the ride on the horse and the cougar came flowing out of Maggie's memory, as if flood gates were opening after a storm. She told Nathan *nearly* everything that had happened between her and Dr. Deihl on that particular day. She confided *almost* every detail of that particular story. Then she laid her head down on the table and wept. She could never tell him *ALL* the details of her experiences with Miles Deihl. The truth would ruin her relationship with Nathan. Maggie thanked God that she was still, technically a virgin.

Nathan walked over and pulled Maggie to her feet. He wrapped his arms around the despondent girl and buried his face in her hair. "Maggie ... I don't blame *YOU* for what happened. Don't cry. We're still gettin' married. I just need to get you away from that charlatan, before he causes you any more trouble." Nathan kissed the top of Maggie's head and held her securely against him. "None of it would have happened if I hadn't left you here, alone."

"Well, now," Dr. Mathison breathed a sigh of relief, "We've got lots to do, Nathan. I'll plan the wedding and you take care of whatever business brought you to town. I noticed those pelts over there. Munson's trading post has been looking for some good skins. What else are you here for?"

"I need a good ridin' horse, a milk cow, and a draft ox," Nathan replied.

"I'm going to talk to Reverend Wilkins about marrying you two... I'll see if he knows anyone who's selling livestock." The doc slapped Nathan on the back, and smiled. "Shall we plan the wedding for tomorrow, Nathan? Maggie? I can get Elizabeth and Suzanne to help with the arrangements."

"Whatever Maggie wants, is fine with me," Nathan said quietly. He seemed to be distracted and in deep thought.

"You are so sweet, Doc!" Maggie said, smiling at Dr. Mathison through her tears. "Tomorrow would be fine with me. The sooner we can leave for Newton, the happier I'll be. Besides ... don't we need to leave before the snow melts?" She laughed. "We *WILL* be traveling in a sled."

"That's right," the doc said. "Oh ... and don't let me forget to give you your metal box, Maggie! You know ..., your dowry?" The doc grinned and winked at Maggie.

"Doc, I'd like to go with you, if you don't mind. I'm still stuck on this side of the river, ya know," Nathan said. "I'd be glad to pay you for your trouble."

"Of course you can go with me, Nathan. Sorry I didn't think of that."

"Maggie, you get your stuff packed. And don't go out of this cabin," Nathan said sternly. "And whatever you do ... don't you dare open the door to Miles Deihl. I'm serious about that!"

Maggie gave Nathan a hug, and then stepped back, looking up at him. "I promise – I won't leave the cabin, and I won't open the door to Miles Deihl."

Nathan and Dr. Mathison loaded the pelts into the doc's buggy and set off for Munro's Trading Post in Zanesville.

"Doc, there's something I have to take care of first," Nathan said thoughtfully, as they crossed the ford to Zanesville.

"You don't even have to tell me what you're thinking, Nathan... I know. We'll find him at McKray's Inn, I'm sure."

"Thanks doc. I just can't let this thing go. Maggie's honor is at stake," Nathan said.

"Well, Nathan ... just remember, the man is dangerous. I got that feeling the first time I met him. He's just plain evil." Doc coaxed the horse up the river bank and on to the road.

When they pulled to a stop at the inn, Miles Deihl's big black stallion was tied outside.

"Damn!" Dr. Mathison exclaimed, "It looks as if that poor horse has been out here since last night. He was here this morning when I came for breakfast ... covered with snow and looking poorly. Seems a shame, to treat such a magnificent animal so badly."

Doc climbed out of the carriage and tied up his horse. He walked around Miles Deihl's stallion, examining its legs. "Look at this, Nathan. This horse has blood all over his front hooves. Dried clear up to its shins."

Nathan knelt down and felt the horse's legs. "There's no sign of injury. This blood came from somewhere else." Nathan stood up and looked at Dr. Mathison. "Too bad this animal can't talk."

"Yep... That would be nice. Something's not right, here, Nathan," Dr. Mathison said, shaking his head.

Just as Nathan and Doc Mathison were getting ready to go into the inn, Sheriff Beymer and Deputy Allen rode up, and jumped down from their horses.

"Good afternoon George ... William," Doc greeted the two men.

"Hi Doc," George Beymer said. "We've got a problem." Sheriff Beymer took off his hat and smoothed his hair back from his face. "Silas

McGregor's dead. Someone slashed his throat. We found him in the ravine on Harvey's path."

"When did it happen?" Doc asked.

"Not sure... Looks like maybe last night or early this morning," William Allen answered.

"Well, now, George," Doc said, taking the sheriff by the arm and walking him over to the big black stallion tied up at the post. "Nathan and I were just talking about the blood caked all over Miles Deihl's horse's front legs. What do you make of this?" Dr. Mathison pointed to the gruesome spectacle. "There's no sign of injury on this animal. He got into a puddle of blood sometime last night."

"Who did you say this horse belongs to, Doc?" George asked.

"It belongs to Dr. Miles Deihl. He's staying here at the inn," Doc answered.

"Hmm... Maybe we should have a word with this Dr. Deihl, William. Let's see what he has to say about this blood," Sheriff Beymer said, slapping his deputy on the shoulder.

Nathan Stillman and Dr. Mathison followed George Beymer and William Allen into the inn. Nathan and Doc found Jacob McKray sitting in his favorite chair by the huge fireplace at one end of the cabin. They pulled up chairs and joined him; making sure they could see what the sheriff and his deputy were doing.

"Nathan!" Jacob shouted, standing up to shake Nathan's hand. "What a surprise. It's good to see you, man!"

"Good to see you, too, Mr. McKray," Nathan replied, shaking Jacob's hand firmly.

"What brings you back to Zanesville?"

"I need some livestock, and I came to take Maggie home with me. We're getting married tomorrow," Nathan grinned.

"Uh Oh… There might be a problem with that," McKray said. "I never did believe Deihl when he said *HE* was planning to wed the lovely Miss Maggie. I suppose Doc told you what's going on?"

"Yep … he told me," Nathan said frowning. "That's why we're here. I feel like I need to straighten this out before it gets out of hand. I want to have a word with Dr. Deihl. Guess I'll have to wait my turn, though." Nathan laughed and pointed to the other end of the cabin where the sheriff and his deputy were sitting with another man. "That must be Dr. Miles Deihl?"

"Yes, as a matter of fact, that's him," Jacob said. "What's going on?"

"Seems Silas McGregor was found with his throat slashed, and Miles Deihl's horse's front legs are caked with blood. Makes for an interesting murder mystery," Dr. Mathison said.

"Is that right, Doc?" Jacob asked, turning to look at Miles Deihl. "He sure was acting strange when he came in here last night. Come to think of it … look over there on the floor by the door. See that red stain – footprints? I didn't notice those 'til this morning. Maybe somebody should check his boots." Jacob rubbed at his chin thoughtfully. "Do you really think he's capable of slitting another man's throat? I mean … he's a doctor for god's sake!! He's sworn to save lives, not take them. I just don't know ...." Jacob shook his head slowly. "Poor old Silas."

"Jacob," Dr. Mathison grabbed McKray's arm, "while they're talking to Deihl ... is there any way you can get into his room and see if you can find a knife? A blood-stained knife, if you know what I mean?"

"Doc ... how can you ask me to do something like that? The man is a customer. He pays me well. I don't think I can do that," Jacob pleaded with Dr. Mathison.

"Jacob?" Doc squeezed McKray's arm hard.

"All right, Doc. But, only because you're my best friend." Jacob got up and disappeared into another part of the inn.

When Sheriff Beymer and Deputy Allen got up from the table where they were speaking with Miles Deihl, Jacob McKray was still not back. Dr. Mathison and Nathan waited until the sheriff and his deputy left the inn, and then approached Miles Deihl, before he could return to his room.

"Dr. Deihl," Dr. Mathison called, walking toward Miles' table. "I want you to meet a friend of mine."

Dr. Deihl stood up and was turning to leave. "I'm sorry, I don't have time to talk right now, gentlemen," he said bluntly.

"Well, that's really too bad, Miles," Dr. Mathison said, "because I thought you'd like to meet the man Maggie Waters is going to marry."

Miles Deihl stopped dead in his tracks. Slowly, he turned to look at Nathan. "Excuse me? Would you mind repeating that? I don't think I heard you correctly."

"This is Nathan Stillman. He and Maggie Waters are getting married tomorrow," Dr. Mathison repeated.

"Yes, there seems to be some confusion," Nathan said sternly. "I understand you're tellin' people *YOU* are marryin' Maggie. I just want to clear that up. You seem to be mistaken. I'd appreciate it, if you would stop spreadin' rumors like that."

"Sir, I don't know who you are, but believe me, Maggie has never mentioned *YOU* to me. And I *AM* going to marry Miss Waters. It must be *YOU* who is mistaken. So, if you'll excuse me?" Deihl turned to leave, again.

"Listen to me," Nathan said, catching hold of Miles' arm. "I know the whole story... I know what you've done and what you've said to Maggie. I want you to understand this... If I catch you anywhere near Maggie, ever again ... I'll kill you with my bare hands. Got it?"

"I don't think *YOU'VE* got it!" Miles said, shaking his arm loose from Nathan's grip. "If Maggie Waters is so in love with you, then why would she be all over me like a bitch in season, huh? Did she tell you that? Did she bother to mention the fact that I could have had my way with her on any number of occasions, but it was *ME* who had to stop *HER*? Did she tell you she practically begged me to fuck her? .... I didn't think so!" Miles brushed the crease out of his sleeve. "Maybe you don't know Maggie as well as I do!" He snickered.

Nathan Stillman was a giant of a man. He stood a good three inches taller than Miles Deihl (who was not a small man), and outweighed him by at least

203

fifty pounds. Nathan was pure muscle, with hands twice the size of an average man's hands. Miles Deihl was risking his life by pushing Nathan's patience, and Nathan had had enough. He snatched Miles up with the ease of lifting a bag of grain, carried him to the door of the inn, and tossed him out into the snow. When Deihl struggled to his feet, Nathan caught him by the back of the neck and rammed his head into a nearby tree, splitting his forehead open from his scalp to his nose.

"I think you need to see a doctor," Nathan said calmly, and turned to go back inside.

Not intending to let Nathan Stillman get away with making a fool of him, Miles pulled a Bowie knife from his boot and rushed toward the big Swede.

"Nathan, look out! He's got a knife!" Dr. Mathison screamed.

Nathan turned, just in time to grab the hand holding the knife. It was no contest, as Miles' wrist twisted and snapped. The knife fell to the ground.

"Oh no... I think you broke your wrist!" Nathan said, nonchalantly. He bent down and picked up the big knife, inspecting it closely. Miles Deihl was writhing in the snow; in pain. "Hmm... Whose blood is on this knife, Mr. Deihl? By the grace of God, it's not mine!"

Dr. Mathison grabbed one of Miles Deihl's boots and pulled it from his foot. It, too, was spattered with blood. Just then, Jacob McKray came running out of the inn to see what was going on.

"Deihl tried to stab Nathan!" Doc Mathison yelled. "Go and get the sheriff. We've got the bloody knife and the boots." The doc pulled Miles' other boot off, and held them up for Jacob to see.

Miles Deihl managed to get to his feet, and ran to his horse, untied him, and jumped on. The stallion reared, and then broke into a run, down the lane and out of sight.

"Doc! We've got to get to Maggie!" Nathan shouted.

Doc tossed the boots and the knife onto the ground at Jacob's feet, and jumped into the buggy. As they tore away, Doc yelled back to Jacob, "Get the sheriff to my office, *QUICK*!!"

Chapter 14 - Maggie

Miles Deihl pounded on Maggie's door with his only good hand. "Open the door Maggie! I know you're in there. Open this door, or I swear I'll kick it in!" he yelled. "You've sure as hell got some explaining to do!" He pounded harder, and then he began kicking the door. "I'm going to wring your neck, you little bitch!"

Maggie was terrified. She didn't have any idea what was going on, but she swore not to open the door to Miles. She ran into Dr. Mathison's office to make sure all the other doors there were locked. She looked frantically until she found his rifle and powder. She quickly loaded the gun and returned to her apartment. Deihl was still pounding and cursing outside her door. Maggie had never known Miles to act this way. He never threatened her before. The girl was frightened out of her wits. She sat down at her table and propped the gun over the back of a chair to steady it. She waited. The door started to loosen from its hinges. Maggie prayed to God someone would come to her rescue. The door was giving way. The door flew open, and there stood a bloody and barefoot Miles Deihl. Horror gripped Maggie's heart – – seeing Miles covered with blood and looking crazed. He was acting insane.

"Don't take another step. Please Miles ... don't come any further." Maggie pleaded. "I honestly don't want to have to shoot you, Miles! Please, just leave! *PLEASE*!"

"Maggie, what the hell have you done?" Miles shouted.

"I said ... don't take another step, or I swear I'll have to shoot you! You're scaring me!"

"You wouldn't shoot me," Miles managed to laugh. He lunged toward Maggie, thinking he could surprise her.

The gun went off, and the ball embedded itself in Miles' right shoulder, knocking him instantly to the floor. Maggie hurriedly reloaded the gun.

"I'm so sorry Miles!" Maggie screamed. "I begged you to leave! Why didn't you go?!" Maggie was shaking violently. "Oh Miles ... you should have left when I asked you to! I'm so sorry – – you made me do it!"

Miles Deihl moaned loudly and struggled to his feet. "OK. Have it your way. Don't shoot, Maggie... I'm leaving, but I'm not done with you," he groaned, and dragged himself out of the cabin.

Dr. Mathison and Nathan were still two blocks away from the office when they heard the shot.

"That's my girl!" Nathan shouted.

"What the hell are you talking about, Nathan? That was a gunshot!"

"Yep... Well, guess who taught Maggie how to handle a gun!" Nathan laughed.

The buggy slid around the corner just in time for the men to see the big black stallion sprinting down the street, away from Doc's office. The rider was hanging limply over the side of the horse's neck. Deihl looked to be half dead and ready to fall off.

"He won't get far," Dr. Mathison said, watching the runaway stallion. He pulled his horse and buggy to a stop, and the two jumped out and ran into Maggie's cabin.

"Maggie!" Nathan breathed a sigh of relief when he saw the girl sitting at the table with the gun. "It's OK, Maggie," he said, gently taking the rifle from Maggie's hands. She appeared to be in shock.

"I didn't let him in, Nathan. He kicked the door in and I shot him in the shoulder," Maggie sobbed. "I didn't try to kill him. I just wanted to stop him." Maggie was in hysterics.

"I know, Honey. You did good. I'm glad he didn't hurt you," Nathan said cradling Maggie in his arms. "We're pretty sure he slit a man's throat last night, and he tried to use the same knife to stab me. You're lucky he didn't get his hands on you, Maggie. Doc's right. Deihl is a dangerous man."

Maggie turned and threw her arms around Nathan's neck. She was trembling. "I love you Nathan. I couldn't bear to lose you. Please don't leave me alone ever again!"

"Believe me, Maggie... I don't intend to ever leave you again!"

Sheriff Beymer and Deputy Allen rushed into the room. "What the hell happened here? Where's Deihl?" George Beymer shouted.

"He took off, headed south," Doc said. "He kicked in the door, and Maggie shot him. I don't think he'll get too far. He's got a gashed head, an injured wrist, and now a ball in his shoulder. You shouldn't have much trouble catching up with him."

The two lawmen ran outside, and mounted their horses. They galloped south on the road, hoping to catch up to Miles Deihl.

"Maggie, get your cloak. I'm going to fix this door and then we have to take care of selling those pelts and rounding up the livestock I need. If it's all right with you, we'll leave first thing in the morning. We can have the wedding in Newton. I just want out of here before anything else happens!" Nathan said. He sounded tired and frustrated.

"Well, if you don't mind, I'm going to go with you to Newton. I'd like to see my friends there, and John. Besides – I wouldn't miss the wedding for anything!" Doc said.

"You know you're welcome to come with us, Doc," Nathan said, holding the door straight, and re-pinning the hinges.

"I suggest we go to Munro's Trading Post first," Doc said. "He might have some livestock for sale, too."

"Good idea. OK the door's fixed, let's go," Nathan said, taking Maggie by the arm and helping her outside. He lifted her into the buggy and Dr. Mathison climbed in on the other side. Nathan laid the doc's gun and powder behind the seat, and out of sight.

By sundown, Nathan had his milk cow along with her calf, his draft ox, and a beautiful, tall and muscular, four-year-old sorrel stud. Maggie put a deposit on a small flock of Merino sheep that Dr. Mathison approved of. The flock would be delivered in the spring under Doc's guidance. Nathan purchased enough grain and hey to feed his animals until they got to Newton. It had been a busy day, and the trio decided to stop at Jacob McKray's Inn and have dinner there.

Jacob McKray greeted them when they walked into the inn, and personally seated everyone. He sat down at their table with them. "I've got some bad news," he said straight off. "The boys couldn't find Deihl."

"What?! That's impossible!" Dr. Mathison exclaimed. "The man was a mangled mess. He couldn't have gotten far."

"Not what I wanted to hear, either," Nathan said. "But we all know he is a sly one. He probably talked someone into taking him in, and patching him up. After all, Doc ... you said he could charm the skin off a rattlesnake!"

Maggie felt a lump forming in her throat. "Nathan, I'm frightened," she said softly, reaching for his hand under the table.

Nathan squeezed the her hand reassuringly. "Maggie, let's not worry about it right now. For all we know, he's out of our lives for good. At least we can believe that, unless we find out otherwise. No sense wasting energy worrying about the unknown. Let's just put it in the Good Lord's hands. I believe He'll take care of us."

"You're a good man, Nathan Stillman ... even if you are a little naïve," Maggie smiled.

"Umm... You're calling *ME* naïve?" Nathan laughed.

"Jacob, I want one of those big juicy steaks of yours. And a pile of mashed taters," Doc said, licking his lips.

"That sounds good to me, too," Nathan added.

"Well, I'll have the same, but not as big as theirs," Maggie giggled.

"Coming right up, folks," Jacob McKray said, leaving the table.

"Look over there! It's Reverend Wilkins," Doc said. He got up from the table and walked quickly over to where the Reverend was sitting.

Maggie and Nathan watched a very animated conversation between the two. Jacob McKray soon joined Doc and the Reverend. In just a few minutes, Doc Mathison, Reverend Wilkins, and Jacob McKray approached Maggie and Nathan.

"Well now... Is this the happy couple?" Reverend Wilkins asked, extending his hand to Nathan.

"I'm Nathan Stillman, sir," Nathan said, shaking the Reverend's chubby hand.

"Nathan... Maggie... We're going to have a wedding. Right here ... right now," Jacob McKray announced. "And the two of you are going to stay in my best room tonight. How does that sound?"

Nathan and Maggie looked at each other in stunned amazement. Neither knew what to say.

"Well? Cat got your tongues?" Doc chuckled. "Might as well get it done, rather than wait. We can still leave first thing in the morning, but then I will be accompanying *Mr. and Mrs. Nathan Stillman* to Newton. What do you say?"

"I think that's very gracious of you all," Nathan said, grinning broadly. "What do you say, Maggie?"

"I love the idea," Maggie said, wiping the tears running down her cheeks with her napkin.

Nathan looked at her tears. "I'm confused... Please tell me those are the crazy happy tears we talked about last night!"

"Yes, Nathan ... they are happy tears," Maggie said, quietly.

"I'll have your animals put in our barn for the night," Jacob said. "Doc are you staying here, too."

"I'd love to, thanks," Doc nodded. "I just need to go to my office and pick up a few things for the trip to Newton. It should only take me about forty-five minutes to get to the office and back. I'll leave as soon as we're done with dinner."

"I'll ride with ya, Doc," Jacob said. "I don't want you out there alone, with that Deihl still on the loose."

"I accept your offer, Jacob!"

While Jacob and Dr. Mathison went to get Doc's stuff, Nathan and Maggie were escorted to separate rooms, where they cleaned up for their wedding. Word of the wedding spread quickly through the town. Elizabeth Williams and Suzanne Jackson arrived with their husbands, and brought Maggie and Nathan gifts of necessities for the ceremony. Samuel Williams brought his straight razor and a clean change of clothes for Nathan. He, like Nathan was a massive man, tall and squarely built. Elizabeth brought Maggie rose water for her bath, and even offered her the use of her own wedding dress and veil. By the time Doc and Jacob returned, all was ready; even the decorations.

"Let the celebration begin!" Reverend Wilkins shouted.

Nathan took his place beside Reverend Wilkins, and Maggie was escorted by Dr. Mathison. The congregation, gathered at the inn, hummed a familiar hymn as Dr. Mathison walked Maggie toward the waiting Nathan.

"Maggie," Dr. Mathison whispered, "I brought your parents' wedding rings... I didn't think you would object." He placed the rings in Maggie's hand.

"You're an angel, Doc," Maggie whispered back.

"Nathan, here is your beloved," Doc said, placing Maggie's hand into Nathan's hand.

Nathan had never seen Maggie look as lovely as she did at this moment. His own eyes were filling with tears, and for the first time, he understood what Maggie meant when she spoke of "happy tears". Just looking at Maggie, in the beautifully embroidered wedding dress and delicate lace veil, took his breath away. Her smooth white skin glowed in the subtle light from the fireplace and the candles. He could barely contain his emotions.

During the ceremony, Maggie fought to suppress the doubts that kept creeping into her consciousness. Those doubts were like thieves, trying to steal her joy.

Reverend Wilkins cleared his throat and repeated, "You may kiss the bride."

Suddenly the reality hit Nathan, and he leaned down and kissed his wife. *HIS WIFE!*

Everyone clapped and cheered. The wedding was over, the honeymoon would begin.

"Drinks for everyone!" Jacob McKray shouted, throwing several jugs and lots of cups upon the bar. "Help yourselves, my friends!"

The world was suddenly filled with wonderment and excitement. Maggie and Nathan were standing on the threshold of their lives together. Nathan scooped Maggie up in his arms and swung her around.

"Do I need to show you the way to your wedding chamber?" Jacob whispered to Nathan. "Follow me, son." Jacob led Nathan down a hallway, through the kitchen, and right into Maggie's old room. "Recognize this Maggie? I thought it would be secluded enough ... away from everyone else. Seemed perfect to me."

Nathan carried Maggie into the room which had been decorated with lace, ribbons, and candles. It looked like a dream land. The warm aroma of rose water, cinnamon, and vanilla beans permeated the air.

"You two have a good night. And congratulations," Jacob said, closing the door softly.

Maggie nuzzled her face against Nathan's neck as he stood there, in the middle of the room with his new wife in his arms. Her senses were stimulated by the scent of Nathan's skin. It was a curious mixture of leather, soap, and pine. She planted little kisses all along his prominent jaw line. She gently kissed the dimples on each side of his mustache, and lingered at the deep cleft in his chin. He could feel his passion being fueled by Maggie's innocent affections, and he was hesitant to respond.

Nathan allowed an old memory to surface in his psyche. He remembered the young widow who played such a significant role in his formative years. It was the summer of his eighteenth year. Her name was Annie. She wasn't what Nathan considered an immoral woman. She had lost her husband to a deadly rattlesnake bite, the year before; after being married for only two years. She employed Nathan to help with putting up hey on her farm; her land was next to the Stillman property. Annie was only twenty-three. She was beautiful, sad, and alone. Annie stole Nathan's innocence and his heart. She taught him to love and to make love. That summer was the pinnacle of Nathan's coming of age, but it ended suddenly and without warning. One day he discovered Annie had left. The cabin was empty, the animals were gone. No one ever heard from Annie Wilson again. It was as if she had never existed. Nathan was left with broken dreams and a void in his life. He had managed to forget his lost love, until this moment, as it all came flooding back into his consciousness. Annie had prepared him for this – his wedding night. She had taught him gentleness and patience, restraint and persistence, stamina and confidence.

Nathan carried Maggie over to the bed and laid her down gently. He pulled his shirt off, exposing his massive bronze chest. He unbuttoned his trousers, revealing his muscular stomach to just below his navel. Maggie watched and marveled at the rippled lines of muscles across Nathan's abdomen. She reached out her hand and touched his stomach. That touch felt like fire on Nathan's skin; his senses were so intensified by his emotions. He lowered himself on to the bed beside Maggie and gathered her into his arms, pulling her tightly against his bare chest. He kissed her gently on the cheek, and then moved his lips to the corner of her waiting mouth. He kissed each side of her mouth, teasing her; tempting her.

Maggie wanted his kiss. She cupped his handsome face in her hands and pulled his mouth down onto hers. Nathan was eager to give Maggie what she wanted. He kissed her deeply. She had never been kissed like that. Nathan withdrew and began the gentle kisses once more. He felt her relax in his arms. He kissed her neck, and moved his lips to her ear.

"Do you have any idea how much I love you, Maggie?" he whispered, allowing the warmth of his breath to cover Maggie's ear. He felt her shiver. "I love you with every ounce of my being," he continued to breathe the words, and he gently bit her earlobe. She trembled. "I intend to show you what love is all about, Maggie."

He moved his lips down her neck and across her shoulder, kissing and nipping at her skin with his teeth.

Maggie caught her breath sharply as Nathan's mouth moved from her shoulder to the barely revealed cleavage, exposed at the top of her gown . Adeptly, and with one hand, he began to undo the tiny buttons on the front of the dress. He slowly pulled at the opening of the tight-fitting bodice, releasing the soft white mounds of flesh that his mouth was seeking. As he covered Maggie's breasts with kisses, he reached down and pulled her leg up over his hip. His hand found the small of her back, and he gently but firmly pressed her body hard against his. Maggie's back arched, as she responded to Nathan's urgency. He grasped Maggie's thigh, pulling her into him, even closer. Maggie released a cry of surprise, as she realized the extent of Nathan's intensity. She struggled. Without warning, Nathan's lips were on hers, covering her mouth, stifling her cries. He kissed her deeply and passionately, until Maggie finally surrendered to his passion this time. She wrapped her arms tightly around Nathan's neck, as he pulled her over on top of him. He stripped the dress from her shoulders and pulled it down past her waist. Feeling Maggie's bare skin against his, ignited an inferno that couldn't be quenched by anything less than complete penetration; but not yet.

Nathan held Maggie's hips in his massive hands, and moved her pliant body in a rhythmic motion, an instinctive prodding; waiting for that receptive cue he remembered so well, with Annie. Maggie intuitively pulled her knees up along Nathan's sides, and he immediately slipped the dress down to her legs. Her body was now completely free for him to possess. He rolled Maggie onto her back and continued to kiss her insatiably. His hands caressed and stroked her bare skin. He touched her in secret places, making her moan and wriggle beneath him. Nathan found his reward in the warmth of Maggie's eagerness. He prolonged his assault on the girl's senses; kissing her and caressing her body. He pushed his trousers down, and off.

Nathan placed one knee between Maggie's legs, and then used his other knee to open the way. Her legs spread easily. And then it began; the exploration; the thrusting; gently and carefully. Maggie grabbed Nathan's back and pulled him to her. He wanted to enter her; but not yet.

Nathan whispered into Maggie's ear, "Maggie, do you want me?" He ran his tongue over her ear, down her neck; and then he was breathing in her ear again. "Maggie, do you want me?" He covered her mouth with his, and kissed her more passionately than he had before. All the while, the probing continued.

Maggie was writhing beneath Nathan's massive body, clawing at his back, trying to pull him in to her. His kisses intensified, and his hands were under her hips now, lifting her up to him; to meet each incessant thrust. Nathan allowed each movement to penetrate just a little further. Little by little, he entered her. She wanted all of him inside her; and her need was excruciating.

"Maggie, just tell me when you want all of me, Honey," he whispered hoarsely.

"NOW!!! Please... Nathan ... now!" she pleaded.

With unrestrained force, Nathan broke through; and plunged into her. He gave Maggie what she had begged him for. She screamed in pleasure and in pain.

Nathan remained motionless for a moment, allowing the girl to recover from his initial penetration. He held her tightly and kissed her deeply; until the passion began to rise once more. Slowly and rhythmically, Nathan moved further into Maggie's acceptance. Soon, she began to move *with* Nathan; the cadence of an instinctive exchange of love and affection. Nathan picked up the tempo, and Maggie responded. She began her own expression of love, and need, and longing. The two were becoming one, and Maggie was completely engulfed in the escalating conflagration that had overtaken her body and her psyche.

Without warning, Maggie's back arched, and she let out a cry that emanated from her deepest being. She grabbed Nathan's buttocks and tried to pull him even further into her. The world exploded. Her body shook with delicious waves of euphoric spasms, as Nathan pushed into her deeper and harder; over and over, until he felt her completely abandon all inhibitions. He released his love inside her; filling her to overflowing.

The marriage had been consummated.

Chapter 15 – Surprises

It was Saturday morning in Newton, and the sky was finally clear. The reflection of the bright sunlight on the snow-covered ground flooded the cabin with a warm yellow radiance, through the greased parchment masking the windows.

John Stillman was feeling more contented than he'd felt in months. He looked into the mirror, and slicked down his golden brown curls with some water. He finally decided to pull his long hair back, and tie it. The ends of his mustache were twisted and waxed. He was bathed, shaved, and dressed; he felt as if he looked "good". It was time to go to Tom McCollough's party. He could barely remember the last party he'd been to. The horse was saddled and waiting just outside. John slipped into his buckskin jacket, grabbed his gun and powder, and left for the McCollough farm.

On the trail to Newton, John couldn't help but feel there was something festive in the air. The birds sounded happier, the squirrels seemed to be more playful; or was it just that his attitude had changed?

When he finally arrived at Tom McCollough's house, Tom ran out to greet him. "Well, John Stillman!! I'm so glad you came. I've got to tell you a secret, before we go inside, though."

"Uh Oh... That doesn't sound good," John said, shaking his head.

"It's my sister Sarah's birthday... This is actually *HER* party. I didn't tell you that because I didn't want you to feel like you needed to bring a present." Then Tom burst into uncontrollable laughter.

"That's the secret?" John asked, looking down from his horse and wondering what was so funny about that.

"No!" Tom laughed even harder. "The secret is ... *YOU* are her birthday present!!" With that, Tom fell down, rolling on the ground, laughing and holding his sides.

Just then, the door to the house opened and a woman stepped out onto the porch. "Tom McCollough!! I think you've had quite enough to drink!" She stamped her foot hard, and put her hands on her hips in annoyance. Tom continued laughing and rolling around in the snow.

John Stillman dismounted and led his horse up to the porch. He tipped his hat to the beautiful redhead, and tied Tiff to the rail.

"I'm John Stillman, ma'am," he said, smiling.

The woman was absolutely breathtaking. She was tall and slender, with a tiny waist and ample bosom. She had copper-red hair, tied up in a bunch of curls at the top of her head. Golden tendrils fell in disarray around her face, and down the back if her neck. Her clear blue eyes widened when John introduced himself. Her cheeks turned a bright pink, and she, too, started to laugh. She stepped down off the porch and extended her hand to John.

"I'm Sarah McCollough, Tom's sister," she said, "I believe *YOU* are my birthday present."

John caught her hand in his, and grinned broadly. He was completely taken by surprise. He turned and gave Tom an incredulous look, then he looked back at Sarah's radiant face.

"I'm honored to be your birthday present, Sarah McCollough!" John laughed. "As a matter of fact, I'm down right flattered to be your birthday present!!" He continued holding onto Sarah's hand. The two of them were totally caught up in each other's gaze. The mutual attraction sizzled; electrified by some unseen force.

Tom McCollough's energy spent, he lay quietly, sprawled out in the snow. "I knew it!" Tom muttered. "I felt it in my bones! I believe in love at first sight!"

About fifteen miles away, on the main trail, Nathan, Maggie, and Dr. Mathison were plowing through the deep snow, on their way to Newton. Nathan and Dr. Mathison were riding horseback, while Maggie managed the ox driven sled, with her little mare tied to the back. The men herded the ox, the cow, and the calf, in front of the sled, to help pack the snow on the path. It was slow going, but at least it wasn't as cold as it had been. Judging from the rate they were traveling, Nathan feared that it may be dark before the group reached the Stillman farm.

"Let's try and pick up the pace," Nathan shouted. "I don't want to be out here in the dark with this calf. It's like bear bait!"

"You're right, Nathan," Doc Mathison answered. "Let's go... Yehaw" doc yelled. He whistled, and swung his hat around in the air. Startled, the cattle began moving along a little faster.

"Maggie ... it's OK to use the whip on that ox's ass, now and then. Get it movin', Honey," Nathan called back to his new wife. He looked up at the sun's position. "It's nearly noon ... if we quicken the pace, we ought to make it to our farm before sundown. We won't have time to spare, though."

Nathan's keen eye caught sight of something ahead, moving at the side of the road, nearly a quarter mile away. He grabbed his gun from the back of the horse and galloped ahead, to investigate. As he neared the spot, he could see it was an injured horse. It was Miles Deihl's magnificent black stallion. Nathan dismounted and ran over to the frightened animal. It was standing still, now, at the side of the road.

"Whoa boy," Nathan spoke softly. He caught hold of the dangling reins and led the horse to the middle of the path. Its right front leg was swollen and bloody. Nathan ran his hand all the way down the horse's leg and didn't feel any obvious broken bones. He checked the stallion's other legs which were fine. The horse had what appeared to be claw marks on its rump, and it was all skinned up along its right side . Nathan concluded that the horse may have fallen. He wondered if it had been attacked by a bear or a cat. The main question in Nathan's mind was more alarming. "Where's your master, boy?" he muttered, looking around for any sign of Deihl.

The others had caught up to Nathan by now, and they were as troubled as Nathan was, at seeing Miles Deihl's horse.

"Good god, Nathan!" Doc Mathison said quietly. "This is all we need. Where do you think Deihl is?"

"I dunno, Doc," Nathan said, looking around. "I don't see any sign of footprints, or blood. Funny ... this fine animal was just left here."

"Well... I figure Deihl fell off... But, you would've thought we'd have found him lying in the road, if he headed this way?" Doc said. Dr. Mathison climbed down from his horse and examined the injured stallion.

Maggie could feel the terror welling up in her consciousness. Just thinking of Miles Deihl caused a strange contradiction of emotions inside the girl. She prayed the man was not in the area. She wouldn't, however, allow herself to wish him dead.

"What do we do?" Nathan asked the doc. "I can't see leaving this animal here... Some predator will finish him off before mornin' ... but if we try to take him with us, he'll really slow down our progress! He's lame!!"

"That's a mighty fine horse, Nathan. Besides, this stallion is going to heal up and be just as good as new. I'm sure of it," the doctor said, pushing at his glasses. "I think you should claim him. Take him home and sell him in the spring when he's sound ... But that's just my opinion."

"Well, that may be the logical thing to do ... but we've got the time factor to consider. It's not safe out here after dark ... especially with Miles Deihl on the loose!"

"Ok, let's take him along for a mile or two and see how he holds up. If he slows us down substantially, we'll turn him loose. How's that sound?"

"All right Doc. Let's do it," Nathan said slapping the doc on the shoulder. He led the horse around to the back of the sled and tied him next to Maggie's mare.

"Nathan, maybe you should bind his leg," Maggie said, looking back at the stallion. "We could put liniment ointment on it and wrap it good, to take away some of his pain."

Maggie didn't wait for an answer. She grabbed her bag and climbed down out of the sled. Within minutes, the job was done and they proceeded on their way. The big black stallion didn't seem to slow them down, because the snow-covered road made it impossible to move any faster.

Nathan and Dr. Mathison kept their guns at the ready, just in case they encountered Miles Deihl.

Chapter 16 – The Arrangement

John Stillman and Tom McCollough sat by the fire drinking and laughing.

"You've got to be kidding!" John said, taking a long drink of the corn liquor.

"Nope... Pa told her ... if she wasn't married and settled by her twenty-fifth birthday, he expected her back in Virginia with him and Mama. She's been here one year, and that was her limit. Believe me, John ... she's a headstrong woman and she's bound determined to stay... Problem is ... she'll never go against what Pa says. That's just how we were raised."

"But what woman in her right mind would marry a total stranger?" John laughed.

"Who said she was in her right mind?" Tom rolled out of the chair and onto the floor. He couldn't control his laughter.

"Well, how do you know she'd settle for ME?"

Tom stopped laughing and suddenly became serious. He looked up at John, "From what I saw, when you two met, it didn't look like she'd be settling! I think she was totally smitten ... right then and there. She's been so damned picky – I've introduced her to some of the most eligible bachelors in the area, and she wouldn't give any of them the time of day. I mean she was down right *RUDE* to those poor chaps!! I think the Good Lord brought you here just to solve this problem! Do you believe in *Divine Providence*, John?"

Both men laughed uproariously. Tom began rolling again. He grabbed his aching sides tightly.

"OK, Tom... I'll do it. But just to keep her here with you. I certainly don't expect her to be a real wife to me. Um... You know what I mean? She can keep her freedom, but I'll give her my name."

Tom sat upright on the floor. His look of surprise was priceless. "You mean it, John?" he asked. Now he was totally serious. "Well, then I'd better go have a talk with Sarah, and explain the game rules to her. I'm sure she'll appreciate your offer to help her out. We'll need to let Reverend Manley know the wedding is on!"

John laughed loudly. "I wondered why Rev. Manley was here! I think I've been ambushed!! But I'll tell ya what ... after all you've done for ME ... this is a small thing I can do for YOU. Besides, your sister is absolutely gorgeous! I can't believe she's single!"

"Well, technically, *NOW* ... she's *NOT* single anymore!" Tom smiled. "And she's no angel, John. I think she's a *she-devil*. Looks can be deceiving... Don't ever forget that. We can get you a divorce whenever you're ready!" He laughed, and winked at John.

John didn't see Sarah again until the ceremony.

Rev. Manley stood beside John, as they watched Tom walk Sarah down the stairs and into the front room. Sarah was wearing an elegant white, silk and lace wedding gown. The dress fit tight, and the bodice was cut low, revealing her generous curves. Silk folds fell from her bare shoulders. Her skin was as white as the snow, in sharp contrasted to her copper colored hair, which fell in golden ringlets, over her shoulders and down her back. The lace veil was attached to a pile of curls on top of her head, and the veil reached clear down to her fingertips. John thought Sarah absolutely radiated beauty and grace. He couldn't take his eyes off of her.

The entire neighborhood had been invited, and John wondered if everyone else knew the wedding was just a charade. Charade or not, the bride was beautiful. Somewhere in John's soul was the sincere yearning for a valid wedding, a real love, and a genuine wife; but this would suffice for now. He was returning the favor of a friend, and he felt good about it.

Tom placed Sarah's hand into John's. "John, I give you my sister, Sarah," Tom said softly.

The ceremony was brief. It was over before John could get a grip on the reality of what was happening.

"You may kiss your bride," Rev. Manley said.

John caught his breath, he wasn't prepared for this. Panic rose in his stomach. He struggled with trying to decide what would be considered appropriate, since his bride was actually a stranger. John had never kissed a woman he didn't even know. Sarah, realizing John's predicament, reached up and caught his face in her hands, pulling him down to her. She covered his mouth with hers, and kissed him warmly. Something stirred in his gut, as she continued to kiss him. Finally he wrapped his arms around his new wife, and returned the kiss. That sizzling energy literally exploded between the two. After what seemed to be a very long kiss, John released Sarah. They both stood there looking at each other in wide-eyed amazement. The people in the room cheered loudly.

The party which followed was a rowdy event. The liquor flowed freely and the dinner was an extravagant banquet. John knew most of the men at the party, but was now privileged to meet their families. He felt honored to be part of such a closely knit community, with so many genuinely good people. He now knew that this is where he actually belonged.

After visiting with the neighbors and accepting everyone's well-wishing and congratulations, John decided he'd better head home, before it got dark outside.

He didn't want to leave without telling his bride good-bye, but he couldn't find her in the crowd.

"Tom... Where's Sarah? I want to tell her good-bye. I've got to get home before dark."

Tom laughed. "Well, John ... I believe your wife is upstairs packing. She's getting ready to go with you."

"What?!!"

"Well, you weren't really going to leave without her, were you?"

"I told you, I didn't expect her to be a wife to me!" John's tone was insistent.

"John, my friend, you need to talk to *HER* about that. Her room is at the top of the stairs to the left." Tom winked and grinned. "Good luck."

John rushed up the stairs, taking them two at a time, and burst into Sarah's room. "Sarah, we need to talk," he said, closing her trunk, abruptly, with one hand. "You really don't need to move in with me. I understand this is a marriage of convenience *ONLY*. You just stay right here with your family. It's where you belong."

"I know what you must think, John," she said softly, looking up at her handsome new husband. "But I'm so grateful for what you were willing to do for me... I decided to take care of you like a real wife would ... should. I honestly *WANT* to be a wife to you."

"But Sarah ... we don't even know each other. How could we live like husband and wife? I've freely given you my name. You can keep your freedom."

Sarah started to cry. "Are you saying you don't want me?"

John's frustration was evident. "NO! That's not what I'm saying! I'm trying to do the right thing, here." He put his arms around her to comfort her. "You're a beautiful woman, Sarah. You don't have to give yourself to a man you don't love! That would be ridiculous! Someday you'll find the right man... We'll get a legal divorce when the time comes, and you can be happily married."

"Just let me try to make you as happy as you've made me, John... Please?" She buried her face in his chest and sobbed.

"Sarah Honey, I can't do that with a clear conscience. You need to save yourself for a man who's right for you!"

Sarah looked up into John's pleading blue eyes. "What if we lived together, and I took care of you like a real wife, accept we agree not to consummate our marriage? You know ... we won't ... um ... we just won't ..." Sarah slid her arms up around John's neck, and hugged him affectionately. "Please, John? Don't make me a laughing stock in the sight of all the neighbors. Nobody knows that this was an arrangement. Everyone thinks we've been courting."

"Oh NO!!" John sighed. "I see the problem now." John reached up and removed Sarah's arms from around his neck. "All right, Sarah. I sure as hell didn't see this comin' ... but we can try and make it work, I guess."

Sarah grabbed John again, and kissed him happily. "You won't regret it! I promise you, John! I swear I will spoil you rotten!!"

"Well, we'll see about that," he muttered, leaving the room.

Downstairs, he found Tom, sitting by the fire, as usual.

"Well, Tom, I sure got more than I bargained for," John said, sitting down heavily, beside his new brother-in-law.

"Yep, well I knew that would happen ... because I know Sarah." He took a long drink from the jug he was holding and then passed it over to John, who readily accepted it and took an even longer drink. "There is something else you need to know, though."

"Good Lord!! What now?!" John exclaimed in exasperation.

"Oh ... not to worry... This is the good part," Tom said, turning to look at John.

"Please ... no more surprises!" John groaned.

"This is the *GOOD* surprise, John!"

"Give me another drink... I don't know how many more of your surprises I can handle!"

Tom started his incessant laughing again, as he handed John the jug. John gulped the liquid so fast, it dribbled from the corners of his mouth, and down his chin.

"OK," John said, wiping his mouth with the back of his hand. "Tell me the *GOOD* surprise."

"All righty!" Tom said, grinning. "I'm glad you're sitting down, John."

"Damn it!! Just tell me what it is!" John demanded.

"OK... You know, Sarah's been an old maid for a long time," Tom began.

"I wouldn't call twenty-five an old maid!" John interrupted.

"Well, now listen," Tom continued. "She convinced my Pa that the men who courted her, didn't like her." He chuckled, thinking how wily his little sister really is. "Pa figured if he upped her dowry, then the guys would find her more attractive." He took another long drink from the jug and passed it over to John. "Anyway ... Pa kept uppin' the ante, and still there were no takers. He just figured he would be stuck with the old maid forever." Tom stopped and laughed until his belly shook. "Finally, he shipped her out here, to see if I could get her married off. Turns out ... I learn she's been shrewd enough to play Pa for all he's worth. She could have married any number of men in Virginia. She was just too damned picky! Here Pa was raising the value of her dowry, and she was still turning down marriage proposals!"

"So... What's that got to do with *ME*?" John said, throwing up his hands in frustration.

"So?" Tom leaned over close to John, and looked him straight in the eye. "It means, John ... you are now a very wealthy man!" He banged on John's forehead. "Is anybody home?" He grinned at John, waiting for his response.

"What did you say?!" John caught his breath sharply. "How *wealthy* is *wealthy*?"

"Um... Let's see... There's twelve hundred acres of prime land which actually borders your farm. There's a fine pair of big black Percheron draft horses, standing in my barn right now... They just arrived from Virginia last week. There's enough money in gold coin to support just about anything you want to invest in. My Pa is actually a very successful plantation owner in Virginia. He raises cotton and tobacco and makes a fortune every year. What Sarah has right now is nothing compared to what we'll inherit when my daddy's gone ... but I don't like to think about that."

"I won't touch her dowry!" John said, slamming the jug into Tom's lap. "But why didn't you tell me this before?"

"Because I wanted to make sure ... if you agreed to marry my sister ... you would do it out of the kindness of your heart and your friendship with me … and NOT for the fortune you actually get for doing it!" Tom stated the facts, looking more serious than John had ever seen him.

"Well … I don't want her damned dowry! I think it's a shame your Pa thought he had to bribe men to care for her!" John grabbed the jug away from Tom and took another swig.

"That's just how it's done, John. Maybe it's an old-school kind of thinking … but that's just how it is."

"I don't like the idea! If I can't support my own wife with my own efforts, and my own money, then I'd say I don't deserve a good woman!" John said indignantly. He jerked the jug out of Tom's hands and chugged on it until it was empty.

"That's why I knew you'd make a perfect husband for Sarah, John. You're an honorable man. She knows how lucky she is. She and I talked a lot about it."

"WHAT?!!" John didn't know what to think. His mind was racing. He felt as if he'd been manipulated. He wasn't sure whether he should be angry or happy.

"I'm ready, John," Sarah called from the stairs.

"I don't know whether to kiss ya or kill ya Tom McCollough!" John said, slurring his words slightly. He shoved the empty jug into Tom's lap.

Tom succumbed to his fit of uncontrolled laughter again.

John stood up and shook his head in disbelief, looking down at Tom. "You sure do take the cake, Tom! I'm leaving!"

John sprinted up the stairs and grabbed Sarah's trunk. He hoisted it onto his shoulder and carried it downstairs. Sarah followed him, marveling at his strength.

"John, I'll have Tom's son bring my carriage around. We can take it, if that's OK," Sarah said, looking up at her husband; studying his face intently. "OK... How drunk did Tom get you?"

"Who? ME? Drunk?" John laughed.

"Yes ... YOU... How intoxicated are you?" Sarah said. "It's all right. I knew he would do that! Will you be OK, though?"

"I'll be fine... After all ... you said you wanted to take care of me," John said. He looked down at Sarah thoughtfully. "I don't know about taking your carriage in the snow. The path to my farm isn't exactly a well-traveled by-way, you know." John rubbed at his chin. "Does Tom have a sled?"

"I think he does," Sarah smiled. "Robby," she called over her shoulder. "Does your dad have a sled?"

"He does indeed, Aunt Sarah," Robby answered.

"Would you please hitch my team to it, and tell your dad we'll bring it back soon?"

"Consider it done, Aunt Sarah."

"John, do you have room in your barn for my team?"

"Well, Sarah Honey, if we can't find room for them in the barn, they can stay in the cabin with us," John said, sounding serious.

"Oh no ..., you ARE very drunk," she sighed.

Robby and John loaded the sled with Sarah's things, and tied John's big gelding to the back. Tom, along with all the neighbors came outside to say good-bye, and everyone had a gift which they placed into the sleigh with the bride and groom. The send-off was first class, as the great Percherons pranced away from the McCollough farm. Robby had put the sleigh-bells on the horses' tack, and spread a warm quilt over John's and Sarah's knees. It was a beautiful afternoon, and John was feeling no pain.

"Are you all right, John," Sarah asked, with sincere concern.

"I've never been better!" he said, slipping his arm around Sarah's shoulders. "Are you warm enough, Sarah Honey?"

Sarah looked at John in surprise. She knew the moonshine was working on his senses. "Um... Yes, I'm fine, thank you," she said hesitantly.

The sleigh moved smoothly over the snow-covered trail, toward the turn-off near Crooks' Tavern. The jingling of the bells reminded John of happy times in Pennsylvania. He couldn't believe how cheerful and contented he felt at this moment. He squeezed Sarah, and pulled her closer to him on the seat of the sleigh.

"You know, Sarah ... this could be a good thing," he said, as if thinking out loud. "It just feels comfortable."

"I know," she replied softly.

"Maybe you'll learn to love me," he said, nonchalantly.

"Maybe you'll learn to love *ME*," Sarah surmised.

Caught off guard, John pulled the horses to a stop. He looked at Sarah in amazement. "You don't really think it would be difficult for me to love you ... do you?"

"Why would you assume it would be difficult for *ME* to love *YOU*?" Sarah grinned.

"Well, I don't think I've never been in love," John admitted.

"I don't think I have either," Sarah confessed. She couldn't help giggling.

"Aren't we a pair?!" John laughed. "Here we are ... married ... and neither of us knows what it's supposed to feel like to be in love!!"

"Well, when you kissed me, I thought maybe I knew," Sarah said, looking away from John's gaze.

"Is that right?" he said, grinning.

"Yes. You didn't feel it?"

"I'm not sure, Sarah. Maybe you should kiss me again... I'll tell you if I feel something," he teased.

Sarah immediately turned to John and slipped her arms around his neck. She offered her luscious full lips up to him, and he seized the opportunity like a ravenous animal. He covered her mouth with his, and gathered her into his arms, holding her tightly against him. He kissed her until they were both dizzy with passion. When he released his hold on her, they were both breathless.

"Oh my... Did you feel that, John?" Sarah asked, gasping and trembling.

"Nope... Better try it again!"

Sarah knew he was lying. She had felt his heart pounding against her body. She leaned close to him and kissed him on the cheek.

"Did you feel that?"

"Sarah!! I'm going to take you home and attack you like a mad-man!" he threatened, lunging at her.

Sarah wasn't sure this time, if he was teasing or not. She moved away from him on the seat.

John put his arm around her and pulled her back beside him. "I'm only joking, Honey. I promised you that won't happen. I gave you my word. You're completely safe with me. Honest!" he said, reassuringly. He felt Sarah relax against him.

"Gidup there!" he shouted, giving the reins a snap. The team trudged on.

As they neared the turnoff by Crooks' Tavern, John saw the other group approaching from the north. He strained his eyes to make out who it could be.

"Good Lord!!" he exclaimed. "It's my brother Nathan!" John stopped the sleigh and jumped out to wait for the others.

As Nathan got closer, he realized it was John standing in the middle of the trail. He galloped up to him and jumped off his horse, grabbing his brother in a bear hug.

"John! I'm so sorry we quarreled! Will you forgive me?"

"Little brother, there's nothing to forgive! And by the way – thank you for the beautiful gelding!"

"What are you doing out here, anyway?" Nathan asked, looking at the sleigh and the Percherons. "What a gorgeous team! Whose are they?"

"One question at a time, Nathan," John said, looking back to Sarah and smiling broadly.

"OK ... what are you doing out here?" Nathan asked again.

"I'm on my way home."

"Whose Percherons are those?"

"They belong to my wife," John replied, cocking his head, and waiting for his brother's reaction.

"NO!! You didn't say *WIFE*!!"

John took Nathan by the arm and walked him up to the sleigh. "Sarah, this is my younger brother Nathan."

"I'm pleased to meet you Nathan. I've heard so many good things about you." Sarah grinned at Nathan and extended her hand to him. She knew he would be shocked.

"Nathan, this is my wife, Sarah."

Nathan grasped Sarah's hand in his, and tried to speak, but his voice was stuck somewhere in his throat.

John instinctively slapped Nathan hard on the back, knocking the breath out of him.

"Um... Thank you John," Nathan said, gasping for air. "It's nice to meet you, too, Sarah." Nathan turned to John with a look of utter surprise. "I leave you alone for a week, and see what you've done!!" He gave John a playful shove. "When did this happen?"

"Today," John replied.

"What?!! You couldn't wait until I returned? I would have liked to have been at your wedding!" Nathan almost sounded angry.

Sarah giggled. "Well, it was a surprise to us, too, Nathan."

"WHAT?!!" Nathan threw his hands up. "How could it have been a surprise to you two?"

"Well, that's a long story!" John laughed. "We'll talk about that later."

The others were at the turnoff now. Maggie climbed out of the sled, and walked up to Nathan.

Nathan put his arm around Maggie and looked soberly at John, not sure how he would react to Maggie's presence, after their argument.

"John, Maggie and I were married last night."

John lunged at Maggie, and grabbed her, lifting her off of her feet. He hugged her tightly and swung her around.

"Maggie!!" he shouted. "Congratulations! This is a joyous occasion. I want you to meet my wife, Sarah," John said, putting Maggie down, and gesturing toward his new wife. "We were married today. And it's Sarah's birthday." John doubled over with laughter. "I was her birthday present!"

Nathan eyed John critically. "Is my brother drunk?" he asked Sarah.

"You can blame *my* brother Tom for that," Sarah admitted.

Dr. Mathison jumped down from his horse and joined the others. He walked up to Sarah and gave her a big hug, and then shook John's hand.

"Tom pulled it off, huh?" Doc chuckled. "He told me he could do it! That old devil!"

"You mean *YOU* were in on it, too?" John said incredulously. "I can't believe it!"

"Well, you boys better get on down the road, before it gets dark, don't ya think?" Dr. Mathison said, wisely changing the subject. "I'm going to stay at Crooks' Tavern tonight, visit with Tom in the morning, and I'll see the rest of you tomorrow afternoon ... or on Monday .... Maybe." He mounted his horse and rode across the road to the tavern.

"John ... if this is your wedding night, wouldn't you like some privacy?" Nathan whispered to his brother.

"Naw ... we don't need any privacy!" John laughed loudly, slapping his knees with both hands.

"Stop your damned laughing and be serious!" Nathan demanded. "What are we going to do? We have two brides, two honeymoons, and one cabin with one bed!"

"No," John said. "We have two brides, two honeymoons, and one cabin with TWO bedrooms, and one bed."

"What are you talking about?" Nathan asked, shaking his head.

"I finished the loft while you were gone. It's right nice. We just need an extra bed up there."

"That can be arranged!" This time, Nathan laughed.

The Stillman brothers, with their new wives, arrived at the farm just as darkness was settling over the valley. Nathan and John carried their brides over the threshold, and then unloaded the sleds. Next, they herded the animals into the barn and secured the new doors which John had hung there.

While the boys were taking care of the animals, Maggie and Sarah were busy putting things away and organizing the cabin.

"Maggie, I brought bunches of food from our party. Are you hungry?" Sarah said, holding up a big basket.

"I'm starved, and I'm sure Nathan is, too," Maggie sighed.

"OK, then... You set the table and I'll start a fire and warm this stuff up. We'll surprise the boys, when they come in!"

"Sarah ..." Maggie hesitated.

"What, Honey?"

"Happy birthday."

"Thank you, Maggie."

Sarah stirred the coals and laid a log on the fire.

"Maggie, if you look in one of those crates, you'll find my dishes and silver."

Maggie found what she needed and set the table, complete with the silver candle sticks and candles.

"That's lovely!" Sarah breathed, looking at the table in the candlelight.

"Where on earth did all of this beautiful stuff come from, Sarah?" Maggie asked, folding the linen napkins and placing one at each plate.

"Well... Don't laugh ... but I've been keeping a hope chest since I was about thirteen. I always loved pretty things, so I collected what I liked, over the years. I know it seems extravagant, but it's just so pretty."

"It certainly is pretty!" Maggie agreed.

Sarah dished up the food into the china bowls and put them on the table. She uncorked a bottle of wine and set it on the table, also.

The door opened and Nathan and John were stunned by what they saw.

Sarah ran to John and looked up at him smiling. "Do you like it? Are you surprised?"

John bent down and gave Sarah a hug. "You really *DO* intend to spoil me, don't you?" he whispered in her ear.

She reached up and pulled his head down to her, kissing him on the cheek. "You bet I do!" she whispered back, and then giggled.

Nathan and Maggie stifled their own giggles, watching John and Sarah crooning to each other.

After dinner, as the girls cleaned up the dishes and cleaned off the table, Nathan read the Bible out loud. It had been a Stillman family tradition for as long as the boys could remember, and one which they both wanted to continue.

When the work was done, and scriptures had been read, it was time to decide who would sleep in the loft, and who would sleep in the bed.

"Let's draw straws," Nathan suggested. "I'll take some straw and cut it. We'll let the girls choose pieces and then see who gets the longest piece. She'll be the one to choose where she wants to sleep. How does that sound?"

"Let's do it," John said.

John cut the straw in four varying lengths, and handed them to Nathan. Maggie and Sarah each got to choose two pieces of straw. Then they compared lengths. Sarah had the longest piece, so she got to choose. To everyone's surprise, she chose the loft.

"Well, Sarah, Honey ... there's no bed up there," John warned.

"I brought my feather bed," she said, grinning up at John.

"Now don't you just think of everything," John teased.

Nathan helped John carry Sarah's things up the ladder to the loft, and get them situated. John had not only put in a floor, and built the walls, but he had even fashioned a type of trap door for privacy, never thinking how convenient it would end up being.

Sarah went up first and changed into her nightgown. She snuggled down in the softness of the featherbed and pulled the quilt up around her. She waited.

Soon John appeared at the top of the ladder, closing the trap door behind him. He turned the lantern down low, and pulled his shirt off over his head. He stood there looking at Sarah, and decided to leave his trousers on – just to be safe. Sarah was in awe of his perfect physique. He was the most beautiful man she had ever seen, and she thanked God for such a wonderful birthday present.

He scooted in, under the quilt beside her, and relaxed with his arms behind his head.

"Happy birthday, Sarah," he whispered.

Sarah snuggled up to John, laying her head on his broad warm chest. "Thank you, John. You made it a perfect birthday," she whispered back.

John felt a restless stirring in his body, as Sarah cuddled against him. Her lips were on his bare chest, now.

Chapter 17 - Lost Control

Morning came quickly and John's body was accustomed to waking up with the rising sun. Even without windows in the loft, John knew instinctively that it was morning. He opened his eyes slowly, surprised to find that somehow during the night he had changed position. He found himself on his right side, up against Sarah who was also on her right side. He had his right arm under Sarah's head and his left arm around her. His hand rested on her stomach. That, in its self, wouldn't have been disturbing to John, but his hand was on bare flesh. He wasn't sure how Sarah's nightgown had been pulled up around her waist, but her hips were against his groin, and it seemed he was holding her securely in that position. His lips were at the nape of her neck, and he inhaled the enchanting scent of her hair, which seemed to be a combination of lilac and fresh air. He didn't dare move. He didn't want to wake her. He wanted this moment to linger a little longer. It felt so right; so comfortable.

Sarah stirred. John held his breath, hoping she wouldn't break the spell. Her hand found his and she covered it with her own, pressing it harder against her stomach. She moved her hips against him and moaned softly. John caught his breath in surprise. He decided she must be dreaming. He gently kissed the back of her neck, and he felt a shiver run the entire length of her body. Again, her

245

hips moved against his groin. Something stirred deep in his gut. He could feel it growing. He knew he should get out of bed and leave Sarah alone, but his flesh wouldn't allow him. He just wanted to enjoy this feeling for a few more minutes. Her body was warm and her skin felt so soft on his hand. He breathed in her scent one more time, and one more time he kissed the nape of her neck. One more time she moved against him. That was it. It took every bit of self-discipline John could muster. In one quick movement, he rolled off the featherbed and onto the floor. He laid there trying to control his pounding heart.

"John," Sarah whispered, "come back to bed."

"Sarah Honey, it's time for me to get up. I've got chores to do," he said in a hoarse voice. He couldn't believe she was awake. Neither was he sure she had been asleep a few minutes ago.

Sarah sat up in the bed and looked down, where John was sprawled out on the floor. She grinned at him impishly. "John, maybe you're too honorable for your own wellbeing."

"What's that supposed to mean?" he groaned.

Sarah crawled over John's side of the bed, and onto the floor where he lay. "It means I wish you would kiss me one time, before you go to work."

Sarah's long red hair was in tangles, hanging down over her shoulders and across her face. John reached up and brushed her hair away from her eyes. Grasping the back of her neck, he pulled her face down to his and found her lips with his mouth. It was a demanding kiss. He kissed her in anger for teasing him. John pulled her over, and on top of him, yanking her nightgown up to her waist. He grabbed her bare hips in his massive hands, and held her hard against him, allowing her to feel the urgency she had intentionally incited. She cried out; his erection was bruising her, but John's kiss stifled her cry. He rolled her over onto her back and picked her up, tossing her into the featherbed.

"Now, go back to sleep, Sarah," he said coldly. He dressed in a hurry and climbed down the ladder.

Nathan and Maggie were already up and dressed. The coffee was made and the fire was blazing. Sunshine was beginning to filter in through the windows. Nathan handed John a hot cup of coffee, and John gratefully accepted it. He sat down in the rocker and stared at the fire, deep in thought.

"Is there something wrong, John?" Nathan asked.

"Nothing I want to talk about," John replied.

Nathan put his coat on and Maggie pulled her cloak around her shoulders. "We're going out to the barn, John," Nathan said, picking up a bucket. "I'm going to teach Maggie how to milk our cow. Would you like to come along?"

"No," John said bluntly.

Once John was alone in the cabin, he climbed back up the ladder to the loft.

"Sarah, please come down here. I want to talk to you."

In a few minutes, Sarah emerged from the loft, and climbed down the narrow ladder. Her eyes were red and swollen, and it was obvious she had been crying.

She stood quietly at the base of the ladder, not sure what John wanted her to do. She stared blankly at the floor.

John took one look at his beautiful wife, and immediately felt agonizing pangs of guilt for what he had done to her. He approached her slowly, but she backed away from him.

"Sarah, I'm truly sorry... I honestly didn't mean to hurt you," John said in a low voice. "It's just that you were trifling with me. I felt like you were tryin' to get me to dishonor myself." John reached out his hand to her. "Please, Sarah ..."

Sarah looked up slowly. Her sad eyes penetrated John's soul. "You don't want me. It's all right. I'm sorry, I thought I could please you," she said in a quiet voice.

John caught her into his arms and held her close to him. "You're wrong, Sarah! God knows I *DO* want you." He tilted her chin up, and forced her to look at him. "I just want to make sure you NEVER do that out of gratitude, or because you feel obligated, or for any reason other than love. Don't you understand?" He felt tears welling up in his own eyes. "I promised you I wouldn't touch you – you're the one who said we wouldn't consummate this marriage ..., remember?"

"That was before you kissed me the second time," she whispered.

"Oh no! Not that again!" John hugged Sarah tightly. "You can't know whether you're really in love based on a kiss!" he said. "Pure lust can masquerade as love. You just can't base *LOVE* on a kiss!"

"Yes you can, John," she spoke adamantly. "If you can kiss me one more time, and then tell me you don't love me, then I promise you... I'll not bother you about it again."

Deep in his gut, John knew she was right. It just wasn't logical, and he was a man who based everything on logic. This, however, defied logic. He knew exactly what she was talking about. He'd felt it, but he refused to admit it. John Stillman was a stubborn Swede.

"OK, Sarah ... explain to me – how I'm supposed to judge whether I'm in love, by kissin' you!" John demanded.

"If you kiss me, and you don't want to ever stop... if the whole world disappears while you're kissing me... if your body aches and you wish you could just melt into my skin and be part of me... if you become intoxicated... if your heart feels as if it's swelling up and may burst. That's how you'll know if you're in love with me."

"Is that how *YOU* feel, when you kiss *ME*," John asked. It was a sincere question.

"Yes."

"How do you know it's not just LUST?" John asked, trying to sound serious.

"Because it feels so pure. It feels like something you would want to last forever... not for just one encounter. It feels as if it's meant to be – as if God himself ordained it."

"OK, Sarah... I'm going to do this one more time, and see what happens."

John slowly lowered his lips to hers. He kissed her gently, barely allowing his mouth to touch hers.

He wanted more. He wrapped his arms around her and held her tightly against him. He kissed her deeply, and it became more urgent. He wanted her closer, but it was impossible, he couldn't get her close enough to satisfy his craving for her. His kiss became a burning passion, and the world disappeared. Nothing existed but this kiss. As Sarah responded to his passion, he became intoxicated by her intensity. Suddenly he felt that his heart would burst inside his chest if he couldn't possess her. Without reservation, he lowered her to the floor and covered her with his body. Nothing else mattered, as long as he could have her. He pushed his trousers down and raised her skirt. It was clear to John; that Sarah wanted him as badly as he needed her. He drove himself into her warm flesh, and she accepted him. She grabbed at his hips to get more of him. He raised her legs so he could go deeper into her. Suddenly the entire world exploded and they spun totally out of control.

Nathan opened the door just as this was happening. Quickly and quietly, he closed it again, before Maggie could see inside. The two hurried back to the barn, not wanting to interrupt or embarrass John and Sarah.

John collapsed onto his side, trying to catch his breath. He couldn't believe the intensity of their lovemaking.

"Sarah... I love you," he whispered.

"I know." She smiled.

John managed to stand up. "Oh my God, Sarah... You're bleeding! I didn't even think about that!" John said looking down at the floor where

Sarah was lying. "That's too much! You're not supposed to bleed so much!"

Sarah giggled. "You're just too passionate!"

"You're a devil, Sarah! Your brother was right. He said you were a she-devil."

"He's always called me that."

"Well, we've got to figure out if you're OK!" John said. He was on the verge of panic. "I'm so sorry, Sarah Honey... I wasn't thinking! You completely messed up my mind! I was just out of control! I should have been careful!"

Sarah struggled to her feet. She was dazed and weak, but otherwise she felt fine.

"John, I'm all right. I think this is normal," Sarah said, looking for something to use to clean up the floor. "Most people make love in a bed, you know? It probably soaks into the sheets, instead of making puddles on the floor. Oh, I hope Nathan and Maggie don't walk in!"

"If you can climb the ladder, Sarah ... you go up to the loft and change your clothes. I'm taking you home, to your brother's house. We're going to have Doc Mathison check you and make sure you're OK. I couldn't live with myself if I've really injured you."

"John ... Dr. Mathison is coming here ... probably tomorrow. Why don't we just wait and see. If I keep bleeding, we'll go today. Please calm down!"

At that moment, the door opened and Maggie walked in with the bucket of milk. She took one look around and went back outside. "Nathan, you need to return to the barn, and stay there 'til I tell you. Don't ask me any questions... Just go back and wait."

Nathan turned back toward the barn and Maggie went back into the cabin.

"Oh God, Maggie... I'm so sorry you had to see this!" Sarah said. She was beside herself with embarrassment.

John was extremely distressed.

"What happened, John?" Maggie asked, although she was pretty sure she already knew.

"Damn it!" John cursed. "I just didn't think! I forgot about Sarah bein' a virgin! I'm such an ass!" John covered his face with his hands. "I think I hurt her bad, Maggie! I don't think she's supposed to bleed so much."

"Well, it sure looks like a lot, to me," Maggie said, looking at the floor and then looking at Sarah's skirt. "I think you tore her up real bad."

Now, tears were running down John's cheeks. He pulled Sarah over to him and held her close to him. "I'm so sorry, Honey!" He said it over and over.

"Sarah, I think you should sit down," Maggie said, pointing at the blood dripping onto the floor from beneath the girl's skirt. "I'm going to send Nathan to get Dr. Mathison. How long will it take for him to get there?"

"It'll take an hour or more! Isn't there something YOU can do to stop the bleeding?" John pleaded.

"I don't think so," Maggie replied. "Sarah, sit down!"

Sarah obediently sat down on the chair. "I really think I'll be all right, Maggie."

John heard a horse outside and he ran to the door. "Oh thank God! Dr. Mathison is here!" he exclaimed, throwing the door wide open.

Maggie ran outside to tell Dr. Mathison what had happened, before he walked into the disaster. "John, go and keep Nathan company in the barn ... right now. I'll let you know when you both can come back in," Maggie shouted.

Doc Mathison walked into the cabin with a huge grin on his face. "Well, well, Sarah. Looks like John did a bang-up job deflowering you!" He chuckled gleefully. "High time someone succeeded!"

"That's not funny, Doc," Sarah growled.

"Well, I hate to have to embarrass you, girl ... but you're gonna have to let me take a look at the damage. Maggie ... put an old blanket or something on that bed." Dr. Mathison ladled some hot water into a bowl, and found a clean cloth. He carried them over to the night table. Sarah climbed up onto the bed and covered her face in humiliation, while the doc examined her. He cleaned the blood away and then waited to see if the bleeding would stop.

"Well, doc?" Sarah spoke through her hands which still covered her face.

"Well, Sarah ... you're torn all right. Good thing it's external – there doesn't seem to be any damage internally. I can stitch it up, or we can wait and see how it heals. Didn't you feel that tearing? Must have been some really wild passion going on here! I can't believe you didn't stop!"

"Shut up, Doc!" Sarah snarled. "It didn't hurt!"

"Must have been some tryst!" Doc laughed. "I've heard about passion like that, but this is the first time I've actually seen the results of it."

It took all of Maggie's will to stifle her giggles, knowing Nathan actually saw it happening.

"Doc, if you tell my brother about this... I swear I'll hunt you down and kill you!!"

"Now Sarah, be nice!" Dr. Mathison grinned. "Well ... what do you want to do? Do you want me to repair it, or leave it?"

"I don't know, Doc? What would you suggest?" Sarah started to cry.

"Well, if I stitch it up, you'll heal faster, but the next time you and John go at it, you'll just end up the same way. If we leave it to heal on its own ... it may take longer to mend, but you probably won't get all ripped up the next time you make love. Which, may I suggest ... you don't do again for a couple of weeks! Stay off your feet for at least three days, too"

"Ok Doc," Sarah conceded. "If that's what you think is best, then that's what we'll do."

"Well, you'll probably continue to bleed a little, but unless you start gushing, you don't need to worry. When's your next menses?"

"Um ..., about two weeks from now," Sarah said.

"Oh dear God," Doc groaned. "I'll bet you don't see that one. Didn't anybody ever talk to you about fertility? Don't you know this was the very worst time for you to have sex? I'd bet my life, you're already pregnant!"

"Oh Lord!" Maggie cried out.

Doc turned around and looked at Maggie through squinted eyes. "Please don't tell me... Maggie didn't you think about that either? So now I've probably got to worry about both of you being pregnant. These Stillman brothers are in for lots of little surprises, if you girls can't think ahead!"

At this point, Maggie and Sarah were both in tears.

"Well girls, I think I'd better go out to the barn and make sure the boys are still in one piece. I can't imagine how rough you two might have been on them!" Dr. Mathison laughed all the way out the door.

"Sarah, how did life get so complicated?" Maggie asked, sitting down on the side of the bed.

"I'm not sure, Maggie... But if we're both pregnant, it means we got that way one day apart. That might be fun ... both of us having babies at the same time!"

"Oh yea... Loads of laughs!" Maggie said, wiping at her tears.

Doc Mathison walked into the barn laughing so hard he could hardly stand. Nathan was sitting on a barrel and John had one of the draft horses in the cross ties brushing him down. Both men looked up when the doc came in. The anticipation was tangible.

"Well, John... What the hell were you thinking?!" Doc asked, giving the man a critical look.

"I wasn't," John replied, his face turning red. "Is Sarah goin' to be OK?"

"Well she'll heal ... but only if you can control yourself for a couple of weeks," Doc said.

"Doc, I tried to control the situation," John said, throwing the brush down, and rubbing his hands over his face. "She's a bit more than I can handle. I swore I wasn't goin' to touch her! I don't even know how it happened!"

Dr. Mathison bent over double; laughing. When he finally caught his breath, he sat down hard, on a stack of bags of grain, and pulled his glasses off. "John ... if we were talking about any other woman, I would call you a liar. But I've known Sarah for a long time, and I know exactly what you're saying!" He laughed harder. "Problem here ... is .... Sarah got more than she could handle." Doc slapped his legs, and laughed so hard he cried.

Nathan looked at them both, trying to figure out what he'd missed. "Will someone explain to me, why my brother would vow NOT to touch his own wife?!"

"NO!" John said bluntly.

"Well... You leave Sarah alone for about three weeks. She's torn up pretty bad, but she'll be fine. She needs to stay off her feet for a couple of days, too."

"Doc ..." John hesitated. "I just hope she'll leave ME alone. She teases me... She knows exactly which buttons to push... She drove me crazy this mornin'. I swear, I didn't have any intentions of doing that!"

"Well, John ... at least she's not a virgin anymore. You surely did take care of that. You boys have another problem to worry about, though." Doc wiped his eyes, and put his glasses back on. "I have a feeling you're both going to be fathers. Probably about July. You're both idiots!"

Nathan jumped to his feet in shock. "What are you talking about, Doc?"

"Seems nobody in this family knows anything about the birds and the bees!" Doc said. "Both those

256

girls are fertile this week ... and you boys serviced them both at just the wrong time. If they're not both pregnant, I'll eat my hat."

Nathan and John looked at each other, blankly.

"Oh well ... that's how I make my living." Doc laughed. "Looks like you boys will be my best customers!" Dr. Mathison pushed his glasses up. "Yep... If you're gonna dance to the music ... you're gonna pay the piper!"

Maggie walked into the barn, still crying. Nathan put his arms around her and tried to comfort her. "I know, Maggie. Doc just told us." He kissed her on the forehead. "No sense worrying until we find out for sure. Besides, I like kids ... and you said you were going to give me lots of children to help out on OUR farm. Do you remember?"

Maggie managed a smile. "It's just so soon... I wanted to help you get the crops in, and put up the fencing for the sheep ..."

"Don't worry about that, Maggie," John said, "I'll help Nathan out with all of those chores."

"You're a sweetheart, John. Thank you." Maggie looked over at the doctor. "Are you staying for dinner, Doc?"

"If that's an invitation, then the answer is YES. I'd love to stay for dinner," Doc said.

"Nathan, will you cut me some venison?" Maggie asked, looking up at her handsome husband. "We'll have a venison stew. Does that sound OK with you men?"

"Come on Maggie," Nathan said. "I'll get the meat."

Once Maggie and Nathan had left for the smokehouse, Dr. Mathison could speak freely with John. "Looks to me like Tom made a good match, John."

"It's amazing, Doc. I wouldn't have believed it myself, but I think I fell in love with Sarah the minute I saw her. Do you reckon that's possible?" John picked up the brush and went back to brushing the horse.

"I've seen it before, John."

"Seriously?"

"Yep. It happened to ME," Doc said. "I jumped right in and never looked back. I'd still be married, but lost her about fifteen years ago, along with my newborn son. I don't want to scare you ... but childbirth is risky business."

"When I saw what I did to her, I hated myself, Doc!" John shook his head in exasperation. "I still can't figure out how she got the best of me!"

"Um... John... I don't think she got the best of you. I think she got the *worst* of you!" Doc laughed. "Don't beat yourself up anymore about this. You didn't mean to hurt her. She's going to be fine, and you've got to remember ... it took both of you to get yourselves into this situation. Looks like you're going to have to be the strong one, now. That's a bull-headed woman you've got!"

"Yep, and I'm gonna keep her!" John grinned.

When Doc and John walked into the cabin, Maggie was busy preparing the stew, and the table was set with Sarah's finery.

"Where's Sarah?" John asked, looking around the cabin.

"She went up to the loft to lie down," Maggie said, stirring the pot which was hanging over the fire.

John disappeared up the ladder and into the loft.

"Sarah?" He turned the lantern's wick higher, so he could see his wife, lying on the featherbed, snuggled into the quilt. He walked over and sat down on the side of the bed. "Sarah Honey, how are you feelin'?"

"I'm fine."

John sat there in silence, not sure what to do. Sarah finally emerged from under the quilt, and crawled up onto his lap, putting her arms around his neck. She hugged him.

"Doc says we might have a baby," John said, brushing the curls away from Sarah's face.

"I know... Wouldn't it be wonderful?"

John was surprised by Sarah's reply. He expected her to be unhappy about the prospect like Maggie was. "I really love you Sarah!" John exclaimed.

"I know."

"I would love to kiss you, Sarah Honey ... but I'm afraid to. After where that got us this morning. You know?" John whispered, nuzzling his face against Sarah's neck.

"Kiss me anyway," she sighed, hugging him tighter.

"Oh no!" John scolded, trying to escape from her grasp.

Sarah wrestled him down onto the bed, giggling, and she kissed him full on the mouth. It was a long, soft, gentle kiss. It was the most loving kiss John had ever experienced. It wasn't a passionate kiss, but a kiss that spoke volumes to his soul. That kiss told him secrets about love, and life, and the hopes and dreams two people in love can share. They relaxed together in silence. It was a warm, comforting silence. Neither of them needed to speak. Being together was all that was.

"Dinner's ready," Maggie called up to the loft.

"You go ahead... Sarah and I will eat later," John answered. "Just make sure and save us some."

Nathan said grace, and Maggie served the stew. After dinner, Doc and Nathan sat by the fire discussing Nathan's plans for the farm, come spring time. Dr. Mathison seemed to be more excited than Maggie was, when it came to the Merino sheep.

"I don't know a thing about sheep, Doc," Nathan said, pouring a little whiskey into the doctor's cup.

"Seems your wife's been studying up on raising sheep. I reckon she'll teach you what ya need to know."

"Doc, did you have enough to eat?" Maggie asked.

"Maggie, my girl ... that was a fine dinner, but if I ate any more, I think I'd burst. Thank you," Doc said, patting his protruding stomach. "Oh! I nearly forgot... Tom McCollough wanted me to tell all of you ... you're invited to his place for Thanksgiving dinner on Thursday."

"I can't believe it's Thanksgiving time already!" Maggie exclaimed. "Too much going on, I guess. I hadn't even thought about it."

"Tell Tom we'll be there, Doc," Nathan said. "That's really good of him to think of us. I mean … I know Sarah's his sister and all, but it's really nice of him to include Maggie and me."

Nathan and Maggie walked outside with Dr. Mathison.

"I sure hate to eat and run, like this, but I don't want to be on that path after dark," Doc said. "Say my good-bye's to John and Sarah, will you?"

"Sure will, Doc," Nathan said, shaking Dr. Mathison's hand. "Now you take care!"

Maggie gave the doc a big hug, and slipped a piece of mincemeat pie, wrapped up in a cloth, into his pocket. Doc winked at her, climbed onto his horse and left.

Chapter 18 – Trouble in Paradise

"Three down, and three to go," Nathan said, wiping his sleeve across his brow. "John, I really appreciate your help. I plan on payin' you for your work. I want ya to know that."

"I don't need paid! You and I are going to be doing a lot of work together around here."

Nathan shoved his hands into his pockets and grinned at his brother. "Good Lord, John ... do you realize that altogether we've got twenty-four hundred acres ... right here in this gorgeous valley?!"

"That's one hell of a lot of work!" John laughed.

"That's one hell of a piece of paradise!" Nathan added.

John cocked his head to one side, thoughtfully. "And then there's your sled business... Speaking of which ... what are we goin' to do with them once they're all made? Are the buyers comin' here to pick them up, or what?"

"I figure we can pull the sleds behind us when we go to Tom McCollough's place on Thanksgiving. The fellas can pick em up there. Tom can collect the money I'm owed and I'll just get it later," Nathan answered. "Let's go get some more wood, big brother."

In the cabin, Maggie was churning the cream; making butter. Fresh cornbread, baking in a pot on the hearth, smelled wonderful.

"Maggie ...," Sarah called from the loft.

Maggie rushed up the ladder, fearing that something was wrong.

"Maggie, I've been thinking... See that trunk in the corner?" Sarah was sitting on the featherbed, cross-legged like an Indian; pointing to the trunk.

"Oh... Sarah you scared me! I worry so about you!"

Sarah giggled. "You are the sweetest thing, Maggie! But please don't worry about me. I'm just fine." Sarah brushed her hair out of her face. "Now... If you look in that trunk, you'll find a bunch of dresses. Oh... And there're shoes, and bags, and cloaks... You can find things that match. God knows I sure don't need all of them. I want you to choose four or five, for yourself... You can have them. If they don't fit, we'll just do some seamstress miracles, and make them fit!" Sarah pretended to sew the air. "Back in Virginia, Pa owns a big plantation. He raises cotton and tobacco. He makes a fortune every year ... way more than anyone needs to live on! Anyway, Ma and Pa always threw big parties, and elegant dresses were ... um ... like an essential. I mean every well-bred young lady had to have the BEST dress in the county!" Sarah laughed, thinking about the shallowness of the idea. "Honestly Maggie ... I don't know how those people got their priorities and their values so messed up." She shook her head sadly. "I've learned a lot since I came out here to live with my brother Tom and his family. I've learned what's *REALLY* important. And I've learned what good people have always known... It's what's in a person's heart that makes a person good. Not money, land, livestock, and certainly NOT clothes!"

"... Sounds as if you've grown wise, beyond your years! It takes an awful lot of fortitude to give up the kind of lifestyle you were used to, and then have to learn to survive out here in this wilderness." Maggie stared into Sarah's eyes, and marveled at her sincerity. "But still ... Sarah ... you have to be crazy to give away beautiful clothes like this," Maggie said rummaging through the trunk.

"Hey! Let's play dress-up!!" Sarah said, crawling to the side of the bed. "Let's pick out what we're going to wear to Tom's Thanksgiving party!"

"Well, how about I play dress-up, and you stay right there in that bed, so by Thursday you can be up and around, Sarah. Since you already know these things fit *you*, we'll just decide what you'll wear... You don't need to be up on your feet trying on clothes!" Maggie pulled a beautiful emerald green satin dress out of the trunk and held it up in front of her. "Oooo... This is the most beautiful color I've ever seen!"

"Maggie! That shade of green matches your eyes perfectly!!" Sarah shrieked with excitement. "Nathan will lose his mind when he sees you in that!"

"Nathan lost his mind years ago, and it had nothing to do with me!" Maggie giggled.

"Try it on Maggie. If it needs hemmed or anything, I can do it while I'm sitting here doing absolutely nothing else," Sarah said, pursing her lips into a pout.

Sarah asked Maggie to find the pink brocade dress, and the matching shoes she wanted to wear.

"Sarah," Maggie said, looking at her sister-in-law, who was sitting there in her nightgown, resembling a straggly-haired orphan. "I have to tell you... I think you're the most genuine person I've ever met. I mean ... being raised the way you were... I mean growing up in such an affluent family ... I would expect you to be spoiled, conceited, and weak... But you're quite the opposite! I really respect you. I also understand why John is so in love with you!"

"Oh Maggie ... do you really think he loves me?"

"What kind of a question is that!" Maggie asked incredulously. "I've known John all my life, and I've never seen him dote over anyone the way he makes over you. It's just not in his nature. It's almost like you've managed to tame the beast!"

Sarah explained the situation to Maggie, from the beginning to the present. Maggie was shocked and amused, listening to Sarah describe the wedding; along with the hilarious events of that day. The girls giggled and laughed until they were worn out.

"What a story that will be to tell your grandchildren!" Maggie said, giving Sarah a big hug.

"I know, Maggie." Sarah tossed her hair back and grinned. "Just please don't tell Nathan. Let's let John do that, when he feels like he's ready."

"I won't say a word, Sarah. I promise. But that sure explains a lot!" Maggie laughed. "Oops! I completely forgot the cornbread! I hope it's not burned!" Maggie hurried down the ladder.

Before Maggie reached the floor, Nathan snatched her off of the ladder, flung the girl over his shoulder like a sack of potatoes, and marched out of the cabin.

"Take care of that cornbread, John," he called, on the way out the door. "Maggie and I have something to take care of in the smokehouse."

"Nathan! What are you doing? It's cold out here!" Maggie scolded, as she squirmed to get loose.

"Don't worry, Maggie... I'm going to warm you up in just a minute." He said, playfully.

"Oh no you won't, Nathan Stillman!" Maggie shrieked. "You know what Dr. Mathison said about this week!"

Nathan set his wife down on her feet and frowned. "But Maggie ... it's probably too late by now. This is like shuttin' the barn door after the horse already ran away!"

"Well maybe it is, Nathan. But, I'd just as soon not take any chances!"

"Well hell! Looks like it's gonna be a damned cold week!" He caught Maggie's hand and led her back toward the cabin.

When Nathan and Maggie returned, John was standing at the table, slicing the hot cornbread. He looked up in surprise. "Good Lord, Nathan! That was fast!" John said, and then chuckled.

"Shut up, John!" Nathan barked.

"OK," John muttered, throwing a spoonful of butter on one piece of the sliced bread, and taking a big bite. "Maggie! This is delicious!" he said, with his mouth full.

Maggie didn't answer, but returned to the butter churn, and began ramming it with a vengeance.

"I'm goin' back out and work on those sleds," Nathan growled. He grabbed a piece of the cornbread and left.

"John?" It was Sarah. She was backing down the ladder; still in her nightgown.

John went over and swung his wife down off the ladder and into his arms. "You ... little girl, are supposed to stay off your feet!" he scolded, grinning at his wife.

"Well, I'm hungry ... and it's dark and gloomy up there, John!" she pouted. "I wish we had a window in that loft." She gave John a big kiss on the cheek.

"Come spring, I'll build you your own home, Sarah. I'll make sure you have lots of windows," he said, trying to see her eyes through the red curls falling every which way over her face. He placed Sarah on a chair and knelt down in front of her. Smoothing the ringlets back and away from her face, he leaned forward and kissed her gently on the lips.

"Sarah, I'll warm the stew for you," Maggie said, standing up.

"It's OK, Maggie," John said. "I'll fix her something to eat."

Sarah had already discovered the warm cornbread on the table. "This is the best cornbread I've ever tasted, Maggie!"

"I'm glad you like it. It was my Mama's special recipe," Maggie said, sitting back down at the churn.

"John, did Maggie tell you we have a surprise for you and Nathan, come Thanksgiving?" Sarah giggled.

"Oh no... Sarah, don't you think I've had enough surprises lately?!" John joked.

It was Thanksgiving.

The Stillman household buzzed with preparation. The chores were finished and the cow had been milked. Although Nathan and John were ready to leave, Maggie and Sarah were still in the loft.

"I'll go get the team hitched to the sleigh, Nathan," John said, pulling his buckskin jacket on. "We'll get those sleds tied up to the back, whenever you're ready." John opened the door to go outside. "I thought it looked like more snow! Look at this, Nathan."

"Well this should be fun," Nathan said wryly, peering over John's shoulder, and looking at the big white snowflakes drifting down through the cold air. "Looks like a wet snow to me. How do we stay dry? It's an hour's ride!"

"Hey! Where's your sense of adventure, little brother? We'll just use the canvas from the wagon. Don't you worry – I'll take care of everything," John said, bounding out of the cabin.

"That woman sure has changed you," Nathan muttered under his breath.

"He's certainly a different character, isn't he?" It was Maggie.

Nathan turned around to see his wife standing at the base of the ladder. He had never seen Maggie dressed in such extravagant finery. "Maggie!" Nathan exclaimed, "where on earth did you get that dress?!

Maggie spun around in a circle; smiling and showing off the flowing silk. "Isn't it lovely, Nathan?!" she squealed.

"NO! It's cut entirely too low, Maggie!" Nathan said sternly. "Do you want men gawking at your breasts?!!"

Maggie's expression changed from joy to disappointment in an instant.

"No, Nathan," Maggie said, looking hurt and confused. "I don't want men gawking at my breasts." She covered her cleavage with both hands. "I wanted YOU to think I looked beautiful." Maggie's eyes were filling with tears, as she stood there devastated by her husband's disapproving glare. "I'm sorry, Nathan, I'll go change."

Nathan grabbed his coat, without saying another word, and stormed out of the cabin.

Maggie obediently changed into one of the simple cotton dresses Caroline had given her. Maggie's sobbing brought Sarah down from the loft. She was dressed in the beautiful pink brocade dress, which also had a low cut bodice. Sarah couldn't understand what had gone so terribly wrong.

"Oh Maggie ... this is my fault. I'm so sorry!" Sarah said, trying to comfort Maggie. "I didn't think Nathan would object. I thought you looked gorgeous. And you look lovely in that dress, too!"

Sarah disappeared back to the loft, only to emerge a few minutes later in a dress similar to Maggie's.

"Sarah! Don't be silly! Go put that pretty pink dress back on!" Maggie said, trying to smile.

Sarah giggled. "Oh NO!! I'm not about to do any more damage to this Thanksgiving! I've caused enough trouble ... but then that's what I'm notorious for." Sarah scurried back up to the loft, and began rummaging through the trunk. "Look at these cloaks, Maggie," she called down to her sister-in-law. "They'll look nice with our dresses! And these bonnets? Come take a peek – Tell me what you think?"

Maggie climbed up the ladder and looked into the loft. "I think you're an angel, Sarah!!" She grinned.

"Well I've been called a lot of names, but that's never been one of them!" Sarah laughed.

The cabin door opened and Nathan walked in. Maggie hurried back down from the loft. She stood silently at the base of the ladder. Nathan looked Maggie over, and nodded approvingly. "That's much better Maggie. Are you ladies ready to go?"

Maggie and Sarah put on the cloaks and bonnets, and went outside. Nathan lifted Sarah into the front seat of the sleigh, beside John, then he helped Maggie into the back, climbing in beside her. The snow was falling harder, now, but John had stretched the canvas over the wagon frame which fit the sleigh perfectly.

John slipped his arm around his wife and smiled at her lovingly. "Well ... what about the surprise you have for me and Nathan?"

"Oh Lord, John!! It didn't turn out to be such a good surprise after all." Sarah turned to look back at Nathan. "It was my fault," she said. "I had some really pretty party dresses I thought Maggie and I could wear to Tom's Thanksgiving party. They were cut pretty low, and I just didn't think." Sarah looked back at Nathan and Maggie again. "I'm so sorry, Nathan."

"Low cut dresses?" John asked, raising one eyebrow. "I always thought dresses would be perfect if they had NO bodice at all!" he joked.

"You're bad!" Sarah said, slapping John on the arm.

"... Sounds to me like you're the one who is bad!" John laughed out loud. "Did little brother lose his temper?"

"Well, I don't think he realized it was *MY* idea. Maggie got a good scolding," Sarah said, apologetically.

"Yep... You really are a she-devil, Sarah!" John chuckled.

Sarah giggled. "That must be why you love me!"

"Hmmm ... maybe," John said, looking thoughtful.

With all the joking in the front seat of the sleigh, the silence in the back seat was colder than the icy wind blowing through the valley.

When the sleigh and the big black Percherons arrived at Tom McCollough's farm, Tom ran outside to welcome them. Nathan had tied four of the finished sleds to the back of the sleigh, for Tom to disperse to the buyers. Upon seeing the literal "train" approaching, Tom couldn't believe his eyes.

"Well now... that *IS* a creative method!" he shouted. "You never cease to amaze me, Nathan Stillman." Tom helped everyone down out of the sleigh, and slapped Nathan on the back. "Nathan, I'll have Robby put the sleds in the barn. I already know why you brought them here," he said. "I was actually going to suggest it myself! Great minds think alike ... and all that stuff."

"Happy Thanksgiving, Tom," John said, grabbing Tom's hand and shaking it energetically.

"And to you, John!" Tom said, studying John's smiling face, and then looking at his sister's radiant smile. "I guess this means you're not angry with me, John?"

"Are you kidding?!" John laughed. "I love you, Tom!" He grabbed Tom and gave him a big kiss on the cheek. Both men laughed hysterically, with Tom falling to the ground in his usual uncontrollable fit of laughter.

"Tom, thank you for the invitation," Nathan said, reaching down, catching Tom's hand and pulling him back up on his feet. "Happy Thanksgiving!" Nathan stepped aside gesturing toward Maggie, "This is my wife, Maggie."

Tom extended his hand to Maggie. "Aw... Maggie! It's so nice to finally meet you. I've heard a lot about you, girl." Tom grinned. "Of course Doc is heart-broken... I don't think he wanted to lose his new assistant!"

"I'm pleased to meet you, Mr. McCollough," Maggie said, forcing a smile. "I want you to know, I think your sister is one of the nicest people I've ever met."

"What ... that she-devil? Maggie, you don't know her yet... Just wait a while," Tom said, laughing. "Or just ask John. I'm sure he knows, by now!"

Sarah was standing behind Tom when he said it. In one smooth motion, she put her foot behind Tom and pulled him off balance. Tom tripped, falling backwards into a snow-bank.

"See what I mean?!" he grunted, trying to stand back up in the slippery snow.

After dinner, Nathan discovered Maggie sitting in a corner all alone, watching the falling snow, from the window.

"Maggie... There you are. I've been looking everywhere for you." Nathan sat down beside his wife. "Why aren't you visiting with the rest of the women?"

"I just don't feel like visiting," Maggie answered coldly.

"Look... If this is about the damned dress ..."

"No, Nathan. It's not about the dress. It's about your *attitude.*"

"Maggie, don't be so touchy!"

"Nathan, don't be such a pompous ass!"

Nathan didn't say another word. He simply got up and walked away to join the others.

The ride home was warm and carefree in the front seat of the sleigh, but the atmosphere in the back seat was tense. John and Sarah giggled and snuggled, while Nathan and Maggie kept their distance from each other. John pulled the sleigh up to the cabin and lifted Sarah down.

"I'll take the horses up to the barn and get them brushed and fed for the night," Nathan said. "You go ahead inside. The fire probably needs a couple of logs. I'll be in shortly."

Maggie was about to climb down from the sleigh, when John realized that his brother had completely ignored the girl. John stepped over and lifted Maggie down. He could see the tears running down her cheeks, glistening in the muted light from the setting sun, which was slipping down behind the hills.

Nathan unhitched the team and led them up the path toward the barn.

"Don't cry Maggie," John said, putting his arm around her shoulders.

"Oh Maggie... I am so very sorry. This is all my fault!" Sarah whispered.

"It's OK," Maggie said. "Maybe tomorrow will be a better day."

Inside, Sarah went straight up to the loft, while John tended the fire.

"Maggie, I'll see you in the morning, girl," John said, mounting the ladder.

Maggie waited until the little trap door closed, then she quickly changed into her nightgown and crawled into bed.

Nathan came back hours later. He sat down in the rocker by the fire and picked up his Bible. As he read, it was impossible for him to concentrate on the book. He put the Bible down and grabbed the jug of whiskey. Nathan sat for a long time, drinking the liquor and staring blankly into the fire. He looked over at Maggie, sleeping soundly in the bed. His body ached to make love to his wife. He was upset and confused; not sure what he'd done to make Maggie so angry with him. He drank some more. After a while, Nathan passed out; there in his rocking chair; where he woke up, as the sun rose the next morning.

A vicious circle was taking its toll on the marriage. It became an every night occurrence, as Nathan began drinking more heavily – more often. As the weeks went by, Maggie became more disenchanted with Nathan; having to put up with her husband's nightly ritual of drunkenness.

It was no secret, in the Stillman household, that Nathan wanted children right away, but Maggie would have no part of it. Because of Maggie's aversion to rushing into "motherhood" there was one week every month, that made Nathan's mood particularly ugly. He loathed the fact that his wife could wield such power over him by withholding sex ... and especially, that she could deny him children.

Chapter 19 – Merry Christmas

"Merry Christmas, Sarah!" John said, shoving a package into his wife's arms.

Sarah pushed it back to John, and ran outside, leaving him in a state of confusion. He put the package on the table and rushed out to see what was wrong. He found Sarah leaning over the side of the porch retching, and holding her stomach.

"Sarah, Honey, what's wrong!"

"I'm sick, can't you see that?!!" she snapped.

"Is it something you ate?"

"John ... you big dumb Swede! I'm going to have your baby!" she cried.

"Sarah Honey!!!" John yelled, picking her up and swinging her around.

"Oh God! Put me down, quick!" Sarah screamed. But it was too late. She vomited all over them both. Sarah began to cry. "I'm so sorry... I tried to warn you."

John put Sarah down, and looked at his shirt. Tears were streaming over John's cheeks.

"Don't cry, John... I said I was sorry. It washes off," Sarah sobbed, unbuttoning her husband's shirt. "Let me have it!"

"I don't give a damn about the shirt, Sarah! I'm just so damned happy!! How long have you known?"

"You're not mad because I threw up on your shirt?"

"Hell NO!!" John was grinning from ear to ear. "I asked you ... how long have you known, Sarah?"

"A week or so... When I started getting sick, I was pretty sure."

John pulled Sarah into his arms and held her affectionately. "Is it going to be a boy or a girl?"

Sarah giggled. "You really expect me to know that?"

John swept his wife up, carrying her into the cabin; dancing around and laughing.

"What's up with you two?" Nathan grinned.

"We're going to have a baby!" John yelled.

"Are we surprised?" Nathan chuckled. "I'm happy for you!"

"That'll make you Uncle Nathan!" John laughed, putting Sarah down on a chair.

"Well, Daddy John and Uncle Nathan had better get the stuff moved out of the loft and bring it down here. The little mother can't be climbin' up and down that ladder!" Nathan said, shaking John's hand. "Congratulations big brother!"

Just then, Maggie came in from the spring house, carrying a bucket of fresh water. "What's all the excitement?" she asked in a tired voice.

"John's going to be a daddy!" Nathan exclaimed, smiling broadly.

"I've known that for a couple of weeks ... Haven't I Sarah?" Maggie grinned over at Sarah.

"Maggie is very good when it comes to keeping secrets – didn't you know?" Sarah confessed.

Maggie gave Sarah a big hug and shook John's hand. "Congratulations, you two! May there be many, many more to come," she giggled.

"Well, Nathan?" John was eyeing Nathan inquisitively.

"Well *WHAT?*"

"Well .... What about you and Maggie? Did it *take?*"

"What the hell are you talking about, John?!" Nathan asked, looking confused.

"Well, Doc said both these gals were probably pregnant! Is Maggie?"

Maggie's face turned beet red as she watched Nathan contemplating John's question.

"Not *yet*, John," Nathan finally replied, shoving his hands defiantly into his pockets. "We may just wait a while, until Maggie feels up to it."

"Maggie's too young to start a family," Sarah interrupted. "Now *ME* ... I haven't got time to waste!! John and I have to make hey while the sun shines – ya know?"

At that, John grabbed Sarah's hand and headed for the ladder to the loft.

Chapter 20 – It's Over

It was a cold evening, during one of Maggie's fertile weeks. Nathan was more intoxicated than usual. He sat by the fire, nursing his jug of whiskey while Maggie slept soundly in the bed up in the loft. Nathan mulled the situation over in his clouded mind. He decided that *HE* was the master of his household, and that *he* would decide whether or not to bring forth offspring. Nathan convinced himself that it was his right to make that decision.

Finally, he got up from the rocker, and staggered over to the ladder that led to the loft. He made his way up and through the trap door, undressed and slid into bed, next to Maggie. She didn't wake up.

"Maggie ...," he whispered. She didn't answer.

Nathan reached for his wife under the quilt, encircling her waist and pulling her close to him. She didn't respond. Finally he pulled her forcefully into his arms and kissed her. Maggie immediately pushed Nathan away, but he wouldn't stop his advance. He slid his hand up under her nightgown. Maggie didn't want to scream and wake John and Sarah. She fought to get away from Nathan – in silence. Before she knew it, he was on her, pulling her nightgown up, and forcing her legs apart. She fought him, to no avail. He held her down with his massive strength, crushing her beneath his body.

"Please don't do this, Nathan," Maggie whispered; pleading with him.

"I love you Maggie. I want you. Have you forgotten you're my wife? It's your duty!"

Those words literally knocked the fight out of the girl. Maggie's body went limp, and she allowed Nathan to have his way with her. She cried out in pain when he entered her, but he didn't stop. Maggie sobbed as Nathan took his pleasure. When it was over, he rolled off of her body and fell into a sound slumber. Maggie cried herself to sleep.

When the first rays of light began filtering into the cabin, Nathan awoke. He couldn't escape his guilt, remembering what he did. Whiskey was no excuse. He had no justification for his inexcusable behavior. He quietly got out of bed, dressed quickly, and left the cabin; not being able to face Maggie should she awaken.

Not long after Nathan left, John woke up. Thinking his brother had started the chores without him, he went straight-away to the barn. When he walked in, he found Nathan sitting on a barrel with his face buried in his hands. He was sobbing like a child.

"Nathan! What is it?!"

John wasn't prepared for the story which came pouring from Nathan's heart.

"I have nothing to say, Nathan. I have no advice for you. That was probably the biggest mistake of your life. You figure it out!" John left the barn immediately because his first inclination was to beat the living hell out of his younger brother.

When John returned to the cabin, Maggie had made the coffee, and poured John a cup. Sarah was sitting at the table beaming at him as usual.

"Here's your coffee, John," Maggie said softly. "Sit down and enjoy it. Sarah and I have been talking about making some curtains. What do you think of that?" She tried to smile.

"Sounds like a good idea," he said, trying not to show his anger. He was shocked by what he saw when he looked at Maggie. She was pale, and her eyes were red and swollen. She hadn't bothered to comb her hair; she looked like death warmed over. And then John noticed the huge purple bruises on her neck. He couldn't take anymore.

"Um... There's something I need to take care of in the barn," John said hoarsely.

Chapter 21 – Retribution

John sprinted back to the barn. He burst through the doors in a violent rage.

"You son of a bitch!" he shouted, grabbing Nathan by the collar. "This is for Maggie!" he growled, letting go a punch which knocked Nathan clear across the barn. He crossed the floor and yanked Nathan to his feet. "This is for me!" he snarled, slamming his fist into Nathan's face one more time. Nathan crumpled to the floor, and John returned to the cabin.

When he walked in, Sarah instantly noticed that John's hand was bleeding, and his knuckles were already swelling.

"Oh my God, John!" Sarah cried. "What did you do to your hand?!"

"John!! ..." Maggie said, catching her breath, as she examined his swollen hand. "What happened?"

Just then, the cabin door opened very slowly, and everyone looked up. Nathan staggered in, his face bloody and bruised. He stumbled over to the bed collapsing onto it; moaning.

Sarah and Maggie looked at John, and then back at Nathan.

"Oh no ...," Maggie sighed. "You didn't have to do that, John!"

"Oh yes I did! I feel much better now."

"I do, too," Nathan groaned from across the room.

Maggie grabbed a bucket and ran outside, bringing it back in, filled with packed snow.

"Sarah, take some of this over and put it on Nathan's face. I would, but I'm afraid I'd finish him off. I'll see to John," Maggie whispered.

Maggie cleaned and bound John's hand, insisting that he keep it buried in the bucket of snow.

She watched Sarah sponging Nathan's swollen face with the icy water from the melting snow. When she couldn't control her rage any more, she grabbed the jug of whiskey and walked calmly over to the bed. She uncorked the jug and poured the entire contents into Nathan's face.

"Maybe this will help!" she spat at him. "Just let me know if there's anything else I can do for you!"

Nathan screamed in pain as the whiskey burned his eyes and seeped into the wounds . Sarah jumped back in alarm.

"Maggie!! What on earth is going on here?!!" Sarah screamed.

"Sarah, Honey ... you don't even want to know. Just leave it alone," John said, shaking his head in disgust.

"John's right," Nathan moaned. "Just let it go. He did the right thing. Gave me just what I needed."

"Well at least you didn't have to *FORCE* me to give it to you!! You horse's ass!!" John shouted.

Maggie put on her cloak and left the cabin. Sarah wanted to follow Maggie, but was afraid the brothers would kill each other if she left them alone. Sarah paced back and forth trying to decide what she should do. After a few minutes, she heard a sound outside, and opened the door, just as Maggie's horse galloped past the cabin. She was heading for the trail.

"That was Maggie!...on her mare!" Sarah cried.

John jumped up and ran out of the cabin, heading for the barn to get Tiff. Nathan rolled from the bed and hit the floor with a thud. Scrambling to his feet, he left too. Then Sarah heard the fighting. She ran outside to find John and Nathan rolling in the snow, gouging and punching each other. Both men were huge Swedes, and Sarah was panic-stricken; watching the two giants wrestling on the ground. Finally, John managed to climb onto Nathan's chest and with one agonizing blow, knocked him out cold. In moments John galloped past, on his way to catch up with Maggie. Nathan lay unconscious in the snow.

"And I thought my brothers were a wild bunch!" Sarah muttered as she tried to revive Nathan. "Get up Nathan! You'll freeze to death out here. Get your ass up!!!"

Nathan moaned and rolled over, burying his aching face in the snow.

John was amazed at how sure footed Tiff remained, as he raced down the icy trail. He could only hope that Maggie wasn't riding hard on the treacherous path. Finally, he caught sight of her. She was sitting on her mare, at the side of the narrow road. She had stopped. John trotted Tiff up beside her.

"Maggie, you can't just run away like this," John said, as calmly as he could.

"I don't know what else to do, John." Maggie sounded surprisingly calm.

"You can come back with me. If you don't want to stay, I can't blame you. But you need to make a plan. You don't just ride off without knowing where you're going or what you're going to do."

"How did you find out what happened?" Maggie asked, wiping at her tears.

"Nathan told me the whole story. He said he was drunk."

"I want to kill him, John!"

"Well, I tried." He managed a chuckle.

"I don't think I'll ever feel the same about him ... not after this," Maggie sobbed.

"I understand, Maggie. He understands it, too."

"I doubt it!" Maggie snarled. "He said since I was his wife, it was my *DUTY!*" Maggie broke down completely, her body shaking with her sorrowful sobbing.

"Well, I know it's no excuse ... but if he was as drunk as he says he was ... he couldn't have been himself."

"Or maybe that's how he *REALLY* is, and the whiskey just brought out the truth!" Maggie cried.

"Come on, Maggie. It's cold out here, and my hand is killing me. Let's go back and decide what you're going to do. If you want to go back to Zanesville, Sarah and I will take you back tomorrow. I promise."

Maggie sat quietly; thoughtfully. "John ...," Maggie finally spoke, "what will I do if I'm pregnant?"

"We'll cross that bridge when we come to it, Maggie. Maybe you're *NOT* pregnant. Even if you are, that doesn't mean you have to stay with Nathan if you don't want to."

Maggie broke down crying again. "I can't raise a child all by myself, John."

"Well then ... consider staying with Nathan until you find out ... whether you are or you aren't pregnant."

"I think I can do that, if you promise not to say a word about this conversation," Maggie said quietly, looking up at John. "I'll just pretend everything is all right. If I'm pregnant, then I'll just have to stay. If I'm not ... then I'll leave."

"Can we go now?" John begged.

"Yes."

When Maggie and John got back to the cabin, Sarah was still trying to get Nathan inside. He couldn't stand up. John jumped down from the horse, threw Nathan over his shoulder and took him inside.

"Sarah, Honey ... can you throw some quilts on the floor there in that corner? Make him a bed. He's not sleeping with Maggie."

Sarah didn't ask any questions. She made the bed, and John put Nathan down.

"I've got to put the horses away and get the cow milked. You see to Maggie" John said, giving his beautiful wife a quick kiss.

"What about your hand, John? You'll need some help," Sarah said.

"Thank you, Sarah Honey, but even though it hurts like hell, I'll still have to get my chores done," John replied, clutching his injured hand.

Sarah turned to her sister-in-law. "Maggie, sweetie ... do you want to talk? I mean ... you don't have to tell me anything you don't want to, but I'm sorely confused by all that's happened this morning."

"Can we wait until later, Sarah? I'm just all worn out. I've got to think about things before I can talk about them."

"That's OK, Maggie. Are you hungry? Shall I start lunch?" Sarah asked.

"No thanks. I don't feel much like eating. I think I just want to lie down. It was a very long night."

"In that case ... I'll just tuck you in." Sarah took Maggie by the arm and led her to her bed. "Now if you need anything, you just tell me." She pulled the quilt up and tucked it under Maggie's chin.

"Thanks Sarah," Maggie said in a tired voice.

Sarah went over to where Nathan was lying, and looked at his face, shaking her head sadly. "Nathan, are you awake?"

"Yes," he managed to speak.

"Are you OK?" Sarah asked, kneeling down to get a closer look.

"My head hurts real bad," Nathan moaned.

"Do you think we should send for Doc Mathison?"

"I'll be all right. I just need to sleep," Nathan said, trying to see through the slits of his swollen eyelids.

John walked in with the bucket of fresh milk, and saw Sarah kneeling beside Nathan.

"Sarah," he said, "I asked you to see to Maggie, not Nathan."

"Well, look at him, John!" Sarah demanded, rising to her feet. "And he says his head hurts. I think he needs to see the Doc."

"He's not injured! He's just got one hell of a hang over. That's all!" John said. "Maybe he'll learn that drinkin' too much has consequences."

Sarah walked over to John and slipped her arms around her husband's neck. "How did you manage to milk the cow with a broken hand?" she asked, smiling up at him.

"It wasn't easy, Sarah Honey. It hurts," John said, trying to sound serious.

Sarah lifted his hand and inspected it carefully. The swelling was down, and the cuts looked more like scratches, now that they weren't bleeding. "My, my, John... You're hand appears to be only bruised ... but maybe you'll learn fighting has consequences!"

"OK, OK... You got me!" John laughed. "But look at this busted lip. Would you kiss me right here, and make it better?" He pointed to his lips.

Sarah was only too happy to accommodate her husband's request. She tried to kiss him affectionately, but it quickly turned to passion. John wrestled free from her embrace, and held Sarah at arm's length, frowning.

"You know better than that, young lady!" he said sternly.

"Sorry... I lost my head!"

"You stole my heart," John whispered, pulling her back into his arms.

Sarah glanced over at Nathan. His body was shaking violently and his eyes looked to be rolled back in his head. His back was stiffly arched, and his hands were in tight fists.

"Oh my God!!" Sarah screamed. "He's having fits, John!"

Hearing Sarah's screams, Maggie jumped from the bed and was at Nathan's side in seconds.

"It's a convulsion!" Maggie cried. "John, get me a dowel, quick! Sarah, help me hold him down!"

John looked around frantically, and then grabbed a stool Nathan had made. With the strength of bull, he tore it to bits, and handed Maggie a small rounded piece of wood, about six inches long.

"Try to get his mouth open, John ... just enough for me to get this between his teeth!" Maggie shouted. "Be careful ... you could lose a finger. He's not aware of what's happening!"

John struggled; trying to pry Nathan's clenched jaws apart. It took all of his might, but he finally managed to force a space just wide enough for Maggie to slip the wood between Nathan's teeth.

"I've seen convulsions like this with fevers ... and I know it happens with head injuries, but I have no idea how to treat it!"

"Did you say head injury?!" John gasped in disbelief. He was sitting on Nathan's chest, at this point, with his knees holding his brother's arms down.

"Yes, if he has a concussion, his brain could be swelling! I just don't know! We need a doctor! We need a doctor *FAST*!!" Maggie shrieked, as Nathan continued to convulse.

As soon as the seizure subsided, John grabbed his jacket and left. Within minutes he was heading to Tom McCollough's farm to find Dr. Mathison.

Tom gasped. "Good god, John!! Doc left early this morning." Tom rubbed his chin thoughtfully. "I did hear there's a doc staying with the Henderson's up in Unionville. He was on his way to Lancaster and had an accident. They took him in until he mends. You might try him. It's a couple of miles up the road. They live right beside the church at the top of the hill, on the main road."

"Thanks Tom... I'll try to find him!" John shouted, turning his horse and racing away.

John found the house and quickly jumped down from Tiff. He ran up to knock on the door. Just as he raised his hand, the door swung open, and a middle-aged woman was standing there.

"Can I help you?"

"Do the Henderson's live here?" John asked, hurriedly.

"Why, yes. I'm Lucy Henderson. What do you need, son?"

"I need a doctor! I mean my brother Nathan needs a doctor. Tom McCollough said there was a doc stayin' here!" John rambled.

The man sitting at the table stood up and approached the door. "I'm a doctor. What's the problem?" he asked, peering over Lucy's shoulder.

"My brother's having convulsions! We got into a fight. I must have hit him too hard!! Oh please .... Come with me. I'm afraid he's going to die!" John pleaded earnestly.

"Calm down, now. I'll get my bag and my horse....I'll be right out," the doctor said, placidly.

The two riders sped down the road, back toward Newton. There was no time to talk. When they arrived at the cabin, John raced up the steps, opening the door wide for the doctor.

The doctor's eyes grew wide in astonishment when he saw Maggie. He struggled with his emotions. The bitterness he'd been feeling toward Maggie, turned into fear, and then the fear changed to tenderness. He was overtaken by the absurdity of the moment.

"Can I be alone with the patient and his wife?" the doctor asked.

Chapter 22 – Fear and Passion

Maggie was speechless; terror gripped her when she saw Miles Deihl. Her heart began racing and she felt faint. Before she could say a word, John threw Sarah's cloak around her, and escorted her outside.

"Maggie, don't say anything, please!" Miles whispered. He knelt down and examined Nathan's head. He pulled Nathan's eyelids open and looked into his eyes. He checked inside his ears, and looked up each nostril.

Maggie was in shock.

"I can save him, Maggie ... but please don't give me up! Don't turn me in... I'm begging you." Miles checked Nathan's pulse. "Do we have an agreement, Maggie?" he asked, gently putting his hand on hers.

"I... I ...," Maggie tried to get the words out.

"I'll take that as a *yes!*" Miles said. "Now, here's what's wrong. It's not just a concussion, Maggie. I think his brain is bleeding and the pressure probably caused the seizures. Are you following me?" Dr. Deihl caught hold of Maggie's arm and shook her gently. "Get a grip, Maggie!" he demanded. "If you want him to live, you're going to have to help me!"

"I... I'm trying," she sobbed. "I'm just... I didn't expect ..."

"Damn it, Maggie! Forget the past for the moment. We've got to relieve the pressure on your husband's brain, or you're going to be a widow!" Miles' impatience was tangible.

"All right," Maggie said weakly. "I'll keep your secret. What do you want me to do?"

"I'll need you to boil the sharpest knife you can find, and the smallest saw you've got. We'll need a sturdy needle and some thread. Oh … and a lantern if you have one, and snow. Thank God for the snow! We'll pack his head in the snow when we're finished. It should help take down the swelling." Miles looked at Maggie inquisitively. "What the hell happened to *YOU*?!!" He touched the big purple bruises on her neck, and didn't pretend not to notice her red, swollen eyes.

Maggie began to cry. She didn't bother answering Dr. Deihl, but got up and started gathering the things he asked her for.

Miles Deihl walked outside, rolling up his sleeves. John and Sarah were walking hand in hand beside the smokehouse. Seeing the doctor on the porch, they rushed back to the cabin.

"Doc! Will he be OK?" John shouted.

"I think I can save him, but I can't promise anything just yet," Miles said. "He has significant pressure on his brain. He's bleeding inside the skull. If I can relieve the pressure, and stop the bleeding, he has a reasonable chance of recovering."

"And if you can't stop the bleeding and relieve the pressure?" John asked.

"Then he'll either die … or he'll be an invalid the rest of his life," Miles admitted. "I just have to be honest with you. I can't give you a guarantee. I'm sorry."

John began to cry. He was overwhelmed with guilt. "I can't believe I did this to my own brother!" he whispered hoarsely. "If he dies ..."

"John," Sarah interrupted, "this isn't just your fault! Nathan's just as much at fault." She hugged John tightly.

"What happened to your brother's wife?" Miles asked. "I noticed the bruises on her neck."

John didn't get a chance to answer.. Maggie was at the door, calling the doctor inside.

"You won't want to come in, until I tell you," Dr. Deihl stated. "I'll let you know how he is, as soon as I can."

John and Sarah retreated to the smokehouse, where it was warm, and the doctor went back inside the cabin.

Maggie had all of the items, assembled on a clean sheet next to Nathan. Miles put an extra log on the fire, to get more light into the room.

"Maggie, you've got to promise me you won't pass out, this time!" Miles said, looking at Maggie's sad eyes. "You need to be stronger, now, than you've ever been in your life. This is going to be worse than anything you've seen me do, yet!" He took her frail hand in his, and he squeezed it affectionately. "God knows, I still love you, Maggie. If saving this man will make you happy, then I'll do everything I can for him ... but I need your help. Can I depend on you?"

"I'll try not to pass out," Maggie agreed in a subdued tone.

"Well, if you start to feel queasy, just breathe hard, through your mouth. Sometimes that helps. Let's get started."

It was a slow, bloody process, as Miles Deihl cut and removed a section of Nathan's skull. He was able to locate the bleeding and once more, Maggie had to help with the cauterization. She finished the process without fainting. The blood was drained and the bone replaced. Miles skillfully stitched Nathan's scalp back over the wound. When all was finished, Maggie bandaged Nathan's head tightly, and packed snow around it.

"Maggie, this may not work. Usually, the bone isn't put back, but if there's a chance it stays in place and mends, your husband could have a more normal life. If the pressure starts to build again, we'll just have to remove the bone and leave it out. I've read about this procedure, but I'll admit it .... this is the first time I've done it."

"I understand," Maggie said weakly.

"Your husband will probably remain unconscious for two or three days, so don't worry ... unless it's longer than that. He'll probably have a terrible headache when he does wake up ... if he wakes up. Here's some bitter powder for the pain." Miles laid some paper packets on the table.

Maggie and Miles cleaned up the mess, washed their hands, then sat down at the table; exhausted. They sat in silence for a long time, each one lost in thought.

"I'm sorry I had to shoot you, Miles," Maggie said, quietly.

"I'm sorry, too. You nearly killed me," he smiled.

"If I had wanted to kill you, you would be dead," she stated defiantly. "Nathan and John taught me to shoot when I was just a little girl. I can shoot straighter than most *men*... So don't think I meant to do anything but *STOP* you. Had I wanted to hit your heart, I would have."

"Well ... in that case, am I supposed to be grateful?"

"No! I just want you to know ... I never wanted you dead."

"And why would that be? Could it be that you cared just a little?"

"Maybe... I don't know... I never understood our relationship... Like some kind of bond." Maggie looked thoughtful. "Miles, did you really kill Silas McGregor?"

"Yes."

"Why?!"

"Truthfully?"

"I'd like to know how a doctor is capable of taking a life, rather than saving one!"

"Because he was making lewd comments about *YOU*, Maggie. He was telling the men at the poker game what he would do to you if he ever got his hands on you. I couldn't stand it! I'd had a lot to drink ... I thought I was protecting your honor." Miles hung his head and shook it sadly.

"What about telling everyone we were going to get married and you were going to use *MY* money to start a practice and build a hospital?"

"Isn't that something you would have liked, Maggie? Truthfully ... you have to admit, we'd make a pretty good medical team. I never meant it in a derogatory way!"

"I just needed to know, Miles."

"And since you want the truth... Your husband split my head open for the same reason I killed Silas McGregor. I'll probably wear this scar the rest of my life in remembrance of *YOU*." Miles ran his finger along the scar, going from the top of his head, straight down to the bridge of his nose. "I said some things I shouldn't have ... about *YOU* ... that's why he rammed my head into that damned tree. I guess I deserved it ... but I was angry. I knew I'd lost you to *HIM*!"

"Didn't he break your wrist?"

"No, but he sprained it pretty badly. If he hadn't, I would have killed him. I actually tried."

"Life certainly gets complicated, doesn't it, Miles?"

"Maggie, I have to tell you... You look like hell!! And how did you get those bruises on your neck?"

"Nathan was drunk last night, and he took me against my will." She stated it flatly; unemotionally.

Miles jumped up from the table, feeling the rage building in his soul. "And you let me save his worthless life?!! What the hell were you thinking? Did you like it Maggie?! Did you enjoy being raped?!!"

"You don't have to speak to me so cruelly, Miles," Maggie said, starting to cry. "Of course I didn't enjoy it! I didn't tell you because I knew you wouldn't help him if you knew!" Maggie stood up and put her hand on Miles' arm, trying to calm him. "John, his brother, found out, and nearly killed him... I thought that was enough punishment. I'm going to leave Nathan if I'm not ..." Her voice trailed off. She couldn't believe she was having this conversation with Miles Deihl.

"You mean your husband's own brother beat the hell out of him because he forced himself on you? Well good for him! Too bad he didn't finish the job." Miles stopped and looked Maggie in the eye. "... and you're going to leave your husband if you're not *WHAT*? Maggie ... if you're not what?!!"

"If I'm not with child," Maggie said in an almost inaudible voice. "He took me, and I think I'm fertile. I didn't want to take a chance on becoming pregnant... Besides I was annoyed with him, and not in the mood... He was determined."

"Oh NO, Maggie!!" Miles snarled. "When was your last period?"

"I think it was a little over two weeks ago."

"Good god!! And he knew it?!"

"Yes."

"Maggie, leave with me! You don't need to stay here ... pregnant or not. I'll take care of you, and if you have his child, I'll take care of it, just as I would my own. Don't stay if you're not happy!" The doctor looked over at Nathan and frowned. "Men do things when they drink... things they wouldn't otherwise do, Maggie. I almost feel sorry for the man ... but I still think you should go with me!"

"I have to think. I'm so confused, now!" Maggie cried. "I thought marrying Nathan was the practical thing to do. I'd grown up with him. I thought it would be a safer choice. I thought I knew him. I didn't know about his drinking!"

"Well you know ... if he regains consciousness, his brother or his brother's wife will describe me.

Once anyone knows who I am, my life will be over. They'll hang me if they catch me. Maggie, you're going to have to decide quickly because I'm going to have to leave the state. If I stay here, now – I'm as good as dead!"

"I just need a little time, Miles."

"Three days. That's all ... then I'm leaving."

"Where will you go?"

"Maybe Kentucky... I'm not sure."

Miles encircled Maggie gently in his arms and held her close. He kissed her swollen eyes. He hesitated. Then, he kissed her on the lips, igniting the same old explosive feelings in both of them.

Miles Deihl stopped, stepped back, and shook his head sadly. "Maggie, I told you a long time ago ... you would be my *undoing*. Just think about what I've said. I'll be back day after tomorrow, unless you need me sooner. I've got to go, now."

"Miles, if it's any consolation ... I have a surprise for you." Maggie laid her hand on his chest. That touch seemed to pierce his heart.

She went out onto the porch and called to John and Sarah. Within minutes they returned to the cabin.

"John, would you show Dr. Smith the black stallion we have for sale. I think he might like taking it in trade for his services."

"Did you say you have a black stallion? I've always wanted a tall black horse!" Miles grinned broadly; his eyes widening in anticipation.

John headed back to the barn and soon he returned, leading the magnificent black stallion. Its leg had healed perfectly. The horse was as beautiful and animated as ever.

"You can't be serious!" Miles gasped, stepping up to the horse and nuzzling his face against its muzzle, affectionately. "This stallion is worth a fortune!" He winked at Maggie.

"If you saved my brother's life, Doc ... there's nothin' I wouldn't give you!" John said, raising his hands into the air.

"Well, we'll see how things go," Miles said. "We'll just have to wait and see. You keep the horse for now. If your brother recovers, I just might consider the trade." Miles walked up to Maggie and whispered in her ear, "So my name is *SMITH*? I'll try to remember that ... especially since the family I'm staying with thinks my name is *BROOKS*." He turned, mounted his horse, and left.

"Thank you Dr. Brooks!" Maggie called after him.

"I thought you called him Dr. Smith, before?" Sarah said, looking confused.

"I was mistaken," Maggie said, taking Sarah by the arm and walking into the cabin with her.

Nathan remained unconscious the rest of the day, and the next. John sat with his brother most of the time, leaving Nathan's side only to gather fire wood, milk the cow, or tend to the animals. On the evening of the second day, Nathan moaned and managed to move his hands. Late in the night, he began talking.

The next day, Maggie knew Miles Deihl would be back to check on Nathan. Nathan was healing and becoming coherent. If he saw Dr. Deihl, there would be hell to pay. Maggie had no choice, but to sedate her husband. She mixed the bitter powder into a cup of water and helped Nathan to drink it. Within minutes, he was asleep.

When Miles arrived, Maggie explained what she had done.

"Well, Mrs. Stillman, I would have liked to have had a conversation with your husband ... just to check and make sure he's rational, but under the circumstances, it seems you've rendered him quite unconscious." Dr. Deihl could barely keep from laughing, as John and Sarah hung on every one of his words.

"I'm sorry, Dr. Brooks, but he was in pain. We can all verify ... he's much better and completely rational ... thanks to YOU!" Maggie said. "When will he be able to be up and around?"

"Whenever he feels like it," Miles replied. "He'll just need to take it easy for a month or so.

Even a bump to the head could be fatal, at this point."

"Well, Doc ... have you decided whether you want the stallion? Or would you prefer gold?" John asked.

"I've thought about that," Miles said, taking some coins out of his pocket. "I'll take the stallion, but I'll also give you fifty dollars in gold. I think that would be a fair transaction for such a magnificent animal." He laid the gold coins on the table.

John stepped forward and extended his hand. "That sounds perfect, let's shake on it."

"I can't wait to ride that gorgeous horse!" Miles said grinning, and shaking John's hand.

"I'll go bring him out for you, Doc," John said, pulling on his jacket. He left the cabin.

"Dr. Brooks, would you like some dinner before you go?" Sarah asked.

"No thank you, but I would like a private word with Maggie, if you don't mind," he replied.

"Of course. I'll go and help John get the horse ready." Sarah put her cloak on and went to join her husband.

Miles pulled Maggie over into the corner, where Nathan wouldn't see them, if he were to wake up. "What have you decided, Maggie?" Miles asked, looking deeply into Maggie's expressive eyes.

"I want to go with you, Miles, but I just don't know how I can do that to Nathan."

"That's easy," Miles said. "Just remember what he did to *YOU*, and then try to figure out *HOW* he could have done that to *YOU!*"

"OK... I'm still not sure I can do it. If you're positive that you're leaving tomorrow, wait by the bridge on the main road, at the tavern ... where this lane turns off the main road. If I'm not there by half past eight in the morning, then just leave without me. I'm going to try, Miles. I swear I'm going to try!"

Chapter 23 – A Difficult Decision

The next morning, Maggie was up before sunrise. She bathed and dressed, then hurriedly packed a small bag with only necessities. She gazed at her father's metal box containing her inheritance. She held it to her heart, wondering how she could possibly do something so wrong; something she knew full well her father would not approve. She stifled her conscience.

Looking over at Nathan, lying quietly on the floor in the corner, she wanted to take back her father's wedding ring. She considered trying to slip it off his finger, but was afraid he would awaken. She tucked the metal box into her bag, put on her cloak, and slipped out of the cabin.

Once in the barn, Maggie saddled her little bay mare and led it down through the meadow to the roadway. Quietly she climbed into the saddle, and left the farm. She didn't look back.

As she rode along the trail, the sun was rising above the hills. The birds were flitting from tree to tree, looking for food, which had become scarce for them in this winter paradise. In the light of the rising sun, the snow sparkled on the ground, and on the bushes, and on the trees. As if diamonds and jewels had been cast all over the earth, everything twinkled with rainbow colors.

It had been a long winter and even though spring was approaching, winter refused to concede.

Maggie could feel the anticipation rising in her soul. She began to question herself. *'Had she made the right decision? Was she doing something she would later regret?'* She stopped the horse and just sat there thinking.

She was amazed at human nature, she was confused about the carnal drive, she was curious as to how she could be so fickle. Maggie wondered how simple misunderstandings could complicate so many lives. She thought about how making snap-judgments and hasty decisions can adversely affect hopes, dreams and future plans. Maggie considered the fact that ordinary people prefer to choose what's familiar instead of taking the risk of choosing the unknown; although the familiar may be the safer choice, it's always the unknown that seizes the imagination and forever flirts with one's fascination. How ironic!

And then Maggie thought about Sarah. Sarah was the one person she knew, who seemed to have a solid grip on the meaning of love and the importance of what lies in the human heart. Sarah didn't see good or bad, nor black or white. She trusted her own judgment and was convinced there was absolute virtue in everyone and everything; in every situation. Sarah always said it was all about one's perception. She said, *'Whatever you're looking for – that's what you'll find.'*

"How long does it take to grow up?" Maggie asked out loud, looking into the sky.

After a time of soul searching, Maggie continued on her way. It was too late to turn back now. She had already been unfaithful to her husband on an emotional level, and nearly physically as well. There wasn't much in her life, at least not in this present phase, which mattered anymore. Maggie knew things were about to change drastically.

When Maggie arrived at the bridge, she checked the position of the sun. It had to be about a quarter past eight. She climbed off her mare and led the horse down under the bridge for a drink of cool water. Maggie decided this would be an ideal place to wait, where no one could see her. Time dragged by, and she kept checking the sun's position. It was past time for Miles to be there. Maggie's heart sank as the realization hit her; he must have changed his mind. Miles obviously wasn't coming. She waited a few more minutes. Still, he didn't come.

Abandoning hope, Maggie led the little mare back up to the road. She hopped into the saddle and turned the filly toward home. Icy tears stung Maggie's cheeks, as she rode along the path. It was a curious revelation for Maggie to realize everything didn't revolve around *her*. The reality crushed her spirit. – Her narcissism was a cruel ruse. Maggie was looking inside herself, and seeing the bitter truth at last. '*She was only a pawn in the game of life, not the queen.*' She began to sob. And to think – she believed the decision was all up to *her* – It was *her* choice, to stay with Nathan or go with Miles. '*How ironic it would be, if she returned home, only to be thrown out by Nathan.*' That would be something she wouldn't expect to happen in her self-centered world; but now she was facing *that* possibility.

Just then, she heard a horse galloping up behind her, and she turned around to look. It was Miles, on his beautiful black stallion, Seminole. He was leading another horse which was loaded with luggage and supplies. He rode up to her and jumped off his horse.

"Maggie, I'm so sorry... I didn't mean to be late." He pulled her down into his arms and kissed her; breathlessly. "When I got to the bridge, and you weren't there, I was afraid you hadn't come." He swung Maggie around, happily. "I was on my way to Stillman's farm to steal you away ... whether you intended to come with me or not!" He laughed, setting her down.

"I waited for a long time, Miles." Maggie wiped the tears from her face.

"Well, no matter... I'm here now. You're coming with me. We've got to hurry, before someone sees us." He grinned that handsome grin of his, and Maggie's heart melted. He kissed her again; hugging her tightly. "Want to ride with me, Maggie?" He didn't wait for her to answer. Miles scooped her up into his arms and set her atop the big black stallion. He tied her mare up beside the other horse, and then climbed into the saddle behind Maggie. The two of them trotted back toward the bridge, on their way to *"who knows where"*.

John rolled over in the bed and looked around. Sarah was still sleeping soundly, but Maggie wasn't in the room; and to his surprise, Nathan was sitting at the table.

"Where's Maggie?" John asked.

"I think she left me," Nathan said flatly.

"What are you talking about, Nathan?"

"She packed her bag, took her money, and left before daylight. I pretended I was asleep. She's gone, and I don't blame her. That's why I didn't try to stop her. I didn't want to play on her guilt or sympathy." Nathan held up a piece of paper. "She left me the land patent. Signed it over to me. Why would she give me all that land, John?"

"That I can't answer. Maybe it's got something to do with love, or decency. Do you have any idea where she went, Nathan?"

"Not sure... but I've got a pretty good idea. Do you know?"

"No. I thought she would wait to find out if she was going to have a baby, and then decide whether to stay or go," John spoke honestly. "If you have an idea ..., then where do you think she is?"

"Someday I'll tell you, John. But not right now."

"I understand, Nathan."

"I've been sittin' here thinkin' about life, John," Nathan said. "Do you realize how much has happened in three short years? Like a lifetime of livin' in three short years! God must have some kind of crazy schedule... It looks as if we're on the fast track."

"Well, when you put it that way, it *is* pretty amazing!" John said, rubbing his chin. "Do you realize you stood on death's doorstep twice in these three years?" John tilted his head to one side. "Make that three times, if you count the injun massacre."

"Yep, I was thinkin' that, too. Maybe I've got nine lives... You know ... like a cat." Nathan forced a grin.

"Nathan, I'm sorry I hurt ya so bad! I just meant to rough ya up, not kill ya!"

"I know that. I also know I deserved a good beatin'. I wish I could apologize to Maggie ... but it's too late. Life will go on. We live and we learn. Isn't that right?"

John looked at Nathan thoughtfully. "Well... Maggie's young and strong willed. She'll survive in spite of what life throws at her. She's always been one of those natural born survivors. I think she's just too young to have good sense. That's been her whole problem. Too bad she couldn't have spent four or five more years with her folks. I just hope she doesn't end up hard, cold, and cynical after all of this."

"Me, too," Nathan said, wiping at a tear sliding down his cheek.

"Nathan, I knew what you did was the biggest mistake of your life. You were the one person Maggie felt she could trust, and you betrayed her trust. I still can't believe you got so drunk you forced yourself on that girl – treated her like a common tramp!"

Nathan began to sob with remorse. "John, if I could undo it all, I would! I never would have hurt

Maggie. It was the damned whiskey! I swear on my soul ... I will *NEVER* touch alcohol again! *NEVER*!!"

"That's one hard lesson learned. Let's just hope the ones yet to come aren't so harsh. Don't ya wonder how much more we have to learn before we're actually considered *WISE*?" John mused.

Chapter 24 – Life Revealed

Spring brought the usual flooding, but this year the creek didn't make it up to the cabin. Nathan and John were relieved; being able to sleep through the nights not having to worry about the constantly advancing water. Soon the soil was warm enough to start the planting process all over again, and the Stillman brothers got their crops in on time this year.

As summer approached, the neighbors all came together, and another cabin was raised. This time, on the six hundred acres Maggie had deeded to Nathan. It was beautiful land, and a welcome respite for Nathan to finally have his own home. He didn't mind living with John and Sarah, but realized they needed their privacy, and now they would need the space, with the baby coming next month.

Nathan could see John's cabin from his new home on the knoll across the valley. Nathan's had been situated on higher ground, so he wouldn't have to worry about the yearly flooding. The brothers built a sturdy bridge across the main creek and cut a road over the land to the younger brother's home. They had to do significantly more clearing, since there was dense timber covering the plat, unlike the land where the original cabin had been built. Felling trees and removing stumps took all spring. The work still wasn't totally complete.

When the brothers weren't working the fields, and tending the crops, they were busy building fencing and shelters for Maggie's sheep, which were due to arrive at any time.

Newton, Ohio – July 26, 1808 – The Stillman farm:

Nathan and John were busy splitting rails for the fences. The sun was hot and the work was hard. Nathan sat down on a stump and wiped the sweat from his face with a handkerchief. He gazed across the beautiful meadow in front of him.

"John, I had a dream last night... It seemed so real ..., when I woke up this mornin' I thought Maggie was with me. I could almost smell her. It was that lavender scent."

"You know, Nathan ..., I think you should quit thinkin' so much about her? You're wastin' time. You need to find another wife. Have a happy life. Stop punishin' yourself. I don't think Maggie will ever come home."

"I think she will," Nathan said, defiantly. "I know she will."

"Nathan, why can't you just forget her?"

"Do you remember the doc who saved my life?" Nathan asked.

"Yes. Dr. Brooks?"

"I saw him. I was barely conscious, but he talked to me, John. Maggie never knew he talked to me. I guess she just thought I was unconscious, and that was that."

"What did he say, Nathan."

"Well, I know I should have told you this before, but I just needed to think about it first."

"For god's sake, Nathan ... what the hell are you ramblin' on about?"

"First of all, his name wasn't Brooks ... it was Deihl."

"You mean that murderer you had the run-in with over Maggie."

"That's the one," Nathan grinned. "He made me promise ... that no matter what happened between Maggie and me ... that I would always take care of her. He said she would probably leave me because of what I did to her, and go with *him*. He told me he was helpin' the Seminole Indians and he said it was dangerous. He said his mother was a Creek Indian – But, anyway... He said he would kill me, if I didn't promise him that Maggie could come back to me, if anything happened to him." Nathan looked at John, and smiled. "What do you make of that, big brother?"

"Did you commit to that promise, Nathan?"

"I'm alive aren't I?" He laughed. "I did... I promised. That's when he told me why he killed that fella in Zanesville. The man was planning to hurt Maggie, and he said he wasn't about to let it happen. It was the strangest damned thing. He talked to me like I was his friend. Miles Deihl said if Maggie went with him and was pregnant with my baby ... I shouldn't worry because he promised to be a good father to my child. He even apologized to me.

For a while, I wasn't sure I didn't dream it all ... but now I'm certain... It really happened. Deihl seemed to be an honorable man, John."

"He threatened to kill you, and you call him honorable?" John laughed.

"I know he was just tryin' to protect Maggie. I think he genuinely loved her all the along; while Doc Mathison was sure he was just usin' her. It seemed like he needed to know Maggie would be OK, no matter what happens. I think the man knows he's going to die young."

"That's pretty amazing, Nathan!" John rubbed his chin thoughtfully. "God works in strange ways. So if Maggie comes back, what will you do?"

"I'd take her back in a heartbeat."

Both brothers were silent – contemplating the story.

"Nathan, he paid for his own horse! Not only did he save your miserable life ... but he wouldn't take his own horse in payment. Remember? I told you he insisted on paying!" John scratched his head. "What kind of man is he?"

"Well, we'll probably never know, John. But I can tell you one thing... I hope Maggie *is* with him. That way, I won't have to worry about her!"

The men picked up another rail and carefully set it in place. One more line of fencing would finish the project.

Just then, the sounding of the bell rang across the valley. It was the signal that Sarah needed John. The men jumped on their horses and raced to John's cabin.

Rebecca Wilson, Samuel Wilson's wife, was the local community's midwife. She had been staying with John and Sarah for the last three days. It was the custom in the wilderness.

The men arrived just as Rebecca walked out of the cabin smiling.

"John, you have a beautiful daughter, and Sarah is just fine," she said, tears running down her cheeks. "I always get so emotional when I'm allowed to experience the miracle of life!" Rebecca apologized.

"Thank you so much, Becky!" John grinned. He gave the woman a bear hug and rushed inside.

Nathan remained outside with Rebecca, giving the new parents time alone, to bond with their new baby.

Sarah was in the bed, propped up on pillows holding the tiny bundle, when John walked in. He beamed with pride; gazing down at his beautiful but tired wife, and the baby girl, nursing at Sarah's breast.

"She's beautiful, Sarah!" John whispered. "Just like her mother."

He knelt down beside the bed and couldn't take his eyes off of the baby.

"What shall we name her, John?'

"Well, Sarah of course ... after her mother," John said.

"Oh, John, couldn't we name her Ann? I never liked my name," she begged. "Ann is such a noble name."

"If that will make you happy, Sarah Honey ... then *Ann* it is!" John smiled.

"I love you so, John! Let's have twenty children! Let's keep having children until we run out of names!" Sarah laughed.

"Sarah, was it hard? I mean, I thought childbirth was terribly painful. Are you all right?"

"It wasn't exactly a picnic, John ... but just look at what I received for enduring it!"

"I know you're going to be a wonderful mother, Sarah. See what one kiss can do?!"

"I told you so!" Sarah smiled knowingly. She looked toward the window and saw Nathan peeking inside, trying to see the baby. "Tell Uncle Nathan he can come in if he wants to."

John walked outside and discovered his brother Nathan, looking in the window, with tears streaming down his face.

"You cry baby!" He laughed, pointing his finger at Nathan. "Sarah said to tell you to come inside and see the baby. But please, Nathan – wipe your nose. I don't want her to see what a sniffling idiot you really are!" John teased.

Lexington, Kentucky – The Palace Hotel:

Maggie's knuckles were white with pressure as she clung to the iron headboard; her arms stretched above her head. It was three o'clock in the morning and she'd been in labor for hours.

"How much longer will this continue, Miles?" Maggie whispered weakly.

"It won't be long, now, Maggie," he said sponging the girl's face with cool water.

"I don't think I can stand any more."

"Be strong, Sweetie."

"I've been with my Pa lots of times when babies were born ... it shouldn't take this long. I'm afraid, Miles." Maggie began to cry, but stopped abruptly as another pain gripped her tired body.

Miles checked his pocket watch. He tried to conceal his concern, as he timed the contraction.

"Try not to tense up, Maggie," he spoke softly. "If you can relax, the contraction will do the work it's supposed to."

Suddenly Maggie began bearing down. Her face turned red and she pulled hard on the headboard. Miles immediately pulled the sheet from Maggie's knees and positioned himself at the foot of the bed. When the contraction subsided, Maggie began to sob again.

"This is it, Maggie... I can see the baby's head. You'll have that baby in your arms in just a few more minutes!" he said, his relief obvious.

Again, Maggie was seized with the overpowering pain and pressure. Once more she involuntarily strained to push the baby from her body. Maggie's water broke.

"Take a deep breath, Maggie... When the next pain comes, push as hard as you can, and don't stop until I tell you."

It began again. Maggie tightened her grip on the iron bed, and groaned; straining. She bore down with all the strength she could recover, and continued to push. The pain seemed to be overpowered by pressure; now; all she could feel was the intense force of the compressing. Finally, the contraction reached its climax, and Maggie released a primal scream which came from deep within her being.

"Stop, Maggie!" Miles shouted. "The head is out."

Maggie let go of the iron bars on the bed and collapsed, nearly unconscious. The pain was gone.

Miles worked feverishly, trying to turn the baby; positioning it so the shoulders could be delivered easier.

"Get ready, Maggie... One more push. The contraction should start any second now. Take a deep breath."

Maggie reached over her head, and again grasped the bars. She sucked in as much air as her lungs would hold, and they waited. When the pain began again, Maggie worked as hard as she could, trying to complete the delivery of her baby. Miles tried turning the child more, but still the shoulders wouldn't pass. The contraction stopped, and the baby remained trapped.

"Maggie ... I promise you, when the next contraction starts, we'll free this baby. When it begins, push as hard as you can, and don't stop until I say so. Your baby's life depends on it."

Miles pulled the sterile scissors from his bag and waited. Maggie couldn't see what he was doing. Just then the next contraction began. Maggie diligently strained and pushed. Miles picked up the scissors, very carefully slipping one blade into the space between the baby's neck and Maggie's skin. He cut quickly, enlarging the opening only enough to allow the shoulders to slip through. He tossed the scissors aside.

"Stop, Maggie!" he shouted.

Miles caught the slippery child, as it came bursting into the world looking more like a six-month-old than a newborn. The baby's skin was blue, and he wasn't breathing. Miles quickly wiped the child's mouth out and briskly rubbed its body with a clean cloth. The baby finally started to cry and Miles started to laugh. He tightly tied the cord with string, in two places, and made the cut between them. The child was free.

"Why are you laughing?" Maggie asked in a barely audible voice.

"Because, Maggie, Honey ... you just gave birth to a bull!" Miles chuckled softly. He wrapped the child in a blanket and held it into the air for Maggie to see. "It's a boy!! He's huge, Maggie. I don't think I've ever delivered a baby this large. That big Swede, Nathan, seems to have reproduced *himself!*"

Maggie was too weak and tired to sit up, so Miles placed the baby into her arms. He was grinning from ear to ear. Bending down, he kissed Maggie gently on the forehead.

"You did a terrific job, Maggie. I knew you could," Miles whispered. "You just relax, Honey, I've got a little damage to repair."

"What kind of damage?" Maggie asked, looking frightened.

"Um... Sweetie, I had to do an episiotomy to get his shoulders through. We almost lost him, Maggie. If I hadn't done it, he would have died."

"What's an episiotomy?"

"I had to cut you, Maggie. Now all we have to do is deliver the afterbirth and get you stitched up. You can nurse your son as soon as you feel strong enough."

Miles sat in a chair by the bed, watching Maggie and the baby sleeping. He thought of all he and Maggie had experienced together, and came to the conclusion that this moment was the most precious. Maggie slowly opened her eyes and looked lovingly at the handsome doctor sitting by her bedside.

"I'm so lucky to have known you these past three years," she said sleepily. "What would I have become without you in my life?"

"Well you wouldn't be the little whore you are now, Maggie," Miles said, and then he laughed.

"That wasn't nice, Miles!"

"It was a compliment, Maggie!"

"Thank you ... I guess ...."

Miles sat silently thinking. Finally, he leaned forward and took Maggie's hand in his.

"Maggie, I thought when you went into labor, the baby was coming early ... but after seeing the size of the boy, and doing some calculations ... I think you should know the child wasn't conceived when you were raped. He would have been conceived nearly three weeks earlier, maybe more."

"And why do you think that should be important to me?"

"Because I wouldn't ever want you to resent the child ... thinking he was the product of violence,

Maggie! This baby was conceived in love. That's important for *HIM* to know."

"Miles Deihl ... you never cease to amaze me! You are the most perceptive person I've ever met, when it comes to human nature. You've taught me so much!"

"Have you decided on a name for him?"

"No, not yet," Maggie said, looking down at the baby.

"I think you should name him after his father, Maggie."

"That wouldn't bother you?"

"Why should it? I would hope that someday he can meet his father. Although I was raised by a step-father, at least I had the opportunity to know my real dad. I'll raise this boy as if he's my own, but we're never going to lie to him, Maggie. He's going to know the truth as soon as he's old enough to understand it. That's only being fair to him."

"All right, Miles. We'll name him after Nathan ... but we'll call him Nate"

Chapter 25 – The Past Returns

September 27, 1810 – Newton, Ohio

Nathan Stillman's beautiful new chestnut mare was particularly animated on this brisk autumn morning. Nathan had finished the chores early, and was headed into Newton to pick up some supplies.

The general store was busy today. The weekly stage from Marietta was due to come through. Lots of Newton residents congregated at the store to welcome relatives and old friends.

Sam Wilson was leaning against the light pole outside the store when Nathan rode up.

"Mornin' Sam," Nathan shouted; dismounting the big chestnut, and tying her to the rail.

"Why Nathan Stillman … you're just the man I was hoping to see!" Sam grinned at Nathan.

"What did I do now?" Nathan joked.

"Well, it's not so much what you've done lately … It's about what you *might* have done about nine years ago." Sam couldn't manage to stifle his laughter. He winked at Nathan.

"You expect me to remember back that far?" Nathan scratched his head thoughtfully. "So what is it that I *MIGHT* have done, Sam?"

"Let's walk over here by the creek, and sit a spell. I don't want anyone to hear what I'm about to tell you." Sam headed for a bench on the creek bank.

"Oh God ... this sounds serious, Sam. Should I go have a drink first?" Nathan was joking, but he was beginning to see that Sam was actually very serious.

The two men sat down, and Sam turned to Nathan, placing his hand on Nathan's arm, in a reassuring manner.

"Well ... here's the story, Nathan. My cousin, William Wilson, died and left a young widow to fend on her own ... this was back in Bucks County. Seems she had lost her entire family in the Indian wars, and had nobody to look after her when she lost her husband. They'd only been married a couple of years. My family was all living in Pittsburg at that time."

"Bucks County?" Nathan interrupted.

"Yep. Does that ring a bell with you, Nathan?"

Nathan's face flushed bright red, as he allowed his mind to go back; remembering his youth.

"You crazy, light complexioned Swedes can't hide your feelings. That red face of yours is a dead give-away!" Sam laughed and patted Nathan on the back. "I don't mean to embarrass you, or condemn you, Nathan. It's just that you need to hear this."

"Go on," Nathan said soberly.

"Well ... My cousin's widow showed up on my Aunt Lea's doorstep out of nowhere. She was pregnant and very sickly. Of course, my Aunt took her in. I guess her daughter-in-law died in childbirth, but left a beautiful baby girl in my Aunt's care."

"Oh my God!" Nathan cried, covering his face with his massive hands, wishing this was just a bad dream.

"That's not the end of the story, Nathan."

"I don't know if I can bear to hear the rest," Nathan replied.

"Well, here it is." Sam Wilson took a deep breath, and sighed. "My Aunt died about a year ago, and the little girl was passed around from relative to relative ... none of which really wanted her, because everyone in the family knew she was a bastard child ... that she wasn't fathered by my cousin, William, who died about two years before this baby was born. Poor little girl." Sam shook his head sadly. He continued. "I had to go back there, a couple of months ago, to settle my father's estate. While I was there, my uncle asked me to go to Bucks County and see if I could sell my Cousin William's farm. It had set empty for years. I just happened to spend some time with the family next door – *YOUR* family, Nathan. By the way, your ma and pa are doing just fine and asked me to tell you to write more often." Sam tried to lighten the mood.

Nathan looked at Sam, tears welling up in his big blue eyes. He shook his head despondently. "Sam ... was that *MY* child?"

Sam put his hand on Nathan's shoulder and shook his head. "Only God knows, Nathan. But from what your family told me ... about the time you spent helping Annie Wilson ... and the fact that the child is a spittin' image of *YOU* ... I'd have to say YES. I believe she is your child. I don't mean to pry, but it *is* a possibility, right? You and Annie were lovers, right?"

"I loved that woman!" Nathan admitted. "She was my first love. Then she just disappeared ... left without a word. I never knew what happened to her. It broke my young heart. I was only about eighteen." Nathan began to sob. "Now I think I understand what happened – I mean *WHY* she left so abruptly." Nathan drew his sleeve across his eyes. "Why didn't she tell me? I would have married her in a heartbeat! She should have known that."

"Well, maybe she thought you were just too young." Sam paused, thoughtfully. "Nathan, isn't it interesting how life can be so mysterious – it's like destiny was at play in this very town ... just to bring us together for *THIS*. If I hadn't actually suspected that little Annie is *YOUR* baby, I would have never approached you with this story. I certainly don't mean to meddle in your life, but this little orphan girl needs a real and loving home. Would you be interested in being a father, Nathan?"

"Of course I would, Sam," Nathan said. "I would love to be a father ... you know that!"

"Yes, I do know that. That's why I just *had* to tell you about this."

Nathan jumped to his feet. "OK," he said, "what do we do to get her here? How do we prepare her for the truth? Will she even want to come?"

Sam stood up, looking at Nathan in amazement. "You're just not going to believe this, Nathan. We both know that the Good Lord works in mysterious ways, right?"

"Yes," Nathan said, wiping at his tear-streaked face.

"Well, I had already made up my mind to adopt that little girl, just in case I was wrong about you maybe being her father. I have to admit that my wife wasn't really up for it ... But when I met little Annie last year, I was smitten ... to say the least. I kept in contact with her – she's so smart! ... she can read and write already .... and she's just about willing to accept anything at this point. She calls me Uncle Sam, and she's coming .... *TODAY!* On the twelve o'clock .... Actually she'll be here pretty soon, Nathan."

Nathan looked like he'd been *"thunder struck"* standing there with his mouth wide open and his eyes as big as saucers. Sam slapped the bottom of Nathan's chin, closing his gaping mouth. Nathan was speechless.

"So what shall we do, Nathan?" Sam asked. "Do you want to meet her today, or would you rather I prepare her, get her settled in, and then bring her out to your place in a week or so? That would give you both some time for it to all sink in ..."

"That sounds like a good plan, Sam," Nathan replied, finally able to speak. "I can't tell you how much I appreciate this. I haven't been this happy for a long, long time. And I had nothing to look forward to. I thought I had nothing to live for. I can't wait to tell John and Sarah!!" Nathan was beside himself. "Can you bring her home a week from today?"

"That's what I'll do, Nathan. Now if you change your mind, be sure and get word to me."

"Samuel Wilson ... There's no way in hell I'm going to change my mind. I just want to get everything ready for her. I want everything to be perfect. Thank you, thank you, thank you!!" Nathan grabbed Sam and gave him a bear hug that nearly snapped his back. Setting Sam down, he remembered the supplies he needed. "Sam, I've got to go, but let's shake on this agreement. You've made me a very happy man."

The two men shook hands; both of them laughing loudly, and obviously satisfied with their agreement. Nathan hurried back to the store to pick up the items on his list.

Just as Nathan finished loading the saddlebags onto his mare, the stage pulled in. Nathan quickly mounted the horse and trotted down the lane, just about thirty yards from the general store. He stopped and turned the mare around. Watching in anticipation, as the passengers disembarked from the stage, his excitement was peaking. One by one, six people emerged from the stagecoach. He saw Sam approaching the coach, just as a little girl with blonde curly hair, poked her head out of the stagecoach door. When she saw Sam Wilson, little Annie jumped into his arms. It was a heart-warming sight, and Nathan began to weep again. He couldn't wait to get back to the Stillman farm to tell John and Sarah the news.

"You devil, you!" John exclaimed. "And I wondered why you were spending so much time over there ... working for free."

Sarah was beaming. "Nathan, what a wonderful surprise. We need to get busy and make sure you have everything ready for your little girl. I'll make a list. You know ... her own bed and dresser, wash stand, those kinds of things. She's just got to have a pretty room. I'll make the curtains."

"Well, do you think I can raise her right?" Nathan asked, rubbing his chin, thoughtfully.

"No question about it, Nathan," Sarah replied. "With our kids, and your daughter, it will be a wonderful, big, extended family." Sarah stopped short. "What will we do with two little girls both named Annie?"

Chapter 26 - "Panther Across The Sky"

November 16, 1811 – The home of Dr. Miles Deihl – Lexington, Kentucky:

Maggie looked up from her knitting, when Miles walked into the room.

"Is he asleep?" she said softly.

"Finally," Miles said, smiling. "He made me read the same story three times, though."

"So that's what took so long?"

Miles reached down, taking the knitting needles and yarn from Maggie, laying them on the table. He caught her hands and raised her to her feet, looking down into her smiling face.

"I've been thinking, Maggie," he said, grinning at her.

"Oh NO! It's been my experience that men become dangerous when they're allowed to think!" she mocked; repeating what he had said to her, so many years earlier.

"You think you're pretty witty, don't you?" He laughed, remembering his own comment.

"I'm sorry... I just couldn't resist!" Maggie gave Miles a big kiss on his cheek. "Now ... what were you thinking, Miles?"

"That boy is so smart, Maggie! He absolutely amazes me. I can't wait until he's a little older...

There's so much I want to teach him." Miles gave Maggie a gentle kiss on her lips.

"I don't want him to grow up too fast. You'll just have to be patient!"

"I always thought raising children would be a wonderful experience. You know ... molding their minds ... stimulating their imaginations... But young Nate has taught *ME* things. I can't exactly explain it, but it's as if he understands everything, on a subtle level, which I'm not in touch with. Does that make any sense to you?" Miles shook his head, struggling; trying to find the right words. "I can't put it any other way than this ... the boy speaks to my soul. That's as close as I can come to verbalize it. He's special, Maggie!"

"You've been a wonderful father to him, Miles. He loves you. Maybe that's what you feel."

"No, Maggie... It's more than that. When he becomes a man, he's got a very significant destiny. That makes our responsibility all the more important. We need to raise him in a way which will help him fulfill his calling."

"Which is *WHAT*?" Maggie looked confused.

"I wish I knew. For now, that's all I'm sure of." Miles wrapped his arms around Maggie and grinned that handsome grin. "That ... and the fact that I love you madly!" he whispered in her ear.

Maggie reached up and slid her arms around Miles' neck. She pulled his face down to hers, and planted little kisses all around his mouth. He kept trying to trap her lips with his, but she was too quick. Finally, he caught her face in his hands, and covered her mouth hungrily with his. The inferno was ignited. Miles wrapped his arms around Maggie and kissed her feverishly. He led her into their bedroom. They both laid down on the bed. He continued to kiss her and caress her until he was confident her passion was as insistent as his own. He took his time undressing her, returning to her lips from time to time; intensifying her desire; rekindling the inferno. Miles began at Maggie's lips and kissed her all over her body, from her head to her toes. He loved making her quiver and moan. He found it tantalizing that she so freely enjoyed the pleasure he loved giving her.

When her passion was at its maximum, Miles stopped, leaving her begging for more. He waited. When Maggie could no longer endure the agony of her need, she rose up like an animal and ripped at his clothes, literally tearing them from his body. She groaned and clawed at him, trying to capture what she desired; what she needed. Miles teased her, tormented her, and provoked her. His own desire was beginning to overtake his resolve, and he surrendered to the wild passion which sizzled and burned between them. Maggie cried out, when he finally threw her down and thrust himself into her. Maggie was insatiable. Now Miles was the one receiving the pleasure, as she absorbed him completely. He let her set the tempo, and he played her body like a fine instrument. She responded perfectly to his skillful domination. Her cries of pleasure became louder as he adeptly ushered her to the edge of ecstasy. When Miles was certain Maggie was ready, he drove into her harder and faster until she let it go. Her body shook in shivers of delight, and her screams penetrated the silence of the night. At that point, Miles couldn't restrain himself anymore. He emptied himself into her; he filled her with himself.

It was at that moment, just before midnight, as Miles was releasing his seed into Maggie, the entire night sky lit up. A huge ball of fire crossed the sky, from out of the southwest, incredibly bright with a weird greenish-white color. The room was illuminated by the flash.

Miles gasped, sitting straight up in the bed. "What the hell was that?!!" He left the bed and ran outside. As the meteor crossed the sky, leaving a trail of fire behind it, Miles' eyes grew wide with wonder. Maggie came out, just in time to see it disappear below the horizon. She, too, stood in awe of its beauty.

"That was exquisite!" she cried. "It's crossing was so *slow!*"

"It's a sign," Miles said quietly.

"A sign of what?"

"You're pregnant, Maggie!" Miles laughed.

"That's not funny, Miles!"

"I'm not being funny. You're pregnant. That was my sign!"

"That was no sign ... That was a meteor ... And I'm not pregnant!"

"We just conceived a son! Maggie ... you're going to bear *my* son!!"

"That's not possible," Maggie said weakly.

"Count the days, Maggie!" Miles laughed harder. "What were you thinking?"

"ME?!!"

"You always keep track of the days, Maggie! What happened – – What did you do?!!" Miles continued to laugh.

"Oh NO!!" Maggie cried. "I forgot! I'm sorry!!"

"You tricked me, didn't you, Maggie?"

"NO!! I swear!! I didn't think ...." Maggie began to cry.

"No ... you didn't think!" Miles interrupted, falling to his knees with the uncontrollable laughter.

"Why are you laughing, if you're angry with me?" Maggie sobbed.

"Because I'm glad you didn't bother to think!" Miles stood up and grabbed Maggie, hugging her, and covering her face with kisses.

"But Miles ... we can't have a baby together!!" Maggie cried.

"Why NOT?!!"

"Because we're not married, and it's not fair to an innocent child to be raised as a bastard!"

Without thinking, Miles slapped Maggie hard across the face with his opened hand, leaving her distraught and bewildered.

Miles' dark eyes drove into Maggie like daggers. "I've met many men in my time ... men who epitomize the term BASTARD ... and yet, *they* had *married* parents!! *NO* child of mine will ever be called a *bastard*, Maggie!" Miles spat out the words, looking at her as though she had committed an unpardonable sin.

Miles turned and went back inside, without apologizing.

Maggie remained outside, crying and trying to understand Miles' unexpected angry outburst. Five years earlier, the girl would have reacted in a tirade to being slapped like that, but she had learned to think; to weigh and balance viewpoints. Miles had taught her to control her childish impulses.

She had seen Miles Deihl angry on only three occasions, in the years she had known him, however this was the first time he was infuriated to the point of striking her. She tried hard to comprehend his displeasure. She realized she would probably never understand all of his idiosyncrasies.

The next morning, Miles was gone; he didn't even say good-by.

Chapter 27 - The Earthquake of 1811

This sequence of three very large earthquakes is usually referred to as the New Madrid earthquakes, after the Missouri town that was the largest settlement on the Mississippi River between St. Louis, Missouri and Natchez, Mississippi. On the basis of the large area of damage (600,000 square kilometers), the widespread area of perceptibility (5,000,000 square kilometers), and the complex physiographic changes that occurred, the New Madrid earthquakes of 1811-1812 rank as some of the largest in the United States since its settlement by Europeans. They were by far the largest east of the Rocky Mountains in the U.S. and Canada. The area of strong shaking associated with these shocks is two to three times as large as that of the 1964 Alaska earthquake and 10 times as large as that of the 1906 San Francisco earthquake.

(http://earthquake.usgs.gov/earthquakes/state s/events/1811-1812.php)

December 15, 1811 - 9:30 pm - Lexington, Kentucky

Dr. Miles Deihl had been gone six weeks, and in his absence, Maggie attended to the office and all of his patients, as she always did. This time was different, however. This time, Maggie wasn't sure whether Miles would come back to her. By now, she was certain that she was pregnant, and she was frightened at the thought of going through it alone.

On the other hand, she didn't see Miles Deihl abandoning his own child. He wasn't that kind of man. If he were indeed convinced she was going to give him a son, then she was confident he would return to claim the child. The question at hand was ... did he really believe he had impregnated her?

Little Nate was asleep in his room, and Maggie was reading one of Miles' medical books. She was having a hard time concentrating on her reading; thoughts of Miles kept interrupting her study. She finally laid the book down and walked outside, onto the porch. It was a cold night and it was late. Things were normally quiet at this time of night, but tonight something seemed different. It was too quiet. The air was too still. Maggie looked up and down the street, as if expecting to see something unusual. The feeling of anticipation was overpowering. She tried to shake it off, but the uncanny sense of expectancy remained.

Maggie decided to try and get some rest.

December 16, 1811 – 2:00 am – Lexington, Kentucky:

It was the noise which awakened Maggie from a sound sleep. The loud rumbling was coming from below, and then the house began to sway. Maggie jumped out of bed in alarm. Her first sensation was a mild dizzy feeling. The floor was slightly moving and she felt as if she was standing on a boat. Suddenly everything changed. A violent shaking knocked her to her knees and she screamed in terror. She had to crawl to get to Nate's room, as the quaking increased in its intensity. By the time she reached the boy, everything was crashing and breaking. The huge dresser in the room was sliding across the floor; first one way, and then back the other. Nate was sitting upright in his bed laughing and clapping his hands together, thoroughly enjoying the excitement and the noise. Maggie grabbed the boy and dragged him down to the floor with her, and the two of them tried to get to the front door without being injured by falling objects. The house was coming apart.

Once outside, Maggie could see other people running into the street shrieking in panic. The earth was rolling in huge crashing waves. Buildings were collapsing, trees were breaking, animals were screaming in alarm, and the air was filled with a thick dust, rising in clouds of perturbed filth. She could barely breathe.

Maggie picked Nate up in her arms and moved to a location where she was sure nothing could fall on them. The earth continued to pitch and lurch. It went on for an indefinite period. Maggie lost track of time in the disaster. She watched as her own home came crashing down like a house of cards. She felt faint. Just as she was losing consciousness, she sensed someone's arms around her. The blackness swallowed her awareness.

When Maggie awoke, little Nate was safely in her arms, and her neighbor, Lettie was sitting in a chair beside the cot she was lying on. Maggie looked around. She was in a tent.

"Lettie, is it over?" Maggie asked weakly.

"No darlin' it just keeps on shakin'," Lettie said. She looked at Maggie, her eyes full of questions. "Maggie, where's Dr. Deihl?"

"I don't know," Maggie answered. "He had to go away on business, but that was over a month ago. I hope he's all right." Maggie could feel a lump forming in her throat. She missed Miles, and she was afraid she may never see him again.

"Well, darlin', don't you worry. Stephen and I will make sure you and little Nate have a place to stay," Lettie said patting Maggie's hand.

The people of Lexington, Kentucky continued to live in tents for the next three months, as the restless earth trembled and shook. Sometimes Maggie allowed herself to think about John, and Sarah, and Nathan. She prayed it hadn't been as bad for them, as it had for people of Kentucky. She wondered whether Miles was alive or dead. She worried that he may have been caught in the quake while traveling on the Mississippi River. Rumors were rampant about how the Mississippi had been thrown from its banks, and how land had risen and sunk along the river. She'd heard that most of the people who died in the quakes were on or along that waterway. News from travelers did little to calm Maggie's fears.

By May, 1812, Maggie and little Nate were living in a rented cabin on the outskirts of the town. Maggie was six months pregnant, but managed to keep Miles' practice going. She made excuses for the doctor; telling people he was delayed along the Mississippi, caring for injured people. In her heart, she knew she would soon have to face the truth. She would need to make plans for herself, her son, and the baby she was expecting. Maggie thought about returning to Pennsylvania, but wasn't sure if any of her aunts or uncles still lived there. She even considered going back to Newton, but she was determined not to go crawling back to Nathan. She still had plenty of money. Miles had insisted on her saving it. Maggie knew she could go anywhere she wanted to go, and do anything she chose to do. She just hadn't yet decided *where* to go, or *what* she really wanted to do.

It was a warm, balmy night. The moon was full and the stars were plentiful in the clear nighttime sky. The spring peepers and the crickets were singing in chorus, while a mocking bird in the distance added to the evening serenade. Maggie could smell the faint aroma of honeysuckle on the breeze. It was a perfect night, but she was lonely, and not even this kind of perfection could lift her spirits. It only reminded her that there had been happier times in her life; but not at this time.

Maggie was exhausted from the day's busy schedule. She bathed little Nate, took her own bath, and went to bed early. Lately, her dreams had been extremely vivid, and she had learned to enjoy them. There was little more in her life which she found pleasurable. She quickly fell into a deep sleep.

She dreamed she saw a Creek warrior approaching her cabin on a magnificent black stallion. The Indian was dressed in nothing more than a loin cloth and leggings. Three colorful feathers hung from the left side of his long, coal black hair. He wore beautifully engraved silver bands around each bicep, accentuating the swell of his muscles. Silver bangles hung from his ears. The warrior's bare chest glistened in the moonlight. His eyes flashed golden, in the glow of the full moon, like the eyes of a wolf on the prowl.

Maggie allowed him to slide into the bed beside her. He lifted her nightgown. She could feel his lips moving on her swollen, pregnant stomach. His hands were caressing her engorged breasts. Little shivers ran up and down her body, as the Indian explored her exaggerated curves. She felt his lips move from her stomach to her mouth, and her lips parted to welcome him. The kiss was too familiar. Maggie stirred. This was no dream. She was going to scream, and the man quickly slammed a hand over her mouth to stifle her cry. Maggie wrestled with the man, trying to free herself. She opened her eyes. To her amazement, this man was not dressed like a Creek Warrior; he was dressed like an ordinary traveler. She was terrified.

"Maggie! Shhhhh! Maggie, it's me ... Miles!" he whispered.

Maggie's eyes grew wide with shock and fear. She blinked hard, not sure she was really awake. She could see Miles' handsome face, shining in the muted light from the full moon. She began to cry. He removed his hand from her mouth and gathered her into his powerful arms.

"My God, Maggie," he whispered hoarsely, "I've missed you!" He buried his face in her hair, and breathed her scent. "I've been worried out of my mind... I couldn't get back. I tried! I swear on my soul, Maggie ... I tried to get back sooner!"

"I didn't think you were coming back!" Maggie sobbed. "I was sure ... this time, you weren't coming back." She slid her arms around Miles' neck and clung to him as if she were a drowning person clinging to a rescuer.

"You're pregnant Maggie!" Miles grinned at her happily. "I knew you were... This is my son, Maggie!" He gently stroked her stomach.

"How did you find me, Miles?"

"After seeing our house in the rubble ... I had to ask a dozen people. I'm so glad you're all right. I've already checked in on Nate. He's sleeping like a log. The little guy must have found that quake pretty exciting, huh?" Miles returned to kissing Maggie's stomach, and speaking a strange language to his son, inside Maggie's body.

In her relief, Maggie totally forgot to be angry with Miles. She relaxed with his kisses and caressing. She decided to just let him enjoy his handiwork. Miles Deihl was completely obsessed by the knowledge that it was *his* child growing inside her this time.

Chapter 28 – Troubled Times

Life's cycles continued in a perpetual procession. As the seasons progressed, planting and harvesting was the goal and the result. John Stillman's growing family exemplified this progression. By the spring of 1812, John and Sarah were the parents of three children; Ann, Jonathan, and Thomas.

The family farms now included the growing herd of Merino sheep, a wonderful orchard of fruit trees, chickens, hogs, and cattle. The crops were larger and the harvests more plentiful. John and Nathan had built extra cabins for hired farm hands that now lived on the farms and rented the cabins. Life was good and the brothers prospered.

Nathan was happily raising his daughter Annie, who was thriving in the beautiful Ohio countryside. Annie was the apple of her father's eye, and she knew it. The two of them were inseparable. Nathan, however, had managed to turn his daughter into a "tom boy" like Maggie was at that age. She could shoot straighter than most men, she could track and bag a buck with ease, and she could sheer a sheep quicker than any of the hired hands.

The last winter had been worse than any other. From October through March, snow covered the ground. When it wasn't snowing it was raining ice. The temperatures had been the coldest that John and Nathan had ever experienced. The brothers were surprised they didn't lose all of their livestock to the foul weather.

To add to the hardships, the unprecedented series of great earthquakes had shaken the land from December, 1811 through February, 1812, leaving the settlers in the area nervous and afraid. Aftershocks continued to rattle the earth on a daily basis.

The War of 1812 began, and added to the local anxiety, with Britain's military support for tribes in Ohio, Indiana, and Michigan. The Creek War in the south was escalating into a full-blown civil war, and Upper Creeks or Red Sticks were allying themselves with England; causing more Lower Creeks to flee into Florida, joining the Seminoles.

Chapter 29 – The Creek Nation – One Family's Story

"I'm so tired, Miles. Can we stop for a while," Maggie asked, stroking her stomach.

Miles pulled the wagon to a stop and helped Maggie down. She was happy to feel her feet on the ground. It had been a long ride from Kentucky. They'd been a week and a half on the trail, only stopping to eat and sleep. Alabama seemed so far away. Maggie wondered if they would ever get there.

It was the first week of July, and the weather was sweltering hot. Maggie blotted her chest with a handkerchief and tied her hair up on top of her head, trying to stay cool. Miles brought her a cup of water from the wagon, but it tasted lukewarm, and not very refreshing. Little Nate had been grumpy the entire trip, but was sleeping peacefully in the wagon, now.

"It should only be two more days, Maggie. My uncle and my cousin will meet us in Monroe County when we get to Alabama. They're camped along the main road. We'll have the ritual ceremony after we rest a day or two." Miles untied the horses from the back of the wagon and led them into the shade. He watered them and the team. Returning to the wagon, he sat down tiredly.

"Are we safe, going that far into the south, Miles?"

"Only God knows," Miles said flatly. "My kin ... those who will be with us in Alabama, are Red Sticks. That means they are actually Upper Creek. They've decided to go against the Lower Creek tribes – my mother's kin. The Red Sticks want to drive out the white settlers along with the Lower Creek people who sympathize with the whites. I'm stuck between the two, Maggie."

"I'm confused and I'm frightened, Miles."

"Well, Maggie, families are pretty damned tight down here, so as long as they know who I am, we'll be OK. I'll just have to make sure my family names are visible. Since my father was part Upper Creek and my mother was Lower Creek ... I should have plenty of protection from both sides. They're at war, though. I told you it was coming. It's going to get *very* ugly." Miles pulled his shirt off over his head and wiped the sweat from his face with it. "As soon as we've got this ceremony over with, and the baby dedicated... I'll take you back to Kentucky where you and the boys will be safe."

"Miles, what makes you so sure I'm carrying a boy?"

"Maggie ... sometimes I just know things." Miles smiled knowingly, and winked.

The next day, Miles and Maggie rolled into Monroe County, Alabama. They hadn't been on the Monroe Road more than three hours when from out of nowhere, a group of men approached the wagon. Miles stopped the horses.

"Miles!" the large red haired man shouted. "We timed it just right, didn't we?"

"Good to see you healthy, Will," Miles said. "This is Maggie. Maggie, this is my cousin *Red Hawk* – only the most powerful man in the south!"

"It's a pleasure to meet you Miss Maggie. My name is William Weatherby."

"Nice to meet you, too," Maggie said, looking confused.

Another man rode up to the wagon, on a stunning white horse. He tipped his broad-rimmed hat and grinned at Maggie. Maggie looked at Miles, and then back at the man on the white horse. The resemblance was striking.

"You must be Maggie!" he said, nodding at her. "I'm Peter McQuinn."

"Maggie ... Peter is my uncle," Miles smiled. "Peter, Maggie wants to know if we're safe here. I told her I possess the best of both worlds. What say you?"

"He's kin, Miss Maggie... It's our obligation to keep him safe. The damned Lower Creeks have the same obligation," Peter said. "This is probably the only *neutral* Creek on the planet! He dances to his own drum beat ... and nobody else's!! He's just like my brother was."

"Yes ma'am! This Creek isn't Upper or Lower ... He just dangles in the middle!" William laughed loudly. "But, we love him anyway ... And so do his Lower Creek relatives. What can we do?"

Miles followed the men to their encampment, and got settled for the evening. Maggie and little Nate were both tired and hot. They cooled themselves in a brook running beside the camp, and then went to sleep early. The men sat up for hours talking. Maggie could hear them clearly, but couldn't understand the language. It seemed strange to her that these were Creek warriors; one was a chief; and they didn't look at all like Indians.

Maggie was surprised that Miles Deihl leaned more toward his mother's people, the Lower Creeks, instead of siding with the Upper Creeks (Red Sticks). After all, it was the white settlers which had murdered his parents, and the Red Sticks delighted in murdering whites. The Lower Creeks adhered more to white ways.

The next day, they traveled on trails which were off the main road. It was midafternoon when the group arrived at a beautiful plantation house, complete with fields of cotton and tobacco. Black slaves were working the fields and the crops stretched as far as the eye could see.

"Maggie, this is cousin William's plantation," Miles said, looking around the land.

"Miles, I'm really confused. None of these men look like Indians to me."

Miles laughed so hard he nearly fell out of the wagon. "You were expecting wigwams, tee-pees? I promise you, Honey ... these guys are for sure, Creek warriors!" He stopped the wagon and lifted Maggie down, and then Nate. "Most Creek people are mingled with Scottish and French blood ... but the Creek blood runs wild in their veins!"

"I want to be an Indian, too," Nate shouted. "Can you make me an Indian, Father?"

"If your mama says it's OK, I'd be happy to make you an honorary Creek!" Miles grinned down at the child.

"Mama ... is it OK? Can I be a hon .... A honer... Can I be what he said?"

"If that's what you both decide, then it's fine with me," Maggie said, smiling at her son.

Inside the plantation house, Miles and his family were escorted to their rooms. It was the most beautiful home Maggie had ever been in. It reminded her of some of the big homes she had seen in Philadelphia, only this one was far more impressive.

There was a soft knock at the bedroom door. Miles opened it and Peter walked in.

"Here's your mother's ritual dress, Miles. I sent a runner to Pensacola to fetch it when you told me the plan. Your cousin Dorian has been holding on to it for years. She said she'd be more than happy to loan it to you for this occasion, but you'll have to take it back to her when you go down there."

"Peter! I can't believe you risked it for *ME*!" Miles picked up the dress and inspected the intricate colors and patterns woven into the material. "My mother must have looked stunning in this."

"As will your Maggie!" Peter grinned.

"Thank you, so much," Miles said, trying to conceal his emotions.

"I have another surprise for you, too. But that comes later, Miles," Peter said. He turned and left the room.

"Miles ...," Maggie began, thoughtfully, "if Peter is your father's brother ... then ... is *McQuinn* actually your surname?"

Miles laughed out loud and slapped his knees. "Maggie, Sweetheart, I was wandering how long it would take you to figure that out." He grabbed Maggie and kissed her full on the mouth. "Nothing gets by you does it?!"

Later that afternoon, a black woman came to the room to inform Maggie she had to try on the dress, so it could be altered for her ritual. Since she was very pregnant, it was obvious some alteration would definitely be necessary. Maggie complied.

It seemed to be one thing after another, all in preparation of the night's festivities. Maggie wasn't exactly sure what would be taking place, and she had seen very little of Miles since their arrival at the plantation.

Little Nate spent his time with one of the house slaves, who'd been assigned to look after him. When he wasn't with the slave girl, he was with Miles. Maggie welcomed the break from her day to day routine of child-raising. Little Nate was a lively boy, and it was all Maggie could do to keep up with him in her advanced stage of pregnancy.

Two Negro women attended Maggie in preparation for the ceremony. She was dressed in the multicolored gown which Miles' mother had worn, and her hair was woven with flowers and ribbons. Her body had been dusted with a golden colored powder, and she was dripping with beautifully engraved silver earrings, necklaces, and bangles. She wore bracelets on her arms and her ankles.

Maggie hadn't seen Miles or little Nate since yesterday, and she was becoming distressed; not knowing what was about to happen.

Peter McQuinn entered the room and when he saw Maggie, he stood frozen – staring at the girl.

"Maggie ... I can't tell you how enchanting you look! No wonder Miles is so taken with you. You are a vision to behold!"

Maggie blushed. "A very fat vision, I'm sure!"

"You have no idea how special you are, do you?" Peter was grinning the same handsome grin she'd seen on Miles' face so many times. "To the Creek ... pregnant women are a very good omen ... like a magical talisman ... sacred to us! Hasn't Miles ever told you that?"

"No," Maggie said softly.

"Well ... little girl ... sit yourself down and let me educate you!" He laughed, taking Maggie by the hands, and escorting her over to the bed. They sat down together, and Peter looked into the girls huge green eyes. "First of all ... *YOU* were destined to be here, in this very place, and at this very time. The day you were born, it was already decided by the Great Spirit. Everything that has happened to you during your lifetime was preordained *for Miles*. He knew it when he first met you. Didn't you ever wonder why he was so tenacious in courting you? I wasn't there ... but I'm positive he was determined to capture your affections the moment he saw you ... it could have been *NO* other way! *YOU* had no choice in the matter, either."

"Well, he *was* persistent," Maggie admitted, giggling.

"It was required of him. He had no alternative, Maggie." Peter grinned, and squeezed her hands. "We Creeks, consider our women to be our most precious attribute. From our women, comes our future. Our women are always chosen for their beauty, strength, and intelligence. Like the fertile soil of our deltas, our women are the gardens which produce our future generations. Every warrior knows it, when he finds his mate. It's the same for the daughters of our chiefs, too. Their mates are selected by the Great Spirit. That's how the blood gets intermingled. It's a predetermined bloodline. It gets stronger and stronger with every new generation. It never happens by accident. There's something in our genes, Maggie ... a sixth sense, maybe... We intuitively understand our destiny and we have a special *knowing*... something which goes beyond just mere understanding... It's hard to explain." His voice trailed off into his thoughts.

Maggie listened intently, fascinated by what Peter was disclosing.

"Maggie ..." he continued, "from what Miles' told me ... there was a faux pas in the *great plan* ... a blunder or a misstep along the way, if you will. I don't expect you to fully understand what I'm about to tell you, but just listen ... OK?"

"All right," Maggie agreed. "This is so unbelievable ... but it rings so true in my heart! Please continue."

"Well … you were raised Christian, right?"

"I was."

"Then you're familiar with the concept of good versus evil and unseen forces which constantly war against each other, right?"

"Yes."

"I'll try to make this simple for you, Maggie. Your son Nathan was meant to be fathered by Miles. Miles knows it, and we – his family know it. The boy has a huge role to play in bringing about an important change in this nation. We're not sure yet, exactly what that transformation entails … but it's inevitable. He's been chosen, Maggie." Peter hesitated for a moment, and then continued. "Because there are forces at work, which don't want this change to come about, *YOU* were used to try and defeat your son's purpose. We're just glad it only delayed things, and didn't permanently ruin the great plans for him. His genes might be Nathan Stillman's, but his soul is pure Creek!"

Maggie was dumbfounded. She sat quietly, looking back over the events of the last few years. Everything Peter McQuinn said seemed to fit.

Peter gently shook Maggie's hands, bringing her back from her thoughts.

"That's not all, Maggie!" He laughed and winked at the stunned girl. "Do you know where your father met your mother?"

"He met her in New York. Her family had come there from Tennessee, I think."

"Do you know what her maiden name was?"

"Colbert. Her name was Margaret Colbert," Maggie answered.

"Well, Maggie … did your mother ever speak of her family in Tennessee?"

"No, she didn't, as a matter of fact. My grandparents … my mother's parents … didn't stay in New York. They left shortly after my mother and father were married. I never met them, and Mama didn't talk about them. I always thought they didn't approve of my parents' marriage, and there was some kind of a rift in the family because of it."

"Maggie, my dear … this may be a shock, but your mother may have been the daughter of a Creek Chief … William Colbert. I haven't finished my research, but I'm sure she was Creek by blood. That's got to be where you get your dark hair and lovely features. Your father could have been a part of the plot to bring your son Nathan into the great plan."

"Are you saying all of this was planned … so many years before little Nate was born?" Maggie asked, looking skeptical. She paused, thoughtfully. "And yes, come to think of it … my mother did have dark hair and dark features. She really was beautiful when she was young!"

"Your father was of Scottish descent, wasn't he?"

"Yes."

"And wasn't he quite prosperous … a strong and intelligent man?"

"Yes. He was a physician."

"It's typical, Maggie … all part of the great plan. You'll learn more, in time. We've got to get you ready for your ritual now, though." He took Maggie's arm and escorted her out of the room and down the massive staircase.

When Maggie was led out onto the steps leading to the garden, she couldn't believe her eyes. Everyone she remembered seeing, visiting the plantation, had been inexplicably transformed from ordinary southern gentry, to what could only be described as a gathering of authentic Creek Indians.

The people were now dressed in traditional Creek attire. The men had painted their faces in intricate patterns and colors. They wore colorful feathers in their hair, and their bodies were adorned with beautiful silver accessories. There was a huge bon fire burning in the middle of the garden. Musicians were playing flutes and other instruments which Maggie wasn't familiar with. And then there were the drums. The drums reverberated a deep throbbing which moved her spirit; the sound was more than a resonance – she could actually feel it throughout her body. Many of the Creek people were dancing in circles around the fire.

Peter held Maggie's arm firmly as they stood at the top of the steps looking over the spectacle below. There was a full moon in the clear nighttime sky and a warm gentle breeze was carrying the scent of night-blooming jasmine; stimulating Maggie's senses. The entire scenario was breathtaking, but alien to Maggie's narrow comprehension of this enigmatic culture.

Suddenly everything came to an abrupt stop. The silence was broken only by the crackling sound of the fire. The dancers fell to their knees. And then she saw him.

A Creek warrior approached on a magnificent black stallion. He was dressed in nothing more than a loin cloth and leggings. Three colorful feathers hung from the left side of his long, coal black hair. He wore beautifully engraved silver bands around each bicep, accentuating the swell of his muscles. Silver bangles hung from his ears. The Indian's bare chest glistened in the firelight. His eyes flashed golden, in the glow of the full moon; like the eyes of a wolf on the prowl. He slid from the horse like an apparition in the shadows cast by the fire and the full moon. It was Miles. He stood motionless at the end of the walkway, in front of the fire. He was waiting for Maggie.

Maggie remembered her dream. Was she dreaming again? She shook her head quickly and looked away. When she gazed back again, the vision remained. Peter McQuinn led Maggie down the steps and along the garden path, up to where Miles was standing. Maggie was mesmerized by Miles' piercing stare. His eyes penetrate her soul; his eyes were glowing with flames of passion which frightened and aroused her. He reached out and grasped her hand, pulling her closer to him. Maggie was bewildered; not knowing what to expect.

Just then, an old man, the *Ancient*, walked up to them. He carried a huge wooden staff which had strange symbols carved into it. He spoke for a long time, but Maggie had no idea what he was saying. Peter pulled a long, red silk scarf from his pocket, and handed it to the old man. The man tied the scarf to the end of the staff and waved it around. He seemed to be showing it to the crowd. That's when the drums started again.

As the drumbeat got louder and louder, William Weatherby, Red Hawk, the chief, approached Miles and Maggie. He was carrying a shiny silver knife. Maggie trembled and looked up at Miles, needing some solace, but his eyes remained impassively fixated on hers. She felt as if she was being pulled inside his being, as he continued to hold her gaze; locked in his. Maggie was drowning in Miles' burning stare, as he became her focus of existence. Something was happening, and her awareness wasn't permitted to participate. She was being possessed and consumed. Her very essence was being absorbed into Miles' soul – – and his into hers.

She barely felt the sting of the blade as it severed the vein on her left wrist. Red Hawk cut Miles' left wrist also, and then placed the laceration onto Maggie's, letting Miles' blood bleed into hers, and hers into his. Their blood mingled; they became one; physically and spiritually. The old man bound their wrists together with the silk scarf; all the while, Miles held Maggie captive in his gaze. The drumbeat seemed to echo between the two of them, rebounding from one heart to the other. The drums grew increasingly louder and the beat more rapid, until Maggie was completely engulfed in the furor. Her consciousness was slipping away from her. She surrendered to it all.

Miles caught Maggie's limp body with his free arm. Peter quickly unbound their wrists and handed the blood-soaked silk to the old man. Once again the old man tied it to the staff and waved it to the crowd. Loud cheers broke out, and the music and dancing resumed. Miles lifted Maggie up into his arms, and holding her close to his heart, he carried her up the stairs and back to their rooms. He laid her gently on the bed, and then stood back admiring her. This is what he was born to do.

Maggie didn't awaken until the next morning. Miles and little Nate were sitting on the side of the bed, both of them grinning at her. She opened her eyes sleepily, trying to decide if she had had another one of her vivid dreams.

"Mama!" little Nate shouted gleefully, "I'm a real Indian now! I'm a brave Creek warrior!" He crawled over to his mother and held his wrist up proudly. It was bandaged, but Maggie could see some blood seeping through.

"Nate!" she cried, hurriedly sitting up in the bed. "What did you do?"

Seeing his mother's unexpected distress, the boy quickly retreated to Miles' lap. "You tell her," he said, looking up at Miles.

"Maggie, little Nate and I are blood brothers now. Our son has the blood of a Creek warrior running through his veins... As do you, my love." Miles grinned broadly, waiting for Maggie's tirade.

It didn't come....much to his surprise.

"That's wonderful," she whispered, her eyes filling with tears of joy.

"She's happy, Nate!" Miles grinned from ear to ear. "She's not mad at us!"

"Yea!! Mama's not mad at us!" Nate shouted, clapping his hands.

"Why would I be angry?" Maggie asked, smiling at Miles.

"Well Maggie ... we never know how you're going to react. Sometimes you really catch us off guard!" He grinned, looking down at Nate. "Isn't that right, son?"

"That's the truth," the boy sighed.

"I'm actually relieved to know it's done," Maggie said.

"Maggie ... what are you talking about?" Miles asked, raising one eyebrow in suspicion.

Maggie giggled. "Your uncle Peter told me a very interesting tale. It had to do with Creek princesses, and little boys with big jobs to do ... and lots of other things about brave Creek warriors."

"Then you approve?" Miles asked.

"Yes! It's already been written," Maggie replied.

Miles was astounded by Maggie's attitude toward the entire incredible set of events.

Maggie was about to get up, when without warning, her body was suddenly gripped by the pains of labor. She fell back onto the pillows holding her stomach in her arms.

"Nate, you run along and find Samantha. Tell her to stay with you. Your baby brother is about to be born," Miles grinned, setting little Nate down and giving him a gentle push towards the door.

Miles went to the bedroom door and called for the midwife who was staying at the plantation. It had all been arranged for Maggie's delivery. He went to the bed and slid in beside Maggie. Sitting up against the headboard, he pulled Maggie between his knees and supported her back against his chest. He put his cheek against hers and hugged her tightly.

"This is how it's supposed to be, Maggie. Put your arms through my legs and use them for leverage when you need to."

"This feels so right, Miles. I feel safe and secure with you holding me like this."

"Are you comfortable, Honey?"

Another crushing pain overwhelmed Maggie. "Oh!!! It hurts!"

"Just relax, Maggie," Miles whispered in her ear.

There was a knock at the door and the midwife hurried in, carrying towels and a basin of hot water.

"I promise you, Maggie... This will be easier and faster than the last time."

Miles continued to cuddle Maggie, and talk to her through the entire delivery, which was extremely easy and quickly over.

"Here's your baby boy, Moon Wolf!" the woman cried, handing Miles his son.

"Look Maggie! He's perfect!" Miles said softly, showing Maggie the newborn.

"*Moon Wolf* ?" Maggie whispered, remembering her dream. She turned slightly, looking Miles square in the eye.

"Well ... umm ..... yes, but you can call me Miles." He laughed, and then winked at Maggie.

The dedication ceremony was short but dramatic. Miles presented the boys to the Creek community, and the old man added Maggie's and her sons' names to the staff, next to Miles McQuinn's name. It was a carved record of the Creek bloodline. The staff passed from generation to generation and recorded every family genealogy and progression. It was the very essence of the Creek culture, and was considered the most valuable artifact of the tribe. No one was permitted to read the names on the staff aloud; especially the original name at the bottom. The original family name was a highly guarded secret.

Chapter 30 – Time Passages

The years flew by and the boys grew to be strong young men and fast friends. Dr. Miles Deihl was a perfect father, spending all of his spare time with his sons. He made sure their education came first – above all things. Miles spent hours with the boys, teaching them and stimulating their young minds; making them curious about everything in life. When the three of them weren't studying, they were in the forests and fields learning about nature. Their father showed the boys how to use a bow and arrow, a tomahawk, and how to shoot a gun.

Miles taught them how to ride Seminole, and they trained the stallion's colt. The horses behaved as though they understood that they were an integral part of the boys' education. The stallions both showed a natural affection for Miles' sons. The magnificent black horses were part of the family, and were loved as family members.

Miles made his usual trips south, but tried not to spend as much time away from his little family in Kentucky. His medical practice had grown, along with the population of Lexington, and Dr. Miles Deihl was a respected member of the community.

On March 27, 1814, General Andrew Jackson's army utterly crushed the Red Sticks. Despite their stubborn bravery, some 800-900 Creeks were killed out of the 1,000 who stood and fought, in a battle earmarked by its savagery. Jackson's army suffered 49 killed and 154 wounded – many mortally. The Battle of the Horseshoe was one of the most bloody and savage battles of the War of 1812; and is perhaps the worst slaughter ever suffered by the Creeks at the hands of an American army. The power of the Creeks was forever broken by the carnage on the banks of the Tallapoosa.

This victory, catapulted Andrew Jackson into the public limelight of the nation. Nine months later, on January 8, 1815, Jackson vanquished the British Redcoats at Chalmette in the Battle of New Orleans. That was the last battle of the War of 1812, and the worst defeat the British suffered on American soil.

The American government was now concentrating on restraining the Seminoles in Florida.

July, 1821 – Lexington, Kentucky

"Maggie, you and I have to talk about Nate," Miles said, pulling Maggie down onto his lap.

"What about Nate?" Maggie asked, giving Miles a lingering kiss on his lips.

"It's time for his initiation, Maggie."

"His what?"

"He'll be thirteen at the end of this month, and he needs to spend his thirteenth year with the elders – It's our family's tradition," Miles said flatly.

Maggie jumped up, stamped her foot, and slapped her hands onto her hips defiantly. She looked at Miles angrily, sparks shooting from her large green eyes.

"You will NOT take my son away from me for a year! Not even for a month! With all the fighting going on down there ... what are you thinking?!"

"He's going with me next week, Maggie."

"No he isn't!" she screamed at him.

"I'm going, Mama," Nate said calmly. He had walked in on the conversation by accident.

"NO!" Maggie cried. She ran from the room in tears. She knew full well, she was outnumbered. Her heart was breaking as she cried herself to sleep that night. Her son, Nate, didn't belong to her anymore. He was more Creek than she had anticipated; a free spirit, true to his destiny.

It was the longest year of Maggie's life. Never had she been separated from her son, let alone for a full year. Miles made extra trips south during that time, to keep tabs on Nate's progress. He wasn't happy about his son being away, but had full confidence in the fact that the Creek elders would look out for the boy's wellbeing.

When the initiation time was over, Miles went south and brought young Nate home. He had grown nearly four inches taller and put on extra pounds. His skin had turned a golden bronze color, and his hair had been bleached nearly white, from spending time in the southern sun. Maggie was amazed at the change in his stature and his attitude. He seemed more confident, and he carried himself with an air of authority. His voice was deeper, and his body was muscular. Nate and the doctor spent hours conversing in the native tongue which Maggie never learned.

In 1825, it was young Miles' turn to go to his initiation. He would be turning thirteen. After seeing all the positive changes in Nate, four years earlier, Maggie handled the situation much better, this time. She didn't want to be separated from young Miles, but she knew it was for the best. Her youngest son was eager and excited to spend the year with the elders of the Creek tribe, and her older son, Nate, was disappointed he couldn't go along.

When it was time to leave, Miles kissed Maggie and hugged young Nate sadly. Maggie knew it was as difficult for Miles as it was for her, but destiny demands its own. Both of their boys would be well prepared for the future, and supremely groomed for the preordination, which would be their destiny.

By the spring of 1827, the boys had been accompanying Miles on every trip he made to the south. Maggie's sons had grown into strong, fine looking young men, capable of handling any situation with confidence and courage.

The boys had learned to emulate Miles Deihl in all circumstances. They had learned to have a deep compassion for their relatives, the Florida Seminoles. At times, that very compassion seemed to border on hatred towards the government's treatment of the Seminole people, however, like Dr. Miles Deihl, the boys both abhorred violence.

Chapter 31 – Lost Love

July, 1827 – Lexington, Kentucky

Maggie heard the commotion outside and was excited to think Miles and the boys had finally returned home. She ran out onto the porch as the wagon rolled to a stop. She immediately noticed Seminole II was tied to the back of the wagon. She thought it odd Miles wasn't riding the stallion, as he always did.

Nate and young Miles climbed down out of the wagon and tied the horses to the bar in front of the house. Maggie didn't see the doctor. Instead of the boys running to greet their mother, such as they always had, they went to the back of the wagon without greeting Maggie. Instinctively she knew something was wrong. She ran down to the back of the wagon. Her sons were pulling a cot from the rear. Dr. Miles Deihl was lying motionless on the stretcher.

"What happened?!!" she cried, feeling the fear rising in her throat.

"Mama, father's real sick," Nate said soberly. "I think it's malaria. It comes and goes ... the fevers and chills." The boys carried the stretcher into the house and put Miles into bed.

"Miles... Miles ..." Maggie gently patted Miles' face. "Wake up, Miles." Tears were streaming down her cheeks.

"Maggie ..." Miles' eyes fluttered open. "Oh God, Maggie ... I was afraid I would never see you again." He forced a smile.

"What can I do to make you well, Miles?" Maggie asked, trying to sound calm.

"Sweetheart, I don't think you can do anything, at this point," he whispered. "I think it's damaged my liver, Maggie."

Maggie looked closely at his handsome face and realized his skin had a yellow tinge to it. Then she checked the whites of his eyes. They were horribly yellowed from the disease. She began to cry.

"Maggie ... crying won't help. You've got to be strong. That's the only way you can help me." Miles began to shake violently with chills. "I won't get better, Maggie. I don't know how long I've got, but there's so much I need to tell you."

"Nate, go and get more quilts," Maggie ordered. "Young Miles ... you go make some hot tea."

Nate brought the quilts and began spreading them over his father's shivering body.

"It's been like this for five days, Mom ... first the fevers and then the chills. He won't eat, and he says he can't sleep. Little Brother and I have done what we could ... but we need quinine."

"Where can we get it?" Maggie asked, looking a bit optimistic.

"Nate, I don't think you'll find it around here, son," Miles groaned.

"Then I'll ride to Louisville!" Nate said angrily. "I don't intend to just watch you die!"

"Son, it's too late. I can tell my liver is finished. Take my word for it."

Nate bit at his lip, trying to keep from crying. He loved Miles, and respected him more than anyone he had ever known. Although Miles had explained to Nate that he wasn't his real father, the two of them had grown closer than most biological fathers and sons. Miles had always considered Nate *HIS* son; as Nate had considered Miles his father. Now the boy was going to have to let go of the most important person in his life. He didn't want to have to say good-bye.

"Maggie... Mix up some of the bitter powder. I ache all over. It might even ease the fever and chills," Miles said, patting Maggie's hand.

Young Miles brought the tea in, and sat down at the bedside. He lifted a spoonful to his father's lips. Dr. Deihl was able to take some of the liquid.

"Thank you, son," Miles whispered. "You boys have been a joy to me... I could have never asked for two better sons than what I have." He sipped some more of the tea from the spoon. "I want you to know that your mother is the only woman I've ever loved, and I expect you to look after her when I'm gone. She's more special than you know ... but you'll understand in a few years. I'll always be with you in spirit... You know that from your training. Now go and unload the wagon and see to the horses, while I talk to your mama."

Young Miles set the cup of tea down, and the boys obediently left the room. Maggie sat down at the bedside and laid her head on Miles' chest. She sobbed; her body shaking with the heartfelt grief.

"Don't give up Miles ... don't leave me. I don't know what I'd do without you!" she cried.

"Maggie, I made arrangements for this very situation, years ago. Nathan Stillman and I made a solemn pledge to each other."

"What?!" Maggie immediately raised her head and looked at Miles in disbelief. "When did you speak to Nathan?"

"I spoke to him before I left his cabin, back in 1807."

"I don't understand!"

"I agreed to let him live, and I would raise his son, if he agreed to look after you when I died. I promised him I would send you back to him. He agreed to take care of my family when I couldn't." Miles began to perspire. Maggie ran and got a cloth and a basin of water.

"Miles, I don't want to go back to Nathan!" she whispered hoarsely.

She sponged the sweat off of Miles' face and chest with the cool water.

"Maggie, it was a gentlemen's agreement. You have no choice. You have to promise me you'll go ..." Miles hesitated, choking on the words. "If I die, please don't dishonor me, Honey!" He looked deeply into Maggie's eyes. "Nathan Stillman made a mistake that he deeply regrets. He loves you Maggie. You need to go back to him and let him take care of you. Give him a chance to redeem himself." Miles paused and took a deep breath. "Another thing – when the boys are older – they've got to retrieve the staff Maggie. I was supposed to, but I don't think I'm going to make it ... so the boys need to do that. It's imperative. The staff can't be lost or fall into the wrong hands, Maggie."

Maggie was mixing the bitter powders in a cup of water. Her mind was racing. She was terrified to go back to Nathan. She raised Miles' head and helped him to drink the solution, hoping she could talk him out of making her return to Newton.

"Please don't talk like that! I'm not going to let you die! I need you! The boys need you! Miles, I can't bear this!!" She began to sob again.

"I love you, Maggie ... but you'll be strong when the time comes. I've completed my destiny. Yours is still ahead. You'll love again ... don't deny yourself the love you deserve, Maggie. And the boys will become strong and powerful citizens. I'll be watching... I promise!" Miles' breathing was becoming more rapid. He was silent for a few minutes, thinking, while Maggie continued to cry. "Maggie, why have you never told me you love me? I've often wondered why you can't seem to bring yourself to *say* it." Miles raised Maggie's head so he could see her face. "I know you've always loved me ... but you've never told me. Will you tell me now ... while there's still time ... so you'll have no regrets when I'm gone?"

"Is your pain easing up any, Miles?" Maggie asked. Her voice was shaking.

"Don't try and change the subject, Maggie. I asked you a question."

"Miles," she began, "... if you've always known how I've felt about you ... then why would I need to *say* it? Haven't I *shown* you? Haven't I SHARED myself with you ... fully and completely?" Maggie wiped her tear-stained face on her apron. "You're the one who told me that real love is *sharing* one's self with another. You said I had *flawed reasoning* when it came to love. I decided when I left Newton with you, that I would just *prove* it to you rather than *say* it."

Miles was silent. His eyes were closed and his breathing had eased a bit. He was asleep. Maggie wasn't sure if he'd heard anything she said to him, in answer to his question.

She got up quietly and left the room. Her sons were standing on the porch looking up into the night sky. When they saw their mother they rushed into the house.

"He's sleeping. I gave him some bitter powder and he fell asleep," she said softly.

"That's good," Nate said. "I don't think he's slept much in five days."

"Mama," young Miles said, looking sad and frightened, "will father be all right?"

"No, Miles," she said bluntly, "your father's dying. I don't know how long he'll remain with us ... but we're losing him. You boys need to prepare your hearts. We'll just pray he won't have to suffer much." Maggie was trying to be strong. She wanted her boys to be prepared, and have no false hopes. "I want you to go to bed, now. If he gets worse during the night, I promise I'll wake you. I'll sit with him."

The boys retired, and Maggie returned to Miles' bedside where she remained the rest of the night.

Maggie had fallen asleep sometime during the night, but was awakened early in the morning by Nate who barged into the room. He was distressed.

"Mama, Old Seminole's going crazy in his stall! I don't know what to do!" he cried.

"Go and get him and bring him to the window, Nate. And get your brother up," Maggie said, checking Miles to make sure he was still breathing. She knew in her heart that the time had come; and she felt that Miles' magnificent black stallion, Seminole, sensed it, too.

She ran over and opened the window as wide as she could.

"Maggie ..." Miles' voice was weak, and his breathing was shallow. "Maggie, come close."

Maggie ran to the bed and threw her arms around Miles, planting little kisses all over his face. She held him tightly; affectionately.

"What, my love?" she asked, whispering it in his ear.

"I understood what you told me last night, Maggie. I understand why you never *said* you loved me. You did prove your love, Maggie. Words would never do justice to the love you've shown me through all these years."

"Oh Miles!" she cried out. "I was so afraid you didn't hear me! I'm so relieved to know you did!"

"It's all right, Maggie."

"Miles," Maggie whispered in his ear, "... you were right... You've always been right about everything! I DO love you! I've always loved you!!!! I LOVE YOU!!!"

"I know Honey... I just wanted to hear you admit it." He smiled. "Remember this... I love you ... and I'll love you eternally, Maggie... That's forever. I've loved you since the first day I met you. I think I was born loving you."

Just then Nate brought Seminole to the window. He was snorting and prancing, and being extremely belligerent, until he put his head through the open window and saw Miles. Miles looked up at his stallion.

"Whoa, boy! Seminole my old friend, you understand, don't you? Our sons will carry on."

The stallion whinnied and snorted, and it was obvious that Miles and the stallion had an understanding between them that defied logic. The old horse settled down and remained calm, as he stood there watching his master.

Nate and young Miles came into the room, and each one of them hugged their father affectionately. Each boy, individually, had a private conversation with his father in the language Maggie never understood. Maggie would never know what was said that day, between a father and his sons. It was private, and personal, and intimate. It was never spoken of again.

A week after Dr. Miles Deihl was laid to rest, his old friend Seminole laid down in his stall, never to get up again. The stallion left behind a beautiful colt out of the pretty bay mare Dr. Mathison had given Maggie so many years before. A magnificent steed, black like his sire, Seminole II was every bit as beautiful and intelligent.

Chapter 32 – The Long Road Home

September 28, 1827

It was a gray and drizzly day. The air appeared frozen by the autumn chill.

Maggie stood alone in her bedroom, gazing into the mirror on the heavy oak bureau that Miles had made for her.

She barely recognized the woman looking back at her. Sunken eyes, and the dark circles beneath them gave her a "death warmed over" appearance; the sparkle had left those eyes. Her once shiny black hair now looked lifeless, and it was streaked with a few dull silver strands. She noticed the dryness of her skin, and the deep furrows beginning to appear on her brow and around her mouth. She wasn't even forty years old yet, but she looked like she was sixty. Maggie had not only lost the love of her life, but she had also lost her zest for living.

She walked over and sat down on the bed beside the little metal box that contained her parent's gold and treasures. Dr. Miles Deihl insisted on her keeping her inheritance for a rainy day. She lovingly held it close to her heart. It was all she had left in the world ... but it wasn't enough to replace her beloved Miles.

"Ma?!!!" It was Nate. "Come on Ma, we've got to get going."

Maggie knew the house was prepared for the winter and all was in order for the trip to Ohio, but she couldn't help feeling like a *calf heading for the slaughter.* She did not want to leave her home.

She heard the heavy footsteps coming up the hall, and she knew it was Nate. Maggie hurriedly shoved the box into her bag.

"I'm coming," she called out, just before he burst into the room.

"Mother, I know this is hard for you, but father was emphatic. He said that Miles and I would probably have to hog-tie you and drag you to Ohio, because of your damnable pride. Now please, get your bag and come on."

"Oh – your father said that, did he?"

"Yes he did."

"And he said it was because of my pride?"

"Yes he did."

"Well, he was wrong, for once!" Maggie snatched her bag from the bed and marched over to Nate. "For your information, young man, I have NO pride left. I have NOTHING left that matters!" Maggie shouted. Tears were streaming down her pale cheeks as she stamped her foot in defiance.

"Let's go," Nate said quietly, as he grabbed Maggie's bag from her hand, and gently took his mother's arm, steering her out of the room.

Maggie hesitated, looking back longingly at the cozy room she and Miles had shared together, for so many years. How was she going to leave all her happy memories behind?

"Mother, what on earth is in your bag? It weighs a ton! Do you really need so much stuff?" Nathan interrupted her thoughts.

"Yes, I need it .... And I wish I could take more!" Maggie wiped the tears from her cheeks with the back of her hand.

Outside, Miles was waiting with the horses. They would be traveling light, and all their gear and belongings were distributed among the three steeds. Nate tied Maggie's bag to the back of the saddle, and then helped her onto the horse. Seminole II stood quietly when Maggie mounted him.

"Finally!" Miles exclaimed in frustration.

"Yep, let's go before Mama thinks of another way to keep us here," Nate said, chuckling.

"Well it's barely five o'clock in the morning, son. I would think we could at least have breakfast before we leave," Maggie said, motioning toward the house.

"It's OK Mama," young Miles reassured his mother, "we'll grab a bite on the way. Nate said we'll stop in Georgetown and rest. He's got it all planned."

"There's a tavern there, and I've heard that they serve a pretty decent meal, Mama. So don't worry." Nate said, trotting off down the street, with Miles and Maggie following.

By the time they made it to just south of Sadieville, it was growing dark. Nate had ridden ahead, to find an Inn where they could spend the night.

Without warning, two riders came out of the forest and stopped on the road in front of Maggie and young Miles. Seminole II reared and snorted as the two men approached.

"Stop where you are," one man shouted, drawing his pistol.

The other man rode up behind Maggie and Miles, pulling a long-rifle from the side of his horse.

"We have nothing of value," Maggie said, reigning Seminole to a halt.

"Well, we'll be the judge of that, Ma'am," the man behind them yelled. "Now untie those saddlebags and toss them down, now."

Seminole was acting decidedly strange, as he continued to snort, whinny, and paw at the ground. It was all Maggie could do to try and control the stallion.

"I said throw those saddlebags down!! RIGHT NOW!!" The man at the rear, gave Maggie a painful poke in the ribs with his long-rifle.

Seminole reared and turned, knocking the long-rifle out of the man's hands. Maggie could barely hold the horse back, as the man jumped to the ground to retrieve the gun. The stallion charged at the man and trampled him, striking him in the head; immediately rendering him unconscious - if not dead.

Young Miles managed to pull his tomahawk from his waistcoat, during the commotion. In one swift movement, he threw it. The tomahawk struck the other man in the forehead, splitting his skull and knocking him from his horse. He lay motionless and bleeding on the road.

Maggie grabbed the reigns of the two horses that the men had been riding, and Miles jumped down to collect their weapons, along with his prized tomahawk. Within minutes Maggie and young Miles were miles down the road and out of harms way ... for the moment. They slowed the horses to a walk.

"Miles, you have the courage and quick thinking of your father. You saved our lives back there."

"I was very frightened, Mama."

"So was I, son. But you managed to keep your wits about you, even though you were scared. That's the important thing." Maggie reached down and patted Seminole on the neck. "... and thanks to Seminole, we got our chance to escape."

"There's Nate!" Miles shouted. He pointed to the shadowy figure riding toward them on the unmistakable white horse that Nate had adorned with bells and colorful feathers.

"No doubt about it," Maggie laughed. "That's a Creek pony, for sure."

Nate rode up to his mother and brother, and then circling them, he asked, "Why are your horses all lathered up ... and where did those other two come from?" He eyed them critically.

"We had a run-in with some very ugly highway men," Maggie said. "Your brother saved the day, though. Everything is all right. The horses were theirs."

"What the .....!!" Nate caught his breath. "What happened?"

"I'll tell you about it later. I'd just like to get off this road as soon as we can. Did you find us some lodgings?" Maggie sounded impatient.

"Yes, I did, and with no time to spare. The inn was filling up fast when I got there … but I was able to get us a room; and I already arranged for our dinner tonight, and breakfast tomorrow morning. It's not far from here, but it's a short distance from this road."

"That's my boy!" Maggie said, smiling at Nate. "This has been a very long day."

"Mama, you'd best turn those horses loose now, before we get to the inn. I don't know what you two have done, but we don't need any more trouble."

"You're right, Nate," Maggie agreed. "You take them, and turn them out back there." She pointed to a clearing in the forest, where it looked to be a good pasture. "Someone will claim them, I suppose."

Maggie, Nate, and young Miles were up at dawn and ready to continue their journey to Ohio. It was a warmer day, and the sun was just coming up over the Kentucky hills as the trio left the inn. Heading back toward the main road, they passed a group of men leading the horses that had been set free the night before; a body was draped limply across the saddle on each horse.

"What happened?" Nate called out as they passed the group.

Maggie just looked the other way and continued on with young Miles.

"Not sure," one man replied. "We found them a few miles from here. Just layin' dead in the road. Funny thing ... they both still had their money on them. We wonder if they had an argument and just did each other in .... These horses were close by, so we reckon they belonged to the dead men. We seldom see trouble around here. You folks be careful now, ya hear? Keep an eye out for suspicious activity. Just in case ...."

"Thanks, we'll be watchful, for sure," Nate said.

Nate hurried to catch up with his mother and brother. "Well you two sure made short work of those bandits, didn't you?" He was shaking his head in disbelief. "Leave you alone for an hour, and just look what you did!"

"Well, son ... it was either us or them. What would you have done?" Maggie looked serious.

"Just kidding, Ma ... I'm glad you two know how to handle yourselves in a bad situation. Father would be proud."

The next two days were easy traveling. The family made good time, and they were able to find lodging early in the evenings. Nate made sure that his mother didn't become overly tired. She continued to look pale and fragile.

On the afternoon of the fourth day, the wide expanse of the Ohio River was in sight. It had been an unusually warm and balmy day for October, but the temperature was dropping dramatically at the moment. Dark clouds were rolling in from the southwest and the distant rumble of thunder could be heard echoing across the Appalachian foothills. The wind was whipping up whitecaps on the surface of the river, like the churning of fresh butter as it begins to thicken. The fragrance of fresh rain was corrupted by the smell of fish from the frothy river, as the wind began to intensify.

Maggie, Nate, and Miles made their way down to the ferry crossing. Portsmouth, Ohio was on the other side of the Ohio River, at the mouth of the Scioto. It was a busy little town with several paddle wheelers lined up along the banks. It was a "picture post card" view from the Kentucky side of the Ohio.

"You can rest here, Mama. I'll go speak to the ferryman and see about our transport," Nate said, helping Maggie down from her stallion.

"Ask how quickly he can get us across. There's a storm coming, Nate. I don't want to get caught by a cloudburst in the middle of that monster river!" Maggie pulled a bonnet from her apron and put it over her hair; tying it securely at her chin. She brushed the windblown strands of curls from her face, and tucked them into the bonnet.

Miles led the horses to a clearing by the road, and secured them to a rail. He settled down in the lush grass to rest, gazing at the river; a look of wonder and excitement written all over his young face.

"Quite a sight, isn't it, Miles?" Maggie sat down beside her son, and surveyed the spectacular scenery before them. "Reminds me of my days on the Muskingum River, in Zanesville. It was every bit as lovely, but not as wide. You'll see it soon, Miles."

Maggie allowed the memories of her younger years to invade her thoughts. Tears began to well up in her eyes.

"What's wrong, Mama?" Miles' voice was full of concern and questioning.

"Oh, Miles …. It's just that remembering the past, sometimes brings to mind the mistakes we made there. I certainly made my share of mistakes – and Zanesville was definitely a proving ground for bad judgment and flawed logic."

"I don't understand, Mama."

"Well, just remember this, Miles… *YOU* are responsible for the consequences of the choices you make … Whether good or bad. Don't ever try to blame anyone else for the situation you find yourself in, as the result of your own free will and choice."

Maggie pulled a handkerchief from her pocket and dried her eyes.

"Sorry son," the ferryman said, shaking his head slowly. "Can't cross this river 'til the storm comes through or blows over. Just don't wanna take a chance on gettin' hit by lightning." He removed his floppy hat and brushed the dust from it. "You might try waitin' it out at Kramer's Tavern … it's just up that road a piece." He pointed to the turnoff up above the riverbank. "Just come on back down here, once it clears up."

"Thank you sir," Nate said, shaking the ferryman's hand. "We'll check back later, then."

They were almost to the tavern when the storm hit. The rain was blowing sideways as the wind tore through the Ohio River Valley. The sign above the door to the building was swinging wildly in the onslaught. Blinding flashes of lightning were almost constant, and were followed immediately by deafening thunder that crackled, crashed, and then rolled off into the distance; echoing across the hills.

Maggie and young Miles hurried into the tavern, while Nate tended to securing the horses in the nearby lean-to.

Maggie found a table in the corner near the huge sandstone fireplace, and she and Miles sat down. They were visibly shaken and out of breath. Maggie pulled the rain-soaked bonnet off, and shook her long curly hair free. She wiped the rain from her face with her skirt.

The wind was screaming through crevices around the windows and doors, and the shutters were rattling and banging against the side of the tavern. The storm seemed to be intensifying, and the myriad of violent sounds was terrifying. Young Miles looked over at his mother; his eyes were wide with fear and anticipation. He gripped the arms of his chair so tightly that his knuckles were white.

Daniel Kramer, the Innkeeper, grabbed a jug of whiskey and a couple of glasses, and rushed over to the table where Maggie and Miles were sitting. "Excuse me, Ma'am ... I couldn't help but notice your distress," he said, in a thick Scottish brogue. "Would you like a little whiskey to calm your nerves?" He set the whiskey and glasses down on the table.

"Thank you, but we don't really care for any whiskey." Maggie stated it bluntly.

"Well, is there anything I can do to help you?" Daniel had a worried look on his handsome face. "You both look so lost and alone, if you don't mind me sayin' now ..."

"We'll be fine. It's just that we got caught in this awful storm ... and my older son is still outside in it. He had to get the horses to shelter." Maggie squirmed nervously in her chair. "I'll be alright. The whole episode just caught me off guard."

"Is your husband outside with your son?"

"No, my sons and I are traveling alone. I'm a widow."

"I'm sorry to hear that. I didn't mean to pry." Daniel gently patted Maggie on the shoulder. "I'm sure your boys are taking very good care of you, but if there's anything I can do, just let me know. My name's Daniel Kramer. I run this place." With that, Daniel returned to the bar; and his other customers.

At last, Nate burst into the tavern; as if being blown through the doorway by a violent gust. He was dripping wet, and had lost his hat somewhere in the storm.

"DAMN!" Nate gasped, brushing his dripping wet, blonde hair away from his eyes. "This is the worst storm I've ever seen!! The horses are none too happy about it... I liked to never get them penned up!" He pulled out a chair and sat down heavily. "I don't think I've ever seen a storm hit so fast and so hard. Never seen so much rain .... Not even in Florida

384

where it rains every day." Nate reached across the table for the jug of whiskey.

Maggie immediately removed it from his reach, and playfully slapped his hand. "You don't need that, Nathan!" She eyed her son critically.

"Just thought I'd settle myself, Mama... That was quite an ordeal!" He managed a nervous chuckle.

"Well, Mr. Kramer brought that over for us, just in case ..." Maggie pointed to the man behind the bar. "He's the owner of this tavern, and a very thoughtful man. He just had no way of knowing how I feel about liquor."

"Well, Mama, that's just how *YOU* feel. I for one, see no problem in having a drink now and then ... for *medicinal* purposes."

Maggie looked worried. "Do you think the horses will be safe?" She changed the subject.

"I'll go out and check on them as soon as it calms down a little, Mama," Nate replied.

"I'd say it had better calm down *a lot*, Nate. I won't let you go back out in this tempest!" Maggie looked around to see if any of the other travelers seemed alarmed. Several patrons were obviously concerned, and although Maggie couldn't hear the conversations, she could tell by their expressions and their hand gestures that this was no ordinary storm.

A pretty young girl in a crisp white apron hurried up to the table and asked if they cared for some stew.

"That sounds wonderful," Maggie replied. "And … just in case we can't get the ferry today … do you have a room available for tonight?"

"I'm sorry, Ma'am, but we don't have any empty rooms for this evening." The girl turned to leave the table.

Nate caught hold of the young woman's wrist, stopping her in her tracks. "Excuse me, Miss … we're not from around here, and I'm wondering if this violent storm is normal for these parts."

"Oh no. This is not normal at all; especially for October. We're all a little worried. Seems it should have blown over by now, but it just looks to be getting worse." For a moment, she looked like she was about to cry. Composing herself, she asked, "Would you like bread and milk with your stew?"

"Yes, please," Nate replied. "My name is Nathan, what's yours?" He smiled at the girl, reassuringly. She immediately relaxed.

"I'm Catharine Kramer. My father owns this tavern."

Now, it was obvious to Nathan, that Catharine was Daniel Kramer's daughter. She had the same curly red hair and beautifully expressive blue eyes as the big Scottish man behind the bar.

"Well, Miss Catharine Kramer … this is my mother Maggie and my little brother Miles. We're from Lexington, Kentucky, and none of us have ever seen such a violent storm. I'm glad we're all safe inside this sturdy tavern."

Catharine nodded first to Maggie and then to Miles. "I'm pleased to meet you all." She then smiled down at Nathan. "I'll check with my father and see if he can't make some room for your family tonight ... just in case the ferry isn't running."

"We would surely appreciate that, Catharine," Maggie said, breathing a sigh of relief.

The meal was served, and as the family ate, the storm raged on outside.

"Mother, I've got to check on our horses," Nate said. "I need to do it now."

"Nathan, I told you to wait until the storm was over. Once it's quiet, you and Miles can tend to the horses."

"Well it's a lot quieter now than it was," Nathan said, placing his napkin onto the table. He stood up and walked toward the tavern door. Miles followed his brother.

Just then the door flew open and Jack Saunders, the ferryman ran inside.

"The river's comin' up!" he shouted. "The dam up in Milton Gorge is cracked ... it could be cavin' in, and the river's comin' up fast!! They sent a rider from the gorge to sound the alarm. If any of you have families along the banks, you better get them to higher ground NOW!!"

"How much time do we have, Jack?" one of the men at the bar yelled.

"Don't know, Sam ... looks like it's risin' pretty damned fast. I'd say we may have about half an hour before a wall of water from Milton Gorge hits Portsmouth, if the dam completely collapses!"

Daniel. Kramer threw down his apron, and ran to the door to look out. He was able to see the ferry landing from the tavern, but he didn't see the ferry; nor could he see the cables. He was silent for a long while. When he turned to his patrons, the color had drained from his face. He looked ashen. "It's over the banks now," he said in a shaking voice. "It's still raining, but the wind has died down. Better get going, if you need to move your families ...." The big Scotsman ran his hands back through his curly red hair in frustration. His eyes, that were usually twinkling and a brilliant blue in color, had turned gray and dull in an instant. People, who knew him, always watched his eyes. They were a barometer of his emotions. Anytime the sparkling blue faded to gray, men moved out of his way.

"Has the river ever come up this far, Kramer?" Sam Guthrie called out.

"Not as long as I've been here," Mr. Kramer said thoughtfully, stroking his beard. "But we never had a dam break, either. We're pretty high here, but if it gets to this road ... then I'd be movin' up the hill!'

Sam Guthrie ran to the door and looked out. "Looks to me like it's got a good twenty-five feet before it gets up to this road, Kramer." He turned to the others; needing some solace, he raised his eyebrows and waited.

"Sam, you and the other locals need to go right now!" Daniel Kramer yelled. "This is not the time to be second-guessing Mother Nature... now get the hell out of here!"

Miles and Nate stood silently, looking at each other in disbelief.

The room was emptying quickly, as the local patrons rushed off to try and save their families and possessions from the rising waters.

Catharine Kramer hurried over to where Nate and Miles were standing. She gently touched Nate's arm, to get his attention. "I'm really sorry you and your family are caught in this mess. My father will make sure you all stay safe. He's concerned that your mother, and you boys, are so far from home."

"We surely appreciate that, Catharine ... Thank you. Now we've got to check on our horses."

"I don't think you need to worry about them, Nathan. My father already had our man, Salvo, move all the horses in the lean-to. He took them up to our barn at the top of the hill." Catharine hesitated. She cocked her head to one side; a questioning look on her face. "Is the big black stallion yours?"

"Yes, um ... well he's my mother's horse. Why?"

"Because Salvo was very impressed with that horse. Said he'd never laid hands on such a beauty. But anyway, your horses are just fine ... The black, the bay, and what Salvo called 'that gorgeous white Indian pony' .... So that's three less things you have to worry about for now." Catharine smiled up at Nathan, nodded to Miles, then turned and went over to the table to speak with Maggie.

Nathan and Miles stepped outside. The storm had finally passed over, and all that was left of the monster torrent was a balmy breeze and a steady rain. There was still, however, the rising river to contend with. It was nearly five o'clock in the afternoon.

"Too bad we didn't make it here earlier. We could have crossed the river and been on our way to

Circleville by now." Miles strained to see through the rain. The river was creeping up the hillside, and it looked to be lapping at the bank, just below the road. "Nate, what are we going to do? How long do you think it'll take for that river to go down – low enough to cross it?"

"I have no idea, Miles. But like Father always said, everything has a reason and a purpose; and everything is part of the plan. Guess we're just where we're supposed to be, right now." Nathan shook the rain from his hair, and headed back inside. Miles followed him.

Chapter 33 – A Great Catastrophe

Daniel Kramer, Catharine, and a tall, muscular black man, were all standing at the table where Maggie was sitting. Nathan and Miles joined them.

"Aw, boys ..." Daniel Kramer greeted them, "we were just talking about arranging for your stay, here; until the river recedes enough for you to cross safely, and be on your way."

"Mr. Kramer was nice enough to offer us lodgings without cost. He says we are his *welcomed guests* for as long as it takes," Maggie said, smiling. "I told him that you boys would help out around the tavern, as long as we're here. Are you agreeable with that?"

"Sure!" Nathan said. "Beats sleeping in the road, isn't that right Miles?"

"Yep – I agree." Miles slapped Nathan hard on the back; but playfully; nearly knocking him down.

"Salvo, here ..." Daniel Kramer motioned to the black man standing beside him, "has taken care of your horses, and he'll prepare a room upstairs for you boys and your mother. It may not be fancy, but I guarantee it will be clean and comfortable ... and hopefully DRY."

"Mr. Kramer, how will we know if that dam has totally collapsed?" Nathan asked.

"Well, son ... if that dam completely fails, unless they get a rider here ahead of the wall of water, we won't know until we're hit with a ten or twelve foot wave. Either way, we'll be OK. This tavern is built of sturdy sandstone, and we have a second and third floor to go to, if need be. It's the people down below ... along the river bank, that will bear the brunt of that kind of a catastrophe. You boys just relax, and try to make your mother quit worrying so much."

"She likes to worry ... says it's her job," Miles quipped, laughing and pointing at Maggie.

After dinner, Salvo escorted the trio up to a huge room on the second floor. There was a fireplace at one end, and a cozy fire had already been started. It gave the room a warm and inviting glow. Three beds had been made ready, and a pitcher of fresh water had been placed by a large bowl on the bureau, along with a stack of clean linens.

Salvo handed Maggie a bell, and smiled at her. "If you need anything at all, Miss Maggie, just step into the hallway and ring this bell. Mr. Kramer wants to make sure you have an enjoyable stay – regardless of the present situation." The Negro hesitated, then added, "He doesn't do nice things like this for just *anyone!*" Salvo winked and grinned.

Maggie felt her cheeks flush; not sure what Salvo was implying. "I really do appreciate the accommodations, Salvo," Maggie said, taking the bell.

Salvo left the room, closing the door behind him.

October 3, 1827 5:38 am – Kramer Tavern

Maggie and the boys awoke to a loud commotion, coming from downstairs. Nathan ran over to one of the windows and peered into the early dawn mist that obscured the landscape.

"Oh my God!!" he exclaimed. "It's up to the doorsill! The river is clear up to the tavern door!!"

Miles jumped from his bed and joined Nate at the window. "Mama!! There must be a dozen horses tied up down there, and they're standing in two or three feet of water!! It's up to their hocks and higher!"

Maggie joined the boys. She caught her breath when she realized what must have happened. A wagon was tied up, just under the window. The water was halfway over its wheels; and she could see the outline of several bodies lying in the wagon bed, covered by a canvas tarp.

Nathan and Miles pulled their trouser over their long-johns, stepped into their boots, slipped the suspenders over their shoulders, and were out the door and down the stairs in an instant.

Maggie dressed quickly, tied her hair back, and ran to the stairway. Afraid of what she was about to encounter, she hesitated. She stood at the top of the stairs for a few minutes, listening to the conversations below. Gathering her courage, she knew what she needed to do.

The scene before her was strangely reminiscent of her experience with the tannery fire in Zanesville, so many years ago. There were dozens of injured people sitting and lying around the room; some looked to be seriously wounded; others only slightly hurt. She was listening to the people talking.

Maggie understood that when the dam completely failed, the onslaught of water had rushed down the ravine and then down the river; ripping away trees, homes, stables, and barns; then, slamming the debris into everything in its path. Too many families had been caught off-guard and victimized by the flood. Maggie was overcome with compassion.

"Miss Maggie!" It was Daniel Kramer. "Your boys tell me that you have quite a bit of medical experience. We could really use your help ... as you can see. What do you suggest we do?"

"Of course I'll help." Maggie patted Daniel on the arm. "Nathan! Miles! Catharine! Come here." She motioned the youngsters over to where she and Kramer were standing.

"I know, Mother ... we're about to set up a hospital environment, aren't we?" Nathan said, looking solemn.

"OK, children ...."

"We're NOT children!" Miles interrupted.

"Well ... whatever you are, I need you to do exactly as I tell you." Maggie looked around the room, trying to decide where to start. "Miles, I want you and Catharine to gather up supplies – we'll need kettles of boiling water in the fireplace, lots of cotton batting and muslin strips, scissors, sharp knives, needles, and silk thread if you can find any – otherwise any thread will have to do .... And lots and lots of whiskey!" Maggie stopped to collect her thoughts, and then continued, "Get blankets, too." She looked up at Daniel Kramer. "We need tobacco ... to pack into the wounds .... It stops bleeding."

394

"I'll get it," Daniel said, without hesitation.

Maggie pulled Nathan aside and in a low voice she said, "Son, I need for you to start at one end of the room and work your way down. I'm leaving it up to you to decide which ones need immediate attention, and which ones can wait. Just do a quick examination, separate the two, and move on. This way we'll have two groups to work on. You and I will tend to the seriously injured, and Miles and Catharine can patch up the ones who are only slightly injured. I'll start sterilizing the scissors, knives, and needles. I think Mr. Kramer can pass the whiskey around, don't you?" She forced a smile.

"Mama ... we can do this," Nate said, giving Maggie a quick hug.

Daniel Kramer returned with a large pouch of tobacco. "Maggie, you're a *god-send*, you know that don't you?" He looked sad and tired. "The problem is ... the only doctors in these parts, are on the other side of the river. We're pretty much on our own over here." Daniel slid an arm around Maggie's shoulders and gave her a reassuring squeeze. "I hate to tell you this ... but we've got a lot more people on their way here, Maggie. I think we'll probably be busy for a couple of days, if not longer. Are you up to it, Sweetie?"

"I promise you, Mr. Kramer ... I'll do everything I can."

"Please ... call me Daniel."

"I'm at your service, Daniel."

"Thanks, Maggie."

Nine days passed, and finally, what had been a steady stream of seriously injured survivors, became only a small number of *walking wounded*. The river was receding quickly, but as the water level dropped, it revealed the real destruction and devastation. The aftermath of the flood was a sad testament to what the breaking of a dam can do to a community. Makeshift morgues and mass burials were commonplace in the region. The sadness of the local people was palpable.

Although the small group of Good Samaritans at the tavern was exhausted, they were satisfied with their efforts; some had been lost, but many had been saved.

Maggie and Mr. Kramer were sitting at Maggie's favorite table; near the huge fireplace.

"Well, Maggie, we survived." Daniel Kramer patted Maggie's hand affectionately. "Everyone I know is thanking God right now, for your being here at just the right time."

"My family calls that *destiny*," Maggie said quietly.

"I've been thinking, Miss Maggie ..." Daniel looked distant. "Would it be in your *destiny* to stay here with us ... rather than continue on to Unionville?"

"You've been so kind to us, and I love you all .... But I made a promise to my late husband that I have to keep. I have no choice." Maggie's face flushed. "Believe me ... I really don't want to go back there."

"Then don't!"

"I wish it was that easy, but it's much more complicated."

"Well, Maggie ... I won't pry, but I will tell you that you're welcome here any time. If you ever decide to come back ... if things don't work out for you back there, you can call this your home."

"Thank you so much Daniel. It's nice to know someone cares."

"Well I *do*, Miss Maggie." Daniel squeezed Maggie's hand and looked deeply into her eyes. "Will you write me when you get there, so I'll know you made it safely?"

"Of course I will."

Chapter 34 – The Continuing Journey

October 19, 1827

Crossing the Ohio River, on the rickety crowded ferry, was an ordeal; as the horses were anxious and animated during the transport. The river level was still above normal and the current was swift. It took an eternity to cross over to Portsmouth, because the ferryman had to keep watch for all sorts of floating debris still cluttering the river. It was the stuff nightmares are made of, when several swollen gray bodies floated by; eyes staring blankly at the sky.

By the end of the third day, the trio had journeyed well into the Ohio Territory. They followed the old Delaware trail up the Scioto River valley to Chillicothe, and then on to Circleville.

They cut across to Lancaster and then took the old Zane's Trace road toward Unionville.

"Mother, it's going to be sundown in another hour. I'm afraid we're going to have to rough it tonight. We'd better start looking for a place to make camp, because I have no idea where the closest inn is," Nate said, looking around the empty wilderness.

"I think you may be right, son. We've been so lucky to find warm lodging every night so far. Looks like tonight we'll be sleeping under the stars."

Maggie laughed and turned to Miles. "Are you up for a campout, Miles?"

"Why not, Mama? At least it's not as cold today as it was yesterday."

"... But we can't be that far from Summerset. I remember going through there with your father." Maggie was trying to remember.

"If you don't mind traveling at night, we could keep going and try to get there." Nate looked back at his mother, waiting for her reply.

"Well, I know there's an inn there. About one more day from there, and we'd be in Unionville. I just know I'd feel safer in an inn ... rather than sleeping along this *god-forsaken* road."

"It's fine with me... What about you, Miles?" Nathan turned to his little brother.

"I'm not afraid of the dark!" Miles replied.

"OK, then it's settled," Maggie said. "If we get too tired, or the horses get too tired, then we will stop and make camp. Agreed?"

A huge golden full moon was beginning to rise above the Ohio hills, and a chilly fog had settled across the road, as the family proceeded toward Summerset. The silence was deafening in the blackness of the night. It was as still as death itself, except for the faint sound of running water nearby.

Maggie stopped her horse and climbed down. She led Seminole II over to the small stream to drink. She knelt down and drank some water from her cupped hand. The boys dismounted and let their horses drink. After a short rest, they were all refreshed and ready to continue.

"I need to walk for a while," Maggie said, "I'm feeling a little stiff from being in that saddle so long." She laughed and rubbed her cheek against Seminole's muzzle; patting him lovingly on his neck. "I think old Seminole would appreciate that, too."

The trio proceeded; walking and leading their horses along the trail, in the muted golden light from the full moon, that was now high in the sky.

Suddenly, Seminole II became anxious; snorting and pawing at the ground. He raised his head high, sniffing at the air in alarm. The other horses also began acting up.

"What on earth ....?" Nate began, but was abruptly interrupted by a bone-chilling scream coming from the forest.

Maggie remembered that sound. It was the unmistakable sound of a panther, and it was nearby. "Don't move!" Maggie whispered. "It's a panther!" Her voice was trembling.

Just then, the cat bounded onto the road, only a few yards ahead of them. It crouched and screamed again. The horses were going wild. The panther inched forward. Miles, very slowly drew his tomahawk from his waistcoat, and raised it into the air; but before he could throw it, a huge gray wolf appeared from seemingly nowhere. It jumped onto the back of the unsuspecting cat. The cat whirled in circles, desperately trying to extricate the wolf from its body. Without warning, the great gray wolf sunk his sharp fangs into the cat's neck; effectively severing the jugular vein and sending blood spurting in all directions, as the panther continued its deadly gyrations. It was over as quickly as it had begun. The cat laid quivering and bleeding in the middle of the road. The wolf stood over it like a sentinel, ready to pounce on the cat if it moved again. He watched quietly until it was dead.

Miles was about to throw the tomahawk at the wolf, but Maggie instinctively screamed, "NO!! Miles!! Don't harm the wolf!"

Miles obediently lowered the tomahawk, and looked at his mother in shocked disbelief.

The wolf looked at Maggie; then at Nathan and Miles. His huge eyes glowed golden in the moonlight. He looked into Maggie's eyes. Maggie was completely captured in his gaze. It was a spiritual *meeting of the minds*, as they were all frozen in time and space.

"Moon Wolf ..." Maggie whispered.

The great gray wolf lowered his head in submission, and backed away slowly. He finally walked quietly into the forest. It was then, that Nate, and Young Miles fully understood what had just happened.

Another two miles up the trace, and they found themselves in Summerset. The inn was warm and cozy. The food was good. Sleep was welcomed.

The family would reach Unionville tomorrow.

Chapter 35 – Higher Ground

October 24, 1827 – Newton, Ohio

It was a sunny October day. The brilliant colors of fall adorned the Ohio hills in shades of red, yellow; gold, and crimson. Sarah Stillman was sitting by the window, inside the large two-story home John had built years ago for his growing family.

Sarah loved autumn. She had watched the colorful transformation from this vantage point, over the last few weeks. The older boys were harvesting in the fields, while the youngsters played on the front lawn. John and Nathan Stillman were engaged in a serious game of horseshoe, at the back of the house.

Two miles up the road, a rider was approaching the Stillman farm. *She was riding a tall, highly spirited black stallion, which ran like the wind. The woman's long black cloak floated behind her in the wake, as the magnificent ghostly steed galloped down the road. The rider and the horse were phantoms, riding through the surreal shadows cast by the golden sun shining through the dense canopy of tree branches above the path. The horse, at times, slowed to rear up, in an intricate ballet, reaching high into the air and dancing on his hind legs along the trail. It was apparent that the rider and the horse were intimately bonded. It was clear that both were free spirits, an enigma to all they encountered, and each possessing the soul of a maverick.*

Sarah stood up when she saw them coming. Like an apparition, the duo glided down the road to the house. Sarah could see two more riders following behind. The woman, cloaked in black, jumped down from the tall black stallion and looped the reins over a post. The other two horses galloped up to the mansion and stopped. Two young men dismounted and waited silently.

Sarah ran outside; immediately recognizing Maggie. The two women embraced each other crying. It was an emotional reunion.

"Maggie!" Sarah cried. "Welcome home! We've waited so long!"

"You really expected me to come back?" Maggie looked stunned.

"Nathan had us all convinced that you really would come back some day," Sarah said, laughing through her tears of joy.

Just then, John and Nathan emerged from the back yard to see what the commotion was about. The men stopped dead in their tracks upon seeing the woman cloaked in black, standing beside Sarah. Nathan looked at the tall black stallion and then back at the woman.

"Maggie?" Nathan gasped in disbelief.

Maggie froze when she saw Nathan. She couldn't utter a word. Her eyes grew wide and she began to tremble. Nathan was approaching her. She backed away slowly.

"It's all right, Maggie," Nathan said. "I'm glad you're here."

"I had no choice," Maggie said, in a low voice. "I promised Miles I would come."

"He was a man of his word," Nathan said, extending his hand to Maggie.

Slowly ... cautiously, Maggie put her shaking hand into Nathan's. He immediately pulled her to him and wrapped his arms around the frightened woman, giving her a reassuring hug.

"You don't have to be afraid of me Maggie. I'll never hurt you again," he whispered. Nathan looked over to where the boys were standing. He released Maggie from his embrace, but continued to steady the trembling woman; keeping his arm around her waist. "Who are these young men?" he asked, smiling.

Young Nathan stepped forward and offered his hand to his father. "I'm your son, sir," he said. "My name is Nathan Stillman – but everyone calls me Nate."

Nathan's surprise was obvious, as he grasped young Nathan's hand and shook it vigorously. Nate had the same strong build and curly blonde hair that his father had. He was every bit the image of his dad, right down to the huge muscular hands. The boy's father couldn't conceal his emotions, and big tears began to roll down his cheeks.

"I wish I had known ... all these years ... that I had a son!" he cried. "I can't tell you how many times I thought about it! I sometimes felt sure you were out there somewhere. Something in my soul kept tellin' me ..." Nathan grabbed his son and gave him a huge bear-hug.

Young Miles stepped forward and shook Nathan's hand. "I'm Miles, sir. Miles Deihl was my father."

"Miles Deihl was an honorable man, son!" Nathan said, patting young Miles on the back. "He was a man of his word, to be sure! I'm pleased to meet you, Miles." Nathan looked at Maggie. "You and the boys are welcome to stay in my home up there on the hill." Nathan pointed across the valley, to the big red-brick farmhouse on the knoll above the pasture. "I consider it your land and your home. I always have. You have a fine herd of Merino sheep, too, Maggie. I've taken good care of them while you were gone." He looked over at Nate and Miles. "Are you boys willin' to help me out with your mama's sheep?"

"Yes sir!" the boys answered in unison.

"Nathan, I don't know ..." Maggie began.

"Maggie!" Nathan interrupted her. "You don't have to make any long-term decisions right now. I just want you to know that I couldn't be happier to see you. I've put the past behind me ... Right now, I'd just like us to be friends again."

There was a long silence. No one said a word. Maggie looked to be deep in thought.

"All right, Nathan... I could certainly use a friend myself."

John and Sarah encircled the new family in a group hug, weeping and laughing at the same time.

"We've all been through our share of hell and high water," John said, wiping at the tears in his own eyes. "But it looks as if we've finally reached higher ground at last!"

"John ... Sarah ... will you make the boys feel at home while Maggie and I take a short ride? We need to talk," Nathan said, taking Maggie's elbow and steering her toward the carriage, tied to a rail by the side of the house.

Maggie didn't object.

Nathan gently lifted Maggie onto the carriage seat. He untied the horse, collected the reigns, then climbed onto the other side. They headed down the drive and turned onto the road that led to Nathan's farm.

Nathan drove the carriage along the beautiful valley creek that Maggie always loved. The afternoon sun was dancing on the rippled water, like diamonds bouncing on a mirror. Multi-colored leaves floated along, punctuating the continuing autumn ballet. There was a slight breeze blowing from the south that made this October day absolutely perfect. Nathan seemed to be lost in thought. Maggie was being drowned in memories. They rode in silence.

The carriage turned, and headed up the lane to the big red-brick farm house, majestically placed on the knoll; overlooking the valley.

Nathan pulled the horse and carriage to a stop in front of the home. He looked over at Maggie. Tears were rolling down her cheeks, as she surveyed the surroundings.

"Maggie, don't you worry about a thing! I don't expect a wife... But I could surely use the company of a friend." Tears were freely flowing down Nathan's red face, now. "I just want to take care of you and the boys. I promised Miles Deihl that I would. I've got a lot of makin' up to do." Nathan wiped his eyes with his sleeve. "And Maggie... I want you to know that I haven't touched alcohol since you left. I just want you to know that .... I'm ... I'm so sorry – I wanted so badly to apologize to you. I just never got the chance. I don't think it would have changed anything if I had, though. The damage was done." Nathan's voice was low and hoarse. "Please, Maggie ... please forgive me?"

"I think I should be the one begging for forgiveness," Maggie stated – almost inaudibly. She didn't look at Nathan, but continued. "I was always over-reacting. Maybe I was just too young and foolish to have even considered marriage .... But I just couldn't stand the thought of being alone." Maggie managed to look up at Nathan. "I was a child, and I acted childishly. I'm so sorry to have complicated your life, Nathan. I never intended to hurt you." Her eyes were full of sadness and sincerity.

"Maggie, Sweetheart ... I knew that. I couldn't believe that you signed your pa's farm over to me." He slid his arm around Maggie's shoulders in a comforting gesture. "When I saw that, I understood how confused you must have been feeling at the time. I never felt any sense of anger toward you. I only hated myself. I still haven't forgiven myself." Nathan reached over and cupped Maggie's chin, turning her face toward him. He looked deep into her sad eyes. "You know, Maggie ... we really *can* put the past behind us, and start our lives over as friends – like when we were growing up. I think we need that. I know I've missed having you around; especially during hunting season. John and I really relied on you to be our 'spotter' and our 'tracker'. We really need you now, with winter coming. Gotta get that venison stored away quick." He managed a chuckle.

Nathan watched Maggie's eyes, as the sparkle began to return. She actually smiled.

"That's better," Nathan said, jumping down from the carriage. "Now I know you're tired from your trip, Maggie, but I really want to show you my handiwork. I built this house myself ... well I did have *some* help." He lifted Maggie down from the carriage, and took her by the hand, leading her up the steps to the veranda at the front doorway.

It was a magnificent double-door entryway. There was a beautiful leaded glass fan-shaped window above the doors, with leaded glass panels on both sides. Nathan opened the door wide, and literally dragged Maggie inside.

"Oh my God, Nathan!" Maggie caught her breath as she looked around. "The woodwork is amazing. And that stairway is beautiful! It's got to be one of a kind." Maggie couldn't hide her astonishment. "Did *YOU* do all of this yourself?"

"Yes I did," Nathan stated proudly. "I knew you'd love it, Maggie." Without thinking, he swept Maggie up, off of her feet and into his massive arms, and began dancing around the entry foyer with her. He abruptly stopped, setting her back down, and looking embarrassed. He sheepishly said, "Ummm ... I'm so sorry, Maggie. I just got too excited. I won't do that again."

Maggie's eyes were wide with surprise, but she was laughing uncontrollably now.

"You have nothing to be sorry for, Nathan. This is absolutely gorgeous, and I don't blame you one bit for being excited and proud to show it off. I love it!!"

"Well, at least I made you laugh ... even if I had to make an ass out of myself to do it."

Maggie threw her arms around Nathan's neck and gave him an affectionate hug. She stepped back, looking at the surprise that had now overtaken *his* expression, and laughed again. "Oh Nathan! I've grown up, and yet you've reverted back to your childhood. Aren't we a pair?"

Nathan took both of Maggie's hands in his, and took a long deep breath. "I can't tell you how glad I am to have you here. I just want you to feel comfortable in your home."

"Well, it's *YOUR* home, Nathan, and it certainly is lovely," Maggie said, still looking around at the marvelously carved woodwork.

"Yes, and he did it *ALL* for *YOU.*" A lovely young woman, with curly blonde hair was standing at the top of the stairway, grinning at Maggie and Nathan.

"Annie!" Nathan shouted. "Come here and meet Maggie."

Maggie watched in shocked silence as the young woman descended the stairway. The girl looked to be in her mid to late twenties. She was as graceful as she was beautiful. Maggie's thoughts were racing;

she was speechless, wondering who this woman was. *'Had Nathan remarried?'*

The girl walked straight over to Maggie and grabbed her, in a familiar "Stillman" bear hug. She took a step back and grinned. "Hello Maggie. I'm Annie Stillman. I'm Nathan's daughter." She then took Maggie's hand and squeezed it. "I've heard all about you. I knew I'd get to meet you someday." She giggled, and looked at her father. "You were right, Papa."

Maggie still couldn't find her voice. Her mind was reeling. Her mouth was agape, and her eyes were full of questioning.

"It's a long and complicated story, Maggie. I'll explain later, but if we don't get back to Sarah and John's place, we'll miss dinner." Nathan chuckled, and then looked at his daughter. "Annie, get your wrap, Sweetie ... you can ride over with us."

Finally able to speak, Maggie smiled at Annie. "I'm honored to meet you, Annie. I have to admit ... I'm surprised, but delighted. I'm glad Nathan hasn't been alone all these years."

"Well," Annie began, "I'm surprised and delighted to see that this house can become the happy home it was originally intended to be." She turned and started back up the stairway to get her cloak, then stopped and turned to face her father. "Papa ... I can't tell you how happy I am for you. I have a feeling that this will be a turning point in all of our lives." She looked happily at Maggie. "Welcome home, Maggie."

Dinner at Sarah and John's was a fun filled event. The conversation around the family table was raucous, and rowdy, and filled with extremes of laughter and tears. It was as if time had stood still while Maggie was gone. She and the boys seemed to fit right in, with a family that had been waiting so long for her return. For the first time in months, Maggie felt happily contented. John, Sarah, their six children, Nathan, and Annie had made Maggie and her boys feel welcome, and completely at home. Maggie hadn't seen her sons laughing and enjoying themselves like this, since before Miles Deihl's passing. At this point, she was grateful to Miles for making her promise to return.

"Maggie, I've been meaning to ask you ... where is your stuff? I mean your household belongings and personal things," Nathan asked, looking at Maggie from across the table.

"I can answer that," young Nate interrupted; grinning. "Trying to tear her away from that house and everything in it was a battle that Miles and I waged for nearly a month. Miles and I were more than willing to load everything into a wagon and bring it, but she wouldn't hear of it. She did everything in her power to stay in Lexington, Kentucky. We had to finally promise her that if she wasn't happy in Ohio, we would take her back ... and leave her there. That's why she left everything there ... just in case she wanted to go back. Or maybe as an excuse to go back ... who knows."

"I can vouch for that," young Miles chimed in. "It's the only time we ever had to argue with our Mama. She's pretty head-strong. Pa used to say she was bull-headed."

"Don't we know it!" The older Nathan stated emphatically, slamming his hand down hard on the table.

John and Sarah laughed so hard they nearly fell off their chairs.

"Well ... I was frightened, and I felt vulnerable," Maggie admitted. She hesitated, and then continued. "I'm actually glad I came, now. I didn't realize how much I'd missed Ohio, this beautiful land, and .... And... all of *YOU*." Maggie lowered her head, trying to hide her tears.

"Maggie, you're family to Nathan and I. You've been our little sister from the day you were born. It only makes sense that you would miss us." John walked around to Maggie's chair and put his hands firmly on her shoulders. "Of course we've had our differences, but show me a family that hasn't." He bent down and kissed Maggie on the cheek. "We've missed you more than you know, and I'm not too proud to admit it."

Maggie was overwhelmed with emotion. As John returned to his seat, Maggie quietly folded her napkin and placed it on the table. "Will you excuse me for a moment?" She could barely speak. She stood up and went outside to try and recover her composure.

"I've never seen my Mama get all emotional like that," young Nathan stated. "It's actually refreshing for a change. She's always been so ... so tough. You

412

know what I mean? It's good to see a softer side of her."

"I know, son. It's not like her at all … Not that I can remember. I'll go talk to her," Nathan said, leaving the table.

Nathan found Maggie standing on the porch, steadying herself at the railing. She was crying. Her body shook with the sobbing. Not sure what to do, Nathan gathered Maggie up in his arms and held her close to his heart. She didn't resist, as she continued to cry, burying her face in his chest. Nathan just stood there, holding Maggie against him; silently praying for the right words; hoping that his support would be of some comfort. Slowly, the sobbing subsided.

"I'm so sorry, Nathan." Maggie was too embarrassed to look up. "Maybe I'm just tired."

"You don't have to apologize, Honey. I know you're tired, and you've been through a lot these past months. It's OK to let yourself mourn. Just let it all go, Maggie. It's OK to cry. You'll feel better after a good long rest, too." Nathan lifted Maggie's chin up, so he could see her face. "Do you want to spend the night here, or do you want me to take you home with me?" Nathan kissed her gently on the forehead. "Just let me know where you'd feel more comfortable right now. We need to get you into bed. I think you're all worn out."

"I don't know, Nathan. I'm so physically and emotionally exhausted, I can't even think straight. Whatever you decide is alright with me."

"Well, I've got plenty of extra room. John and Sarah actually don't … you know … with six kids

413

and all. Annie is really excited to have you home with us. She told me that she already likes you. Once we get back to the house, we can have rooms ready for you and the boys, in less than twenty minutes. I have four big bedrooms, you know. What do you want to do?"

Maggie wiggled away from Nathan's grasp, and placed her hand on his heart. "Nathan, if it's really not too much trouble for you, we'll go home with you. I just can't impose on Sarah and John. But ... but ... do you have any tea?"

For some reason, known only to Nathan, Maggie's reply struck him funny. Nathan broke out into laughter that nearly took him to his knees. It was an unexpected response from Maggie. As he was trying to stand up, the entire family came out onto the porch to see what was going on.

"That's my girl, Maggie!" Nathan exclaimed between fits of laughing.

On the way back to Nathan's house, the carriage moved along the lane quietly, with young Nate handling the reigns. Nathan and Miles rode in the front of the carriage with Nate. Maggie rode in back with Annie. Maggie was so tired, that she rested her head comfortably on Annie's shoulder. Annie slipped her arm around Maggie in an affectionate gesture that touched Maggie's heart.

Once inside the big house, Annie took charge immediately. She gathered a pile of clean linens from a cupboard, along with some quilts.

"OK boys," she called. "Where ever you are, come and help me. Let's get these beds made."

Nathan and Maggie had retreated into the huge kitchen. Nathan made the tea, while Maggie relaxed in a beautiful, handmade rocker, in front of the gigantic fireplace.

"Nathan, I just have to tell you, one more time … your home is wonderful. Everything seems so perfect. It's just so beautiful."

"Thank you, Maggie. Wait 'til you see *YOUR* room." Nathan handed her a cup of tea and sat down in a chair next to her.

They relaxed, and drank the tea in silence. There was nothing else that needed to be said, right now.

|

Chapter 36 – Acclimation

October 29, 1827 – Nathan Stillman's Farm

The sun was rising over the Ohio hills. The sunlight was casting intricate shadows onto the walls and floor, through the lace curtains hanging at the windows. Maggie snuggled down into the cozy bed, and pulled the quilt up under her chin. There was a chill in the air, but she just didn't feel like climbing out of bed to add a log to the fireplace. Just as she was drifting off, back to sleep again, there was a soft knock at her door.

"Come in," Maggie called, not caring who it was. She just couldn't make herself get out of her nice warm bed.

The heavy door opened slowly, and Annie struggled to enter the room, carrying a tray full of food, along with a coffee pot, cups, and a little pink rose.

Maggie bolted out of the bed to help the girl. "Oh my gosh, Annie, you don't have to spoil me like this!" Maggie held the door open for Annie, and then she cleared the little night table so that there was room for the tray. "Where on earth did you find a rose in the late fall?"

Annie giggled, as she unloaded the tray. "I grow them in the greenhouse Papa built for me. I'll show you, later."

Maggie was busy stirring the coals in the fireplace. "Annie, I haven't seen much of your father the last few days. What's he been doing?" She picked up a log and laid it on the coals. "As a matter of fact, I haven't seen much of any of you ... including my boys." Maggie turned around to look at Annie.

"Well, everyone has been pretty busy. With winter on our doorstep, there's lots to do. Papa is teaching the boys how to finish the harvest, how to care for the sheep, check the fences, you know. Don't you remember?" Annie sat down on the side of the bed and cocked her head to one side. "They've also been hunting, and butchering. Curing the meat and hanging the pelts ..." Annie jumped up and pulled a chair over for Maggie.

Maggie threw her shawl around her shoulders and sat down at the little table. "And what have you been doing?" Maggie asked, pouring herself a cup of coffee.

"Apple butter. I really hate making apple butter," Annie grimaced.

"Awww ... that I remember. I always thought that was a nasty, boring, chore."

"I'm glad you understand, Maggie." Annie grabbed a biscuit and took a big bite. "Seems like all I've been doing is canning and preserving for the last three months. We've got enough food put up, now, to feed a small army all winter." She poured herself a cup of coffee, and refilled Maggie's mug for her.

"Who taught you to do all of that?"

"Aunt Sarah mostly. Papa taught me a lot, too."

Maggie put some scrambled eggs and some bacon on a plate. She buttered a biscuit and spooned a big dollop of apple butter on it. "I've just got to try your apple butter, Annie." She took a bite and closed her eyes in delight. "Ummmm ... this is delicious."

Annie grinned an approving grin. "I'm glad you like it, Maggie."

"Everything is good." Maggie said, with her mouth full. "You're not only spoiling me ... you're going to make me fat!"

Both women laughed.

As Annie was cleaning up the table and piling the dishes back on the tray, she suddenly looked sad. Maggie noticed it, instantly.

"Annie, what's the matter?" Maggie asked, catching Annie's wrist, and stopping her.

"Oh, Maggie, I was just thinking. Maybe you could talk some sense into Papa for me."

"About what?"

Annie sat down heavily on the side of the bed. "I want to get married."

"Well, Annie, you're certainly old enough. What's stopping you?"

"Papa doesn't like my beau."

"Oh NO!! I know how that goes, Annie. Fathers never think *anyone's* good enough for their little girls. Surely you know that." Maggie patted Annie's hand reassuringly. "What is it that he doesn't like about the man?"

"Maggie, to tell you the truth, I honestly don't know. I think he wants me to be an old maid."

Annie wiped her eyes on her apron. "He's never said *why* he doesn't like Paul, he just forbids me to see him."

"But you see him anyway, huh?"

"Oh my God, Maggie ... please don't tell him. He'd kill me." Annie jumped to her feet in a panic. "How did *YOU* know?"

Maggie laughed, covering her mouth to quiet it. "Because I've been in your shoes, Sweetie. I know how you feel. And I did my share of sneaking around behind my Pa's back. And I wasn't even seventeen." Maggie laughed harder. "I guess I was head strong, just like I've been accused of being."

Annie grabbed Maggie and hugged her tightly. "I'm so glad you're here, Maggie. Maybe you can make my life happier ... like you've made my Papa's life happier."

"I'll certainly try, Annie." Maggie picked up the little pink tea rose and held it to her nose. The scent was sweet and spicy. "Have you talked to your Aunt Sarah about this?"

"No."

"Why not?"

"Because she would talk to Uncle John, and he would tell Papa."

"Well, Annie, you could be right. I know Sarah would never cause you grief on purpose, but I'm sure she *would* confide in her husband. And you're right. He would discuss it with Nathan."

"So Maggie, will you help me?"

"Honey, I'll try, but give me some time. I don't know how Nathan would react to me interfering in family business. I'd like to meet your beau, before I do anything to get myself in hot water with your Pa. OK?"

"You're a jewel, Maggie. Thank you!" With that, Annie picked up the tray and headed for the door. Maggie jumped up and opened the door for the girl.

"I'll keep your secret, Annie. I promise," Maggie whispered.

Ever since Maggie arrived at the Stillman farms, she had been spending her time exploring the beautiful big house; wandering around the huge yard; relaxing in her pleasant, sunny room; and trying to figure out where everyone was, and what they were doing. She had been left alone for the most part, and now that she was well rested, she was beginning to feel lonely.

Rummaging through her bags, Maggie pulled out her riding clothes and boots. She dressed in a hurry, fixed her hair, and left the house. In the barn, she saddled Seminole II, and climbed into the saddle. There was no one around. She trotted her stallion to the edge of the knoll, and looked across the valley. It was a chilly morning, and the fog was just beginning to lift. The landscape was enchanting.

"I was just coming to check on you." It was Nathan. He had ridden up behind Maggie while she was daydreaming.

She caught her breath in surprise.

"I didn't mean to startle you, Maggie."

Maggie laughed. "I was lost in my imagination. I didn't hear you coming."

"Getting restless, are you?" Nathan pushed his hat up off his forehead, and grinned at Maggie. It was the same handsome grin Maggie remembered so well. At this moment, he was absolutely beguiling.

"Well, I decided to go sightseeing. I wondered what everyone has been so busy doing."

"Sightseeing, huh?" Nathan paused, thoughtfully. "I suggest you be very careful, Maggie. We have a lot of men working this farm, and not all of them are *gentlemen*." He removed his hat, and brushed the golden curls away from his face. "I know you're a big girl now, and can take care of yourself, but I just want you to be always aware of your surroundings." Nathan winked at Maggie. "They're not used to seeing such a beautiful woman out here all alone.

Maggie blushed. "Aww, Nathan, such flattery!" Maggie looked up at him shyly. "But, believe me ... I learned that lesson the hard way ... many years ago." Maggie smiled sweetly, as she reached down and pulled a revolver from her boot.

"That's my girl!" He laughed loudly; in unrestrained amusement.

"I thought you'd approve," Maggie said, grinning at her guardian. She shoved the gun back into its hiding place.

"Nathan, how are you getting on with the boys?"

"Maggie, those boys of yours are quite the workers. Did you know that? Smart, too. I've been showing them how this place is run. Teaching them some things. I only have to explain something once, and they pick it up immediately. I never have to repeat anything."

"That's been a big part of their Creek training, Nathan."

"They've told me all about that, Maggie. I can't tell you how impressed I am. Those boys are way mature for their years. Miles Deihl must have been a wonderful father."

"Yes. He was."

"Just so you know ... I appreciate what he did for you and the boys." Nathan rubbed at his chin thoughtfully. "He certainly changed you."

"How so?" Maggie asked quietly. She continued to gaze over the valley.

"I'm not sure how to explain it. You just seem so much more mature than I remember. More grace. More poise. I've noticed that you think before you speak."

She turned and looked at Nathan. "Well, Nathan, doesn't maturity come with age?"

"Not necessarily, Maggie. Besides, you haven't aged at all, but you've definitely acquired some wisdom over the years... It's a quiet, graceful kind of soulfulness."

"Oh please, Nathan. I'm the same Maggie I've always been. Maybe you're just seeing me for the first time. I mean ... seeing me now, without any clouded emotional attachment to distort your perception."

"You're wrong, Maggie."

"You know, I could say the same thing about you."

"Yes you could. And I'd accept it ... if you said it." Nathan laughed, eyeing Maggie suspiciously. "Would you say that you can look at me now, without any clouded emotional attachment to distort your perception ... or would you say I'm wrong? Which is it, that you could say the same about me?" Nathan trotted his mare around Maggie, in a circle, waiting for her reply.

Maggie thought long and hard about what Nathan had just said.

"When did you become so philosophical, Nathan?"

"Awww ... the old trick of answering a question *with* a question, when you just can't answer the question." Nathan held Maggie captive with his penetrating stare. "I'm the same Nathan I've always been. Maybe you just didn't realize that you married a philosopher."

Nathan slapped his horse's rump with the reigns and headed down the lane. "See you at dinner, Maggie," he called back to her, still laughing.

Maggie just sat there, dazed and confused. "What on earth was that about?" she asked herself out loud, shaking her head slowly. "Oh God ... he's got me talking to myself, now!"

Maggie headed for the top of the highest hill she could see. She was sure that from a vantage point like that, she would be able to survey the entire farm. It took about thirty minutes to finally reach the summit, but the view from there was extraordinary. Never in her life had she felt so close to nature. Being alone in this space, at this time, gave her a sense of pure freedom that she'd never felt before – not in her entire lifetime. This was a magical place. The varying colors of the leaves on the trees were so intense that she couldn't believe the scene hadn't been painted by the hand of God Himself. She inhaled the cool fresh air that seemed to be scented with those very colors ... or was it just her fanciful imagination?

Looking over the rolling hills below, Maggie spotted the flock of Merino sheep. Hundreds of them were lazily grazing on the other side of the creek. They reminded her of popcorn, strewn all over an emerald colored carpet. She wanted a closer look.

She made her way down the hill and across the creek to where the sheep were. Maggie knew better than to startle the flock, so she kept her distance. They looked so fluffy and soft. She wanted to dismount and take a closer look, maybe even pet one of the creatures, but she knew better. It was difficult to control her impulse.

This was *her* dream ... her very own sheep. Could she actually allow herself to claim them? Nathan had cared for them for years. He had done a very good job with his breeding program; increasing the flock every year. No ... Maggie knew she was only dreaming about a dream.

From there, Maggie explored the orchards. – Acres and acres – every kind of fruit tree imaginable. All of the trees had been meticulously picked clean of their fruit, except a few pieces left behind, here and there. Maggie grabbed an apple to snack on. She tried to imagine how many wagons, filled with fruit, had been sent to market. It had to have been a very lucrative harvest.

Maggie rode over to Sarah's home, and she spent the rest of the day catching up on events with her beloved sister-in-law. She had always loved Sarah like a real sister, and it seemed that nothing had changed between them, even though they hadn't kept in touch over the years. The two of them were like little girls; giggling, sharing secrets, and making up new dreams for the future.

Maggie was so grateful that Sarah had carefully avoided any mention of her personal life with Miles Deihl, or her feelings about Nathan. Sarah was the epitome of grace, and tact, and loyalty.

The ride home was a beautiful way to end the perfect day. Maggie rode along the creek bank, remembering the long walks she used to take there. She rode slowly, listening to the singing water, cascading over the rocks; inhaling the fresh damp air; watching the woodland creatures scurrying along the water's edge; and experiencing the sunset. Maggie felt like she was definitely at a turning point in her life. It was a spiritual kind of change.

Chapter 37 – Nightmares and Sweet Dreams

November 18, 1827 – Nathan Stillman's Farm

It was a cold and windy night. The first winter storm was blowing into Ohio with a vengeance. It was raining ice and the temperature was dropping quickly. Maggie was grateful for the fireplace in her room.

She tied her long dark curls up, on top of her head, with a ribbon, and bathed in front of the roaring fire. Climbing into her bed, she couldn't help but feel a little apprehensive, as the wind was howling even more viciously, now; outside the four big windows in her bedroom.

Just then, there was a knock at her door. Maggie sat upright in the bed and pulled the covers up to her chin.

"Come in," she called.

The door opened, and to her surprise, it was Nathan.

"Maggie, I didn't want to bother you, but I've decided that with this wind and sleet, we should close the shutters on all the windows. I don't need any broken glass." He looked at Maggie intently. "You look a little pale. Are you alright?"

"I'm just a little unnerved by all of that noise."

"Well, bear with me while I get the shutters closed, and I'm sure you'll find it to be much quieter."

Nathan had to open each window and use a long rod, to catch each shutter, pull them closed, and secure them. By the time he had finished, he was drenched. His hair was dripping in ringlets, and his massive hands were stiff from the icy cold. The room was a mess. Things had blown off the dressers and tables, and the ashes from the fireplace were everywhere.

Nathan stirred the coals and laid a couple of logs on the fire. He stood up and turned to Maggie. He broke into fits of laughter as he stared at the lump in the middle of the bed. Maggie had pulled the covers over her head; attempting to escape the whirlwind which had overtaken the room.

"You can come out now, Maggie."

Maggie slowly emerged from her makeshift shelter. Looking around the room, and then seeing Nathan so completely disheveled, she bit her lip. "Umm ... that went well," she said calmly.

She scooted out of bed and grabbed a thick bath blanket from the bureau. "Give me that wet shirt."

Nathan complied, pulling the shirt up over his head. He handed it to Maggie. She hung the shirt over a chair by the fire to dry. Wrapping the blanket around Nathan's broad bare shoulders, she had forgotten how muscular and perfect his body was. She marveled that he was still one of the handsomest men she had ever laid eyes on. She reached up to brush the dripping ringlets away from his big blue eyes. In that moment, and for only an instant, their eyes locked. It was a secret and silent communication.

"Sit down here and warm yourself up, Nathan. I hope you don't make yourself sick doing this." She was furiously drying his hair with a towel.

"We should have closed those damned shutters before the storm hit. We just didn't see that storm coming," he admitted, shaking his head.

"We never *did*," Maggie replied. "Seems to be the story of our lives, doesn't it?

Nathan looked at Maggie in astonishment.

Maggie and Nathan sat by the fire discussing the farm, the sheep, the boys, the marketing process, and a myriad of other non-personal topics. Finally Nathan stood up and ran his hands over his hair, smoothing it back. It was finally dry. He looked at Maggie and smiled.

"Maggie, you look like a little girl, sitting there in your nightgown, with your hair all piled up on top of your head. All you need is a teddy bear to complete the picture." Nathan reached down and stroked Maggie's cheek affectionately.

"You're not going to try closing more shutters are you?"

"Yep. I've only got about ten to go. The windows downstairs were easy. I did them all from outside." Nathan frowned. "Yours were the first, up here. There must be a better way!" He managed a smile. "I'd better get busy, Maggie. Would you like me to tuck you in, little girl?" He gave her a sideways glance, as he picked up the shutter rod.

"Ummm, no thank you. That won't be necessary," Maggie said; blushing.

"Well, have a good night, Maggie ... and sweet dreams." Nathan picked up his shirt and threw it over his shoulder. He left the room.

Just as he was closing the door to Maggie's room, he nearly ran right in to Annie; startling both of them.

"Papa!" Annie exclaimed. "What happened to you?" She eyed him critically. There he was ... half dressed, his hair in tangles, and his cheeks flushed crimson.

"Would you believe I got caught in a whirlwind?" he asked quietly.

Annie stood there silently for a moment, shaking her head in disbelief. Finally, the girl decided to leave well enough alone, and continued down the hallway toward her own bedroom. "Sweet dreams, Papa," she giggled.

Nathan went downstairs and opened the big front door. He was thankful that the storm seemed to have subsided, and now a gentle snow was falling. He decided to forget about trying to close the other upstairs shutters. He would just call it a night. He retired to his room, across the hall from Maggie's, and soon fell into a sound sleep.

They were swarming everywhere; like ants. Maggie could hear the yelling, the screams of terror, the moaning and sobbing of the dying, and the gun shots. She smelled smoke, and she saw brilliant, deadly flashes of light in the midnight sky. She tried to move, but she was paralyzed in her own terror. Suddenly she saw three Shawnee renegades creeping toward her. One of them raised a tomahawk over her head. It was dripping blood, and she felt the still-warm drops falling onto her face, as she looked up. Just as he was about to bring the weapon down on her skull, she sat straight up and let out a blood curdling scream.

Maggie woke up and looked around, in a confused daze. She was shaking and crying hysterically.

The door to her room flew open and the entire family was at her bedside. Nate and Miles were frozen in fear, not knowing what might have happened. Annie just stood there with her hand covering her mouth. Nathan sat down on the bed and pulled Maggie into his lap, cradling her and rocking her like a baby. He held her tightly; securely.

"It was just a dream," he said calmly. "Maggie, you're OK. It was only a dream."

Maggie continued trembling and sobbing. "It was so real!" she cried. "The Shawnees were everywhere. People were dying. And the blood .... It was warm. It was dripping on my face! Oh My God!!" Maggie swiped at her face, as if to wipe off the droplets of blood.

Nathan looked up at Annie and the boys. "I'm sure she had a nightmare about the massacre that killed her family," he explained quietly. "That's exactly how it happened, and she was there. She saw the whole thing." Nathan smoothed the hair back from Maggie's feverish brow. She was soaked with perspiration. "You kids can go ahead back to bed. I'll stay with her. I promise ... she'll be just fine." He looked down at Maggie who seemed to have lapsed into shock. He'd seen the same thing on the night of the massacre. "I'm surprised these nightmares haven't happened before now, after what she endured that night." He could feel a tightness growing in his throat as he remembered that awful night.

Maggie just stared into space, trembling and sobbing. It seemed like an hour before she finally stirred.

Maggie struggled to sit up. "I'm so sorry. I didn't mean to scare anyone." She sobbed. "It was just so real. Like it was actually happening to me; all over again."

Everyone was relieved that Maggie had snapped out of it, and was able to speak.

"It's OK Mama," Nate said, patting Maggie affectionately on her shoulder. "We didn't know what happened. I'm glad it was only a dream; and not something worse."

Miles bent down and kissed his mother on the cheek. "You're safe now, Mama. Try and go back to sleep. Nathan will take good care of you."

"Good night boys. I love you," Maggie said weakly.

"Goodnight Maggie," Annie said, laying her hand against Maggie's cheek. The girl's voice was full of compassion.

"Good night, Annie."

The children left the room, quietly closing the door behind them.

Nathan continued to hold Maggie, trying to stop her trembling. Once she finally relaxed, she felt like a rag doll in Nathan's arms.

"Maggie, you're drenched with sweat. Where are your clean nightgowns?" He slid her off of his lap and sat her down on the edge of the bed.

"I'll get one," Maggie answered quietly. She tried to stand, but her legs wouldn't cooperate. "I can't believe this happened!" She sounded angry now, and it was a good sign.

Nathan poured some fresh water into the big bowl and found a sponge on the wash stand. He rummaged through the drawers until he found a fresh nightgown and a clean bath sheet. He laid them on the wash stand beside the bowl.

"Now all we have to do is get you over here. You'll feel better once you freshen up."

"I can do that," Maggie said. "Just give me a minute 'til I get control of these damn legs." She managed a smile. "They're still a little shaky."

Nathan pulled Maggie to her feet and steadied her for a moment. It appeared that she was able to walk.

"Maggie ... I'll just wait outside while you bathe. Call me if you need me."

"Why would you do that?"

"I don't know, Maggie. I'm just trying to be considerate, I guess."

"Don't be silly, Nathan! After all ... we're both adults here – and we've been married. You don't *have* to look. Surely you have control of your own eyes! Or you can simply turn your back. Besides ... it wouldn't be anything you haven't seen countless times before." She laughed. "It's not complicated. Relax!"

Maggie was standing at the wash stand now. Without saying another word, she pulled her damp nightgown up and off, over her head, tossing it into a pile on the floor.

Nathan was caught completely off guard. He felt like the wind had been knocked out of him. He collapsed into the rocker, by the fireside, and he couldn't resist looking at Maggie as she was sponging down her beautiful body. He couldn't take his eyes off the spectacle in front of him. His heart was racing, his breathing became heavy, his hands were sweating. He began to laugh.

"What's so funny, Nathan?" Maggie asked indignantly, looking back at Nathan through the mirror in front of her. "Are you laughing at *ME*?" She whirled around to face him.

He looked stunned. A long silence followed as he tried to find the right words.

"It's not *you* that I find amusing, Honey ... It's just that I can't believe I'm having a reaction that I can't control over here. It's *ME*. That's what's funny. I haven't felt this in years and years. It's just pretty damned surprising. That's all." He drew his sleeve across his mouth. "Please, Maggie, you'd better put that nightgown on, as fast as you can." Nathan stood up and walked toward Maggie. "I think you've forgotten .... I *am* a man." He looked serious now.

Maggie hurriedly squirmed into her fresh nightgown and grinned at Nathan. "I didn't forget."

Nathan caught Maggie's wrist and pulled her into his arms. "Maggie, are you trifling with me?" He looked down at her and grinned. "Or is this a symptom of shock? You're teasing me, aren't you?"

Maggie looked confused. "I'm not teasing you, Nathan."

"Then what did you just do?" He continued to hold her against him. "Did you intend to arouse the monster in me?" He couldn't contain his amusement any longer. He released Maggie and fell backward onto the bed in fits of laughter. "Maggie, I've got to warn you ... if you play with fire, you're liable to get burned."

Maggie remembered hearing that statement before. "I'm sorry Nathan. I didn't think it was a big deal. It's just my body. It's nothing you haven't seen before. I'll try and remember to be more modest from now on. I promise." Maggie seemed sincere and a little frightened.

"Well, Honey, I guess I should thank you for reminding me that I *am* still a man. Good God! I haven't felt those urges for a long time. I thought I was past that. You pretty much ignited an inferno in me." He rubbed his chin; thinking. "Damn, you're beautiful, Maggie." Nathan looked her square in the eye. "I just had to tell you that."

Maggie's cheeks turned red. "Um.... I think you're a beautiful and handsome man, too, Nathan .... I just had to tell you that." She giggled, and jumped onto the bed beside him.

Nathan rolled over onto his side to face Maggie. He lifted himself up on his elbow and studied her intently. "I can see you're feeling much better now. I think I should go, so you can get back to sleep."

Maggie's expression changed instantaneously. "I don't want to go back to sleep, Nathan. I'm afraid it will happen again. I don't think I'll ever go to sleep again!"

"You'll be fine."

Maggie started to cry.

"I thought you were all grown up, Maggie," he teased. "What's become of the poised, graceful, *mature*, Maggie?"

"That's not fair, Nathan! You have no idea how terrifying that was for me."

"Well, Honey, just because *YOU* don't want to sleep, doesn't mean I can go without sleep. I've got work to do in the morning. What would you have me do?"

"Stay with me, Nathan." Maggie was pleading. "Just sleep here, so I know I'm not alone. I can't bear the thought of being alone right now."

Nathan ran his hands roughly through his hair, and took a deep breath. "All right, Maggie. I'll stay."

"Oh thank you, Nathan!" Maggie said breathlessly. "I'll put an extra quilt on the bed, so that I can sleep under one, and you'll sleep on top of it ... It will be completely innocent. I know you remember how we do this, right?"

"Yes, Maggie ... I remember." His exasperation was obvious.

Chapter 38 – Happy Thanksgiving

Thanksgiving, 1827 – Nathan Stillman's Farm

Two big sleighs slipped smoothly along the lane, on the way to Tom McCollough's house. The entire Stillman family had been invited to the annual Thanksgiving feast hosted by Sarah's brother Tom and his family.

Everyone was in a festive mood. Nathan followed behind his brother, as they glided along the road. John and Sarah's sleigh seemed to be overflowing with rowdy children of all ages. At one point, Nathan and Maggie had to stop and pick up the one who fell overboard. Everyone laughed till their sides hurt. Sarah and John didn't even seem to notice that they were missing little Joseph.

Remembering her last trip to this Thanksgiving Day party, so many years ago, Maggie was determined to dress as conservatively as possible. She had selected a beautiful dark navy blue satin dress. It had a very high neckline and long puffy sleeves. It was trimmed in delicate ivory lace, with a huge bow on the back. It did, however, fit tightly, and it emphasized her tiny waste and ample curves. She was sure that Nathan would approve this time. He hadn't seen it yet. He'd been outside hitching the horses to the sleigh. When Maggie came outside, she had her cloak on, which covered the dress. She could only pray that this Thanksgiving would be happier than the last one they spent together.

The sleighs pulled up to the McCollough home, and everyone eagerly climbed out. Nathan tied the reins to the rail and then lifted Maggie down. Nate helped Annie. Miles helped himself.

Once inside, introductions were in order. Tom McCollough's list of friends had grown over the years as the town had grown, and Maggie didn't recognize most of the people at the dinner. The boys melded right in with the other young people there. Sarah was kept busy chasing her brood around, and Annie had disappeared with a handsome young man. Maggie assumed it was Paul. Nathan and John were in the middle of a very animated conversation with three other gentlemen.

Nathan turned and saw Maggie standing alone in the foyer. He excused himself from the conversation and walked over to her, his brilliant blue eyes twinkling as he eyed Maggie from head to toe.

"Maggie, you look absolutely breathtaking. Have I told you lately how beautiful I really think you are?" He winked at her, playfully.

Maggie just smiled and blushed as usual. "Nathan, I don't know a soul here," she said. "Everyone seems to be busy with their own agenda, and I feel just a little awkward."

"Maggie! I've never known you to be shy. Come over here with us. Do you feel like discussing politics?"

"Oh no ... you go right ahead Nathan. I'll find someone to talk to. I'll be OK. I promise... Just enjoy yourself." Maggie laid her hand on Nathan's chest, and looked up into his mischievous blue eyes. "By the way, Mr. Stillman ... you look extraordinarily handsome today!." Maggie winked at Nathan and grinned; mocking him.

Nathan laughed and returned to his debate.

The food was wonderful, and the alcohol was free-flowing. Everyone seemed to be having a wonderful time. Maggie had managed to talk to some of the other women, but she found them either boring or pretentious. She put a huge piece of chocolate cake on a plate, and returned to the foyer. She sat down to enjoy her dessert.

"Excuse me ma'am, mind if I join you?"

Maggie looked up to see a very handsome man smiling down at her.

"Well, ummm ... I ..."

"Thank you, don't mind if I do," he chuckled, pulling up a chair across from Maggie.

The man sat down and just stared at Maggie. He didn't say a word as he studied her. He was blatantly inventorying her body. Maggie was becoming agitated.

At that moment, from seemingly out of nowhere, Nathan appeared. "Aww, Geoffrey ... I see you've met my wife, Maggie."

The man jumped to his feet to face Nathan, but he had to look up. "I actually hadn't gotten the chance to talk to her, Nathan. I just this minute sat down."

"Uh huh ... And did she invite you to sit with her?" Nathan asked.

"Actually NO ... she didn't. I just assumed she was a single lady, and ...."

"Well she's not," Nathan abruptly interrupted the man.

"I apologize, Nathan. I had no idea you were married." The man was obviously uncomfortable. Little beads of perspiration were popping out across his forehead. "I haven't seen you around with the pretty lady."

"We've been married for nearly twenty years. And I have to admit, she doesn't get out much. She's terribly shy ... you know." Nathan looked away, and then back at the man. "I usually keep her locked up in the barn when I come into town ... the rest of the time she's locked in the bedroom." He said it as seriously as he could. "I only beat her when she talks to strange men." He bent down closer to the man. "She didn't talk to *YOU* did she?" he asked in a low gruff voice.

"Oh no ... no she ... She didn't say a word, Nathan!"

"Well that's good. I hate it when I have to beat her!"

"I see. Well it was a pleasure meeting you Mrs. Stillman. ... Good seeing you Nathan ..." The man turned on his heel and made a hasty retreat.

Nathan began laughing so hard he couldn't stand up. He rolled onto the floor holding his sides. Maggie was struggling to control her own fits of laughter, when Tom McCollough walked up to the pair.

"Hmmm ... whatever it was, it must have been good," he stated, looking down at Nathan in amusement. "I don't know, Maggie ... it's usually *ME* who laughs so hard I can't stand up. I wish John could see this!"

"I *am* seeing this, and I can't believe what I'm seeing." It was John. "Has he been in the sauce, Maggie?"

At that point, Maggie let go; totally out of control. She laughed so hard she nearly rolled off of her own chair.

John and Tom looked at each other incredulously, and then they, too, began laughing.

"Please ... someone, get me out of here, before anyone else sees me, and labels me a lunatic!" Maggie begged. She was barely able to get the words out, while laughing so hard.

John quickly grabbed Maggie's hand and whisked her outside, to protect her reputation.

Even then, Maggie couldn't stop laughing.

"What the hell did you two do in there? What happened?" John just couldn't imagine what could have been *that* funny.

Just then, Nathan staggered out onto the porch, holding his sides, and still laughing.

Maggie looked at Nathan, and it started all over again; both of them being overtaken by laughter.

Maggie regained some control and grabbed John's arm. "Do you .... Do you know a man named ... a man named Geoffrey?" She continued to giggle.

"Oh no ... that pompous ass that thinks he's some kind of a lady killer?" John asked, looking down at Nathan.

"That's the one!" Nathan said, trying to recover. He grabbed the porch railing for support. He finally stood up. Tears were running down his cheeks, and his face was beet-red from all of the commotion.

"Well what happened?" John insisted.

"Yea ... this has got to be good!" Tom said, shaking Nathan by the shoulders. "Tell us, man!"

Nathan breathed deeply, calming himself as much as possible. "You would have had to be there! The guy was trying to seduce Maggie." He started laughing again, but John grabbed him by the collar and straightened him up.

"You would have had to be there to appreciate it. It was hysterical," Nathan said, breathlessly.

Maggie continued giggling in the background.

John and Tom just stood there staring at each other with blank looks on their faces. It was obvious that they would never hear the entire story.

"Nathan ... Maggie .... You two need some serious help," John said dryly.

John Stillman and Tom McCollough went back into the house, returning to the party.

"Oh Maggie ... aren't we a pair?" Nathan breathed, slipping his arm around Maggie's shoulders. "I can't tell you when I've had this much fun."

"I know ... I haven't laughed so hard in years. Actually, I don't think I've *ever* laughed so hard. Now I'm just totally exhausted." Maggie rested her head against Nathan's chest.

"Papa! Maggie! I've been looking everywhere for you two," Annie called from the doorway. "Aren't you cold out there?" Annie bounded out of the house and ran up to her father. "I need to borrow Maggie for a few minutes. Is that alright with you? I mean ... can you part with her for a while?" Annie winked at her father, who still had his arm around Maggie, holding her against his chest.

"Only for a minute!" Nathan laughed. "Then you get her right back to me."

"Papa, you're such a fool!" Annie giggled.

"And while you're at it, can you round up the boys? I'd like to get home before dark," Nathan said, releasing Maggie.

Annie and Maggie disappeared into the house, leaving John alone with his thoughts.

Annie grabbed Maggie's hand and literally dragged her through the house, and into the kitchen. Standing by the fireplace, Maggie saw the tall handsome man that she knew immediately was Annie's beau, Paul. He was extremely tall, with straight dark hair and bright hazel-colored eyes. His eyes were expressive, and exuded emotion. His full mouth was accentuated by big dimples on each side. He was well dressed, and projected an appearance of authority.

"Annie, this is Paul Hamilton. Paul this is Maggie, my guardian angel," Annie stated gleefully.

Maggie extended her hand to the man. "I'm so happy to finally meet you, Paul."

"I've certainly heard a lot about *YOU*, Maggie. From what I hear, you're a very fascinating woman," the young man said, smiling, and shaking Maggie's hand.

Maggie was immediately impressed by the man. Not only was he handsome, but he had a very firm handshake. Her father had always stressed the fact that a weak handshake was the sign of a weak person. He also had a strong jaw; a sign of strength of character.

Paul continued to hold Maggie's hand in his. "Maggie ... May I call you Maggie?" he began. "There's so much I'd like to tell you. Annie says you're the only one we can trust ... and you're probably the only one who can help us."

"Of course you can call me Maggie!"

"Well, I've tried to speak with Nathan about Annie and me, but he doesn't want to hear me out. He refuses to discuss the issue. I really want to marry her. We've been courting for four years now. I absolutely detest going behind Nathan's back the way we do. We're just about at our wits' end over this." Paul hesitated, shaking his head sadly. "We don't want to go against Nathan's wishes ... Annie doesn't want to see her father hurt ... but we're actually considering eloping. God knows Annie's old enough to do as she pleases. We'd just rather have Nathan's blessings. I don't know *WHY* he's so against our relationship."

"He's never given you a reason?" Maggie asked.

"Never," Paul replied, releasing Maggie's hand and reaching for Annie.

Annie looked up at her beau. She was beaming. It was obvious that they loved each other deeply.

"I don't know what to say, Paul," Maggie said, laying a consoling hand on his arm. "Please don't elope .... At least not yet. I need some time to talk to Nathan. I've got to figure out how to approach the subject. I think it's high time Annie *was* married. If she wants children of her own, she'd better get on with it. Nathan needs to understand this."

"Speaking of children," Annie interrupted, "Danny ... Mary ... come here," she called loudly.

Two adorable children scampered into the kitchen, and ran up to Annie; giggling, and grabbing at her hands. The boy looked to be about seven years old, and the little girl was about five.

Paul looked down adoringly at his offspring. "They're mine, Maggie." He patted the little boy's head, affectionately. "I lost my wife when Mary was born. I've raised them all by myself. They adore Annie. None of us could live without her."

"And I love them!" Annie said, kneeling down to enjoy a group hug with Danny and Mary.

Just then they heard Nathan calling for Maggie from the front of the house.

"Ooops!" Maggie exclaimed. "It was nice meeting you, Paul. I'll see what I can do for you." Maggie looked over at Annie. "Get the boys, Annie and meet us outside, OK?"

"Thank you Maggie. It was an honor meeting you," Paul said.

Maggie hurried out of the kitchen to find Nathan, before he found her.

Maggie was sitting at her dressing table, already in her nightgown, brushing her long black hair, when Nathan knocked at her door.

"Maggie," he called, "can I come in?"

"The door's open, Nathan," Maggie called back to him.

Nathan opened the door and walked into the room. He had that broad mischievous smile on his handsome face. Maggie continued brushing her hair. Nathan pulled two chairs over to the fireplace. He stirred the coals, and threw an extra log on the fire.

"Come sit with me, Maggie. I just don't feel like going to bed yet."

Maggie laid the brush down on the dressing table. She gathered her curls up on the top of her head and tied them with a bright red ribbon. She joined Nathan by the fire.

"Are you OK Nathan?" she asked, sitting down in the big rocker.

Nathan propped his feet up on the stool and leaned back in his chair.

"I'm fine. I just wanted some company," he said, eyeing Maggie admiringly.

Maggie pulled her shawl around her shoulders and smiled back at Nathan.

"You were so quiet on the way home from Tom's ... I wanted to make sure *YOU* were OK," Nathan said.

"I'm just worn out from your special kind of humor, Nathan." Maggie had to laugh, thinking of the lies Nathan had told that poor man.

"That was fun, Maggie." Nathan gazed into the fire and smiled.

"Well, you surprised me! I'm just glad you aren't going to lock me up or beat me tonight."

Nathan started to laugh uproariously.

"Nathan ..." Maggie hesitated, then continued. "I'm so glad we can be friends again. I would have never dreamed it could happen. I really *do* appreciate *YOU.*"

"You're my little sister, Maggie. We grew up together. How could we ever stay mad at each other?"

Maggie was silent. She was considering the term *'little sister'*. She wasn't quite sure she could settle for that. She wrestled with the strange emotions that were overtaking her senses. She tried to deny the fact that she was so attracted to Nathan. He was completely different than he had been, in his youth. He was even more handsome, now, in his maturity; he seemed so much wiser, mellower, and he was a lot more fun than he used to be. Miles Deihl had only been gone a little over six months. *'Was she fickle or just lonely?'* A tear slid down her cheek. Maggie quickly tried to conceal her feelings. She turned her face away from Nathan's view. It was too late.

Nathan jumped up from his chair and was kneeling in front of Maggie. "What's wrong, Maggie Honey? Why are you crying?"

Maggie couldn't bring herself to answer. She continued to look away from Nathan; afraid that he would look into her eyes and see the secret she wanted so desperately to hide.

"Look at me, Maggie," Nathan demanded. "If you don't tell me what's wrong, there's no way I can fix things. I don't want you to be sad." His voice was full of sincerity.

Slowly, Maggie turned and faced Nathan.

Nathan's piercing blue eyes penetrated Maggie's very soul. She knew he was seeing more than she could ever verbalize. He cupped her face in his massive hands and shook his head sadly.

"I can't do this, Maggie. You're tearing my heart out." Nathan dropped his hands to his sides. He got up and walked toward the door. He reached for the doorknob and then stopped and turned around.

"Maggie, if you have something you need to say, then this is the time to do it," Nathan said softly.

"Nathan, wait." Maggie cried. She pulled the shawl tightly around her body, as if it were her security blanket. "I'll tell you what's wrong." She stood up and walked over to where Nathan was standing, and she looked up at him.

"Well?" Nathan waited for her reply.

"This is hard for me to admit, and it's probably not a good thing to say ..." Her voice trailed off into another long silence. She fumbled for the words ... no words seemed to be the *right* words.

"Maggie!"

"OK!" Maggie struggled with her truth. "I just want to be loved, Nathan."

"Everybody loves you, Maggie."

"I want *YOU* to love me, Nathan."

"I never stopped!"

"I don't want to be loved like a *little sister*, Nathan." Maggie lowered her head in humiliation.

Moments passed as the reality of what Maggie just revealed sunk into Nathan's consciousness.

"Maggie ... I'm confused." He managed a smile. "Maybe you could just *show* me what you want? You've left a hell of a lot to my imagination. I certainly wouldn't want to insult you by assuming I understand what you mean ... if you understand what I mean ...."

The silence was deafening, as Maggie tried to come to terms with her own need.

"Well?" Nathan waited.

Maggie stood on her tiptoes and slipped her arms around Nathan's neck. She kissed him on each corner of his mouth and then covered his lips with hers. She kissed him softly. Her shawl fell to the floor as she pressed her body in against his. She couldn't stop the passion that was rising in her psyche. Maggie kissed him deeply and urgently.

Suddenly Nathan responded with an intensity of passion that far surpassed Maggie's. He wrapped his massive arms around her and crushed her against his eagerness. He kissed her until her entire world was reeling and she could no longer stand. He swept her up in his arms and carried her over to the bed.

Morning came too soon. As the light from the rising sun crept into the room, Maggie slowly opened her sleepy eyes. She was surprised to see Nathan still there, beside her. He was propped up on his elbow, wide awake, and smiling at her.

"Nathan ..." she said in a sleepy voice. "I was afraid you would leave."

Nathan leaned over and kissed Maggie on the forehead. "I wanted to make sure you weren't going to beat yourself up over this. I want you to know that last night was incredible. I know how your complex mind works, Maggie." He laughed, and brushed the curls away from Maggie's face. "Just remember this .... You didn't do anything wrong, and neither did I. Affection can take many forms, and this was just one of them. What you did, Maggie ... took courage and honesty. I love you for that. God knows I didn't have the courage to tell you ... all the times I wanted to make love to *YOU*, since you've been back."

"Oh Nathan ..."

Nathan leaned over and kissed Maggie. It was a lingering kiss, full of emotion and tenderness.

"Well, Honey ... I've got to get to work. I just wanted to make sure you understand that I've wanted to make love to you for a very long time. I just didn't have the courage that you have."

Nathan was up, and dressed, and out the door, before Maggie could say anything.

Maggie laid there for a long time; replaying the experiences of last night in her mind. She couldn't believe what she'd done ... but not one ounce of her being was sorry she'd done it.

'Now that we've crossed the line ... where do we go from here?' she asked the universe.

Chapter 39 – A Merry Christmas

December, 1827 – Nathan Stillman's Farm

The back door flew open, and Nathan bounded into the kitchen, brushing the snow from his shoulders; removing his hat and shaking snow all over the floor; and stomping the ice from his boots.

"Good morning ladies!" he shouted jovially.

Maggie and Annie looked up from the breakfast table in surprise.

"Where have you been, this early in the morning, Nathan?" Maggie asked.

"You wouldn't believe it in a thousand years!" he shouted.

"What, Papa?!" Annie jumped to her feet, running over to Nathan; yanking vigorously on the sleeve of his jacket. "What are you so excited about?"

"Can't tell you, Annie, Honey …. It's a surprise for *YOU!*" Nathan was beside himself in his secret zeal. "…. But I can tell Maggie!"

Nathan snatched Maggie's hand, pulled her up from the table, and literally dragging her out of the kitchen and up the stairs – away from where Annie might hear. Once inside Maggie's room, Nathan threw his hands up into the air – in pure glee, bringing them down hard on his skull. "You won't believe it!" he shouted.

"Nathan … what on earth has gotten in to you?!"

"OK ... OK ...." Nathan tried to calm himself down. He took a deep breath and sat down. "Maggie, I know that Sarah told you all about Annie, and how she ended up here with me, right? Before I talked to Sarah, I had been wondering why you never asked me to explain ... now I understand. You've known all along."

"Well Nathan, I didn't want to question you. I know it was a very personal subject. But, yes ... Sarah told me the entire story."

"But here's something Sarah never knew ...."

"What's that?" Maggie sat down across from Nathan.

"Do you remember telling me how you met young Mr. Paul Hamilton, and what a good man you think he is ... and what a wonderful husband he'd make for Annie?"

"Yes, I remember telling you that," Maggie answered, shaking her head *'yes'*.

"Do you remember asking why I wouldn't consent to Annie marrying such an eligible bachelor?"

"Yes, but you changed the subject and wouldn't give me a valid reason for you to deny your own daughter a chance for happiness ... and a family of her own!" Maggie was obviously growing agitated, thinking about Annie's situation.

"Well ... calm down, Maggie ... and listen to me." Nathan reached over and covered Maggie's hands with his. "*Our* Annie's mother .... Annie Wilson's maiden name was Hamilton."

"So what?" Maggie quipped.

"Annie Wilson had a very young brother named Paul – Paul Hamilton. Her family was from the next county over, from ours. The entire family was killed by Indians except for Annie and Paul. They were raised by separate sets of relatives. I never met Annie's little brother, but she talked about him sometimes." Nathan was still trying to calm his excitement. "You know, Maggie ... Paul Hamilton ... our Annie's beau, is in his late thirties, right?"

"Oh my God ... Nathan!" Maggie gasped. "I see what you're saying."

"Yes, but Maggie ... Annie's beau is *NOT* her uncle, like I feared!" Nathan jumped up from his chair and became very animated again.

"How do you know? I mean ... are you sure?"

"I've been writing letters back home, for months now. I've been trying to find Annie Wilson's brother, Paul Hamilton. Well I finally found him!!!" Nathan sat back down.

"So you're sure that *our* Annie is *NOT* related at all to her beau?"

"Exactly! Not only that ... but *our* Annie's uncle will be at the wedding." Nathan was grinning from ear to ear.

"Wedding?" Now Maggie was becoming excited.

"Yep. I went out to Paul Hamilton's farm this morning, after picking up this letter." Nathan pulled an envelope from his pocket and handed it to Maggie. "... and he and I had a very long heart to heart talk. I explained everything to him. He understood ... thank God. We're going to announce the engagement on Christmas Day. Are you up for planning a party, Maggie?"

"Oh Nathan!!" Maggie cried, jumping into Nathan's lap and hugging him tightly. "I can't wait to plan a party for Christmas Day! An engagement party!"

"Well ... Paul and I want this to be a complete surprise for Annie ... so don't let the cat out of the bag ... OK?"

"She'll be so happy! ... and God knows she deserves to be." Maggie could barely contain her own glee, now. "I can keep a secret, Nathan ... but can I at least tell Sarah?"

"If you're sure Sarah and John will promise to keep it a secret .... Go ahead and tell Sarah."

"Nathan, that poor girl has been heart broken, because you wouldn't give them your blessings. She is so loyal to you ... she was willing to forego her own happiness in order to keep from hurting you. They both have gone out of their way to prove their respect for you!"

"Maggie it just broke *my* heart to refuse my blessings to those kids. I've never heard a bad comment about Paul Hamilton ... Annie's beau. He has a fine reputation, and he's an upstanding member of the community ... but how on earth could I have admitted my suspicions ... I just wanted to be sure, before I gave a reason for withholding my approval. I'm glad I kept my big mouth shut. I can't tell you how relieved I am. All I've ever wanted for Annie ... is to see her happy."

Maggie buried her face in Nathan's neck, and hugged him. They both wept with joy.

It was Christmas Day. Maggie had managed to acquire the most beautiful decorations she could find, and had worked for two weeks getting everything organized and prepared. She and Sarah and Annie had been cooking and baking for days. Nate and Miles were in on the secret, and they had made space in the barn for gifts and other surprises. Nathan cut a huge pine tree and dragged it down from the hills just last night. He, John, and the boys were putting the finishing touches on the seven foot Christmas tree. The inside of the house was decorated beautifully, and the outside was covered in wreaths and dried flowers. Over three hundred invitations had been delivered, and nearly all had responded that they would attend the celebration. Never before had there been such a festive occasion at Nathan Stillman's home.

Maggie, Annie, and Sarah had convinced Nathan to allow them to wear some of the timeless, elegant dresses that had been packed away in trunks for twenty years. He had actually stated that it was unnecessary for them to even ask his approval; having forgotten his reaction to the low cut dresses, so many years ago. It was his contention, now, however, to make them as low-cut as possible. (Funny how time changes a man.)

The dresses had been cleaned and altered for the women last week. Maggie finally got her chance to wear the gorgeous, dark emerald green gown she'd fallen in love with, years ago. Sarah had on that lovely pink brocade dress that accentuated her red hair and ivory skin. Annie was a vision in the melon-colored satin that fit tightly at her waist and plunged dangerously low on her bosom. The dress revealed more of her womanhood than Nathan was used to seeing, regarding his daughter; but he managed not to put a damper on this occasion, for Annie's sake.

It was noon, and the guests began arriving. As the carriages and wagons pulled up to the house, Nate and Miles ushered the people to the front door, then took their rigs up to the barn, and secured the horses. They piled all the engagement gifts onto a cart for later.

The food was displayed on a long table in the dining room, and everyone was asked to help themselves; buffet style. Seating was no problem, since Nathan and John had crafted benches along all the walls. This was a feast that dwarfed the biggest dinner Tom McCollough had ever endeavored; and he was notorious for his parties, all over the county.

Once the dinner had ended, everyone congregated in the huge living room, around the magnificent Christmas tree. Annie was at the piano, playing Christmas carols, and everyone sang along.

While the guests were participating in the entertainment, Nathan stole Maggie away from the group.

Taking her by the hand, he led her into the kitchen. "Maggie ... I've got a special surprise for *YOU*." He pulled her into his arms and kissed her passionately, leaving her breathless and stunned.

Recovering her composure, she was finally able to speak. "Umm ... that *was* a special surprise." She laughed.

He grinned mischievously, and ran his index finger slowly across the swells of her exposed bosom. "That's absolutely lovely, just in case you want to know if I like what I'm seeing."

"Thank you, Nathan ... you devil." Maggie teased. She couldn't imagine what he had up his sleeve, but she knew he was up to something.

Nathan began digging in his pockets, as if looking for something. Maggie watched him in amusement. Finally, he seemed to have found what he was looking for.

"Nathan? What on earth are you doing?"

Nathan kneeled down in front of Maggie and took her left hand in his. Looking up at Maggie, he grinned that handsome grin she'd learned to love.

"Maggie .... will you marry me?" He held up a diamond ring that was the most beautiful piece of jewelry Maggie had ever seen.

Maggie fainted.

Nathan was able to catch her before she hit the floor, just as Annie came into the kitchen.

"Oh my God! What happened?" she cried, looking down at Maggie, and then at her father. Then she saw the ring. "Guess your big surprise was a little over the top, huh, Papa?"

"Well, I didn't expect this ... did you?" Nathan muttered, trying to revive Maggie.

"I don't know ... when you told me what you had planned, I actually thought that it might be a better idea to give her some notice .... or warning." Annie couldn't stop giggling.

Maggie began to stir. She looked up at Annie's and Nathan's concerned expressions, and began to laugh. "It's good to be loved!" she giggled.

Nathan helped her up and on to a chair. Annie was frantically fanning Maggie's face to help her get some needed air.

"Oh my gosh ... I'm so sorry. I don't know what happened." She looked confused. "Now ... where were we?" She grinned at Nathan.

"Maggie, Honey ... I was asking you if ..." – Suddenly the kitchen door swung open, hitting the wall with a loud BANG.

"Maggie! I can't believe you're back! I'm so happy for this family!" It was Dr. Mathison.

Maggie jumped up and into Doc Mathison open arms. They hugged each other happily.

"Oh Doc!" Maggie cried, "I was afraid I'd never see you again." Big tears were now streaming down Maggie's cheeks, as she embraced her long lost friend.

Doc Mathison looked over at Nathan, who was standing there looking absolutely bewildered. "Nathan ... did I interrupt something?"

"Naw, Doc ... nothing that can't wait until later." Nathan managed a smile.

"My Lord, Maggie," Doc said, "You're more beautiful now than you were twenty years ago." He looked at Annie. "And Annie, look at you! I've never seen you look so lovely."

"Would you expect anything less from my girls, doc?" Nathan joked.

Just then, John entered the kitchen. "Nathan ... don't you have announcement to make? I think it's time."

Annie laughed. "Oh Uncle John ... I think his announcement is going to have to wait. Maggie didn't take it so well."

John looked at Nathan, his confusion obvious.

"I'll be right there, John," Nathan said. "Annie is the one who's confused." He laughed. "Just get everyone together. I'll just be a minute."

Annie shook her head in disbelief. "This family has to be insane," she muttered.

"OK everyone, let's go in to the living room." Nathan ushered everyone out of the kitchen.

The entire group of guests and the family were gathered together, and the anticipation was palpable. Nathan stood in front of the Christmas tree with his left arm around Maggie, and his right arm around Annie. Annie still looked confused. Maggie was beaming.

"I want to thank you all for being part of this wonderful occasion," Nathan said. "Now it's time to congratulate my lovely daughter, Annie, on this the day of her engagement." He looked down at Annie's stunned face.

Annie looked up at her father in amazement. She still didn't have a clue what he was talking about.

Just then, Nate and Miles opened the double front doors, and in scampered two adorable children who quickly spotted Annie and ran up to her, delightedly.

Annie's jaw dropped. Now, she was the one who was utterly bewildered. She was trying to make sense of what her father had just said, and the presence of the children; when suddenly her whole world took a turn into a fantasy that she had only dreamed about. Annie looked up, just in time to see her handsome beau, Paul Hamilton, walk through the doors.

Paul walked straight up to Annie, knelt down on one knee, and presented her with a beautiful diamond engagement ring.

"Annie Stillman, will you marry me?" he asked quietly, looking up at his beloved, with tears in his eyes.

Annie fainted.

"Oh NO!" Nathan exclaimed. He picked Annie up and placed her in Paul's arms. "Here, Paul ... you take her." He laughed uproariously. "Nothing seems to be going the way I planned it."

Paul just stood there, holding his Annie in his arms, and looking down at her adoringly. She finally began to recover.

"Pinch me, Paul," Annie whispered.

"Why would I do that?" he asked, grinning at the girl.

"Because I want to make sure this is *real*. I'm afraid I may be dreaming."

"It's *real*, Annie. Your father and Maggie arranged all of this just for *YOU*." He kissed Annie on the forehead. "Now ... will you answer my question?"

"YES … YES … YES!! … The answer is YES!" Annie screamed in glee.

Paul set her down and kissed her full on the lips. He slid the diamond ring onto her finger and kissed her again.

The crowd cheered and applauded the happy couple. Little Mary and Danny jumped up and down, happily clapping their hands. Nathan, Maggie, John, and Sarah were all crying tears of joy.

Miles opened the big doors again, and Nate pulled a wagon into the living room that was overflowing with engagement gifts for Paul and Annie.

Paul stepped forward and addressed his new family and friends. "I don't know how to thank you all for making this the happiest day of my life. I just want you to know, that Annie and I have waited a very long time for this dream to come true. It's been hard, but we were able to hold on to our faith and hope. We have certainly been blessed today. Thank you all."

Everyone cheered and applauded again.

Chapter 40 – Mixed Messages

January, 1827 – Nathan Stillman's Farm

January had been bitter cold, but not nearly as bad as the year before. The Stillman families had managed to have an ample supply of food, firewood, and feed for the livestock put aside for the entire cold weather season. Everyone had had the good fortune to stay healthy throughout the bad weather.

Maggie reigned Seminole II to a stop, when she saw Nathan approaching.

"Good morning Nathan," she called to him; waving, as he advanced.

Nathan rode up to her and stopped. He looked concerned.

"I've been looking everywhere for you, Maggie!"

"It was such a nice day, I decided to ride in to town and pick up the mail. I had some shopping I wanted to do, too."

"Maggie, you didn't have to do that. It's a long trip in this cold! You know I always pick up the mail."

"Well, Nathan... this morning, I beat you to it." She grinned at the handsome Nathan.

"You should have told me you were going, I would have ridden with you. Besides, I was worried, when I couldn't find you."

"I didn't want to bother you."

"You always *bother* me, Maggie!" He winked at her. "But that's not the kind of *bothering* you're talking about... I know."

Maggie's cheeks flushed, as she realized what Nathan was referring to. "You're absolutely incorrigible, Nathan Stillman!"

"Seems this poor man just can't help himself." He laughed. "Every time I look at you, Maggie, I just want to grab you and have my way with you!"

"You behave yourself!" she teased.

"If you say so," Nathan said. "But you never know what you could be missing."

Nathan began riding in circles around Maggie, as she sat there on her horse. She was getting dizzy, trying to keep him in her line of vision. He continued to circle her, watching her intently, like a predatory animal, assessing his prey. "Wouldn't you like to give me a '*good morning kiss*' – just a little one?" Nathan said, trying to look innocent.

"Well now... I can't very well give you a kiss, when you won't stand still. Besides, you're making me light-headed." Maggie grabbed at Nathan's coat, as he passed by; trying to stop him; but she missed.

"I have that affect on *ALL* my women!" Nathan said it proudly. "For some reason, they just swoon over me."

"I'm talking about that *circling* thing you always do. It's really distracting." Maggie giggled. "...And it makes me dizzy."

"It's just my way of mesmerizing you, Maggie," Nathan said. "I'll hypnotize you, and then I'll completely dominate you for the rest of your life." He sounded serious.

Nathan stopped his mare, and bent over toward Maggie; close enough for her to reach his lips with hers.

Maggie leaned into Nathan's kiss.

Back at the house, Maggie sat down at the kitchen table with a big cup of coffee.

Sorting through the handful of mail, one letter in particularly stood out. It was addressed to Nathan Stillman, and it was postmarked Ashland, Kentucky. She couldn't help but notice the smell of perfume on the envelope. Her curiosity was nearly more than she could suppress.

Just then, Nathan walked in. He poured himself a cup of coffee and sat down at the table across from Maggie.

"What's this, Nathan?" Maggie held the envelope up for Nathan to see. She looked a little annoyed.

Nathan looked at it, then back at Maggie's inquisitive expression. "What?" Nathan questioned. "It's obviously a letter." He laughed.

"Who's writing to YOU from Kentucky, Nathan?" Maggie leaned over and waved the letter under his nose. "And why does this envelope reek of perfume?" Maggie demanded.

Nathan began to laugh. "Am I detecting a hint of jealousy here, Maggie?" He could barely contain his amusement.

"When you referred to 'all your women'... I thought you were joking!" Maggie said, indignantly.

"I was!" Nathan was suddenly overcome by a fit of laughter.

Maggie stood up angrily, slapping her hands onto her hips.

Young Nate walked into the kitchen just then. "What's so funny, Nathan?" he asked, watching his father, who was helplessly bent over from laughing. Then he looked at Maggie. Her face was scarlet; and it was obvious that he'd arrived just in time to stop his mother from attacking his dad. She looked furious.

Nathan managed to snatch the envelope that was laying on the table; and he held it up for Nate to see. "I believe this is *YOURS*, Son".

Recognizing it immediately, Nate grabbed the letter, grinning. "I've been waiting for this!" he shouted. "She doesn't usually wait so long before writing back."

Maggie collapsed onto her chair. Her embarrassment was tangible. She was speechless.

Nathan looked over at Maggie. He wasn't laughing, now. "Maggie... these kids have been keeping in touch, ever since Nate's been here. It's usually a weekly thing." He reached over and patted Maggie's hand. "Unless Nate had told you... you had no way of knowing; since I'm always the one to ride in and pick up the mail." He smiled across the table at Maggie. "I have to tell you though... I liked seeing you get jealous when you thought I was corresponding with another woman." He laughed. "I even enjoy seeing you angry sometimes... You're radiant when you're mad."

"You mean you're not upset with me?" Maggie asked weakly.

"Hell NO!" Nathan exclaimed. "I'm flattered!"

Now, Nate understood what he had walked into. "Sorry, Mama. It's from Catharine. I just didn't think to tell you about us writing to each other... It wasn't a secret or anything. Remember the pretty blonde at the inn... during that awful storm? Remember Daniel Kramer and his daughter, Catharine?" Nate ripped the letter open. He was grinning happily. He read Catharine's note silently.

Suddenly Nate's expression grew dark. He sucked in his breath and he bit at his lip.

"What is it, Son?" Nathan said, watching Nate's countenance change dramatically; from joy to despair.

Nate pulled out a chair and sat down heavily.

"What's wrong, Nate? Is Catharine all right?" Maggie asked

"No... Mama... I don't think she *is*," Nate answered quietly; still looking at the letter.

"Nate... do you feel like talking about whatever it is?" Nathan asked. He laid a consoling hand on Nate's shoulder. He waited for Nate's reply.

"Daniel Kramer's dead." Nate stated it bluntly.

Maggie gasped, and covered her mouth with her hand. Her eyes grew wide.

"It happened three weeks ago. Catharine says it was his heart. She said that she and their man, Salvo, had been trying to keep the inn running... she says she's just plain worn out."

"That's awful, Nate!" Maggie whispered.

Nate continued. "Catharine says she has no relatives nearby.... They're all in Maine; and she's never met them. She said she has no friends, because she never had time to make any – she was always working.... Helping Daniel with the inn." Nate rubbed at his forehead. "Mama... she says she's all alone, and she just doesn't see how she can continue on without her father."

"Oh my God..." Maggie cried. "I remember how alone I felt when I lost my parents... so far from home, and not knowing a soul."

"I need to think about this," Nate said quietly. "I feel like I want to help her.... Take care of her... I think she was asking for my help. Maybe it was a subtle request, but I got the message."

"You're a good man, Nate." Nathan said. "You'll make the right decision. Just think long and hard about what you want to do... what you need to do."

Nate got up and walked out of the kitchen.

Miles appeared in the doorway, nearly running in to Nate. He stopped and turned; looking back at his brother, Nate, who didn't acknowledge him at all.

"What's wrong with Nate?" Miles asked.

There was a long silence as Miles waited for an answer. He was a perceptive young man, and he instinctively knew that Nate was completely preoccupied with something serious.

"Your brother got a disturbing letter from the little gal in Kentucky," Nathan answered.

"Oh... He's such a lovesick fool!" Miles responded. He proceeded to pour himself a cup of hot coffee, then he sat down at the table, joining Maggie and Nathan.

He was filthy dirty and his dark hair was covered in dust and cobwebs.

Nathan looked at Miles and chuckled. "So did you get those pens all cleaned out and ready for our new lambs to arrive?"

"What a mess!" Miles said, taking a long drink of hot coffee. "Those mama sheep had better appreciate *MY* labor." He looked at Nathan and grinned. "To answer your question... yes. All the pens are clean and ready. I even put in fresh bedding."

Nathan nodded his approval.

"So, Miles... you knew about Nate and Catharine?" Maggie said, eyeing her younger son suspiciously.

"I knew about it when we were still back there at the Kramer Inn," Miles said. "I even caught them spooning in the barn one night!" He laughed. "Yep... Nate was sure crazy over Catharine. She *is* a beauty, though.... And she's just plain nice. I figured they'd end up together – one way or another. It just felt to me... um...like they belonged together... even back then – from the very beginning."

"And I'm the last one to know," Maggie muttered. "Everyone knew about this but me. How is that possible?"

"Guess you've just been too wrapped up in your own romantic fairy tale, Mama." Miles winked at Nathan and grinned.

Nathan grinned back at young Miles. He knew the boy was wise beyond his years.

"Miles Deihl!" Maggie exclaimed. "What kind of a remark is that?"

"Umm... Mama... I think it's called honesty." He sounded just like his father when he said it. "A person would have to be blind, not to see what's been going on around this house between you and Nathan." He laughed. "...and just for the record... I want you to know that I whole-heartedly approve." He leaned over the table toward Maggie. "My father was a visionary, in case you've forgotten. He told me the entire story. He also told me exactly what was going to happen, and what to expect."

"Your father was an incredible man, Miles," Nathan said.

"This conversation is over!" Maggie said brusquely. She quickly left the kitchen.

Nathan laughed loudly, and reached over to shake Miles's hand. "Miles... you never cease to amaze me. You're a fine young man, and I'm honored to be in your presence."

"Thank you, Nathan," Miles said, smiling. "My father told me what a good man you are... and he was right." Miles was quiet for a moment. "He referred to you as a man *'with the heart of a lion -- close to the earth, but bonded to Heaven'*. ... I never fully understood what he meant by that... but I think I know, now."

"Hmm... I can't see how he would come to that conclusion, Miles."

"We'll both fully understand, when the time comes. I know my destiny, Nathan. I know that I'm supposed to keep my Mama grounded... you know... My father told me that *'she has a tendency to exist in a mythical world that has nothing to do with cold reality'* – It's my job to force her to look at life logically... that's what my father concentrated on. I can't allow her to lie to herself, I have to make sure she doesn't revert back to her childish behavior... in her imaginary world – those are *his* words. I guess when she witnessed the massacre... when her family was killed... she tried to invent a world that she was more comfortable in." Miles looked at Nathan grimly. "It took him a long time to force her to grow up, and adjust to reality.... that's exactly what he told me – *his* exact words... Are you following me, Nathan?"

"Are you really understanding what you're telling me, Miles? There is so much truth in what you just said... and on a very deep level!"

"Of course I understand," Miles replied.

"Good Lord, Miles... that's a huge responsibility for such a young man. But it's refreshing to see that you can stand up to your mother's misconceptions... and point them out with logic and composure." Nathan said it thoughtfully.

Nathan studied Miles's eyes, intently. "So much wisdom and insight, for someone so young... You're definitely one of a kind, Miles Deihl. NO..." he corrected himself, "you're the *second* one of a kind." He chuckled. "Your father was the *first*." Nathan reached over and put his hand firmly on Miles's shoulder. "I can't tell you how much I respect you, son."

"I'll take that as a compliment," Miles said, smiling.

Miles rose from his chair, shook Nathan's hand, and left the kitchen.

Nathan was left alone with his thoughts.

Chapter 41 – Minor Setbacks

January 25, 1827 – Nathan Stillman's Farm

Sarah had just arrived. Annie and Maggie were glad to see her; and they were grateful for her help. The girls were in the dining room working on the final wedding plans.

The ceremony was going to be held at the little church in Unionville, and the reception would be celebrated at Nathan Stillman's home. This gathering would be small compared to the engagement party. Annie wanted it to be more intimate; with only family and close friends attending.

Twenty days to go -- and so much to do. The long table was covered with odds and ends; ribbons, bows, documents, and clothes. Most of the handwritten invitations had already been delivered, but there were a few more to do. The tasks for the day were to finish the invitations, alter the clothes, and finalize plans for the reception.

Annie's wedding dress was hanging on the hall tree at the other end of the room. The wife of one of the farmhands had generously offered it to the bride-to-be. It was a pretty, white, cotton dress, covered in hand-embroidered flowers, and trimmed with ruffles.

"I have one more surprise I need to bring in," Sarah said, heading for the door.

"Oh Annie... I believe I'm more excited about the wedding than you are," Maggie said. She was beaming, as she shuffled through the pile of beautiful bonnets Sarah brought.

"I doubt that, Maggie. It's just so difficult for me to believe that dreams really do come true – I'm numb." She ran over to Maggie, grabbing her, and giving her a big hug.

Maggie embraced the girl tightly. "I think I understand, Annie."

Annie stepped back and looked at the woman she considered her surrogate mother. Tears were rolling down her cheeks. "I've been walking around in a daze since Christmas. I'm afraid something will happen to spoil it all... Or it's only a dream, and I'll wake up; and it will be gone."

"Nothing will stop your wedding, Annie!" Maggie shook the girl gently. "Worrying about something spoiling it only steals the joy of looking forward to it! Enjoy your excitement... let it flow, Annie. If anything is going to ruin your wedding, it will be *you*... you're wasting energy worrying about unlikely circumstances, when you could simply allow yourself to be happily dreaming about your future with Paul!"

Annie looked sad. "I know you're right, Maggie... but when I was a very little girl, I trusted my fantasies. Every time a new family took me in, I allowed myself to get excited...to believe that it was going to be forever... But it always ended the same. My life was just a never-ending series of disappointments, until Uncle Will found my father." Annie wiped her tears with her hanky. "Yes, I *did* finally get my dream – *a real family*; but the pain of so many rejections has never really healed. Maggie.... I don't think I could bear any more agony like that!"

The front door flew open, and Sarah wiggled through it. She was carrying a huge, bulky package that barely fit through the door.

"OK, girls," she said breathlessly, "I'm going to need some help unwrapping this." She giggled, and tossed the bundle onto the floor.

"What is that?" Maggie asked, eyeing Sarah suspiciously. She had learned, years ago, that Sarah was completely unpredictable when it came to surprises.

"Open it and see!" Sarah cried. Her excitement was palpable.

Maggie and Annie tore into the package, like children at Christmas time; opening the largest presents first.

Sarah held her breath in anticipation.

Annie gasped, as she pulled the *'surprise'* from the paper wrapping.

She held up an elegant, floor-length, white silk and lace wedding gown, adorned with seed pearls and sequins. Maggie grabbed the delicate lace veil that matched the gown.

"Oh my God!" Maggie whispered. She was utterly astounded by the elegance and beauty of the gown and veil. "That has to be the most beautiful wedding gown I've ever... and I mean *EVER* seen! Was it your wedding dress?"

"Yes it was," Sarah said proudly. "Daddy spared no expense when it came to my gowns." Sarah directed Maggie's attention to Annie.

Annie was holding the dress up to herself, waltzing around the big dining room, and grinning from ear to ear. She appeared to be looking into her future.

"I wanted *my* daughter, Annie, to wear it at her wedding, but being the down-to-earth girl that she is... she declined." Sarah giggled. "She said it would seem pretentious."

"I'll bet you looked gorgeous in it," Maggie whispered; not wanting to distract Annie from her blissful fantasy.

Finally, Annie carefully laid the gown across a chair, gazing at it dreamily.

"Do you like it, Sweetie?" Sarah asked.

Annie ran over and threw herself into Sarah's arms. "Oh Aunt Sarah... It's beautiful!" she cried. "Just looking at it makes me feel like a princess. I love it... and I love *YOU*." Annie turned and looked at the dress again. "Thank you so much, Aunt Sarah!"

"Well Sweetie... that's a very nice wedding dress that Eleanor Stevens gave you... but I like this one better." She giggled. "I just want you to have a fairy-tale wedding, and you'll not only *feel* like a princess in that gown... but you'll *look* like a princess in it... I promise."

"I can't wait to see you in it, Annie," Maggie said. "Go try it on. Let's see how it fits."

Annie grabbed the gown and ran from the dining room.

Maggie and Sarah sat down at the table and began working on the remaining invitations.

"So my brother let you out of the house for a while, did he, Sarah?" It was Nathan. He was standing in the doorway smiling at the women. Nate was with him.

"Looks like we've got an extra wedding dress, here. I'm thinking we could put that one to good use," Nathan said. It was a veiled warning; considering the announcement young Nate was about to make.

Maggie stood up slowly; preparing herself for what she already knew was coming.

Just then, Miles appeared at the door, dropping a couple of heavy saddle bags onto the floor. "OK... I'll go saddle the horses, and meet you guys outside," he said. "Now you be gentle with these men, Mama." Nate gave his mother a quick kiss on the cheek, and disappeared.

Sarah gave Maggie a confused look.

"I'll explain it later," Maggie said, looking at her sister-in-law.

"Mama...," Nate began, "I decided that I could get to Catharine a lot quicker than a letter would reach her." He waited for some response from his mother.

Maggie was silent.

He continued. "I'm going to try and get her to come back with me... and marry me." He said it slowly and distinctly. He waited.

Still, no response from Maggie.

"Mama... if she won't come back with me... I'm just going to stay there and try to help her. She can't run that business alone." Nate rubbed at his chin, like his father, Nathan, did when he was thinking. "Nathan and Miles are coming with me. We're going to try and help her sell the inn, if she agrees to come back here and marry me."

Maggie found her voice at last. "I see you've thought this through and made your decision, Nate." She put her arms around her son, and held him tightly, while looking side-ways at his father. "How long do you think you'll be gone?"

Nathan looked surprised by Maggie's placid reaction. He picked up the saddle bags and threw them over his shoulder. He leaned down and gave Maggie a long, lingering kiss.

"Nathan and Miles will be here for Annie's wedding... no question about it. I'm just praying that Catharine and I will be back with them," Nate said; answering his mother's question.

"Well, Nate... my prayers will be with you." Maggie looked at Nathan sadly. "Nathan...I know you'll take good care of my boys, but please be careful."

Nathan bent over and whispered in Maggie's ear. "I love you Maggie."

The men left.

Maggie was stunned by Nathan's words. She suddenly felt off-balance and giddy. She hurried over to the table to sit down.

"Would you like to talk about it, Maggie?" Sarah asked; sitting down beside Maggie, and putting her arm around the shaken woman.

Two weeks passed with no word from her boys or Nathan. Maggie was feeling lonely in their absence; even though Annie and Sarah were keeping her busy with the wedding plans.

She tried not to worry. She knew her boys were well trained to survive just about any threat. Nathan was strong, responsible, and competent. She reminded herself of that, on a daily basis. It was when nighttime came, and darkness fell over the valley, that being in the big house without Nathan and her sons, seemed to overshadow her optimism. Nightfall was something she dreaded.

Chapter 42 – Running Out Of Time

It was the day before the wedding. Annie was too preoccupied and excited to consider the fact that her father may not make it back to give her away at her wedding. Maggie was glad for that. She didn't want Annie concentrating on anything but her imminent marriage and her future happiness.

All of the plans were finalized. It had been a long, exhausting day. Annie was worn-out, and she retired early.

Maggie was beside herself with apprehension. She sat down at the big windows in the living room and watched as daylight was fading into dusk. She was losing hope.

Feeling particularly restless, she decided to make herself a cup of hot tea; to try and relax. Maggie was in the kitchen busying herself, when she heard the familiar sound of horses approaching. She ran to the front door and threw it open.

Maggie was overjoyed to see Nathan and Miles, and she wasted no time running out to embrace them both.

Suddenly, she realized that Nate wasn't with them and her heart sank.

Nathan could tell by Maggie's body language that she was about to break down. He knew how much she loved both of her sons. He could actually feel what she was thinking. Nathan placed his hands on Maggie's shoulders and turned her to face the road.

There in the distance, she saw a heavily loaded wagon rolling down the lane. She looked up at Nathan beaming.

"She came?!" Maggie shouted.

"Yes she did, Maggie." Nathan said, proudly. "I have to tell you, Maggie... that is one fine woman our son chose. She's beautiful... she's smart... and like Miles says... *she's just plain nice.*" He put his arm comfortably across Maggie's shoulders. "Catharine is perfect for our Nathan!"

"I'll take the horses up to the barn and get them fed and bedded down," Miles said. He led the horses away, leaving Maggie and Nathan to wait for Nate and Catharine to arrive.

"Nathan, I can't tell you how worried I've been... what on earth took you so long?

"It's a long story, Maggie," He said, kissing her on the cheek. "We pretty much killed two birds with one stone. Gawd! What a nightmare... but I won't get into that." He grinned at Maggie."

"Well....? What happened?"

"It took a couple of days to convince Catharine to just sell the inn and marry Nate." He laughed, thinking about his son's tenacious persuasion abilities. "Maggie, that boy was relentless!" Nathan looked at Maggie, shaking his head. "He literally wore the poor girl down. She had no choice, by the time he got done with her!"

"And....?"

"And then Nate and Miles decided to take Catharine to Alabama... to their Cousin William

Weatherby's plantation and have a Creek marriage ritual performed... *AND*... to retrieve the family Staff."

"WHAT!?"

"Yep... they left me in charge of finalizing the sale of the inn, and wrapping up loose ends. We had no trouble finding the buyer." Nathan strained to see Nate's wagon approaching through the darkness, which had quickly settled over the valley. "I pretty much had to decide what Catharine would want to bring, and what she'd be better off selling. So that was MY job, while they were gone."

"Oh Nathan, what a job that must have been."

"There's more, Maggie." Nathan laughed, and put his hands on Maggie's shoulders to brace her. "Seems Miles' Uncle Peter gave Miles his very own squaw." Nathan laughed loudly. "He told Miles that she was his on loan... or to keep if he liked her! Needless to say... there were *TWO* marriage rituals performed." Nathan slapped his knees in delight. "She's absolutely gorgeous... I mean to say—She's definitely a keeper! That's why Miles went ahead with the ceremony. Guess he wasn't interested in *just* a loan."

"Nathan! Miles's barely eighteen! He's too young to be married!"

"Too late, Maggie... what's done is done," Nathan said. "Anyway... we all decided to go ahead and have a Christian wedding here... for the boys. We'll just do it tomorrow, after Annie's wedding and before the reception. What do you say, Maggie?"

Maggie was staring off into space. Her disbelief was conspicuous.

Just then the wagon turned off the lane, and started up the path to the house.

Nathan had to shake Maggie; to help her recover her composure.

Chapter 43 - Valentine's Day

It was Valentine's Day. The sun was just coming up, when Maggie was awakened by a knock at her bedroom door. Before she could respond, the door opened and Nathan walked into the room, carrying a large package.

"Good morning, my Maggie," he said, smiling mischievously.

Maggie raised herself up on one elbow and tried to focus her sleepy eyes. "What are you up to, so early in the morning?"

"This is the big day, Maggie!" he exclaimed. "Our children are getting married, and I couldn't be a happier man." He stopped and rubbed at his chin, thoughtfully. "Well.... There is something that would make me a *completely* happy and contented man." He walked over and sat down on the side of the bed. "This is for you, Honey," he said, handing Maggie the package. "I bought you a present in Lancaster. Open it, Maggie."

Maggie grinned at Nathan, and began tearing the wrapping from his gift.

"What is this?" Maggie gasped. She lifted the beautiful new wedding gown away from the paper, and held it up. She looked over at Nathan in surprise.

Nathan pulled Maggie out of the bed and stood her in front of him. He put his hand on Maggie's arm to brace her.

Nathan dug into his pocket and pulled something out; hiding it behind his back.

"Nathan Stillman... what on earth has gotten into you? And why are you giving *ME* a wedding gown? And what are you hiding behind your back? And why are you holding on to my arm so tightly?"

"Maggie... can I just address *ONE* question at a time?" He laughed, and winked at the confused woman.

"Well... I think that long trip must have affected your senses." She giggled.

"The wedding gown is for you to wear at the wedding."

"Why would I dress like a bride at our children's wedding?"

"Because, you'd make a beautiful bride, Maggie!"

Nathan slowly brought his closed hand around for Maggie to see. One by one, he opened his fingers; until there in the palm of his hand, she saw that gorgeous diamond ring. It was the ring Nathan wanted to give her on Christmas Day. "I was hoping you and I could renew our wedding vows, Maggie." Nathan looked down at Maggie's wide-eyed wonder. "Well... what do you say, Maggie? Will you marry me again?" He tightened his grip on Maggie's arm.

"OWWW!" Maggie shouted loudly. "Why are you squeezing my arm so tightly?"

"Because the last time I tried to give you this damned ring you fainted. I just thought I'd keep you steady this time." He broke into his usual fit of laughter. "Will you marry me or not, Maggie?"

Maggie's eyes filled with tears of joy and she threw herself into Nathan's arms sobbing.

"Maggie!" Nathan literally shouted, "will you marry me again?!"

"YES! Yes! I'd love to!" Maggie shouted back.

The door to the bedroom suddenly flew open, and the entire household ran into the room, to see what the commotion was about.

The children watched as Nathan slipped the ring on Maggie's finger.

Chapter 44 – Spring is in the Air

Spring, 1828 – Nathan Stillman's Farm

Nathan Stillman's big house was full to overflowing with an extended family he'd only dreamed of. He felt that his happiness was complete. Everyone had settled in with ease. The daily routine ran as smoothly as a well-oiled machine.

"Rise and shine!" Nathan called from the hallway. He took the steps two at a time. Reaching the landing, he shouted even louder, "Get up! Breakfast is waiting."

One by one, Nate, Catharine, Miles, and Belle emerged from their rooms.

"Breakfast is on the kitchen table, kids. I'll be down as soon as I can get Maggie out of bed." He feigned exasperation; and then chuckled.

Filing past Nathan, the boys shook his hand, and each girl gave him a kiss on the cheek; all of them smiling brightly. Nathan stood there grinning, and wondering what he did to deserve being such a lucky man. His blessings were too numerous to count.

He bounded into his bedroom and scooped the sleeping Maggie up into his arms and out of the bed. "Time to wake up, Honey! Time's wasting and we've got work to do." He looked down into Maggie's startled face, in amusement. He carried her out of the room and headed down the stairs with her.

"Nathan... I need to get dressed," she muttered, sleepily.

"Naw... you can get dressed after breakfast."

"You want me to cook breakfast in my nightgown?"

"Why not?" Nathan laughed.

"Because it's not respectable, Nathan! What will the children think?"

"Well, Maggie... You don't have to do a thing. I already have breakfast on the table!"

Maggie kissed him lovingly on the cheek. "You're a mad man, and I love you!"

Nathan carried Maggie into the kitchen and plopped her down on her chair. The group at the table giggled and laughed, seeing Maggie in her nightgown, with her hair disheveled and uncombed. Nathan sat down beside her.

"Well, good morning children," Maggie grinned. She looked around the table. Everyone was already enjoying the meal. "It's a good thing you people left some for *ME!* I'm famished." She reached over and put her hand on Nathan's arm. "I don't know what to say... this is beautiful, Nathan. Thank you. I love you so much!"

"Dig in, Maggie.... you can show me how much you love me, later." He said it with no compunction.

Everyone roared with laughter, at Nathan's candid remark.

"Nathan!" Maggie shouted. "You're shameless!"

"I know, Maggie... you just bring out the best in me."

Maggie's face turned scarlet.

Nathan stood up and looked down at his family. "I have an announcement to make."

"I knew there was a catch to this!" Nate said, grinning.

"Well... It's time to get the sheep sheared," Nathan said. "It's a chore that has to be finished before the lambing begins. I was out checking the ewes yesterday, and it looks like we're going to have babies, sooner than we expected. It's a good thing Miles has the pens all prepared for our new lambs. The men started the roundup this morning before daybreak."

"How many are we expecting?" Nate asked.

"I counted about a hundred twenty-five pregnant ewes, Nate"

"How many sheep need to be sheared?" Miles questioned; pretending to count on his fingers.

Nathan laughed. "Miles, you don't have enough fingers *or* toes.... We've got about three hundred seventy sheep to shear. Of course we've got plenty of help... with the hired hands." Nathan walked around the table, watching the boys' reaction. "Here's the thing... I always try to make this a festive occasion. It's gawd-awful hard and dirty work, so I do what I can to keep my men happy.... You know... show my appreciation. We can make this fun."

"Let's see... if I understand what you just said," Nate turned, and looked back at his father, "...this is *gawd-awful, hard, dirty work...* and we're going to make it *fun?*"

"Yep. We have contests with cash prizes for who can shear the most sheep -- And for the fastest...we time them. We'll serve a barbeque at the finish of every day. Last year we had a barn dance on the weekends. It took us nearly three weeks.... Shouldn't take us more than a week.... Maybe ten days this year. We sold off a fair number of our older sheep because the price of wool had dropped." Nathan smoothed down his mustache and rubbed at his chin thoughtfully. "I'm not so sure we'll have the auction this year, though. The government's going to put a big tax on imports, so that should drive the prices back up, here in the states. John and I will just have to talk about that." He looked around the table. "So what do you say?"

"I'm up for it," Miles agreed.

"Sounds good to me," Nate added.

"Well... what I'd like for you kids to do, is put your heads together and see what else we might consider doing... My men and their families have always seemed to enjoy it. Just let me know if you can come up with anything that sounds like fun."

"We can do that!" Nate said. He was beginning to look excited.

"OK, then," Nathan said, clapping his hands together. "I've got to get this event organized as fast as possible... before those mama ewes start going into labor." He laughed. "You boys want to ride into town with me? If you do.... Then let's go!" Nathan gave Maggie a quick kiss 'good-bye' and left.

Nate and Miles followed Nathan out of the kitchen; in a scramble for the door.

"All right, ladies," Maggie said, "I'm going back to bed, if you don't mind. I really wasn't ready to get up this early." She smiled, and padded off toward the hallway in her bare feet; the hem of her nightgown dragging across the floor.

Ben Stevens, the farm's crew leader, met up with Nathan and the boys, at the main road.

"Nathan, I've got some disturbing news," Ben said.

"What's that?" Nathan stopped his horse and looked at the man intently.

"We were up in the north pasture and we saw a huge gray wolf."

"We haven't seen wolves around here in years! Any signs of more... where there's one, there's usually a pack."

"That old wolf just sat over there on the top of the hill, watching us. He was alone."

"Any dead sheep?" Nathan asked.

"We haven't found any yet."

"Don't harm the wolf," Miles interrupted.

"*WHAT!?*" Nathan cried. "You've got to be kidding, Miles!" Nathan looked at the boy incredulously.

"The wolf won't harm the sheep... if anything, he'll protect them," Miles said.

"Miles... wolves can absolutely decimate our flocks...and in short order! Before we were able to run them out of this part of the county, we had to literally stand guard, to protect our investments .... Day and night!"

"I've seen the wolf," Miles said. "He's always alone. He's not a threat!"

"I've run into him, too, Nathan," Nate added. "I've seen him several times over the last few months."

"*WHAT?!!*" Nathan shouted. "Both of you saw that predator and didn't tell me?!"

"Well... you haven't found any carcasses... right?" Miles asked.

"Not *yet*... but that doesn't mean there aren't any. There's a lot of land here...and hundreds of sheep." Nathan took his hat off, and scratched his head, thoughtfully. "Why do you suppose my men haven't seen that creature before now.... if you boys have been seeing him since you got here?"

"Maybe it's up to the wolf.... where and when he reveals himself," Miles answered.

"I'm sorry, Miles, but that makes no sense at all," Nathan said. He was becoming agitated.

"Nathan, please... promise you won't go after the wolf." Nate was sincerely begging his father. "... and tell your men to leave that animal alone, if they see him."

Ben Stevens interrupted the conversation, "That's the craziest thing I've ever heard! You boys are out of your minds! You've probably never had to deal with wolf packs before.... They're nothing less than fur-covered *demons!*"

Nate ignored Ben's remark. "Tell you what, Nathan... give us your word that no harm will come to that wolf, and we'll promise you... if you ever find *any* evidence that he's attacked the flocks... Miles and I will hunt him down, and kill him ourselves." Nate turned to Miles, "Are you in agreement, Miles?"

"Yes, I agree, Nate." He turned to Nathan. "If he was killing your sheep, Nathan, surely you would have seen some indication of it by now! ... Just wait and see if we're right or wrong," Miles pleaded.

Although Nathan was visibly irritated, he sat quietly, for a long while, considering the boys' adamant appeal. It was beyond his understanding, and defied his solid sense of logic, but he couldn't shake the feeling that this wolf embodied some sort of special connection to both Miles and Nathan.

"All right, boys.... You have my word. No harm will come to *your* wolf." Nathan extended his hand first to Nate; and then to Miles. They shook on it – It was a gentlemen's agreement.

The boys rode on ahead, and Nathan turned to Ben. "Well... you've got your orders, Ben. Nobody... I mean *NOBODY*... is to interfere with that wolf. Got it? Make sure you tell the other men."

"What the hell, Nathan?!" Ben shouted. "Have you completely lost your mind?"

"Nope... I believe it's an *Indian* thing. You and I don't have the spiritual capacity to comprehend the mysteries!" Nathan laughed, and trotted off to catch up with his boys.

Nathan and the boys made sure the various pens were solid and stable, as the farmhands separated the sheep, and herded them into the specific enclosures. It was the third day of the roundup, and there were still several flocks to bring down from the hills. The shearing and festivities were set to begin in two days.

Maggie, Catharine, and Belle were in charge of preparing the food. Annie had been baking for days, and Sarah was appointed *'chief overseer'*-- since she had participated in this event many times. John Stillman was busy working on the scheduling for each man who had signed up for the shearing competition. He would also run the annual auction, held at the end of the festivities.

Nathan, John, and the hired hands made sure to shear the pregnant ewes before the anything else was done. It was imperative to get the job finished before the real mayhem started. Working day and night, the men managed to finish the chore.

The carnival atmosphere of the shearing event was chaotic, boisterous, and at times pure pandemonium.

In the shearing sheds, it was an actual *bloody* battle as the farmhands tackled the job of collecting the fleeces from the rams; especially the older ones. It often turned into a brutal wrestling match between beast and man. The younger ewes weren't as difficult; however, it *could* turn into a challenge at times.

The grounds were alive with a party atmosphere. Children played games and women joined groups to keep the shears sharpened, serve refreshments, and keep the rinse tubs filled with clean water at a tent, which was set up as a kind of first aid station.

Maggie was kept busy taking care of wounded shearers; putting poultices on bumps and bruises, cleaning and bandaging scrapes and scratches; and at times, even stitching up deep cuts, and tending to more serious injuries.

"Well, Maggie... Honey... how's your day going?"

Maggie looked up from her task to see her handsome husband standing outside the tent. She hurriedly finished bandaging a man's head, and sent him back to the battlefield. She ran out and grabbed Nathan in a typical *Stillman bear hug*.

"I had no idea how dangerous shearing sheep is!" Maggie cried. "I even had to stitch Nate's shin, where a ram kicked him!" Maggie looked distressed. "It's a wonder his leg wasn't broken."

Nathan laughed. "He wanted to try his hand at it, Maggie.... He needs to learn."

"I was surprised how upset he was... when he realized he couldn't get back in the game. He acted like he was having the time of his life." Maggie shook her head in disbelief.

"That's my boy!"

"That's for sure! He's as insane as his father."

"You should see young Miles tackle those big rams, Maggie! He's a natural."

"Well he hasn't shown up here, yet... so that's a good sign." Maggie managed to giggle.

Nathan looked around and spotted Eleanor Stevens. "Eleanor, can you cover for Maggie?... I'm going to steal her away for a while," he shouted.

"Of course, Nathan," she said, scurrying over to the tent.

"Come with me, Maggie... I've got something to show you."

Nathan led Maggie along the path to the shearing sheds. Inside she could hear cheering and yelling. There were people rushing around outside, carrying newly sharpened shears and brushes; while others tended to lining up the sheep waiting to be sheared.

"This is a huge operation, Nathan! I didn't expect anything like this."

"Wait 'til you see how meticulous the accounting is, Maggie." Holding Maggie's hand, protectively, they went inside one of the sheds.

Maggie watched a man finish his task. The naked ram was herded through a gate and into another pen outside. The man picked up the fleece and took it to a long table where he cleaned off all the dirt and discolored wool. He then rolled it up neatly and attached a tag to it with his name on it. Another man, holding a stop watch, added the time it took for the shearing, and he initialed it. The shearer then grabbed the rolled up fleece and headed out another door.

Nathan and Maggie followed him.

There were numerous wagons lined up at the other end of the shed. Some were already filled and covered with canvas to keep the wool dry; in case it rained.

Nate and Miles were standing at the end of the wagon, currently being loaded. Miles was operating the scale for weighing the fleeces, and Nate was recording the information for every bundle.

The man with the fleece laid it on the scale, and Miles called out the weight to Nate. Nate removed the tag from the roll and wrote down the man's name, the time it took for the shearing, and the weight of the fleece. Ben Stevens took the fleece from the scale and placed in the wagon.

The next man stepped forward with another rolled up fleece.

"What do you think of the *Stillman shearing operation?*" Nate chuckled.

"I can't believe how complex it is... nothing like I expected," Maggie said.

"I have to tell you... I'm impressed. That's for sure!" Miles added.

"Well, it took John and I years to get this farm running like the well-oiled machine it is now. It's been a work of pure trial and error up until now," Nathan said proudly.

"Nate, how's your leg feeling?" Maggie asked, bending down to feel for any swelling.

"It's fine, Mama. Now, I've got work to do... so quit babying me!"

"Spoken like a true man, Nate!" Nathan slapped Nate on the back and led Maggie up the hill, toward the house.

"Where are we going, now?" Maggie asked, looking a little surprised.

"All work and no play will make my Maggie a dull girl."

Maggie looked up at her handsome husband, recognizing that mischievous grin. "Nathan Stillman!! You're incorrigible!"

"I can't help it, Maggie! I'll never get enough of you."

Following the shearing, the ewes were giving birth. The sheds were filled with new life.

It was sunrise; and everyone in Nathan Stillman's home was congregating in the kitchen, getting ready for another glorious day.

"How many lambs have we got so far?" Nate asked. He poured himself a big mug of coffee and reached over, filling up his father's cup.

"As of last night... we had eighty-seven. Seems to be a good year for twins and females."

"Good Lord! That sounds like a lot." Nate's eyes were wide in wonderment.

"Well, don't forget, Nate... we started with a hundred and twenty-five due to lamb." Nathan took a long drink of the coffee. "Now we're going to have a bunch of fertile mamas." He laughed.

"Hmm...," Nate looked over at Miles, Belle, and Catharine, who were huddled together, whispering. "OK... Miles, do you want to break the news to him, or shall I?"

Just then, Maggie walked into the kitchen; half-awake as usual. "Good morning, everyone." She smiled and collapsed into a chair. "What news are you breaking?" She giggled.

The back door flew open and Annie rushed in. "Sorry I'm late... the kids didn't want to get out of bed this morning!" Paul, little Mary, and young Danny walked into the kitchen behind Annie.

"The coffee's hot... help yourself," Nathan shouted, standing at the stove. He poured a cup for Maggie. "What brings you kids out here so early in the morning?" Nathan set the cup in front of Maggie, and sat down beside her.

Annie hurried over and joined her brothers and sisters-in-law in their ongoing secret discussion. Nate joined the group. Paul just stood behind Annie, beaming.

Nathan and Maggie watched; their curiosity was unbearable.

"What is going on with you people?!" Nathan demanded.

Finally, Nate stood up. "I've got an announcement to make."

Miles, Belle, Catharine, and Annie stood up; joining Nate and Paul. The girls were radiant and the men were looking pleased and proud.

"Well.... ?" Nathan said impatiently.

Maggie was still struggling to wake up.

"We're pregnant!" Nate said.

Nathan's eyes grew large and he swallowed hard. "Who's pregnant?"

"All of us!" Miles cried.

Maggie suddenly snapped to attention.

Nathan jumped to his feet. "Wait a minute... are you saying all three girls are pregnant?"

"That's right," Nate replied. "Must have happened on our wedding night."

Maggie fell off her chair in a dead faint.

Chapter 45 – The Wolf and the Bear

The crops were flourishing and the weather had cooperated. The fields were alive with germination, and the earth was giving birth to itself.

Nathan surveyed the landscape from the top of a remote hill. He had decided to check the back pastures, where he seldom rides. He found himself at a purely magical spot. From that vantage point, he could see the entire Stillman properties. It was breathtaking.

As he sat there on his big chestnut mare, his attention was drawn to movement in the valley below. He saw a ewe and her lamb that had somehow been separated from the rest of the flock. Nathan was just about to head down the hill, to drive the sheep back to their group, when he saw the bear. A massive black bear was bounding across the creek and heading right for the unsuspecting sheep.

Nathan drew his rifle from behind him. Praying that he was in range, he aimed.

Suddenly, from out of nowhere, a huge gray wolf jumped between the bear and the sheep.

The bear stopped and stood up on his hind legs. The wolf crouched; ready for the attack. The startled sheep ran the other way; away from the two predatory animals about to engage.

Nathan slowly lowered the gun. He couldn't comprehend what he was seeing. It defied everything he knew about nature. It actually appeared as though the wolf was protecting the sheep.

He watched the wolf slowly circle the bear, while remaining in the crouched position. Minutes passed as the two animals continued to threaten each other. The wolf kept slowly circling. The bear eventually seemed confused. He came down on all fours. At that moment, the wolf lunged at the bear, sinking his fangs into the bear's throat, under his head. It was impossible for the bear to defend himself, as the wolf clung to the underside of his opponent. His claws dug into the bear's shoulders, as he ripped away at its neck. The more the bear shook and tossed its head, trying to extricate the wolf, the more damage it inflicted on itself.

Nathan couldn't help thinking that what he just witnessed was an ingenious move by the wolf. Even at a distance, Nathan could see the blood gushing from the bear's throat in copious amounts. The wolf hung on; showing no mercy; waiting for the bear to bleed to death. It was no contest. The wolf was a sly and deliberate creature. The bear was weakening. Just as the bear began to collapse, the wolf released his death-grip on the animal. He backed away slowly, remaining in a crouched position; ready to attack again if need be. The black bear laid there in the pool of blood. He didn't move.

Nathan was sure the wolf would go after the sheep, once the bear was dead. He waited and watched. The wolf eventually stood up and sniffed at the air. The bear was indeed dead. The gray wolf looked up the hill at Nathan, as if he had known all along that he was being observed. He tossed his head, shaking the blood from his fur, and he trotted off; across the creek and into the forest.

It took a few minutes for Nathan to absorb the reality of the extraordinary execution he had just witnessed. *'Naw...'* he said to himself. *'Couldn't be.'* He gathered his wits about him, and headed down to get a close look at the bear.

"What the hell?!!" Ben Stevens shouted, running over to the road.

Nate and Miles looked up from their work to see Nathan casually riding toward them. He was dragging a huge, male, black bear behind him. The other farmhands immediately dropped their hoes, and joined Ben.

"Bagged yourself a bear, huh, Nathan?" Ben sad, laughing.

"Not exactly, Ben," Nathan replied.

Ben walked back and examined the bear. "This bear's got his throat clean torn out! What the hell did that?"

"The wolf," Nathan answered.

Ben slowly looked up at Nathan; his eyes were as large as saucers. "How do you know?"

"Because I watched the wolf do it."

Nate and Miles just looked at each other and smiled.

The men stood mesmerized as Nathan re-counted how it happened; blow by blow. Far-fetched as it sounded, the proof was there in front of them.

"Yep.... Seems we've got ourselves an unlikely sentinel." Nathan smoothed his mustache and rubbed his chin thoughtfully. "Guess my boys were right about that old wolf."

"Well, I'll be damned!" Ben exclaimed. "I would have had trouble believin' it, even if I saw it happenin'..... It's unheard of!"

"You're right... it was pretty unbelievable." Nathan looked at Nate and Miles. "You two... and I... need to sit down and talk about this." He reached back and untied the rope from his saddle. "Who's going to skin this bear?" He threw down the rope and trotted away.

Maggie was in tears, while Sarah tried her best to console her friend. "Please stop crying! This is something to be celebrating. I was forty-five when little Joseph was born. You're only what... thirty-seven... thirty-eight ?"

"Forty!" Maggie cried. "I just turned forty. I'm going to be a Grandma, Sarah! This can't happen." She put her head down into her hands and sobbed.

"Maggie... just think how happy Nathan will be when you tell him."

"This is like déjà vu, Sarah.... Everybody gets pregnant on their wedding night!"

"I know, Maggie. I was thinking about that, too. It's one of those serendipity things. You know... fate... destiny? I can't help but feel like this is a blessing, Honey."

"*Fate... Destiny,*" Maggie echoed Sarah's words. She stopped crying and became very quiet. Those words had a significant meaning for her.

"Are you OK, Maggie?"

"I was just remembering something... Miles always spoke of *fate* and *destiny*, as if it was some unescapable trap.... that you have no choice in matters where they're concerned."

"You've lost me, Maggie."

"Sarah, do you remember when you got pregnant on your wedding night, and Nathan was upset because I *wasn't* pregnant?"

"Yes, I vaguely remember how disappointed he was... when he found out you weren't, after Dr. Mathison had said you probably were.... Why?"

"Because that's why Nathan got so drunk the night he decided he was going to impregnate me, whether I was willing or not." Maggie wiped her tears with both hands. "I told him I was too young to start having babies." She paused, and managed a giggle. "Don't you see how ironic it is?! It had to have happened on our *second* wedding night! Now, I would be more than willing.... But I'm too old!"

Sarah laughed at the thought. "OH Maggie! You're *NOT* old! Enjoy this happy time. Your life is getting *back* on track, now.... I see what you're saying – destiny *WILL* have its way, eventually. This is actually unbelievable! It can't be just coincidence! You've been given a *second* chance to show Nathan how much you love him!"

Maggie sat quietly, thinking about this strange turn of events. Her musings were abruptly interrupted when the screened door squeaked open, and Nathan walked in to the house.

"Nathan!" Sarah cried, "I'm glad to see you."

"Just had to find my Maggie, Sarah. I have a tale to tell her that she'll never believe."

"How did you know I was here?" Maggie asked.

"Your carriage was tied outside. I saw it." He laughed.

"Well, I think we've got a tale to tell you, that *you'll* never believe!" Sarah announced.

"Really... what's that?" Nathan said, sitting down on the sofa beside Maggie.

There was a long silence.

"Well? My story can wait. What is it that you two have cooked up now?"

"Go ahead, Maggie... tell him!" Sarah was bouncing up and down in her chair, with excitement.

"OK..." Maggie hesitated. "Nathan, this is going to shock you.... I'm glad you're sitting down...."

"Maggie! What is it?!" Nathan interrupted.

"I'm.... I'm...." Maggie stammered. "I'm going to have your baby."

Maggie and Sarah watched a myriad of different expressions cross Nathan's face; one after another: shock, surprise, confusion, astonishment, doubt, and finally sheer ecstasy. His jaw dropped and big tears began rolling down his cheeks. It was obvious that he was speechless.

"Oh please tell me those are *happy tears*, Nathan." Maggie was crying now.

Nathan grabbed Maggie and pulled her into his lap, hugging her tightly. They both continued to cry. Seeing them like this touched Sarah's soft heart, and she began to cry, too.

Just then, John walked in. He looked at the three of them, sobbing their hearts out, and for no apparent reason, he began to cry.

Sarah jumped to her feet and punched her husband in the shoulder. "John Stillman, are you making fun of us?!" she cried, indignantly; through her tears.

"No, Sarah, Sweetie... I'm just such a sucker for *happy tears*. I was just moved by what I was seeing."

"...And how do you know these are *happy tears*?!" she demanded.

"Don't you think I've lived with you long enough to know the difference by now?" He put his arm around his wife and pulled her close to him. "So what's the occasion?" he asked.

"Maggie's going to have a baby!" Sarah whispered.

John looked at Nathan and his mouth dropped open.

"Yep!" Nathan finally found his voice. "I've got two children... and I wasn't there when either of them was born. I missed the most important years of their lives. Now it's like I've been given one more chance to get it right!" He broke down sobbing again.

"Nathan.... I don't know what to say, little brother.... Except maybe congratulations?"

"Well... it's not like he did this all by himself!" Maggie giggled.

"OH... I'm sorry, Maggie," John said, wiping at his eyes. "Congratulations to *YOU*, too!"

Chapter 46 – Absolution

It was September, and the harvest season was just beginning. The crops were plentiful this year, and the Stillman brothers were thankful. Annie, Catharine, Belle, and Maggie were blossoming in the seventh month of their pregnancies. It had been a year of abundance, and a time of convergence.

"I'm so tired, Nathan," Maggie said, struggling to get her expectant body out of the chair. "I think I'll just go to bed early, if that's all right with you."

Nathan took hold of Maggie's hands to help her up.

As Maggie rose, she felt something snap, and without warning, her water broke. She was panic-stricken. She was afraid to move.

"Nathan! Get Sarah! *QUICK*!!" Maggie cried.

Nathan was beside himself. He had no idea what was happening. He helped Maggie back down into the chair, and ran to the stairs.

"Nate!" he shouted, "Get down here, NOW!!"

Nate was instantly at the landing, along with everyone else.

"Go to John's place and bring Sarah here.... as fast as you can. Something's happened to Maggie!"

"My water broke... that's all. Except it's too early... It's just way too early." Maggie began to cry.

Nate was out the door and on his way. Nathan did what he could to comfort his wife. Miles, Belle, and Catharine didn't know what to do. The stress in the room was intense.

Nate returned with Sarah in no time. Sarah rushed in and seized control of the situation.

"It's too late to turn back now... this baby is coming tonight," she said calmly.

"But it's too soon," Maggie whimpered.

"Maggie, you're seven months pregnant... this baby will be fine. Maybe small, but everything will be OK." She smoothed back Maggie's curls, and squeezed her hand. "Nathan, go get a big kettle of water boiling. Catharine, grab some old sheets and put them across the extra bed upstairs. Belle, go find me some string, some scissors, and some whiskey."

Nathan looked at Sarah and managed a grin. "Damn, Sarah... you sound just like big brother, John." He turned and headed for the kitchen.

"Don't you worry Maggie... this will be over before you know it. Are you having any pain yet?"

"No... not yet."

"Good. I'll be right back. Just try to relax," Sarah said patting Maggie's shoulder.

Behind Maggie's back, Sarah grabbed Miles and dragged him into the hallway.

"Miles," she whispered, "I want you to ride into Uniontown and try to get the doctor there to come back with you. I don't remember his name, but I know there's a new doc there. You'll just have to knock on doors and ask." Sarah looked shaken. "I don't want Nathan to know I'm worried, Miles.... I just want to make sure we have a doctor here, just in case anything goes wrong."

"Is Mama going to be all right?"

"We'll just have to pray for her, Miles. Now *GO!*"

Sarah returned to Maggie's side. "Any pains yet?"

"No."

"The bed's ready, Miss Sarah," Catharine called from upstairs.

"Nathan," Sarah called, "we need to get Maggie upstairs."

Nathan came in and gently scooped Maggie up in his arms. He carried her upstairs, and laid her onto the bed.

"I love you, Nathan," Maggie whispered.

"... and I love you with every fiber of my being, Maggie."

Sarah let out a little cry when she saw the blood in the chair, where Maggie had been sitting. She ran up the stairs and burst into the bedroom. "OK, Nathan... you and Nate, and the girls should just go into the kitchen and have some tea. I'll call you if I need you."

When everyone had left the room, Sarah closed the door softly. She sat down on the side of the bed and stared at Maggie. Her eyes were full of questions.

"What's wrong, Sarah?" Maggie asked.

"Maggie, you've delivered lots of babies... with your pa. And I've had six of my own... I'm not sure if you're supposed to be bleeding right now."

"I didn't know I was bleeding, Sarah!"

"Well... let's get you out of your dress and into a nightgown. I'm not sure how bad it is... but you sure left a puddle in that chair downstairs!"

Two hours passed. Maggie continued to bleed; and still no pains. Sarah had kept checking the bedding to try and keep track of how much blood Maggie was losing. Nathan, Nate, Catharine, and Belle didn't have a clue that there was a problem. Everyone thought Miles had gone over to keep John company, since he had to remain at home with his children.

"Well, Sarah... I think this is *bad*," Maggie said weakly. "I'm not sure what's causing this, but we both know... it's not normal."

"I just don't understand why your labor pains haven't started."

"Maybe they have.... And I'm tougher than I look?" Maggie smiled.

There was a knock at the door and Sarah ran over and opened it. It was Miles, with the doctor from Uniontown.

"Sarah, this is Dr. Roberts," Miles said.

"Oh! Thank God!" Sarah said, literally pulling the doctor into the room. "This is Maggie."

"Well, if you'll give me some time alone with our mother-to-be... I'll see if I can help," Dr. Roberts smiled, and motioned Sarah and Miles toward the door.

Downstairs, in the kitchen, the group was surprised to see Sarah and Miles walk in.

Nathan jumped to his feet. "Is Maggie OK?"

"She's in good hands, Nathan. Miles brought the doctor from Uniontown. He's with her now. We'll just have to wait and see what he says." Sarah sat down heavily on one of the chairs and began to cry.

"Oh my god, Sarah.... What's wrong with Maggie?" Nathan gasped.

Nate started for the door, but Miles stopped him. "The doctor's examining her right now. You can't go in, Nate."

Minutes passed, and then an hour. The family tried to be brave, but each one of them was beginning to expect the worst, since Sarah had described the mysterious bleeding.

Finally the doctor walked into the kitchen. He had a solemn expression on his face. Everyone remained silent; afraid to ask if Maggie was going to be all right.

"She's lost quite a bit of blood....I'm going to explain the problem as best I can, and I'll tell you what to expect," Dr. Roberts said quietly. "Mr. Stillman, you can go up and speak with your wife. She understands the situation, and she also knows that the two of you have a decision to make. She wants to see you... she'll tell you what you need to know."

Nathan wasted no time. He took the stairs two at a time, and rushed into the bedroom to be with Maggie. She looked pale and fragile.

Nathan sat down carefully on the side of the blood-soaked bed. "Oh Maggie... the doc said you wanted to tell me what's wrong. Honey...are you going to be OK?"

"No, Nathan... I don't think so," she said weakly. "I've lost way too much blood, and...."

"WHY?!!" Nathan asked in a hoarse voice. The knot in his throat was tightening.

"Nathan... the doc thinks that the placenta has broken away from the uterine wall. That's why the blood. I'm hemorrhaging. Our baby can't get any nourishment or fresh blood, if that's what's happened. Our child could die if we don't do something quickly."

"Maggie, you know I don't understand those medical terms! Just tell me what we can do about it."

"I don't know about you, Nathan... but I think we need to save our baby... and as soon as possible!"

"How do we do that, Maggie, Honey?"

"The doctor will have to cut into my stomach and uterus, and remove the baby that way."

"My God, Maggie! Can you live through that?"

"Probably not... some have, though." She was growing weaker. "Nathan, my pa did a couple of these procedures... I helped him. The babies survived, but the mothers didn't. One bled to death and died immediately... the other one just died slowly from infection."

"We can't let him do it, Maggie!" Big tears were rolling down Nathan's cheeks.

"Nathan, we have no choice, except to let the baby die inside me... and then I'd probably die anyway from infection." Maggie was trying hard not to cry. "We've just got to be strong, Nathan. If we can save our child.... and if I die... it will mean that I've completed my destiny. I'm not afraid. I just don't want you to be unhappy. I love you more than you'll ever know, Nathan. You're the most loving, kind-hearted soul that God ever put on this earth.

I'm just so grateful that I got the chance to redeem myself."

"Are you in pain, Maggie?" Nathan whispered, his voice shaking with emotion.

"No... that's the strange thing. I'm just so tired and weak...and I'm freezing." It was becoming an effort for her to speak; she could barely whisper.

Nathan grabbed two more quilts and spread them over Maggie. He tucked them in; tightly around her shivering body.

"I can't bear this, Maggie! I lost you once.... I don't want to lose you again." He bent over and kissed Maggie's lips. They felt cold.

"Just remember how much I love you...and...." Maggie lost consciousness.

Nathan ran to the top of the stairs and shouted for the doctor.

Dr. Roberts ran into the room, and over to Maggie. He checked her pulse and put his ear to her chest, listening for a heartbeat. He stood up slowly; sadly.

"I'm sorry, Mr. Stillman... your wife is gone."

"NO!!" Nathan screamed.

Sarah came into the room. She took one look at Maggie and she knew it was over.

Nathan fell to his knees, and his entire body quaked with his uncontrollable sobbing.

"We need to get the baby out as soon as possible, Mr. Stillman! Do I have your permission?" The doctor gently shook Nathan to get his attention. "Please, Mr. Stillman... we're wasting time. Can we take your child?"

"Yes.... Go ahead... it's what she wanted." Nathan could barely speak between sobs.

By that time, Nate and Miles were in the room.

"Will you young men help your father downstairs, please?" he said, looking at Nate. "Miss Sarah... are you up to helping me with the surgery to save this baby? I mean... do you have the stomach for it?"

"I'll help you, Dr. Roberts," she said quietly; tears running down her face.

Once downstairs, Nathan embraced the boys, and they all wept together; openly.

"I'm so sorry about your Mama... I know how much you boys loved her. I just want you to know that she was always incredibly proud of both of you."

Nathan needed to be alone. Nate and Miles understood. Nathan knew they were battling their own shock and grief, but at least they had their wives to comfort them.

He went outside and sat down on the steps of the porch. He tried to remember every word Maggie said to him, while she lay dying.

It seemed like hours passed. Nathan was numb from his anguish and his grief.

"Mr. Stillman?" It was the doctor. He stepped outside, and Nathan rose to his feet.

"Is it over, Doc?"

"Yes, Mr. Stillman... and you have a very healthy baby boy."

"Can I hold him?" Nathan asked in a detached tone.

"Well, Mr. Stillman... you also have a very healthy baby girl. They're small, but they're both perfectly healthy." The doctor smiled, waiting for Nathan's reaction.

Nathan looked toward the doorway, to see Sarah standing there, smiling through her tears. She was holding the tiny bundles; one in each arm.

Nathan rushed past the doctor to get to his newly born children. Without saying a word, Nathan positioned his arms for Sarah to place the babies in them; which she did.

Peering into the tiny faces of his brand new babies, Nathan remembered what Maggie had said to him years before: *'...You need a wife ... and lots of children to help out on our farm.'*

"Thank you, Maggie," Nathan whispered.

.....and just then, echoing across the hills, Nathan heard the sorrowful cry of the wolf.

Hear the voice within yourself, which in silence is as clear as the sound of the wolf howling in the night.

ABOUT THE AUTHOR

Ramsey Keller says:

I never write "formula" novels ... they're just too predictable. Also, I can't abide by any one genre. I just don't fit in a box."

I consider myself a "storyteller" and as the story plays out in my mind, like a movie, I just write what I'm seeing.

I like to combine action, romance, humor... and a little erotic spice; but only if it's an integral part of the story

Also written by Ramsey Keller:
A Romantic Sci-Fi Thriller
"Song of the Benjai"

The most powerful emotion in our reality is LOVE.
The most formidable human instinct is the sexual drive.
Some unions are conceived in Heaven; some are devised in
hell. Kyate, Master of the Deis Warriors, has been
deployed by the Galactic Council of Deis to command the
Deis fleet and protect the carrier of a "special gene".

Kyate, Master of the Deis Warriors, and spiritual
teacher in his own right, had been deployed by the
Galactic Council of Deis to command the Deis fleet and
protect the carrier of the god seed. The Province of
Ulonica, on the planet Earth, was under siege. The
Alicupions and the Drothuarians were battling for control
of the planet, by securing the only pure Benjai DNA
remaining -- The Princess Zeidra.

Kyate was first a spiritual master; and secondly he was a
warrior monk; but his true identity was known only to one
mortal.

Kyate's passionate obsession with Zeidra is nearly his
ruination; and he almost destroys her.